THE BRIDGE BETWEEN TWO RIVERS

BY ALEXANDER VIKARE

Second Edition

For they say that the course of human life resembles the letter Y, because every one of men, when he has reached the threshold of early youth, and has arrived at the place "where the way divides itself into two parts," is in doubt, and hesitates, and does not know to which side he should turn

-- Lactantius

TABLE OF CONTENTS

PROLOGUE:POP STYLE

Crows screeched across the skyline of the valley and dark clouds hung overhead, bearing the lightning and rain that was soon to come. A lone figure stood at the edge of a lookout upon a large barren hill, gazing out across the Y-shaped bridge that spanned across two mighty rivers. The corners of his long, dark overcoat flapped, and the wind whistled in his ears, sending a chill up his spine. *Home*, he thought to himself, *it's been too long. Around the world, and back again, yet here I am once more—where It all started.*

The man shimmied the wide brim of his purple fedora lower and pulled the corners of his collar closer. The soft fabric of his peacoat kissed his neck and made him tingle; he shivered again. *It's going to be a cold winter, but perhaps back in this place, at the crossroads, I can find a way to fix it all; to begin anew.*

Cars bustled across the bridge below, and his eyes lie fixed upon the turns. Following a clunker here, a truck there, and the occasional semi heading for the 9 by 7 gap of doom beneath the rails. *Knock the top clean off, which way to go,* he whispered and wondered to himself.

A child draws a bird, two strokes laid with the pen, a skipping rock upon the surface, the waters ripple again. It will be my symbol. Crucified upon the Y, I will find my way to fly.

His eyes flicked towards the clock tower of the courthouse; another rush of wind blew. The arms lie frozen, seeming to be stuck behind the clasp. *The hands of time. Backward or forward, there are three. The long on twelve, the short on three, the second hand spinning itself free. Right on eight; there lies infinity.*

A train screeched down below in the distance, the waters of the dam crashed ahead, and the center column of the bridge loomed; *the old crow's perch.* The street lamp flickered, and the shadow beneath grew quicker. *He's signaling me; it's time I meet with him again.*

The engine of a dark blue 1969 Chevy Caprice cracked and rumbled. The kraken of death lie on the trunk. *Ghost Rider; the shadows forever chasing.* The man bit his lip as he hit reverse to make the turn. *I think I know which way to go.* His foot pressed against the pedal, and the tail end of the trunk swung in reverse. The beat to Kim Wilde's "Cambodia" dropped in synthetic waves and vibrated through the antique interior as the wheels turned.

A single candlelight burned in a dark room. A round, black mirror lie in the man's palms. The obsidian glass glimmered, and the man fixed his gaze; visualizing the symbol, a key for a gate. *Into the void I stare, the land I bear, carrying paradise in one hand, and a scorching flame in the other.*

His posture lie fixed as he focused his will; channeling his intent towards the vision. *Be direct and let go of the desire; the essence of the intention shall be thy wings. Bearing gifts of karmic reward, or whips of harsh punishment. No matter, it's all a mere lesson; a judgement of time.*

The mirror became a dark pool, and the man's tethered soul dived in. Body stiff, eyes still fixed and frozen.

The fall was far, and his consciousness drowned within the waters. A gate to the Otherworld was opened.

Back within the void, he took a breath and gazed above. The melodious hum of the vacuum of space beyond pervaded his presence, and thunder cracked. It was as if he were in a dream. An old crone's bark echoed across the vast deep.

"Wanderer in the Wilderness; where hath thou been?"

Thunder charged again in its echo. The stars mirrored the sky in the thin pool below. They all twinkled a different color and shade; none alike to another. *But pairs, yes. You can always find a pair; two twins of another. Mirror souls. The crow caws after the other through one single syllable.*

Fog grew at his heels in the infinite puddle, and he held the amulet of nine stones; it glowed like a lantern before his gaze as he edged forward. *Hold thy token tight; it is a key,* a whisper came, *it is thy shield.*

A red door with a golden knob stood alone, untethered by itself in the distance. His boots clonked and echoed; splashing across existence, edging forward towards the entrance. He gripped the knob and turned it slowly. The hinges on the door creaked, revealing a room. It was dim, and the air was faint. The room was lit by large candlelight burners lining the walls, and as the door opened, a checkerboard floor was revealed. A red carpet ran from the edge of the door leading towards a large square oak table in the middle. A shade sat at the other end grinning under his wide brimmed purple fedora; it was the man in the hat.

The Wanderer slid slowly into the room, and his heels clonked across the tile. The man in the hat cackled, and hollered, "There he is! King of the Road!"

He snapped his fingers and sung along to Dean Martin's tune by the same name. The Wanderer pulled the chair out on the other end of the table, and the legs ran across the floor, screeching along with the man in the hat's laughter.

The Wanderer sat with his chin down and his shoulders slumped; staring emptily upon the dark etching of a map engraved upon the table; *a mystical maze. We have much in store.*

The man in the hat's cackling halted, and he threw a leg across his knee. A Zipo lighter with an ace flicked open, and he lit up a cigar. Smoke danced before his yellow eyes and curled around the brim of his hat.

"So how was Europe?" he asked.

The Wanderer lifted his chin up, and the light shone dimly across his face. Shade sat under his eyes.

"Good one. You know I haven't made it there yet."

The man in the hat leaned forward in his chair, the light from above only illuminating his chin below.

"Ohhh—well, why not? I guess your precious little book didn't sell as well as you thought it would, did it?"

The Wanderer sat frozen, eyes flickering hopelessly across the table.

"No, it didn't. I put all the good I had, my whole heart, into that book, and nothing came of it. Do you know how scared I was sharing what was personal to me with people like that? I thought if I opened my heart to the world, something would come of it; that the magic of the act alone would flow on its own, but it didn't. All this time I felt like my story mattered, that it meant something, but it really doesn't. That kind of story doesn't speak to people. Nobody really cares."

The man in the hat puffed a reply, "Ah, but you've heard all those words before, haven't you? What goes around always comes back around. Am I right? And the fact that nobody cares, well, your grandfather told you that. Pawpaw told you about how people could be, didn't he?"

"Shut up!"

The Wanderer flung out of his chair and snapped. Heaving, he tried to contain himself, but the river of his grief washed over his anger.

The man in the hat didn't even budge. He just sat back with his arms hugging his elbows grinning; chuckling under his breath.

"And I thought I was a fool. Oh boy, you sure do take the cake."

Pools grew in the Wanderer's eyes, and he shook shaking his head.

"Don't say it. I don't want to talk about it."

The man in the hat jumped up from his chair and spread his arms out like a showman.

"Well, why not?! It's what everybody's been dyin' to hear!"

He tilted his head, and continued, laughing, "Or nobody. Y'see, that feeling, that phrase, 'nobody cares', well, that's passed down, my friend. Think on that and you'll find a clue."

"A clue to what?"

The man in the hat winked, "Better to see it deciphered in the long pages."

The Wanderer shrugged his shoulders.

"I don't get it."

The man in the hat snapped back, "Well, you don't have to! Truth is found within association; identifying what is akin within the crystal cube, it all obeys order, but everything lies divided within the chaos."

"You're not making any sense."

The man in the hat sat back down in his seat, and shook his head downward; disappointed. With a thought, he jerked his head up again and grinned.

"But, ahhhh, we've gone off point. You thought you could run away, didn't you? Escape the burn, you thought. Why don't we see it all again?"

The man in the hat pulled out a pocket watch with a phoenix and a dragon upon the covering clasp, and flipped it open, dialing the hands backward.

The Wanderer pleaded, "Please don't. I just want to be done with it."

The man in the hat cackled and threw the watch across the mapped maze on the table. Images erupted in the clouds upon the empty ceiling above, and I saw it all. Disconnected, watching the bitter heartbreak play out again.

I am known as the Wanderer. Allow me to tell you my story.

I stood at a window, staring out of a high rise room I'd booked at the Delano. *Las Vegas, this is always the city that will remind me of you.* I just sent her the text and the picture.

I stood there smiling, gazing out at all the lights, filled with joy thinking to myself, *Wow, I really did make it far on that trip.* I laughed and thought more. *Everybody thinks I'm cool, and some folks are even calling me the road warrior now. I guess I'm gonna make it. This book is going to do so well. I just know it. It'll sell like crazy, and there will even be a movie made about it. I saw the title and all pop up in the same styled letters on Netflix—in a dream, that is.*

The lights twinkled before me, and my cheeks grew warm as I pressed my hand on the glass. I saw the dark shadows of the mountains beyond, and my mind was taken back to 29 Palms; *the Place Between the Stones, Oasis of Mara. What really happened out there? It didn't make any sense. But I felt it. Oh yes, I felt it.*

My phone vibrated, and it was hit with a reply.
Who's this?

I shuddered, and my heart sunk; my fingers typed back in panic, but to no avail. She changed her number.

Hours later I stare out of the window still, joy below in the city, but showers above. I cried, and whined into the phone, "B-but grandma, I don't know why. I d--don't know why she would do this to me."

My voice grew drawn out and hoarse as I shook. The lump in my throat was just too heavy.

"I thought it would make a difference. I thought it would matter, b-but it didn't. I went all that way, all that way," I sobbed ghastly across the line," I went all that way for nothing."

I dropped the phone, and my fingers ran down my hot cheeks, shivering. A swollen face glared back at me through my reflection in the window. I didn't even look like myself. Pools of tears exploded out of my eyes, and the constant stream ran further down my face. Hollow gasps drug and hung in my throat. "Ohhhhh, noooo. No, no, no. Why? Why didn't it make a difference?"

I went on crying like that for days. We went out to Vegas for my mom's 50th birthday. That was why I returned to the place nearly a year after the trip. I ruined it for everyone. I'd nearly drunk myself to death. Nobody asked if I was okay. They just thought Vegas had gotten to me and I'd lost myself to the party. It was all a cover. I couldn't keep myself together enough to be around them. I wasn't any good to anyone.

The last lamp of hope I had was in the book. I released it June 28th, 2021; exactly a year later, on my father's birthday, to honor him. It also marked the last day of the trip. It was when it all happened in the desert; I was reborn, but only to crumble yet again in despair. When the book was released, barely anyone cared. People that I thought would read the book didn't, but others did, and they absolutely loved it. *She did, too; the first draft anyway. That's*

12

what didn't make any sense about the ghosting. It all came out of nowhere.

The man in the hat snatched at the watch on the table and flicked it closed; tucking it back in the pocket of his long, dark coat. Then, he laughed, "Ohhh, what a drama queen, or king; I guess it doesn't matter these days. Boy, you sure know how to be dramatic."

My head hung low again, and I muttered, "Say whatever you want about me. I don't care."

The man in the hat continued, humming a low chuckle in his throat. Flailing his arms about and talking with his hands.

"She wouldn't even spend ten dollars to buy the finished copy. And you spent all of daddy's money on this grand adventure to win her over; you had to go and make a big spectacle out of everything. Ohhhh, I bet it sure would be nice to have all that money now."

I sunk in shame within my seat, and muttered back, "Nobody will ever know how much that road trip really meant to me. I—I j-just wanted to have the adventure that I'd always dreamed of; a traveler's journey. They always said it was blood money; grandma did anyway. I just figured I'd use it on something to make my dad proud, and on t-that trip all along the way, I felt closer than I had to him in years. It was almost like he was there with me. I can't find him anymore. I haven't felt his presence since; he feels so lost to me now. I—I t-think I crossed some sort of barrier I can't find my way back from. It's like the last shred of innocence I had has been spoiled rotten; trapped in that book. I can't look at anything the same anymore. I—I am p-penniless. Penniless and poor now."

The man in the hat jerked his head forward at the other end of the table and snapped, "Awwww, things not working out at grandma's? You just can't seem to be able to fill papa's shoes, can you? Well, you shouldn't have spent all you had to impress some pretty little dame, you fool."

The man in the hat's teeth clicked, and he chattered, "There's so much that I can see that you don't know."

The man in the hat's cackling echoed across the hall, and he snapped, "It wasn't about being ready. You just didn't have enough stones in the bank; ya ain't rich boy! Just a penniless author with throwaway books in the dumpster. Why, you even threw a whole box away yourself to be rid of it, but you won't delete it. You can't seem to let go. You—"

"I really did pour my whole heart out into that first book," I interrupted, "I'm not upset about how it all turned out; you can't convince someone to love you. They either do or they don't. I just can't see that guy anymore, who I used to be. He was vibrant, running around in a jean jacket outfit with palm trees on his shirt; ready to take over the world, but the journey broke him. Not just by a false quest for love, but by being a ghost. His book is there, but nobody sees it. He's just another heart-broke version of myself; lost to the past. The boy who wrote, 29 Palms, is dead."

The man in the hat replied in a mimicking, sad tone, "Oh, I'm really sorry about that, kid. He was one of the good ones."

"Sorry for what," I replied. A subtle growl rose up in my throat, and my eyes went void, "You didn't kill him. I did."

I cleared my throat and continued, "I've let that story go. I had to. I've never felt more worthless and inadequate in all of my life."

A whisper spoke in my ear, *There is no tugging at the rug, you just simply have faith in the steps.*

I paused for a moment, surprised by the words. *The voice is still there; maybe there is hope. It just spoke to me.* The man in the hat noticed, too. He knew in that moment I hadn't fallen completely.

The man in the hat teased, "Still no bad words about it all? I know the spite in your heart. Don't forget I see and I know."

I sat solid at the other end of the table. A shred of faith had returned, and I replied, "None at all. Everyone deserves to be happy."

I looked downward towards the right at the shadow of the burning flames upon the checkerboard floor. I could feel it again; the longing pull upon my soul.

"Now all I have to do is find my true love. Not by chasing, but by letting go. I don't care if I find someone because I-I c-can feel it still, the faith again."

The man in the hat sat still at the other end of the table; he wasn't smiling anymore at all. His fingers tapped upon the maze.

"Hmmm, you seem to have it all figured out."

Suddenly, he leaned quickly across the table, and his shallow cheeks punched up into a clenched grin. The man in the hat snapped through his teeth, "Why are you here, then?!"

"I never wanted to come back, to this place, but I had to; so I can recover myself."

To save a seed, it must first be plunged into darkness. There it hungers, where it feeds, there it grows. It fights its way through the shadows in the tunnel, towards ascension, so that it can bloom anew. A long night to understand the true light.

Laughter erupted from the other side of the table, and the man in the hat flicked his cigar into the burning fireplace to the right.

"Is that so," he snapped.

"Yes, it is," I replied, "And you're going to help me."

The man in the hat cackled, "And why would I do that?!"

His voice lowered to a soft hum, and his voice croaked slightly.

"I'm very disappointed in you, y'know. You forgot to include me in the palm trees book.. When you left home ten years ago-you pushed me down like a repressed memory; you treated me like I didn't exist. Oh, you're such a good guy. You've never done anything wrong, have you? Ahhhh, look at you. If they all only knew how rotten you really are."

"But that's the thing," I replied. "I remember I left to find answers to what happened to my father, but there's so many gaps missing."

The man in the hat propped his elbow up on the table, snickering and continued, "I'll give you a free pass. I was only jerkin' your chain. I was in the book. It was fun disguising myself as the strange old man. Remember? Near the ghost town? Why, I even laughed for ya. You were scared shitless and shakin' in your drawers, boy. Then there was Bangor, Maine, oh yes, you talked about our last encounter there. Thank you, thank you, you're far to kind. Hold the applause everyone—but then there was Vegas; that's when you began to hear my voice again."

"But why," I asked.

"Because of the amulet you used to bind me. You blessed it in the waterfall, and each time after, you fed me more and more energy from the land; oh and that museum, Lord the house. You're a whore for energy just like I was, boy. You can feel it and you consume it. It's like a drug. There's a lot more to that amulet, y'know. You should've never commissioned the druid to build it; you should've just left it in your dreams. It came from beyond the Biahelek, the Valley of Lost Souls even. It hails from the forgotten time; when serpents flung from the sky. You were lucky the void chucked it at you when it did; I almost had you, but when you put the hat on, it was complete."

16

I stood atop the tower; dark overcoat flapping in the wind, dancing around on the edge, eyes hidden by the shadow of the purple brim, looking down upon the skyscrapers in the grand city I was in. The beat to Kanye West's "Flashing Lights" began to spin.

"Oh, you played a few games of your own. You loved it; damned if you'll admit it, but I know. You got bored, and couldn't avoid the draw. You had to come back home for me. You couldn't escape the fall."

The man in the hat puckered his lips and cackled; making a kissy noise, "Awwww, I love you, too."

"Don't flatter yourself. I'm back here to fill in the missing gaps between what really happened back then. It's the only way I can rediscover the lost part of myself. You're the key, and the only guide I have to it. You're the Wanderer Within the Void."

The man in the hat grinned, "I'm the key? Why don't you just pray to God? Ask that fella for aid."

"I can't," I replied, "not like you mean. I peered too far past the curtain of known reality to look at anything the same; the way everybody else does. The vision I had, the place I was taken to, for a moment I felt all things within everything. The word wasn't the word, and all was within all. It was a whirlwind, a backwards spiral throughout time."

The man in the hat tapped his chin as he grinned, and said, "Sssooo, what are you saying? You don't believe in God?"

"I do, but not in the way everybody else does. I think in a different language I can't hope to describe. It's like everybody is watching the same play, but they all view it from different angles. I see God in literally everything. All is symbolic towards the greater truth. It's comforting, but terrifying all at the same time. I miss the depth of the deeper feeling I used to have in it all—the faith and the belief."

The man in the hat slammed his fist upon the table, and yelled, "Okay, alright! We all get it, you know everything! You understand the world better than everyone else, blah, blah, blah. Good for you, pal; steal the show. Nobody cares! Don't you get it?! Nobody gives a fuck!"

I sat coolly at the end and shrugged my shoulders, "I know they don't. I don't really care either, but I got all these stories; all these books floating around in my head. I don't know what it is, I just can't help myself. The first book fell flat, but it was the start of something. I have to see the work done; there's still so much more to come."

The man in the hat replied, "Ahhhh, so you're here for a story. You sure you're ready? It's not a pretty tale; just another fool's journey. Shall we begin?"

"Yes, I'm ready. It's the only way I can fix the second book."

"Well, take my hand then, friend. It's story time. Pick up that old journal of yours and get your typing fingers ready. Let us see, between the two of us, and answer the question of the mantle. Who is the true Prince of Fools?"

CHAPTER I:

LET ME RIDE

Life is a circle and no matter what you do things always tend to come back around. Back to the same old town and the same old ground. It ain't too bad, I guess. I mean, my roots are laid down in this town of mine. Being back around the fam; everything seems fine, and it's just like old times, but I want something new and something true. I guess I just want something to do.

My pencil tapped against my knee rapidly as my leg bounced nervously. The teacher's drawn out voice dragged, and his footsteps paced across the room. *Squeak, stomp, tap;* voices muttered, chattering, and rapping. My eyes jerked towards the clock, *tick, tock, tick. The bell better come quick. My heads about to split.*

The teacher's monologue faded past the spinning hands on the wall, and chattering filled the room. The whispers grew faster and pervaded the class; dragging against my eardrums like nails on a chalkboard. I chomped the corner of my lip hard and my eyes fluttered rapidly across the faces in the room. *I can't stand crowds. The energy, it's just too much for me.*

Imagine being struck by lightning in your seat, only you can't move, do, or say anything about it. *Don't make a move; they'll all think you're crazy if you do.*

Your breath races, and you struggle constantly to catch it. The pores widen, and your face grows numb. Hair stands up on the back of your neck, and the corners of your eyes tighten. Ringing ensues, and the lights brighten. *The buzzing of the bulbs, and it all collects; flowing together.* It hurdle's into your soul and nails away at your life force. *There's too many people in here, I can't take it. The constant chatter is too much, the quick moving lips, locks that drip, somebody took a slurp, then a sip. It's too much, I can't take it. I can't—wait. Somebody's watching me.*

I snuck my gaze towards the side slow. A girl with a slight shade of freckles running across her cheek was glaring at me. She jerked her gaze away and giggled. I cowered and flicked my head down. *Do I look stupid? Do I look ridiculous today? Do I—*

My cheeks blushed, and my mind chattered; eyes dancing across the orb on the desk. *Well, she is pretty. Maybe she likes me.* The turn came quick, killing the light.

But she doesn't like you, and you know it. Nobody could like you, nobody's ever wanted you. Your shape is abnormal, and your form is frail. You're hideous, boring, and disgusting. You're the epitome of air. Nothing is there.

My cheeks sunk, and my eyes grew heavy, then hot. *But I wish she did; I wish there was somebody.*

Laughter erupted from the corner, and the cracking of a ruler snapped.

"Quiet! Dammit! Quiet, I said," the teacher hollered.

"If you won't be quiet in my class, you can exit the room!"

Chuckling grew in the group, and steam blew out of the teacher's ears.

"You think this is funny?! You think this is a game?!"

He charged towards the loudest participant; a fat kid named Michael.

"Ha! Ha! Laugh it up, Michael! Ha! Ha! If you like laughing so much, you can do it for the rest of the week in after school detention, buddy!"

Mister, whoever—can bland be a description?

Mister Bland meant business, and he was fuming. Michael snickered back in his face," After school detention? I don't care. I ain't gonna go. What you gonna do? How you gonna make me?"

Mister Bland jerked himself straight and tightened up his stance. His fists balled up, and his cheeks grew red as he shook.

"Why I outta—"

Then he erupted, and snapped; jamming a finger in Michael's face.

"You're damn lucky we don't paddle here anymore. Because God give me the strength; I would tear right into your ass, boy!"

Michael twisted his neck, mimicking a cast look of confusion, "Tear into my ass?"

He jumped up from the desk, and stepped to Mister Bland, getting in his face, "Go head tan me up then."

My eyes shuffled in confusion; mustering what I could to follow along. I threw my hand over my mouth and muffled my laughter. I always have a way of coming up with funny scenes throughout the day for entertainment. The world is wild, there's plenty of opportunities for inspiration; *fuel for the fool.*

Mister Bland edged closer towards Michael, clenching his teeth, and flaring his nostrils. *He's just like a dragon; a fire-breathing dragon.* The scene grew intense, and my knee bounced onward. In anticipation, the classroom grew still.

Mister Bland edged his nose into Michael's face, and the tension grew. *I can feel it. I can feel it in the air.*

Suddenly, the bell rang, and seats shuffled. Legs on desks dragged, and both of them disappeared. *Awwww, I wanted to see a fight.*

I got up and snatched up my trapper keeper, then the pencil on my desk. The chattering began again, and everything was buzzing. Elbows bounced together and shoulders shuffled. *Giggling, wailing, barking,* the sea was maddening. *All the noise, noise, noise. Dammit, with the sound,* I thought to myself.

I shimmied into the hall quickly, hugging my trapper close to my chest like it was a teddy bear. My chin edged downward, and my eyes fluttered across the crowd. Legs kicked, elbows bumped, and suddenly there was a shove. I fell to the right, and there was another bouncing me back to the left.

"Hey, what the—"

I was caught in the middle of two fat girls fighting.

"You wanna talk shit come on," one hollered.

The other threw another shove, and yelled, "Come on with it, then!"

The chattering grew louder, and the humming of the lights burned. Another shove, another struggle. I tried to wiggle through the crowd, but I couldn't. *There's too many, too many of them, all at once. I can feel it all in the air. The constant hum, I need some rum. To drum it all down, yes, I do.* When I'm sober, sometimes it can be too much for me to handle. All the waves constantly flow; it's like living underwater, within the sea. Everything is touched—it is all connected; some are conductors, and others are vampires..

Another shove came, and I was caught in the middle. They got closer, and I was sandwiched between the two. I struggled with my elbows, shaking, nervously clenching my teeth, and tightening my jaw. The barking gnashed at my ears.

"Okay, now," I struggled further; trying to shimmy away, still caught in the middle of the brawl.

"Okay."

I'm trying to be nice about it.

A wobbly arm jiggled across my nose; caking musty, slippery sweat across my face. Some had even gotten in my mouth.

Ewwww. I snatched my neck around in disgust, then jerked and shoved my way out from between the two with all the force I had, and screamed, "Alright! Damn, man! Holy fuck; get away from me! Everybody please just get away from me right now!"

The noise still buzzed, but it grew lower. The girls stopped fighting, and I screamed, "Geez, man! Why does everybody have to act so crazy all the time?! I've had it with this shit!"

I clenched the sides of my hair and dug my nails across my face; screaming again, "I've had it with this place! I've had it dammit! I've had it!"

I went straight towards the bathroom and pulled the dish soap out of my trapper keeper. I don't know why, but I always have to play a joke on somebody, *it's a sickness.* One time, I even put in the time to heat up a Snickers bar with a lighter and throw it in the urinal. It was mayhem, and I loved the screams. I pulled the bottle out and drizzled the dish soap all across the tile floor. *Drip, drip, slip, slip. Somebody's about to fall.* I love accidental things that interrupt plans. Except when I'm on the receiving end that is. I don't know why. I guess I'm just a nutcase.

I turned to run down the hall towards the exit, but the janitor, with gray hair and a closely manicured beard, stopped me along the way, and asked, "Where will thee go?"

I threw my hands up, and shook my head, then snapped, "I don't know, dude. I just gotta get out of here, far away from this place. If I disappear, tell the staff or whoever I went to California or somethin'. I don't know, man."

I marched down the hall and flung open the swinging glass doors at the front. A lady teacher screamed after me, "Where do you think you're going, mister?!"

The question alone annoyed me. I turned around and screamed, "Leave me alone, you evil old hag! I can't take it in this place anymore! I quit, I tell ya! I quit!"

Her voice rumbled and echoed after me as I turned, "You can't just go home whenever you want to, kid! That's against the law!"

I carried onward towards the parking lot, not caring for a thing at all. She kept hollering in the distance, not taking a further step out of the door. She didn't care to chase me, only scream.

I yelled back over my shoulder, "Bye! Bye! Bye, bye now!"

She slammed the door, giving up, and my shoulders relaxed. The wind swept me away, and the birds tweeted. I closed my eyes and drew a relaxing breath in. *Finally, calmness.*

Fallen leaves rattled and twirled; the chilled air kissed me upon the neck, and I exhaled in relief. *Finally, some peace and quiet, but what to do now?*

Once I got close enough to the car, I flicked the bill of my hat up, and grinned as I clicked unlock, and swung open the driver door. *I love this ride.*

It was a 2004 silver Nissan Altima. I bought the car with straight cash. In a way, it felt like my dad had bought it for me, even though he wasn't there with me when I got it. But he was; at least I'd like to think I felt him. I'd trade it all, to get you back. *I don't care about the money. I'd burn it all if it would make a difference; if only for a second.* My mom still controlled the fund, though, so I wouldn't blow it all. I wasn't trustworthy enough.

I shimmied around the purple flat bill of my cap to the back; it was custom. Not straight back, more to the side. *Yeah, like a helicopter.* The word Joker faced the front now in the rearview, running across my forehead. A clown smiled on the front towards the back.

Where to go, I thought to myself as my back fell into the seat. *There's nothin' to do in this town.* That may be, but I love the place. I don't know. I guess there's just something special about it.

Of course, there's the Y-Bridge. We're the only town in the whole wide world that's got one. I like it; sort of symbolic, if you ask me. *It doesn't matter which way you're goin' there's still two ways you can turn. Threefold.* Putnam Hill Park is the best place to go if you want to get a real good look at it. You can look out across it all up there, the stretch of the Y; where two rivers clash over the heart of a city that refuses to die.

It's magical, to say the least. My favorite part about the view isn't even the town, though, it's the looking out into infinity, the beyond, where the birds fly, and the clouds rise. To a place where dreams really do come true. Like a promised land, y'know? I don't know. I guess somewhere past the crows is where I wanna go.

I know heaven on Earth doesn't exist, but I guess I've always imagined that special place for me to be out west—in a little town called 29 Palms, to be exact. In a way, that's where it all started for me. I wasn't born there, though. Nope. Zanesville is pretty much all I really know, but mom told me she was pretty sure that's where I was conceived. I'm not sure. I guess, I dream about that space in the desert so much because it was a place where the three of us were truly all together and they were happy, even if you can't see me in any of the pictures.

My dreams go far, a lot farther than I've ever really gone. The furthest I made it was about an hour outside of the 'Ville in the middle of nowhere. I hated the start of it. Y'know, switching schools and all. I'd went to school with the same kids since kindergarten, but here I was, seventh grade, and starting over again. It felt ridiculous.

I might be stuck out here, but I'm not dressing like them. I'm too fat to wear tight preppy clothes like that, even if that's the type that gets all the girls.

I had to have my own style, but it didn't get me anywhere. It just left me ostracized amongst the crowd; abandoned. *There I go being dramatic again.* I solemnly correct myself. I did end up making a lot of friends, but I only really hung with a few. I'm very selective of the people I choose to affiliate with; the energy has to be correct in order for me to relax around them. We were a solid crew, practically OGs together. We massacred grunts in Halo on the daily.

My mom moved me and my little brother Paul out there to help us stay out of trouble. I guess she didn't want us to grow up like her. At least that's what she said, but who knows? It might've just been her boyfriend at the time that wanted us all to leave everything we knew behind. That tends to happen.

I never took a liking to the guy; always on that high horse of his. I was so glad when they broke up. The guy was pretty ugly and on top of that, he was a weirdo. He never had anything nice to say. *Thank god that was all over with. Tick tock, tick tock, goes the clock; off and away flies the flock.*

If only Derek would hurry up and get to the parking lot. After all, I didn't want Miss Cringle to make her way down and scream at me some more. *Highly improbable either way.*

I slid the screen up on my phone like a secret agent man and jammed away at the keyboard and texted Derek, *If you still need a ride, I'm leaving now.*

That would be good enough. I'm not much of a texter; only have a handful of numbers that will actually commute.

I only waited two minutes and called him. I'm quite the impatient type of guy to tell you the truth. I hate waiting on folks; always gotta stay on the move. The line rang and Derek picked up, "What's up, bubbies? I'm headed down your way now."

I couldn't figure out why he always called me "bubbies." Damn near everybody was calling each other that since I got back home. Derek was one of the few buddies I had left to call me that, though. Most of my old friends I grew up with were on some funny acting shit since I got back to town; like I'm not the same kid they grew up with and I'm different now. *Oh well, I figured, who needs 'em?* Derek was like a brother to me at this point, anyway. When it comes to friends, sometimes it's more about quality rather than quantity, I like to think.

Derek appeared at the window, with his fitted cap on, and a wide grin on his face; he said, "You scared or somethin'? Why you got the door locked for?"

I hit the unlock button, and he hopped right in. I said, "Yeah, I had to make sure the staff wouldn't lynch me. I'm a man of precautions. This teacher lady was pissed when she caught me walking out."

Derek laughed, "Why didn't you just creep out the side like me? Walking right out the front like that, you were asking for it."

I cranked up the Altima and laughed. "I was tryin' to make a statement. I'm my own boss now. They don't tell me what to do."

Yeah, that's right. I just turned eighteen.

Derek laughed, then he pulled out a bag of some high-grade mids and tossed the bud across a magazine. He said, "You got the shells, bubbies?"

I pulled 'em out of the console right away. It was time to get high and touch the sky. *Finally.*

I told Derek, "You already know I do. They're the maple syrup-flavored zigzags, too."

Derek clapped and rubbed his hands together, laughing still, and said, "Just like breakfast."

I dashed the Altima out of the parking lot and agreed all the way, "Damn right because we're just gettin' started."

CHAPTER II:

I WANNA GET HIGH

Derek and me were so smoked out I had to roll down the windows so I could see; we were still cruisin' around town after all. Smoke billowed out from all corners of the car. The air rushed through and got it a sweet taste of some afternoon tune. Three sheets to the wind never felt so true and we hadn't even pulled up to the State Street Market to get our bottles of Wild Irish Rose for us two.

Derek laughed through all the haze that was blowing away.

He tried to speak, but all the coughing caught him up. He finally stammered, "Fuck, man—the cops see all this smoke—man fuck the cops, I ain't seen one in weeks, we're out anyway."

I panicked immediately, "What?! We're out?! We smoked the whole bag already?"

Derek rested his bloodshot eyes against his palms and managed to muffle, "Yeah, and we used up all the shells already, too."

It was unbelievable. We smoked three breakfast blunts at the snap of a finger, just like that. I was feeling so stupid I couldn't even think. All I could do was worry, lose myself to the paranoia, and drive around in circles.

I stare out towards the never-ending houses that ran down the street smothering me within an illusion of claustrophobia and panic. *Shit, all I got is a twenty,* I thought to myself, *low, but it should be enough.*

I murmured, "Geez, man. We gotta get more or we're gonna be bored. I can't sit sober with myself. I'll go crazy. I'll—"

Derek interrupted, "Man you buggin' right now, bro."

Then he laughed, "We're gonna get more, man, just calm down. First things first, though."

I looked over at Derek. He was grinning from ear to ear. I waited for him to say more, but he kept staring. *Quite unnerving to tell you the truth.*

I looked back at the road in silence and back at him again, repeatedly. It all felt like an eternity. A whole alternative universe could've been created within the timeframe. I finally broke the silence and snapped, "Well, what do ya mean first things first, man? You're just over there staring at me, got me waitin' on what you're about to say and shit."

Derek bounced back in his seat, howling. The afternoon rays bounced across his face from behind the red and yellow leaved trees that lined Brighton Boulevard, making him look like some sort of mad psychedelic cartoon weaving its way into the fabric of the Altima's interior.

He finally broke free from his own madness and said, "I'm just fuckin' with you, man. What I mean is, first things first, we gotta take this Biggie CD out, bro. That shit is played out."

Nobody around my age likes the same type of music that I do. Y'see, I like the old school stuff, real rap, not the "hip hop" stuff or whatever everybody else listens to today. Back then, rappers taught you how to make money. Folks these days teach you how to be an addict, and I'm trying to figure some shit out. I wanna know how to get it. What he said was unspeakable; I couldn't believe it. Biggie was like a prophet or somethin'.

"What do you mean Biggie's played out? He's the best there ever was, man. I mean I got Jay-Z, Pac, Nas. Whatever you want it's in the CD book in the back."

The clapping of the pages were already moving and falling past Derek's fingertips before I got another word out. That book of mine has the best of the best in it. Pretty much all nineties rap. I keep my secret mixes behind the CD's I know nobody would care to touch. I'm a rocker, too, I just don't let anybody know it. Eighties songs are pretty much my favorite, even the pop songs.

They're all bootlegged, though, so I'm pretty much a thief, I guess. I mean, if a good up and comer releases a debut, I'll buy it so I can help someone make their dream come true; it makes me feel like I'm a part of making them into a star, but as far as the ones with millions go, they pretty much got their money. They're doing a hell of a lot better than me.

Derek flipped onward through the endless pages and said, "Man, you might got it, but you don't know nothin' about no Pac or Nas. You get more into that Eminem shit, just admit it."

He had me a little there. I mean, after all, I loved listening to the greats, but when it comes to the big three that are still around, Jay-Z, Kanye, or 50, I don't know who I like more honestly. I mean, Jay came out on the scene with his own record label. That dude done had money, he was getting' it, and he's my teacher. When I listen to his music, I gotta make a dollar doin' somethin'. It's motivating, and it gives me that drive. *I gotta keep it movin', I gotta get it.*

When Kanye came on, nobody believed in him. Kanye might be my favorite because he's from the Midwest, he gets it; Chi Raq and all that. Kanye had a dream and he beat all the odds. He made it happen. When I hear his music it helps me believe in myself because I wanna be just like that. With 50, that dude is strong, and to me he's sort of the best. I mean, who had a bigger debut than "Get Rich or Die Tryin'"? Nobody. "Power of the Dollar" sunk when he got shot. Columbia dropped him, but he still picked himself back up. 50 Cent is a modern day hero, and he knows the flow. He knows when to step off one industry and climb into another. He's definitely one of my heroes, and Em put him on. Eminem was the biggest underdog. Everybody took him for a joke, but he made it happen, and I hate to admit it, but we're a lot alike. Maybe not the same life, but we're both crazy.

When I listen to their music, it helps me feel strong like them inside, but when they talk about getting money, and I pull out my own pockets, I don't have shit. *I need to get mine somehow*, I'd think to myself, but it never seems to work out.

I've tried about everything I can think of. From bootlegging movies and sellin' them to folks or even brewin' up some fake moonshine. *A little juice, fruit, and a lifted bottle of Everclear, you can get about 6 jars outta that, ten a pop each;* gotta be careful with that, though. Don't sell the fake stuff to the backwoods folks, they ain't too much into playin' about their liquor. I've seen the movie "Deliverance", I know how they are, and those folks don't play, but here in town, nobody really cares; *too sleepy from the heroin, I guess.* Don't worry yourselves. I'll never mess with the stuff. Xannies are kinda fun, though. I have to admit. *I like 'em.*

Derek kept flipping through the pages and said, "All this shit is old. You got anything new? Didn't you say you burnt Flockaveli the other day?"

I rolled my eyes at the oncoming yellow lines of the road faster than the wheels were carrying us.

"Yeah I did, man. It should be in the back of the book."

Derek was excited. He threw a stack of pages to the left and the weight landed in his lap with a thud. Before I knew it, Biggie was out faster than you could say big poppa and the clicks of guns and rounds sounding off percolated across the speakers.

The beat dropped and Derek flipped his hat back to get in the mode. He spit the words to "Bustin' at Em" flawlessly along with Flocka. He already knew the entire album by heart. Dude was talented, I gotta admit. He could put some words together, at least I think. I mean, most of the time I'm so faded I don't know what he's talkin' about, but it sounds good and he sure can match a beat.

My eyes skipped across the dash. *We gotta figure something out here.*

We still didn't have a plan. So I turned the music down and asked Derek, "Okay, first things first is off the list now, so like what are we gonna do about the weed situation, man? We're dry on everything and I'm ready to smoke again."

D's vibe dimmered. *How selfish of me.*

"You gotta calm down, man. You ain't even givin' anybody time to hit me back yet."

Derek tapped his fingers against his chin and stare out the window, then he said, "We could always roll up the block and see if Tony's home. He's usually wit it."

I hit the brakes at the red light and wavered away from the idea.

"I guess, but Von lives a little closer. He might have some smoke."

Derek shook his head.

"Man, he don't ever have any money. You oughta know he ain't got none. I'll try to hit Tony up first and see if he's home."

The phone rang, and a part of me hoped that it would keep on doing just that. Y'see, the thing is, Tony's cool and all, but he cracks too many jokes sometimes and it seems like they're always on me. If it's just us, sometimes he's cool, but if anybody else is around, he goes out of his way to front me out. It's sort of my fault, though, because I let him get by with it. I don't have a lot of courage when it comes to standing up for myself. My friends are few and I don't want to lose 'em by stirring up an issue.

Tony answered on the other end. I could barely make out his voice from the driver's seat. Derek smiled and said, "What up, bubbies? You got any smoke?"

I heard a muffled response drag its way into Derek's ear, then he said, "Ight bet, we about to pull up, then."

Click.

"He's home. He said Kayla's about to roll through and drop 'em off a twenty. You got ten or somethin' to put on it? Y'know how he can be sometimes."

I nodded my head as I turned the wheel at the light to pass the Fair Grounds on the right.

"Yeah, I got about twenty left to work with until I get some more CD's or somethin' sold."

I rolled my eyes. Not just over bein' nearly broke, but because I didn't really like puttin' in on a sack with Tony. He likes to short the bag sometimes, even if you go even, but in this type of case I didn't really have much of a choice.

Tony lived down in brick city, or what folks around town call the Manor. It might sound fancy, y'know with the name and all, but it's not much to look at; pretty much just a bunch of old brick buildings clustered together with a load of crazy folks running around hollerin' at each other all the time. The place makes me a little nervous to tell you the truth. I've heard a lot of crazy stories about it.

I'm not sure how true it all is, but back in the day, or in the eighties you could say, the Jersey boys used to run the whole complex, like the place was the Carter from "New Jack City" or somethin'.

Those dudes were mean, the bad boys in town, and not too many folks were keen on messing with them. Maybe they were tough, or maybe they weren't. Either way, it didn't matter to my grandpa. He got into it with a couple of them one time and they thought they had the stones to take the old man down, but unfortunately for them, even bein' in his fifties, he was still kickin' ass like road house. He beat the brakes off a few of 'em all on his own, and to hear my uncle tell it, that was the day he knew his dad wasn't somebody to mess with. He's a solo wrecking ball, a hero in the town.

The Manor wasn't much to worry about these days, though, but I gotta admit, the roads make it a twisty place that's hard to navigate, especially if you're high; *everything looks the same.*

"Hey, man, you was supposed to go left that way," Derek said sharply.

I threw my hands up and hit the brakes.

"Man, I don't know where I'm goin'. This place is like a fuckin' maze."

Derek pointed to an open spot by the curb and said, "Don't worry about it, just park there. His place ain't too far. We can just walk from here."

Each of our doors slammed, one after the other, and I jogged my way over to the sidewalk to follow Derek. A girl in sweats and a ponytail passed us as we walked. She gave Derek the look. He didn't even acknowledge her.

Must be nice, I thought to myself. The girl wasn't much to look at I'll admit, but that's the part that hurt. She didn't even notice me. I was below her standards, and I knew it; *a bottom feeder.*

Derek turned up the walk fast, and banged on the screen door to Tony's apartment; I followed.

Tony flung the door open, halting the rattling.

"Damn, man, why you knockin' like you the cops for?"

Derek weaved his voice into a Jamaican accent, mimicking this dude named Max from the movie "Shottas."

"Who done killed my kid, bruddha?"

Tony busted out laughing and they each clapped up hands. When we shake, we wrap up knuckles, and at the end we make a gun out of our fingers. *Bang; guns for life.*

Tony looked past Derek's shoulder at me and grinned. His eyes landed on my shoes.

"Damn, look who got the new elevens. Mama get paid today or what?"

Here we go, I thought.

Exhaling, and nearly breaking a sweat, I replied, "Uh, no. I mean, I've had these for a while. My uncle gave 'em to me."

Tony nodded, "Yeah, yeah, I bet. What size you wear again?"

Derek grinned, clicking his tongue against his teeth, and said, "Man, stop playin'. We gonna smoke or what?"

Tony cackled, "Nah, Kayla ain't here yet. I don't know where that bitch is."

Derek shrugged his shoulders.

"I guess we'll just chill, then."

We sat out front and hung out. There were only two plastic chairs. Tony took one, Derek took the other. I stood for a while, but then I figured I'd take a seat, too. The ground was all that was left, so I just popped a squat and propped my back up against the bricks and got settled. My hands shook as I lit up another smoke. My high was drifting away into the cloudy sky and the edginess was beginning to roll back in. As long as I'm drunk, high, or both, I can handle being around other people, but without it, I start to come undone.

My anxiety gets so bad when I'm sober I get all twitchy, my mouth goes dry, and I damn near feel like I'm about to lose my mind. My heart races and I nod, all the while praying for a break in the conversation so I can make my escape.

"S-sorry, I g-gotta use the b-bathroom," I'll usually say, or sometimes I don't make an excuse at all. Deep breaths and a run for the door. Once I'm alone again, I'm at peace, but only for a moment. That's how the split goes. I hate to be alone, but I can't stand to be around other people. The only way I can find my balance is through the buzzy stuff. It makes me happy and helps me be who I wanna be; *my one true self.*

Suddenly, Tony tapped Derek on the elbow and nodded towards this kid walking down the street in old worn out Champion gear.

"Look at fat boy, over here," Tony said with clenched teeth. Then he hollered, "Ey, Malik!"

There wasn't a response. Apparently, the kid had some ear buds in and they were turned all the way up. You could see the cord on his mp3 player bouncing off his belly, but that didn't matter to Tony. He hated to be ignored.

Tony jumped out of his chair, and Derek tensed up gripping the edges where his arms rested.

"Come on, man," Derek pleaded under his breath, but Tony wasn't listenin'.

He cupped his hands around his mouth and hollered again.

"Hey, Malik!"

Everybody in the Manor had to hear him that time. Malik sure did. He nearly jumped out of his shoes. The poor kid looked like a deer caught in the headlights.

Malik's jaw dropped, and he pulled one of his earbuds out.

"H-hey, Tony. What's up?"

Tony stomped closer and said, "You know what it is. What you got on that fifteen you owe me?"

Malik's feet shuffled and his eyes danced around. I felt sorry for him because he reminded me so much of myself.

Malik stuttered, "W-well, I, umm, I—I don't have it right now. My mower broke on me and I ain't been able to cut any grass the last few days, b-but I promise I'll have it to you next week a-as soon as I get the starter rope fixed."

Tony shook his head, "Nah, you ain't got till next week. I need somethin' now."

Suddenly, he grinned and pointed to the mp3 player clutched in between Malik's fist. The kid knew what was coming next. We all did.

"What about that?"

Malik stammered, "W-what?"

Tony clicked his tongue behind his teeth.

"Don't play dumb, fool, give it up."

Malik's eyes shuffled from left to right.

"Come on, please, Tony. My mom got this for me last Christmas and I finally got all my favorite songs on it. I promise I'll have your money next week."

My stomach churned. *I hate confrontations like this.* I knew Tony didn't give a damn about the fifteen dollars, but he was trying to flex, like he always does. It was like a habit, something he had to do. Malik shuffled in his shoes.

Tony snapped, "I don't give a fuck. I want it now."

Derek jumped up from his chair and said, "Come on, man. Why you trippin'? Just let 'em go, he ain't doin' nothin' to you."

Tony turned his head and looked at Derek. He was grinning from ear to ear. I knew he didn't care. It was all just a big joke to him. He bite his lip and winked, then turned back to Malik, and stepped closer to him. Malik backed away, edging off the sidewalk, and took off into the road. A car's brakes squealed and a horn sounded. The poor kid tried to rush off so quick he about got hit.

Tony howled in laughter and flipped around towards us.

"You see that?! His dumbass about got smeared."

He hollered after Malik again.

"Run, Forest, run!"

He shook his head, chuckling as he sat back in his chair. Derek tssked through his lips.

"Man, you didn't have to do all that. What if that car would've hit him?"

Tony waved his hand in the air, flopping it back in his lap.

"He's the one who ran," Tony laughed, "plus that car wasn't goin' fast enough for him to get hurt."

"Unless it ran him over," Tony continued chuckling, "now that would've been a show."

I gasped under my breath and my eyes felt hot. *Don't think about it, don't think about it too much,* I repeated in my head. *I need to get away from here.*

I was glad I was sitting behind them so I could hide; they couldn't see my face. *No, nobody can see what's inside. I just wanna get high.*

CHAPTER III:

LOST IN THOUGHT

Kayla pulled up a few moments later after the fiasco with Malik and to tell you the truth I was glad, it felt like the Calvary had arrived. She stepped out of her blue Ford Focus and was on a mission; her and a friend.

"What ya'll doin'? Just chillin' makin' the women do all the work," she joked.

Tony said, "It's about time. Shit, I was about to call old girl from around the corner and have her hook me up."

Kayla bit her lip and mashed down her eyebrows.

"Boy, you stupid. You know you can't do better than me," she laughed.

Derek was eyeing her friend, though. I could tell he wanted her from the start.

"What up, Kayla," he said," who's your friend?"

Kayla grinned.

"Don't worry about her, she don't want a dog like you, anyway."

Kayla's friend blushed, then laughed and said, "Stop it. I can talk for myself."

She hesitated and bit her lip just like Kayla when she looked at Derek chillin' in the chair, loungin' out in his fitted cap and loose jeans.

Tony snapped, "Well, damn, talk then, girl. You gonna give my boy some or what?"

Kayla shot back, "Stop trippin', Tony. We ain't with the joke's today."

Tony threw up his hands in defense.

"Damn, sorry. You ain't gotta get all snappy with me. I was just tryin' to hook my boy up, that's all."

He paused, scratched his chin, and said, "Speakin' of that. You got the hookup? You got the smoke?"

Kayla grinned and pulled a twenty sack out of her pocket. She threw it in Tony's lap like it was nothing, and said, "There it is, lazy, grand daddy Kush. You tryin' to roll up or what?"

Tony didn't like bein' called lazy; I could tell. He scooped up the sack and inspected it.

"You better watch who you callin' lazy girl. I ain't tryin' to play no games."

Kayla smirked and stepped over to Tony. He was still flopped down in his chair next to Derek, and I was sitting behind them in the shadows under the broken light. *There, but still unnoticed.* Kayla leaned down and gave him a kiss. Tony's lips caught hers and they got all mushy mouthed together.

"Damn, girl, you sure know how to bring that fire. Thanks," Tony remarked.

Kayla blushed, then she looked up and saw me.

"Is that who I think it is? Why you bein' so quiet in the corner?"

I was already startled and shaken, but when Kayla put the spotlight on me, it shocked me.

I pressed my back up further against the bricks, still in the mud, and stuttered, "Y-you remember m-me?"

Kayla laughed, "Yeah. You was in Miss Tipton's class. We were in kindergarten together and went to Wilson.

You were shy back then, too, but we was still good friends. What you been up to?"

I couldn't believe it. She remembered me. My cheeks grew warm and I said, "N-nothin' much, really. Just h-hangin' out."

Kayla smiled.

"Well, it's nice to see you again. It looks like you're doin' okay, 'cept for hangin' out with these fools," she laughed.

Derek looked back at me from the top of the edge of his chair and grinned.

"You know, Kayla," he asked, "why didn't you say anything?"

I stuttered, "I m-mean, I w-wasn't for sure we knew each other, but I guess we do."

Tony flipped around in his chair and gave me the dead eyes.

"You tryin' to hit on my girl in front of me, homie? That ain't cool."

I froze, startled in the headlights, but then Tony laughed, "I'm just bullshittin'. Don't worry, ain't nobody worried about you."

Kayla smacked Tony on the shoulder and said, "Stop bein' mean. We're just old friends and I haven't seen him in a while, that's all. We gonna smoke or what?"

Tony rubbed his arm and grinned.

"Fo sho, just let me grab the shells inside, girl. Be patient."

Derek turned around at me and winked. I felt relieved. Tony didn't mention a thing about money. He was always happy about free smoke; I was too.

Tony went inside and everybody followed. His place was pretty tidy as always, his mom kept it clean because word was she had OCD, which was always hard for me to imagine because I knew Tony didn't give her any breaks. It didn't take Tony long to roll up. The girls sat with Derek on the couch, and I sat on the other side at the kitchen table all by myself. Tony snapped from his chair, "Ey, ya'll got a lighter or somethin'? I ain't got nothin' to spark this up with."

Derek threw him a lighter from out of his pocket, and Tony lit the blunt. His mom might have been a neat freak, but she didn't care about her place smellin' like weed. She done gave up on that.

Tony licked his lips as the smoke crept out of his mouth. He held it all in the best he could and coughed.

"Damn, that grand daddy don't play," Tony said as he passed the blunt to Derek on the couch. D clapped his hands first and smiled. There was no more hesitation. He hit the blunt and coughed, too.

"God damn, where ya'll get that from," Derek looked at the girls and asked.

Kayla rubbed her legs and smiled, "We got it up in Newark earlier. Me and my girl here was shoppin' at the mall and ran into somebody we knew and they hooked us up. It's good, right?"

Derek passed her the 'rillo.

"That shit hits different. It—"

Tony interrupted, "What you doin' hangin' out with other guys up there for?"

Kayla gave him a damning look and twisted her neck.

"Ain't nobody hangin' out with anybody, stop trippin'. You know him anyway; he knows all about you. He was one of those boys that always be wearin' black and blue."

Tony retorted, "Oh, those my people, then. It's all good."

Kayla exhaled the smoke and coughed, "Yeah, so stop trippin'."

Tony grinned and said, "Girl, don't tell me what to do."

Kayla passed the blunt to her friend beside her so she could hit it, but she refused.

"Nah, I'm good. I gotta go home in a little bit. You know how strict my mom is."

Derek laughed, "Come on, a little hit ain't gonna hurt ya. What's your name, anyway?"

"It's Alyssa," the girl said.

"Oh okay, Alyssa," Derek said, "Don't worry, I got you covered. Ain't like mama's gonna know. Just take a little hit. Where you live, anyway?"

Alyssa blushed, then smiled, "Down on Matthews Street, what's it to you?"

Derek fixed his hat and grinned, "Just wonderin' that's all."

He definitely gave her the eyes when he said it, and she gave them right back. I always thought those kinds of looks were funny. *Damn, he's so brave,* I thought to myself. I wouldn't dare give somebody that type of look I'm too afraid of getting' laughed at. Something like that would make me crumble inside. I'm rejected every time I try, so I don't even go there. *Best to keep the head down.*

Derek startled and shook me back to the present.

"Ey, man, you there or what," he laughed, "it's you're hit."

Tony wasn't paying attention anymore. He was getting' wrapped up whispering in Kayla's ear about something. She shoved his shoulder and giggled, "Stop it."

The sight of it made me sick because I knew behind her back Tony did her wrong.

My lips shook faintly as I smiled.

"B-bout time," I replied.

My nerves raced as I stood up. Blood rushed to my temple; pushing a cold sweat across my forehead. Nobody was watching, but it felt like everyone was. *What if they all look at me and stare*, I thought to myself, *I just wanna hide somewhere.* I gulped at the chance of it. The couch felt so far away. I took a deep breath and collected myself. *I can make it a few steps.*

Nobody's going to look, none of them are going to hurt you, but—they might laugh at you, I thought with the first step.

Tony's going to tell a joke about me, then the girls will laugh, I thought with the second. *Oh, my god do I have dirt on the back of my pants from sitting on the ground? What if it looks like I—no, no, no, don't think it, you can make it. Just breath.*

My mind continued to ramble. The thing never shuts off. *It's like there's a devil inside of me.*

My feet shuffled quickly across the carpet towards the blunt and I snatched it out of Derek's hand and took the biggest hit I could.

"Damn, man," Derek chuckled," I didn't know you was that ready to smoke."

He tapped Alyssa on the arm, cutting his eyes back and forth between her and me.

"My boy here is like the smoking king. Look at 'em."

Alyssa smiled, but I could tell she wasn't interested at all. She didn't even care to look at me.

The Kush burned in my lungs, but I couldn't cough. *No, you can't cough. You'll look weak and they'll all make fun.* A scene from the movie "Carrie" came alive in my head and I heard her crazy mother scream, "There all going to laugh at you!"

"No, they won't mama, they're good people, they're all good," Carrie pleaded.

I choked on the smoke and cackled. It was nearly uncontrollable.

Everyone else laughed, too. My body tensed up.

Tony yelled, "Oh shit! It done took off with 'em."

He threw his chin up and looked at Derek, grinning, "Smokin' king my ass."

They're all going to laugh at you. The whiny voice in my head came again.

I heard Kayla retort, "Stop bein' mean, Tony," but I didn't care to look. I was too nervous; *the wave didn't come yet.*

I took another long drag without even thinking about it. My sides nearly split because I wanted to laugh again. *They're good people, they're good. But don't laugh,* my mind rambled, *they'll all think you're mad if you laugh again,* the voice said.

"Ey, ey, ey," Tony snapped, "You makin' the blunt run hittin' it like that."

My right hand dangled the rillo at my side, and my left clenched at the shirt on my chest as I coughed uncontrollably again. *Much, much better.* I didn't care what Tony had to say anymore.

He leaned from the couch and snatched the blunt out of my fingers, then let off a scowl.

"Shit, you tryin' to smoke me up like a vacuum or somethin'," Tony snapped, "must like suckin' on things."

Everybody busted out laughing in the room, but I didn't even care. I floated back to the kitchen chair and let the head change settle. I'll admit, I laughed, too, but then I got brave.

"You're just mad, 'cause you know I could out smoke you any day," I chuckled and snapped. I sunk back into the chair.

It didn't bother Tony, he was calm, too.

"Oh yeah, we'll see about that someday," he retorted before the rillo hit his lips and he took another puff. Then he hissed as the smoke exhaled, "You done met your match."

46

Kayla giggled as Tony passed her the blunt.

"Both of ya'll ain't got nothin' on me. I'm the smokin' queen."

She took a second hit and studied me while she did it. *What's she thinking about,* I thought to myself. *Do I look stupid because I'm high? Do I look dumb right now?*

The anxiety monsters were crippling me. *I need a drink to go on top of this to settle everything. The weed just ain't enough,* I thought to myself.

Suddenly, the air grew thin, and the lighting in the room seemed to change. *Is it all in my head or am I trippin'?*

Something was watching us, or at least it felt that way. I looked past the calendar on the wall, October 14th, 2010. My mind took note, but suddenly I saw a shadow stroke. The silhouette moved from the corner of the room and rushed its way down the hallway. My muscles tensed, but I didn't dare say a word about it. I knew it wasn't the weed either. *The shadow people are back,* I thought to myself, *I better stay away from the mirrors.*

Suddenly, I heard Alyssa cough again, which pulled me out of my thoughts. Then Kayla asked me, "So, where's your girl at?"

I wasn't sure who she was talking, too, so I didn't answer. My fingers tapped nervously against my bouncing knee and my eyes fluttered across the carpet, getting lost in each strand.

"Hey you there," Derek called out, joking. He cupped his hand around his mouth as if he were shouting for someone lost out at sea. Then he said, "Kayla's talkin' to you, bro."

I came, too.

"What's up?"

Kayla asked again, "So where's your girl at? You got one or what?"

I gulped, and my eyes burned. They were already getting dry from the smoke.

"Uhhh, n-no. I don't have one. I don't have a girlfriend or anything."

Kayla nudged Alyssa on the arm and flashed her a quick smile, then said, "Well, my girl right here is single. Why don't you talk to her?"

Alyssa looked at me and mushed her upper lip; she looked disgusted, but then her eyes fell on Derek next to her. She blushed.

"No, thanks. I think I'm already taken."

Derek leaned back and grinned so hard you could see the whole gap in his front teeth. He's a comical guy when it comes to just about everything, and I think that sort of abrasiveness even caught him off guard. He fluttered his eyebrows up and down at Alyssa, then leaned closer to her.

"Okay, then," Derek said as he slid his hand over, across the leather armrest, to grip hers.

Kayla clicked her tongue across the back of her teeth and rolled her eyes. Then she continued talking to me.

"Don't worry, I got somebody else I can hook you up with. She's a real nice girl, you'll like her. Her name is—"

Tony interrupted, "Ain't nobody tryin' to hook up with your hoe ass friends."

Kayla slapped him across the shoulder and he felt the burn; I could tell.

"Owww, why you hit me for?"

Kayla snapped, "Don't talk about my friends like that. They ain't hoes, they just haven"t found the right one yet."

Derek nodded at me to pass the blunt again. His focus had shifted more towards the show than Alyssa. I'll admit mine had, too. I crept over and took the rillo again. I didn't want to risk disturbing anything. I took another drag and watched.

Tony scowled at Kayla.

"Shit, all of 'em, the same way. What about old girl that you used to run around with? I can't even remember her name. She be suckin' dick for cigarettes and everything. What you tryin' to do give somebody AIDs?"

Derek busted out laughing, and Alyssa's mouth fell open in shock.

Kayla patted her on the leg for reassurance.

"He ain't talkin' about you, don't worry."

Then she snapped back at Tony, "I know exactly who you're talkin' about and it ain't like that. You know Mikey made that shit up 'cause my girl left his ass. He shouldn't have been cheatin' point blank, period, but, no, that ain't the girl."

Kayla unruffled her feathers and calmed back down, then she gazed back at me and said, "Don't listen to what these fools say. Birds of a feather flock together, and I ain't no hoe, and my friends aren't either."

Kayla took a deep breath and her tone grew warm.

"I'll find the right girl for you, I promise. I got your back," she winked.

Tony snapped, "Ey, man, you gonna pass me the blunt or what? I've been waitin' for years over here."

"Oh shit, sorry my bad."

I got up and handed Tony back the rillo. The clocked ticked on the wall. Fifteen minutes past two.

"Fuck, I gotta go," I panicked.

Derek wiggled in his chair.

"Why what's up?"

"I gotta pick up Paul from school. I almost forgot."

Derek nodded, "Shit, okay, then. Just get at me later, then. We'll just be chillin'."

Derek shouted after me, "Ey! Don't forget Ellie is havin' a party at her house later. You gonna show up?"

My hand fell on the doorknob and twisted it halfway. Then I turned around.

"Yeah, for sure. I'll text you later and let you know somethin'."

Derek nodded, "Okay, then."

I jerked the door open, but then Kayla called after me, too.

"Don't forget, I'm gonna hook you up."

I wanted to plant a joke on Tony before I left, it nearly killed me not to, but I had to go. My head shook up and down, and I pressed the screen door open.

"O-okay, see ya around."

CHAPTER IV:

FIRST OF THE MONTH

Now my little brother Paul ain't really little and he's just a few years younger than me; thirteen, to be exact. He started middle school when we moved back and, just like me, he's already having problems with girls. He's sort of going through the overweight phase too, like I did around his age, but he doesn't take any shade if anybody tries to give him any for it—unless it's from me, that is. I try not to mess with him too much, but it's fun, and I get bored. I don't know. What else is an older brother supposed to do?

The wheels stopped, and I pulled into the church parking lot across from the school right on time. Paul was crossing the road, and I waved him over. He hopped in real quick and said, "Damn, man; It smells like weed in here! You gonna let me have some or what?"

My throat squealed in a maniacal laugh. He was firing on all cylinders already; talkin' all quick and fast like. It didn't help I was blown. I looked over at him and said, "Absolutely not. Mom would kill me if she found out I let you smoke with me. I mean, she did call the cops on me when she caught me smokin' that black-n-mild out back a couple of weeks ago and everything."

Paul shook in his seat, laughing.

"I tried to warn you when she pulled in, but you acted like you didn't even care. That was all your fault."

My head fluttered from side to side as I backed out of the parking spot and said, "I know, man, but callin' the cops on me for smokin' a black? I mean, for real? She's always gotta be so dramatic about everything."

Gets on my nerves, I thought to myself as my hands turned the wheel and I rolled my eyes.

"Oh well, it is what it is, I guess."

I pulled on to Blue Avenue, and Paul asked, "So where are we goin'? You goin' to Uncle Stallone's cookout?"

Now, we just liked to call my mom's older brother Stallone, but that wasn't really his name. In a way, he sort of looks like Rocky from the movies, sort of Italian, y'know, and he's kind of known as an action star himself around town. Not because he was in the army or anything. He just used to be a little nuts in his younger days.

One time he either got cheated on a bet or cheated somebody himself and a few folks in the pool hall tried to gang up on him. They might've had four on their team, but Uncle Stallone had about sixteen hard cue balls on his, plus a pool stick. I don't even have to say what happened next, but everybody got cracked and he used to pitch, too. After that day, word got around and everybody knew. Don't mess with Stallone because he's packin' those missiles.

I smacked the steering wheel and yelled, "Shit, I forgot!"

Paul replied, "Well, bub, you look crisscrossed right now, honestly; just tellin' you the truth. You got any shades or anything, man?"

"Yeah, I do. I ain't worried about it, though. Is mom gonna be there?"

Paul shook his head.

"No, she's gotta work tonight, but you're lucky she's not."

Feeling a tinge of panic, I turned a quick glance at Paul and asked, "Why? Did she say something to you?"

"No, I haven't talked to her today," he continued laughing, "you just look toasted, bub, that's all."

I felt relieved at that as I thought, *Gee thanks for noticin' pal.* Then the panic settled right back in. *I wonder if the school called her today?*

When we pulled up to Uncle Stallone's down on Echo Avenue, I put my shades on anyway because, to tell you the truth, I didn't want anybody to know that I was burnt.

As soon as Paul and I got out of the car, I could already smell the burgers cooking outside and I could hear the O'jays "Love Train" humming from the radio in the backyard. That meant that grandpa and grandma were there too because if they weren't, the eighties station would be playing. Uncle Stallone loves doing the moonwalk when Michael Jackson's singing.

A little kid came darting up to us on his bike from down the street to say what's up to Paul. He had friends everywhere already, even if he didn't actually grow up in the 'Ville. Hell, I did, and he already had more than me. He's the friend kind of guy and I'm the loner type of dude, I guess; complete opposites, everyone says, but that doesn't mean we can't make one hell of a team sometimes. The boy said, "Hey Paul, you gonna go down to Corey's house and play some PlayStation with us?"

Paul replied, "Yeah, I will. I'm gonna say hi to my uncle really quick and I'll be down."

The boy rode back down the street with that.

I looked over at Paul and said, "Don't bring that kid up here if you go down there to hang out."

Paul grinned, "Who Corey? Why not? Because he always calls you Vanilla Ice?"

"Yeah, I don't like that. He's so annoying."

53

Everybody was excited to see us once we got out back to where the action was happening. To the left of the back patio, my mom's younger brother, Shua, was chillin' with Uncle Stallone's two oldest sons, Zeus and Tommy. Now, Zeus wasn't my cousin's real name, but we all called him that because he was the most cut up guy around town; still is, in fact. He was like the Hulk on the football field back in his day and his brother Tommy was, too. Uncle Shua was pretty good too, and that was one thing that always got me; they were all great at something.

They each graduated ten years ago, and they had always been some of my biggest heroes. I always wanted to make my mark out there on the turf, but I wasn't born with enough heart to make it happen. It always made me feel like a failure because that was the reason why I couldn't wait for high school; so I could be a star, just like they were. That didn't happen, though. The closest I got to making it was being offered the team manager position. I couldn't even cut it being a second stringer.

On the back patio was the card table and, of course, Uncle Stallone was dealing out a hand of cards to a couple of my aunt's brothers, and grandpa; he was at the end of the table, lounged back, looking calm, cool, and collective. He had his poker face on, plus his hat and shades. Of course, he would be in the game with everyone.

He was one hell of a shark back in his day, when it came to the cards, and he still was all the way. He's known for so much more than that, though. He used to be the man around town, ya see, and pretty much ran the whole show. He wore a white turban back then, and he always had a pocket full of dough. He was quick in the mind and even quicker on a motorcycle. Folks still to this day like to say, "Old Geno could ride from Zanesville to Cambridge in less than ten minutes on that motorcycle of his."

The only thing is, it took a little over thirty minutes to reach Cambridge from Zanesville. He had to have shot like lightning across the highway to make that ride in under ten minutes. He might be old now, but folks still respected him all over town. He's great, kind-hearted and will do good by anybody that does right by him, but he also isn't one to tango with if you get on his bad side. Bad, bad, Leroy Brown isn't one of his favorite songs for nothin'.

Uncle Shua shouted, "Hey, come here a minute, man!"

I was still stoned a little, and I wanted to keep my distance, but Uncle Shua was pretty cool and I knew he wouldn't put me on the spot if he noticed I was high. Now, Tommy, however, is a different story. He'll front you out to everybody. Not in a snitch kind of way, but he likes to mess with folks, especially if you're high. He'll blow your buzz in a minute if he catches the slightest opening for a jab.

I walked over to Uncle Shua, Tommy, and Zeus and said, "What's up, ya'll? What ya doin'?"

Uncle Shua leaned forward with his elbow on his knee to scratch his ankle and said, "Not shit, man. You watched "The Town" yet?"

That was everybody's favorite movie at the time; at least all the folks I knew, anyway. I replied, "Hell yeah, man, that movie was good, wasn't it? I downloaded it the other night and watched it on the computer."

I made a gun out of my two fingers and smiled.

"We outta start pulling heists like that, man," I joked.

Tommy interrupted before Uncle Shua could say a word.

"Hell, we couldn't count on you if we were in a bind. Your pants would hit the ground before we'd even get in the bank."

Uncle Shua leaned back in his chair, laughing.

I shot back at Tommy, "Whatever, man. You'd be the first one to get caught if we had to run from the cops."

Zeus sat still, except for the constant bouncing of his leg. He's always tense and ready to go. If anything pops off, he's the guy that's first in line to lead the charge.

Tommy wiggled around in his chair a little and said, "Okay, tough guy. Try to beat me in arm wrestling, then."

Tommy flexed his arm up and said, "Oh yeah, you don't want none of this."

He was right, I didn't. Tommy could break my arm with the flick of his wrist if he really wanted to. I saw him stick one arm in a dryer and lift it right up over his shoulder one time. He was a titan, all three of them were, and I knew not to mess with Tommy when it came down to it. Right before I could make a comeback, though, Tommy's wife Nicole opened the screen door to the patio, and yelled, "Tommy, come in here a minute!"

Tommy spun around in his chair, irritated, and yelled, "What?! Why?!"

Nicole rolled her eyes and replied, "Just come in here for a minute."

Tommy wiggled around and shook his head.
"Whaaaat?!"

He put some emphasis on the "t" at the end. Nicole had him on the edge.

Nicole put a hand on her hip and rolled her eyes, "Stop being stupid, Tommy, just come here. Your daughter made a mess in the kitchen and she won't listen to me."

Tommy jumped up from the chair and threw his hat on the ground.
"Dammit!"

He charged his way inside to assess the situation. The poor guy's relaxing periods always get interrupted. His daughter Keekee is a five-year-old blonde headed heathen, and her favorite phrase is," Crip crap."

Nobody knows what it means, and there's no hope of deciphering it. Perhaps it's gang lingo of some kind. It does have the word crip in it, but I'm not sure. All I know is no matter what, the kid does whatever she pleases and doesn't care too much about the consequences; a true rebel without a cause. You can definitely tell she's one of us.

After Tommy went inside, Zeus laughed, "Bub's a nut, ain't he?"

Uncle Shua laughed, "Fuck yeah, he is."

I glanced around the backyard, but I couldn't see Paul anymore. I asked where he was.

Uncle Shua replied, "Yeah, he went with Marcus down the street to that kid Corey's house, I think."

I looked around again. Everyone wasn't out back. I asked Uncle Shua, "Where's Aunt Jane and Gabbie?"

Uncle Shua replied, "Her sister needed help with somethin', and Gab wanted to go with her. They'll be here later on."

Aunt Jane was Uncle Shua's wife, and she's really cool. She loves to have a good time, and she's been around for as long as I can remember. Her and Uncle Shua have been together since seventh grade, and Gabbie is their daughter together.

She's around seven years old now, and she doesn't talk much. She reminds me a lot of grandpa because he's the same way. They both have their hidden gifts, too. Grandpa has the eye, folks say, because he was born with a veil over his face, which in the olden days meant you could see into other worlds. I think Gabbie can, too. There's a funny little trick she can do. She can tell you what's going to happen before it does sometimes.

I still didn't see grandma either, so I asked Uncle Shua about her, too.

"Where's grandma? What's she doin'?"

Uncle Shua replied, "She's just hangin' out in the house watchin' Scarface."

I laughed, "Again? What is it with her and that movie?"

Uncle Shua only shrugged his shoulders, then a glint on some glass caught my eye. A dazzling mason jar filled full of white lightning was sitting next to his chair. I grinned like the Grinch and pointed at it, "Is that what I think it is?"

Uncle Shua looked down and picked up the mason jar.

"Yeah, it's that lightning in a bottle. You can have some if you think you can handle it."

Suddenly, my aunt Louise hollered from the grill as she slapped together a burger and shook salt across it.

"Uh uh! Don't give that boy any of that! Your sister will kill ya!"

Uncle Shua yelled back, "Come on, it ain't gonna hurt him any!"

Grandpa chimed in from the card table, "Let the boy have a drink. It'll put a little hair on his chest."

All the guys at the table laughed. Uncle Stallone grinned and shook his head, but he didn't care either. They were cool about it. I was either gonna do it there or somewhere else.

Uncle Shua handed me the jar and said, "Just take a sip, man. That's all you'll need, anyway."

I snatched the mason jar, smiling ear to ear. I didn't take a sip, either. I took a whole gulp. Zeus said, "Damn, man! You can definitely tell your one of us."

Uncle Shua shook his head when I handed him back the jar.

"I tried to tell ya, man. We'll see how you feel in a minute."

I didn't feel much at first. I just carried on bullshittin' with Uncle Shua and Zeus, but when I went over to see what was up with Uncle Stallone and grandpa at the card table, the shine really started kicking in. They could see it written all over me immediately. Uncle Stallone looked up from his cards and said, "Well, how you feelin'?"

I chuckled a little and replied, "I ain't gonna lie. I'm feelin' pretty good right now. I'm ready to get fired up."

Uncle Stallone laughed, "Well, don't be goin' and gettin' the red ass on everybody now."

The Dude was sittin' there, too. We call him the Dude. I'm not sure why, but he's my Aunt Louise's brother, and he's a pretty stand-up guy. If you need anything, ask the Dude and he's got you.

The Dude chimed in, "Yeah, you don't want to end up like Bob did the other night. They threw his ass in the drunk tank and I had to go down there and bail 'em out."

I took my shades off laughing, "What did he do?"

The Dude put his cards down on the table and replied, "He was showin' his ass down there at Terry's. Got into it with a guy and tossed 'em across the DJ's stage."

The Dude didn't say another word about it. He shook his head and re-dealt the cards.

Uncle Stallone broke out grinnin' and laughin' as he flicked his smoke into the ashtray. Grandpa just sat there staring at his cards, smiling. Then suddenly I felt my phone vibrating in my pocket and when I pulled it out I saw that it was the call I'd been dreading all day; it was mom. *Oh man, I hope the school didn't call her,* I thought.

I walked out front towards the road to answer the ring.

"Hey, mom, what's up?"

Mom didn't sound happy at all. I could already tell from her tone. All she said was, "Well, is there anything you wanna tell me?"

She knows, I thought, *the damn school called her.*

I still played dumb with her anyway. I mean, I had to at least know for sure what she knew before I went and sold myself out. I replied, "Uhhh, no nothin' I can really think of."

Mom didn't miss a beat. "Oh really? Well, tell me why you cussed at a teacher and left school today."

Oh boy, she's got me against the ropes. What to do, what to say, I thought. All I could come up with was, "What? I didn't cuss at anyone."

Mom wasn't buying it, "Uh-huh, I bet. Well, why did you leave school then?"

She might be fast, but I'm quicker, I thought. *I got this.* I replied, "Well, after I signed up for online classes, the lady at the front desk told me I could leave, so I did. I thought I was allowed to."

Mom sounded pissed. She screamed into the phone, "Online classes?! For what?! And you can't bullshit me because I know ya. You're gonna take your ass back to school tomorrow and apologize to that teacher."

"You think you're slick, but you're not," she snapped.

I scrambled against the assault.

"I'm bein' serious, mom, I'm not lyin'. I don't really have any friends here since we moved back and I don't really get along with anybody at school. That's why I figured I'd just finish senior year online. The lady told me I might even graduate early. I thought you wouldn't care."

Mom still wasn't letting up, and she kept screaming into the phone, "Well, I'm gonna tell you something right fuckin' now! You're gonna finish school! I don't know what kind of game you're tryin' to play here, but it ain't workin'. You better take your ass back to school tomorrow!"

She wasn't gonna tell me what to do. I had enough of that growing up and I wasn't backin' down. I kept my composure with the bite of a nail and said, "Well, I want to do the online classes, so that's what I'm going to do. I don't have any friends there, mom. I'm a complete outsider. I'll even get better grades online, too, you'll see. I'm not gonna dropout, the Marines will never accept me if I do."

Mom snapped back, "Uh-huh, yeah, we'll see. I have to get back to work, but we're not done talking about this. Bye!"

If you could slam a cell phone down into a receiver like you could with the old house phones, that's what she pretty much did. I figured I'd light up a 'port out front after all that to calm my nerves, but then I saw one of Uncle Stallone's younger kids, Marcus, runnin' up the sidewalk with his shirt off and his baby weight shakin' around everywhere. When he finally made it to me, he was out of breath and said, "Paul, just got into a fight with Corey down the street."

Still trying to catch his breath with his hands on his knees, he said, "Paul busted his nose pretty bad."

I took a puff off my smoke and a cigarette wagged around in my mouth.

"What? Paul got his nose busted, or he busted Corey's?"

Marcus shook his head, still trying to catch his breath, and eventually found the air to reply.

"No, Paul busted Corey's. His dad and brothers are really mad."

Flicking my ashes into the wind, I said, "Well, where the hell is Paul? Is he alright?"

Right after I asked, I saw Paul riding up the street with his shirt off on a bike that definitely wasn't his. A kid on the porch pointed at him as he rode by, and screamed, "Look, mommy, boobies!"

Paul was a little chubby, and his smile blew away when he caught the insult. The kid was a little boy, though, that didn't know any better, so Paul didn't stop and say a thing.

Once he got in front of Uncle Stallone's house, he did a burn out and looked to me with a big grin on his face. Paul said, "How you like my new bike?"

I asked him, "Where did you even get the thing? Ain't that the same bike Corey always rides around?"

Paul wheeled the bike up into the yard and said, "Yeah, it used to be his bike, but I bet him I could beat him in Madden; so it's mine now."

Still perplexed and halfway through a smoke trying to figure it all out, I asked, "What about the busted nose and everything I'm hearin' about?"

I paused, grinned, then laughed, "Did ya get him good?"

Paul was a little out of breath, too. It all came together when he said, "He thought he was gonna be tough and get all in my face because I beat him and he tried to tell me I couldn't have the bike. I told him a bet is a bet, and he pushed me. So I broke his nose and took his bike. He got his ass beat twice today."

Suddenly, I spotted a few folks walking up the road like they were the warriors coming out to play or something. Right then and there, I knew things were about to escalate quick. Apparently, the Dude made his way out on the front porch for some reason and he asked, "You alright, Paul, what's goin' on?"

All of a sudden, a middle-aged balding guy with a gut and sunburn across his forehead came storming up to us all and yelled, "I'll tell you what's goin' on! This little punk right here broke my son's nose and stole his bike. So we have a problem here and it looks like you want one, too!"

That was the wrong thing for him to say. After all, the Dude might be old, but he used to be a wrestler back in his day. I think he might've even worked with Jake the Snake

before, but I'm not really sure. Corey's dad thought he was
bringin' a problem, but he's the one that really found one.
The Dude didn't hesitate at all. He whipped his shirt off
showin' off his own gut and yelled, "You ain't gonna fuckin'
mean mug me, buddy! I'll come down there after ya!"

The sound of a whip, or thunder cracking, tore
through the air as if the gods themselves had come to
unleash their fury. It wasn't the gods, but worse. That
crackling sound was Uncle Stallone's screen door splitting
into pieces from Zeus kicking his way through it and
stomping his way out onto the front porch. He dug his nails
into the front of his shirt and ripped it off like Superman
and yelled, "Do we gotta fuckin' problem out here?! Ain't
nobody gonna come up here to whoop on my little cousin
without goin' through me!"

Corey's dad and his two older sons cowered so low
within Zeus's shadow if they were liquid they would've
evaporated. Tommy stepped outside behind Zeus, too.
Then, Uncle Stallone and Shua came out front from the
back. Corey's dad just threw up his arms and said, "Look, all
I want is my son's bike back. This kid, whoever he is, stole
my son's bike and all I want is to get it back."

Uncle Stallone looked at Paul, bewildered, with his
mouth agape, and asked, "Did you steal his son's bike?"

Paul stuttered a little, which wasn't usual for him, but
he was on the stage now and he had to explain.

"N-n-n-no. I bet Corey I could beat him in the game,
and I did. He just didn't want to give me the bike I won, so I
took it."

Uncle Stallone shook his head at Corey's dad in
disgust and said, "Just give 'em the bike back, Paul. I don't
want all this shit up here."

Paul wheeled the bike over to Corey's dad. All the
sunburnt fella gave was a "thanks" and walked off with his
sons. Uncle Stallone put his hands on his hips and shook his

head at the ground. Then he started in on Zeus, "And look what you did, ya fuckin' idiot! You split my screen door in half and everything!"

Zeus just stood still and replied, "Well, sorry dad. I thought somebody was out here tryin' to jump Paul."

Uncle Stallone kept shaking his head, "So that means you kick the screen door open like a maniac, come out here and rip your shirt off?"

Uncle Stallone just walked up the steps and across the splinters of what once used to be his screen door. Tommy looked at Zeus and shook his head in disgust.

"Why did you have to break dad's screen door like that for? That was stupid."

Zeus followed him in and shot back, "Fuck you, bub."

Uncle Shua stood at the gate to the backyard laughing with grandpa.

He asked me, "What was all that about?"

Paul gave him the rundown, and we all laughed about it even more. Of course, grandpa asked Paul, "Did you get him good?"

Paul smiled as he bumped fists with him and said, "Yeah, I got him good."

It was all hilarious, and it wasn't the first time something like that had happened. I mean, every time we all get together, things always turn up to one hundred somehow, but I was so glad it didn't turn into an all-out brawl because I hate fighting. I definitely would've thrown in my own stones if it came down to the nitty gritty of it, but I've always preferred to be someone's friend. Only thing is, some folks don't want that. They'd rather be an enemy, so you have to treat them accordingly. *Peace before war, love before blood.*

After all the ruckus, I sat down to chill with Uncle Shua and drink a little more. At first, we didn't talk about much at all, but suddenly, in the distance, I spotted an old crow. It was cawing away; perched up on the corner of an old brick garage house that lie across the street. The air suddenly fell still and the noise all around, lowered down into a dimmer. All that could be heard to me was the caw of the crow. The sound stung my mind and I saw him again. The man in the hat. He was there staring away, crow cawing upon his shoulder. His eyes hid beneath the shade of his dark purple brim, and I could hear his chattering.

Your wandering calls to me. I feed like a wolf from the hunger. You couldn't banish me forever. A little boy's wish is never everlasting. You know it. You can feel it and you crave it. Why, you--

His words cut like a knife in my mind. I had to silence the voice in my thoughts. He was there, then wasn't. *Poof, then stay. I wish he'd just go away,* I thought to myself.

Suddenly, Uncle Shua asked, "Hey, man, you alright?"

I jerked my head out of my palms and smiled to cover up the fear.

"Y-yeah, I'm alright."

Then I remembered something suddenly that I'd always wanted to ask Uncle Shua.

"Hey, man, d-do you r-remember telling me about the crow that u-used to talk to all you guys down in Race Circle or somethin' like that?"

Uncle Shua nodded, "Yeah, I remember. That thing wouldn't even fly south for the winter. None of 'em do around here. But yeah, it used to hang around and talk to us when we were kids down there in Bona Field Court."

I gulped, looked towards the ground, and in an instant I looked up again.

"Didn't you say it had a split tongue, too? What did it used to say to you guys?"

Uncle Shua paused, shrugged his shoulders, then replied, "I can't even remember, man, but it could carry on conversations with us."

"You mean, you don't remember anything it said?"

Uncle Shua shrugged his shoulders again.

"No, none of us really can. It's like all of us forgot."

I knew that was true because I asked my dad's brother, Uncle Luke, about it, too. He said the same thing. They all saw it there. The crow on the branch. Split tongue weaving and flapping about its beak; saying something, something nobody can recall.

Uncle Shua paused, and the color flushed out of his face. The shine didn't seem to have him warm anymore. He replied, "Yeah—that was—weird. I'm surprised you remember that."

Suddenly, a croaking shriek startled us both from above. A pack of crows lie nestled within the branches of the old pine tree towering behind us. There wasn't a leaf left on a branch. *Death. It's all dead. The spring, the shine, the man inside. It's all withered away—and the town. It's stuck in a never-ending state of decay itself. Ever since him, ever since the curse on the bridge. The night when the crows cawed. There they found him.*

Everyone else didn't notice a thing. I looked wide-eyed at Uncle Shua and said, "That's weird, man. I mean, what are the odds of that happenin' while we're talking about that old crow of yours you saw?"

Uncle Shua shook his head, gazing up at the dying limbs.

"I don't know, man. It probably doesn't mean anything. They're all over town this time of year."

The crows are cawing again. There's something out there. Something out there in them woods. It was like a voice from somewhere unknown came to answer my question. I looked at Uncle Shua and said about the same.

"The crows are cawing again today. They always do that around this time of year. It almost seems like I see a pack of them everywhere I go."

Trying to lighten the mood, I laughed, and said, "Who knows? Maybe they're following me or somethin'?"

Uncle Shua looked at me and said, "Maybe they are."

CHAPTER V:

I GOT 5 ON IT

After a while, I figured I'd sneak off to the car to tap a roach I left in the ashtray a little. I had a getaway to plan. I knew my aunt would be on me about driving after drinking earlier, but I didn't even have that much; only a little. That wouldn't really matter to anybody, though—I did. That's all that mattered.

I flopped in the driver's seat, and my fingers dashed towards the ashtray. Only the roach was gone and the console hung open. My money was missing. Somebody took me for all I had, and it was very recent. I could still smell their sour scent in the car. I cut my eyes and thought, *Winston.*

He wasn't the only thief around that broke into cars, but he was the most active. He always hung out around Echo Avenue and Putnam. I knew he had to be around somewhere still; lurking in the shadows. I hopped out of my car and studied the scene. Night was nearing its edge, and the clouds were billowing away towards the setting sun in the distance. He'd be hard to find in the dark. I'll catch up with him eventually, I thought to myself.

I snatched the door to my car back open, flopped in, and punched the dash. *Why did I leave my money in the car?* I thought to myself. I didn't have a wallet, that's too old man for me, plus I was afraid of it falling out of my pocket.

Stupid; why my car? I thought to myself, *the fiend finally got me.*

Paul ran over and hollered, "What's wrong, bub, what happened?"

I gritted my teeth and balled up my fists.

"Don't worry about it! I-it's—"

Then I let it out; I couldn't help it anymore. I screeched and hollered like a madman.

Uncle Stallone stood on the porch, shaded by the night. All that could be seen was an ember dancing in the dark. Suddenly, the man behind the smoke asked, "What are you hollerin' about down there?"

My cheeks burned, and I bite my lip. *Gnawing away in fury over it all.*

Uncle Stallone hollered again, "Huh? Are ya alright?!"

I nodded my head as my nails dug into the corners of my crossed arms.

"Yeah, yep! Everything's fine! I'm all good!"

Uncle Stallone said, "Huh, what did ya say?"

I didn't have time to repeat myself. I had to find Winston. Normally, I'm not a confrontational person. I abhor it in a way actually, but give me a few drinks and I'm hell on wheels. I got the power to do anything when I got the juice.

The dirty bum was long gone, though, and I knew it. He was as fast and slippery as a fox. Regardless, I'd either find him or come up with a plan to make some money with Derek.

He texted me earlier and told me he was at Von's up on Cliffwood and he'd be hangin' out there till whenever. I still had to plan my escape from Uncle Stallone's, though. *Be as subtle as possible.*

I hopped back in the driver's seat. It was all I could think to do. Uncle Stallone hollered something, but I couldn't make it out. I'd already slammed the door. *Furious.*

Paul was on the other side of the street staring at me from the sidewalk, mouth agape, with a longing in his eyes. He thought he was gonna get to hang out with me tonight, but I couldn't do it. Staying up playing video games didn't cut it for me anymore. Those times were fun, but goin' out on the town was better; a real adventure. I pulled into drive and stomped on the gas.

My mommy is going to be so mad at me, I thought with a grin. I knew somebody would tell on me. I just didn't know who. Truth is, though, I sort of like ruffling her feathers a little every once in a while. Everyone's really. Gotta keep things interesting, if you know what I mean. I might be shy when I'm sober, but I'm a real wild card when I'm buzzin', so I don't have much of a choice in that regard.

I whipped a left off Pine Street, still fuming madly over the theft. The revving of the engine hummed in my ears. *I'm gonna get you back for this one, Winston,* I thought to myself. I'd spot him crawling out of a window or poppin' a hub cap off somewhere. It was all just a matter of time.

I darted the Altima down Cliffwood past the pines and boarded-up houses, gripping the steering wheel and locking in the moment. I tore into Von's yard and jammed the car into park. I shot air through my teeth in a fit of frustration as I shoved the door open and stepped out onto the lawn.

I could hear Von's grandma from the window scream, "Dammit! Vonte, you need to tell that crazy ass white boy to stop tearing up my fuckin' yard when he's pulling in. This ain't Country Club Drive, we ain't got muthafuckas to come fix it all back up for us around here!"

Struck by the arrow and keeled over, dead. Just because I'm white doesn't mean I live on Country Club Drive. I mean, mom did move us by Country Club Drive when we moved back to town, but that didn't mean we were rich. We just wanted to feel a little fancy, I guess, that's all. We still couldn't get in to the actual club even if we tried.

My feet squished in the mud as I approached the door. Head hung low and ashamed. *I lost myself again;* I thought to myself. Von swung the front door open before I could even reach for the nob.

He hollered, "Damn, bro! You can't be tearin' up the yard like that when you're pullin' in."

I stood at the narrow and pleaded in defense, "Fuck—man, I'm really sorry, but I just got robbed and I—we gotta find this guy. He's gotta be around here somewhere."

Von stood there in the doorway in black sweats and white Nikes; suddenly poised up and ready to go. He shrugged his shoulders and threw up his hands.

"Who? You got robbed? What he look like?"

"He's this dirty guy," I attempted to explain, "he wears a toboggan hat with holes in it and he never takes a bath. We gotta find him, man. He took my whole fifty--or I mean, twenty, bucks."

Von laughed and pointed, "You lit right now? You sure you didn't just lose the money?"

I pleaded, "Nah, no, man, I ain't; just buzzin' I guess, really. The console was open in the middle when I got in the car. He had to take it."

"Why him, though?"

He was annoying me on purpose. I could tell from the smile on his face.

"What's with all the questions, man? You gonna help me find the guy or what?"

Von lit up a square and retorted, "He wears a toboggan?"

"Yes, a toboggan hat with holes in it," I whined.

Von changed his voice to mimic mine.

"A toooh-baaahgan hat with holes in it?"

I wrung my hands together in frustration, scratching away nervously at my empty palms. *I got the itch.*

"Yes! A toboggan hat! Stop playin' man. You gonna help or what?"

Von waved his hand and walked further down the walk towards me; puffin' away.

"You need to smoke, and chill, man. That money's gone. Ain't no way we gonna find him. You talk to D yet?"

I threw my arms up in the air in frustration.

"I thought he was with you? Where did he go?"

Von kept his cool; his mood wouldn't waver.

"I don't know. He went to meet up with this girl named Alyssa or somethin'; said he'd catch up with us later. You wanna come in and hang for a minute?"

It was whatever. I was cool with coming in and all, but he knew and I did, too, that his grandma was gonna have my ass as soon as I walked in—and she did.

After the door swung closed and we were in the living room, she started in immediately.

"You gonna fix my yard, boy, or what? You can't be goin' around town tearin' people's shit up and expectin' to get away with it."

I sighed and cast a somber look, "I'm really sorry about your yard. I didn't mean to tear into it like that. I sort of forgot that it was muddy out. I was just upset, and I needed a friend to talk to and I knew Von was home. So that's why I rushed in like that be-because—"

Grandma wagged her finger and shook her head in her chair and said, "Boy, you ain't bullshittin' no one. Tell me what's really goin' on. I can tell you're upset."

She was right, I was very much so. I huffed and shrugged my shoulders.

"Well, I ain't gonna lie. Somebody broke into my car and stole all my money. That's what I'm pissed about. It wasn't much, but still—I'm broke as fuck right now and—"

Grandma snapped, "Language! Don't be using those curse words in my house!"

I hung my head, chin nearly touching my chest, and said, "I'm sorry. I just gotta calm down a little, I guess."

I hung my head lower in despair.

"I guess I'll have to let it go—I don't know. I just hate it. I have the worse type of luck sometimes."

Grandma looked mad. She was definitely down. By the look in her eyes, she looked like she was nearly ready to beat Winston down herself. *Stone cold.*

"Well, don't get down on yourself, sweetheart. You best not be up to getting' into any trouble, anyway."

Her tone was soft for a moment, but then it grew hard again. She leaned up in her chair and pointed her finger at me.

"'Specially with my grandson. His ass is on probation and he don't need no more messes. I ain't gonna see him go backwards over nothin'."

Grandma folded her hands, shook her head, and said, "Uh-uh, not on my watch."

I darted my eyes at Von as quick as I could to check and see if he had an escape plan. He did or his eyes wouldn't have narrowed and he wouldn't have smirked. Lucky for him, grandma got locked back into Judge Judy and didn't even notice. Telephones still hurt when there flung whether your old or young, and she'd do it. I saw it all before.

Grandma jerked her gaze from the TV back to me, hands still folded in her lap, and she asked, "Well, are you havin' dinner with us tonight? You lookin' too skinny boy, you need to eat somethin' at least."

Everyone thinks I'm too skinny. I don't like to eat much because food makes you gain weight and I can't afford to turn into a fat boy all over again. I have enough problems getting' girls as it is—still a virgin, in fact. I can't even count myself as a man yet. Nobody knows, though. *No, I can't tell anybody.*

I smiled and replied, "Nah, I'm good. I ate earlier. Thank you, though. I'm just gonna go out for a smoke. You comin' Von?"

Von grinned and nodded his head. *Captain Obvious.* Grandma noticed, too. She snapped at Von, "You better not be plannin' anything, boy. You still got a few things to do around here."

Von interjected and promised her that he didn't. For some reason, she actually believed him.

Didn't matter either way. She was out like a light before we left. I asked Von, "Damn, she was all fiery and alive like twenty minutes ago, now she done went zombified. What did you do to her, man?"

Von grinned at her, sleeping in the chair, and shook his head.

"That whiskey be knockin' her out sometimes. She had five glasses before you got here."

"Five tall glasses, for real? Your grandma is a legend."

Von tssked through his lips.

"Hell nah, half cups. That's all she needs. I'm glad she's asleep, though. I'm tryin' to go out with ya'll tonight. D said Ellie knew about a party goin' on somewhere later on."

Von paused and pulled out a pack of smokes and packed them on the side of his fist as he started for the door. I just stood there staring at grandma slumped in the chair. Still laughing under my breath, but then a slight tinge of worry crept under my skin and I asked Von, "Man, you think she'll be alright? I mean, what if she falls out of the

74

chair? Maybe we could pick her up and lay her on the couch or something?"

Von swung the door open behind me and I heard him say, "You talkin' crazy. We ain't touchin' her ass; she'll wake back up. If she falls, she falls, she's got a life alert button for a reason."

"Man, that's fucked up, though. I mean—"

Von wasn't trying to hear it.

"Stop playin' and come on. She'll be fine. Ey, you hit up D yet, to see where he at?"

I turned my back on grandma in the chair as Judge Judy swung and struck her gavel on the TV.

"No, not yet. I'll give him a call, though."

The wind blew and my skin grew cold when I walked back outside, feet stomping in the mud with a phone ringing in my ear. *Come on, man, pick up, pick up.* The call went to voicemail. Not once, but four times, then Derek finally answered. He was breathing hard, like he'd been jogging for hours. Derek shouted on the other end, "Man, you just called me like four times. If I don't answer on the first. I'll get back to you. Alright? What you need?"

I choked and grumbled my laugh away. It was hard to bear, but I made it through.

"Well, man, you said you wanted to link up later. I'm at Von's right now and we're just chillin' waitin' to see what's up with you before we take off. He said somethin' about Ellie's friends havin' a party later. What's up with that? We goin' or what?"

Derek still struggled to catch his breath. I heard Alyssa's voice in the background sounding all sensual.

"Who are you on the phone with? Get back over here."

Derek grumbled, "Just chill, ight. It's my boy from earlier, that's all."

Derek made a sucking sound against his teeth into the phone and continued,"Yeah, we goin' to link up with her later, but I ain't got no money. I mean, I can get you back later, though. I always do."

He always did, too. Derek wasn't a bum, but he didn't know or have a clue yet. So I had to tell him.

"Shit, man, see that's the problem right now; what I've been tryin' to get ahold of you about. That guy, Winston, got me, man. Right outside of my uncle's house. I didn't even know until I got in the car. We gotta find him. He's got my whole twenty bucks. I'm all tapped out now."

Von French inhaled off his port, and said, "Why'd you leave your car unlocked, anyway? You know Winston ain't the only one that breaks into rides around here."

I darted my eyes towards the passenger seat and cut them angrily at Von. I shot back, "Well, I thought I fuckin' did, Mr. Obvious. I guess it didn't lock all the way—I don't know, dude. Alright? I'm tryin' to figure it out, though, so just chill, man, fuck."

I shook my head back towards the windshield; staring out of it menacingly, hoping to spot Winston somewhere. *The shadows lie still.*

Derek was losing it on the other end. Cracks of static rippled my eardrum. Derek replied, "Ya'll are retarded. But, hey, man, I'm with you. We're gonna find Winston and get your money back. Just pick me up. I'm at Alyssa's right now. She lives right down from Von's on Matthews Street. Just pull up and we'll be out."

"Bet."

I clicked the phone and hit reverse. My wheels spun and dug holes further into the muddy yard as we spun off and away to pick up D down on Matthews Street.

When we pulled up, a light flicked away in the window and a flame shot through the room. Derek wailed and jumped through the window. Thank god he only dropped a few feet out of the first story. He would've been a goner if he would've hit his head any harder.

A girl, Alyssa I take it, leapt through the blinds with gritted teeth. Her nails tore at the paint on the edge of the windowsill. She watched him with fierce malice as he fumbled around on the ground.

She's a dragon—a fire-breathing dragon.

I almost thought she would come for him, almost have him, but there she stood. She pointed her middle finger at Derek with a straight and sharp motion, like a wagging nail. Then she snapped, "Fuck you, motherfucker! Go hang out with your faggot ass friends, then!"

Derek pulled himself up out of the yard in a panic as he rushed towards the car. Von snapped on the other side, "What did that bitch just say?"

"She called us faggots, apparently," I replied with mashed down eyebrows. *That wasn't nice.* Then I hollered back, "Hey, man, we're not gay. Just because we're cool and we hang out all the time, I mean, it doesn't mean we're gay. We're not suckin' on—"

Alyssa screamed, "Shut the fuck up! You skiiiinnny loser!"

Gee whiz, what got into her? She seemed so nice and content earlier.

Loser was sounded out with a lot more annunciation than I expected. Apparently, she had put some real thought into her opinion of me; which was a surprise because I hadn't thought that much into her at all.

Derek scrambled and flipped open the door to the backseat and hollered, "Step on it! Drive, man, drive!"

I did. I got some fast reflexes when it comes to rather itchy situations, been in plenty of them, so we sped off and away. Gone from Alyssa and that—*flame. What was the flame about?* I wondered, so I had to ask.

"Holy cannoli, man, what happened back there? I saw a flame in the room and heard you scream, jump, then that's it. What did she try to do? Burn you or somethin'?"

Derek heaved in the back seat and nodded his head.

"Hell, yeah, she did. The crazy bitch tried to light me on fire with some hairspray. She just put it in front of her lips and blew."

I nearly split open when he said that, and Von did, too. Derek heaved, "Hey, that shit ain't funny, though. She almost burnt my face off."

He tapped me on the shoulder when I turned the wheel onto Baker Street and spun my way up the block.

"Forget about that. What's the plan? I mean, Winston stole all the money you had. I'm broke, and I know Von ain't got no money."

Derek shook his head.

"We ain't got nothin' for smoke. I mean—"

Derek paused, then narrowed his eyes at the dancing lights in the rearview mirror.

"You thinkin' what I'm thinkin'?"

I tapped my left hand on the steering wheel as Von took another puff off his 'port in the shotgun seat. I huffed, "No, not really. I ain't a mind reader. I mean, I was thinkin' we could just hunt down Winston and get my money back. That's the only option we have really or I could try to sell some movies or somethin' real quick. We could always try that."

"We don't even know where he is, though, and nobody's tryin' to buy any CD's, man. You barely even sell any, just to your folks. That's about it," Derek uttered from the back seat.

He was right. Family was the only people that would buy. I was too nervous to approach anybody else.

"What you wanna do? Just ride around and hope we see him? Man, that ain't no plan. We can get it now, then get him later."

Derek shrugged his shoulders in the back.

"We gonna have to do the change game again. That's the quickest way to get what we need tonight."

Please, not the change game. I hated it the first time we did it. I nearly bit into my fingers once my nails were gone. It was a scary charade to pull off, but I knew in my heart I might have to break down and do it again. I could already feel my buzz wearing off and if that happened, I'd be useless and afraid at the party. *I can't handle myself without it.*

Derek interrupted the anxiety train screeching through my mind.

"You down or what, man?

Von took a long drag, and let out a billow of smoke as he choked, "Shit, I'm sittin' here, too, and I'm down. What ya say, bird? We gonna go up north and hit the cars or what?"

"I don't really want to. I mean, what if we get caught? I don't want to go to jail over a bunch of change, man."

Von laughed at me.

"We ain't gonna get caught, bro, I promise. Tell 'em D."

Derek edged his head forward through the middle and pressed further.

"Yeah, we just gotta be fast, that's all. Don't worry one and done that's it. We just gotta pick out a good one."

I grinded my teeth and wrung my hands on the wheel as we approached the stop sign at the end of Baker Street.

I don't like stealing from people; I thought to myself, but it wasn't really morality that got me. The fear of getting caught scared me to death. I hate that feeling, fear, that is. It seems to hold me back so much.

Just do it, a voice whispered in my ear, *like he said; one and done, that's it. Don't tangle yourself in a knot about it. Don't think—just do.*

Goosebumps ran up my arms as I flipped the blinker, signaling a right turn on Pine Street towards the Y-Bridge.

I exhaled with spite and reluctance.

"Fuck it, I guess. We ain't got nothin' else to do."

Von clapped his hands and started dancing as he broke out singing the chorus to Waka Flocka Flame's "O Let's Do It."

Derek hollered from the back, "Ey, yeah, play that shit!"

We listened to that song repeatedly the whole way to the north-side — towards the cars with all the change. When we pulled up on the first ride, I pulled my Joker hat down lower to hide my face and brought the music down to a mere murmur with a shift of the knob. I cut the lights off, too, and pulled under a tree where it was dark enough to hide. *Just like last time.* I still kept the engine running, y'know, just in case we had to make a quick getaway.

Derek fumbled around in the back and pulled his hood up. He tapped Von and I both on the shoulder and said, "Ight, I'm cool with going first, but ya'll two are gonna have to get out and scoop some coins up, too. I ain't gonna get stuck doin' all the legwork."

Von crossed his arms and snapped, "I'm on probation, man, I can't be gettin' caught in the mix right now—"

I turned my head slowly, grinning a little at Von from the corner of my eye.

Yeah, you're scared, too, just admit it.

Derek snapped, "Your already in the mix; You're in the car. You got next and if we still ain't found a good one yet after him, it's you."

I stuttered, "Man, I-I'm drivin', though. A-ain't nobody else getting behind the wheel, but me. I'm not with this thievin' type of shit, anyway. It's not my s-style."

Derek shook my seat from behind and snapped under his breath, "You always let me drive, though. How's now different?"

I huffed through my teeth and hissed in disgust. I shook my head and said, "Fine, but we're only aimin' for change. Most folks forget about it and don't use it, anyway. Leave the big bills alone. If we gotta steal, we should at least have a little sympathy. I mean—"

Von interjected, "Sympathy? Are we gonna just keep talkin' or what? Shit, I'm hungry. I ain't tryin' to sit here all night."

Derek made a loud shhh noise as he silently swung the door open. He walked normally at first, towards the sidewalk, hood up and hiding his hands in his pockets. Then he crept low as he approached the dark Honda Acura. *Hopefully, the alarm doesn't sound.*

To my surprise, the first time we played the change game I thought for sure we'd get caught or shot, but more folks left their cars unlocked than I expected. Outside the garages even. It was almost like they wanted you to steal from them.

Tax the rich. Now that's a fun game to play, the voice in my head said.

Derek was slow about opening the door, but he was fast when it came to sliding in. My fingers tapped nervously about the steering wheel as my eyes darted in every which way. I tried my best to play the perfect lookout. All I could see were trees and one-story homes nestled up in groves. *Everything is wide open.*

Von chain-smoked away on another square beside me, not breathing a word; simply finding comfort in the silence.

Derek slid out of the car suddenly and hopped back down on the sidewalk; stood straight up and walked as inconspicuous as ever back to the ride where Von and I waited. He threw himself into the back quickly. I pulled off slowly and flipped the lights back on to dispel the suspicion. Derek fumbled, "Shit, all I got is around twenty on it or outta the car, I mean. Ain't much, but it'll get us another sack at least, and some Fours maybe."

He paused and counted the change in his hand. It clunk and clanged around in his palms, then made a jingle when he plopped it all into his pocket.

"We might need more, though. Ya'll ready for another one? Who's got next? I did my part."

The air grew still, and neither Von nor I said a word. All I did was turn the wheel.

"Well," Derek continued, "who's goin'?"

Without even thinking, I blurted out, "It ain't gonna be me. So, y'know, I-I don't wanna be doin' this, anyway. We're gonna get caught doin' this stupid shit, guys."

Von snapped in the passenger seat as we weaved around in circles within the dark sub-division.

"So I guess it's me then? Huh? I already got strikes on me, man. I shouldn't even be ridin' with ya'll. I'm on fuckin' probation I—"

"Yeah, we get it," Derek interrupted, "you're on probation, but as far as it's goin' right now--you're the only one that ain't pitchin' in. Do your part, bro."

"How's that?" Von snapped, "Bird ain't done shit either."

"We're in his car, though. That's him pitchin' in right there. We're rollin' on his gas. I just went, so that means—"

Von smacked the dash and threw a tantrum beside me.

"It's me, then?! Why did ya'll even pick me up then? You knew I didn't have any money!"

"You never do," Derek replied coolly.

Von clenched his fist and nodded his head. His fuse was always easy to light.

"There you go, startin' in again. Like you always do. Just because you got a job at Captain D's, it don't mean you're better than me. I ain't on no slave shit, that's all. I see what I want and I take it that's all that's to it. Only reason I ain't got my bread up now is 'cause of the probation. You just—"

Derek snapped, "That's what you always say, though. Man, you got caught up on some stupid shit. What was it again? Oh yeah, you got caught up in a yard tryin' to steal a basketball. That's the dumbest shit ever to get charged on."

Derek chuckled and tried to go on with his tirade, but Von wasn't having it. He punched the dash and hollered, "I wasn't tryin' to steal nothin' though! I picked the ball up to test the bounce out, and they told the cops I was in the yard stealin'. That's all that happened. When I'm really grindin' I don't get caught."

Von shrugged his shoulders and continued, "Just got caught up on some fuck shit, that's all."

Suddenly, Derek tapped my shoulder from the back seat for me to pull over to the side, but we were still out in the open. It might've been dark, but being directly under the moonlight we could still get made. Derek grinned and pointed towards a gray Ford F-150 with a rebel flag bumper sticker.

"That's you. Go get it, mastermind."

Von jerked in his seat and swung an elbow towards the glass.

"Why that one?!"

Von hollered, "You got me fucked up. They probably got the whole KKK up in that muthafucka or somethin'. I ain't doin' it."

Von crossed his arms in rebellion against the plan.

Derek chuckled, "Why not? You said you never get caught. So it shouldn't be a problem, for real. You're just scared. It's okay. I get it."

Von mashed his brow down and flashed an angry glare at D. Then he said, "I ain't scared. Nothin' can get to me."

Von took a deep breath and uncrossed his arms. His hand clicked the door handle open, and he whispered, "Watch me work."

He was shivering when he got out, and it wasn't even that cold out. It scared him he didn't have to lie. Honestly, I was, too, the whole time in fact, but my adrenaline helped me mask everything. I was on point and in control—unless we got made, that is.

Von crept low all the way towards the truck right out in the open. *Come on, man, creep behind the bushes or somethin'.* The only way he could've been seen any clearer is if somebody shined a spotlight right on him.

"This fool is so stupid," Derek cackled, "He ain't got no sense to him at all, but damn!"

Derek paused, then pointed, "Look at that. He got to the door."

I could see him—barely after he got in. The truck had tinted windows, so it was super dark. It felt like he was taking too long. *Snatch and run, man, come on.*

When D and I heard an alarm go off, we panicked. We both went a-gasp and looked at one another. At first, we didn't know where the sound was coming from, or maybe we didn't want to admit it to ourselves. Von set the alarm off.

It all went haywire in an instant. The outside lights kicked on atop the garage and blare down upon the truck.

Von still wasn't out yet. He was wrestling his leg around the cab. I could see his teeth gritted together from afar as he struggled, then he fell right out of the driver's seat onto the pavement.

Suddenly, the screen door on the house flung open and an older fat gentleman in a wife beater appeared. He either had dookie or burrito stains all over the front of him. I didn't want to know. There was only one thing to do.

I stomped on the peddle towards Von as he sprinted away from the driveway. The fat guy screamed and chased after him with an aluminum ball bat in his grip.

"Goddammit, get back here, ya filthy thief! You ain't gonna be stealing on my wagon tonight, boy. How about I steal a chunk off your ass instead?!"

The fat man waddled after Von with his little leaguer gear in tow. Von yelped. The tires of the Altima squealed to a halt just as we reached him. *To the rescue.*

Derek hollered, "Come on! Get in!"

He swung the door open to the back right on cue and Von leapt in nearly head-butting Derek on the nose when he landed on the seat. I burnt rubber at the wheel as we took off into the night. I could still see fat boy Charlie Brown chasing us from behind, but there wasn't any catching us. *We were gone.* His hollering disappeared to a faint whisper, and it bleeped out as if it were never there.

I exhaled deeply, relieved, then I said, "Gee whiz, man, that shit was close. You alright?"

Von fought to catch his breath; all he did was nod. Then Derek gave him the third degree.

"You a fool, man. How did you set the alarm off, mister expert?"

Von snapped, "Yeah, the alarm might've gone off, but you're wrong. I did better than you."

Bewildered, Derek and I both asked, "How," at the same time. Then, Von pulled out a wad of bills and said, "Shit, I ain't had time to count it all yet, but there at least gotta be a couple of fifties right here."

"Damn," I blurted, "We're set tonight, then! It might've been an itchy escape, but we made it alright."

I laughed, "Shit, I think I'm the only one that hasn't fell yet tonight."

Jinx. The third is always the worst.

Derek nodded at the wheel.

"Ok, then, King Von, you got it tonight. Ya'll still down with hookin' up with Ellie and goin' to the party ?"

Not a question at all. *Of course.*

CHAPTER VI:
ROLE MODEL

Cars whizzed by, the window was down, and the cool air felt right; we'd made our escape, and we were practically rich for the night. *We're thieves and degenerates. I don't deserve this money; I don't deserve any of it. The score was nice, but what would happen? How would I pay the price? Yes, there's always a cost and a charge to everything; a shadow to the figure, an action with a surprise. I shouldn't have been a part of it. I should've just—*a dark chattering voice gnawed at my heart; twisting within my soul.

Ahhhh, but no. It was fun, wasn't it? A real thrill. You know you like it; it's the art and act of freedom. Life can be quite a drag after all. Ya gotta get your kicks and giggles somehow, boy. You'd be as stale as a cracker if you didn't. You'd—

Don't speak back, just play another song in your head to drown the devil out. My skin grew cold, and a streak beneath my skull burned. *It's there now, forever. I can't get him out. No, it's not. It's make believe. He's not real. None of them were, none of them are. Ghosts aren't real. I have to forget; I have to escape. I just need another drink.*

I leaned from the back and edged between Von and Derek; they were in the front.

Lil Wayne was "Bill Gatin'" across the speakers. The drumming of the beat was setting the board.

"Guys, I don't know about you, but I need a fuckin' drink, man. I'm gettin' a little antsy back here."

Von retorted back, "Hell yeah, I heard that. Ya'll wanna get a bottle of Hen?"

Wrinkles of disgust ran across my face, and I shivered.

"Uhhhh, hell no. That's all you guys, man. Last time I had that I woke up in a puddle, drenched and soaked. I pretty much pee peed all over myself because I was so lit I passed out. If that wasn't bad enough I had to leave the scene with dicks drawn all over my face."

Derek busted out laughing. Von chuckled to himself, turning his head towards the middle.

"Say what? You pee peed yourself?"

"Yeah, I pee peed all over myself. The Henny demon got me, man."

It was crazy. Drool ran down my cheek, the hair fairy got me, and someone drew all over my face. I felt like a zombie; soaked in my own waste. When the lady screamed from the sidewalk, and her little yorkie barked, it split my eardrums, and I let out a dying groan to go along with her shrieks as I wiggled into my car.

"Call the ambulance," I squealed, "I'm dyin'! Dyin' I tell ya!"

I had my fun, and I stopped acting goofy. I left her bewildered, with no explanation regarding my horrid condition or antics. It just wasn't her concern; none of her business.

The story made my friends laugh a little, and it helped take my mind off the guilt of the crime. *If you're feelin' blue; have a laugh or two, and if you ain't got nothin' to do, act out a joke to brew.*

The car teetered and wobbled as we climbed out of the ride; red lights blinked on the State Street sign.

"So what ya'll wanna get?" Derek said. I shrugged my shoulders. We were still undecided. Von didn't respond; he jerked the door open, and the bell jingled. Derek followed, and I piled in after him next. *Don't look at the chips,* I thought to myself; my stomach growled. *You don't need anything to eat. It'll kill the buzz.*

Derek and Von went towards the counter, and I darted for the coolers; *where is the Wild Irish Rose?* The wild fruit kind is my favorite, and it'll get ya lit; that's why I love it.

I heard Von raise his voice at the counter.

"Man, I came in here and bought the shit before? I mean, what the fuck's the problem now?"

The guy behind the counter was hard to understand, but his tone was direct, and his glare ran agitated, perhaps a tad confused. He was the man who never smiles. I'm serious, he never has. Never in a family photo, never at the beach with his friends, never at the fair. It all depends; I'm not sure, but the guy was a hard sell, and I knew we were screwed. I shook the bottle of Wild Irish and the light red liquid swished and danced around within the glass. *I feel so thirsty. He won't sell it to me. I know it. I clutched the bottle tight to myself and cut my eyes. Perhaps I should steal it.*

Von barked in the store, "This is bullshit, man! How you gonna think I'm not old enough?"

The man, who never grins, jammed his finger across the counter, and rambled quickly, "Get out of my store right now!"

"Whatever, man," Von threw his hands up in defeat and tssked through his teeth, "I'll just go somewhere else. I can't stand ya'll's asses around here, anyway."

Von marched for the door, and Derek hollered after me, "Hey, you comin', man? They ain't gonna sell anything to us here."

I hugged the bottle and whimpered, *but we can't leave. These bottles are my friends.* My shoulders slumped, and I hung my head. *The charade is over; it's all a loss.*

I placed the bottle sadly back down on the shelf; where my hopes and dreams for the night now lie. *I could steal it, but that's not right. That's—*

Oh, but you just did, a voice said, *Don't act like you don't remember. Is the memory already growing faint? You have a skill of forgetting and throwing away things. Whatever protects the self image, I presume, that's just what you do. Go ahead and take some candy.*

But I can't. My mind rambled, even if I wanted to. *The guys staring right at me now.* Just leave, just walk out, and I did. It was awkward. I was mean mugged all the way to the door, but it was cool. I'd done the right thing. *I'm a good guy again now. A true law-abiding citizen.* I proudly got into the backseat and Derek cranked the engine. The groaning in my stomach swallowed my happiness away. *I'm so hungry, I need something to eat. But no you don't. You just need another drink.*

It didn't take us long at all to get to Ellie's house. She lived on Ohio Street right up from grandma and grandpa's on Luck Avenue. When we pulled up, the place creeped me out like it always did. Ellie lived in a Victorian-style house, I guess you would call it, but there were plenty of houses on the south end of town, just like it. White paneled siding, green shutters, a nice little porch, and whatnot, but still— there was just something about it; some strange tune to the entire area, in fact. Sometimes if you listen long enough, you can hear it in the wind. It's something dark. Just look at a black-and-white photo taken downtown; the older it is, the stranger it gets.

My grandpa had told me a lot about the old days of Zanesville. This one time we were watching this movie called Hoodlum, y'know, the one where Laurence Fishburne plays Bumpy Johnson—but anyway, there was this shootout happening in the street with Tommy guns spraying everywhere and bodies droppin' left and right. It was a bloody scene to say the least, but when grandpa told me that sort of stuff used to happen in Zanesville, I couldn't believe it. He told me, "They used to call this place Little Chicago. Al Capone even stopped here to eat every once in a while."

Grandpa was born in like 1932, so I figured he might've met old Capone himself, but he said that he never had. Still, after he gave me the rundown on the shootouts that used to happen in Little Chicago, I had to ask him, "You ever get into a shootout like that?"

He didn't say a word; just looked back towards the road, the wind blown. I was lying on the porch swing next to him, book in hand, and I was curious. I couldn't help myself, so I pressed him further. Glimpses of his story flashed through my mind, and I saw things, *yes, I saw things*, and I wanted to have an answer to match the scenes and images flowing through. That only happens with a select few. I repeated myself differently.

"Come on, grandpa. I want to hear some of your stories."

He just sat with his hands in his lap, gazing out, and said, "They don't care about our stories, Hawke."

He paused in thought, and cleared his throat, then said, "Y'know, there were black cowboys, and gangsters, too. They don't ever talk about it. You don't ever see them make movies about that."

It made me sad because I knew he really believed it. That's why he liked "Hoodlum" so much. He couldn't believe the main characters represented him. Nobody cares, and he was right. I did, but I knew what he meant. Nobody cares about the average story.

I hold many perspectives. I can see it all from different angles. The man in the hat was always distant around him, around grandpa that is. Almost as if he were afraid of him, knew him maybe. *I didn't know. I don't—*

"Hey, man, you got a square," Von asked. I pulled one out of my pack, squiggling around.

"Sure, here ya go, buddy."

Back to reality, I guess. Drivin' on by, we pulled up; the car parked.

Ellie wailed from the porch, "Took ya'll long enough!"

Derek put the car in park and yelled back, "We had to make a few stops along the way stop trippin'! You got some smoke, though?! We still gotta pick some up."

Ellie shook her head and took a long drag. Apparently, she was irritated. I stuck my head out the rear window and heard her say under her breath, "Took all that time and didn't even get any weed yet."

Ellie stood firm in the shade on her porch, her hat shadowed the cast of her eyes. She flicked her ashes and said, "Don't worry about it. Just come on in. We gotta pregame before we get there, anyway."

Sounds like a plan.

It didn't take long for us to get a smoke fest goin' on. That's just how we always do, but before we did, D and Von started playing Madden. It got a tad heated, as always.

Von screamed at the game when the referee blew his whistle. Ellie cracked up. When she laughs, it makes you wanna laugh because she's just cool like that. She sort of looks like a chick version of Chris Tucker to tell you the truth and is damn near just as funny as him, too.

I walked in the room after takin' a twinkle and said, "Damn, Von you getting' your ass whooped by Derek already?"

I was feeling good again. Ellie had over a fifth of Yeager. It might've been a gallon; I already had a few shots of it. The taste was so lovely. *I have satisfied my hunger, but I still desire more. I'm as hungry as a wolf.*

Derek pushed on Von's shoulder, laughing, and Von snapped, "Nah, this muthafucka is always cheatin'. That's why he's winnin'."

Von spun around towards Ellie on the couch behind him and said, "He changed the settings on my shit when I went to get a drink didn't he?"

Ellie was packing a bowl full and looked up at Von all wild-eyed smiling and said, "Stop trippin' because you're losin'. You just ain't got the skill for it, that's all."

Derek howled in laughter. Von threw his controller on the ground and turned the PlayStation off. Derek stopped cackling right away and threw his hands up in the air. He asked Von, "Why did you have to go and turn the game off like that for?"

Ellie sparked up the bowl. Smoke slowly crawled out of her mouth and she said, "Because he's a sore loser that's why."

Then she snapped, "You better watch tossing my shit like that because if you're breakin' you're buyin'. Just sayin'."

Von stood up, obviously pissed off and annoyed at this point and replied, "Nah, it ain't like that. I'm just tired of playin'. We gonna smoke or what, though?"

Obviously. Ellie passed the bowl to Derek instead and said, "Stop bullshittin' you could've just paused it."

Von rolled his eyes and watched Derek take a hit. He chuckled when the smoke raced from his lungs; choking on the fumes.

"Your always trippin', man. Just calm down, and ease it down a little, my kid bruddha. Everything is gonna be alright."

There's that voice again. I chuckled on the couch when he did it. He was terrible with Jamaican accents.

D passed Von the bowl, and he took a hit. When he was done, he did like he always did. He French inhaled the smoke back in as it crept out from behind his lips. I busted out laughing, "Von, you always look like super crazy when you do that, man."

Von handed me the bowl and said, "What you think Wiz was talkin' about in the song? That's the way your supposed to do it, man."

Ellie cut in laughing, "Nah, you just tryin' to look cool. You ain't got it like, Wiz."

I smirked and sparked up the bowl. *Time to get on my level, though.*

The sour diesel stung my tongue as it shot into my throat, suffocating my air ways and filling me up like a hot-air balloon. I was bound and determined to reach the sky. I let the smoke out and said, "We gotta get us some more drinks somewhere. I mean, we got money for a bottle. Ellie could buy it."

Derek jumped up and replied, "We got a bunch of Fours already. Ellie picked 'em up earlier."

It appears the change game wasn't that necessary. I floated towards the sky and snapped excitedly, "Oh shit you do?! Well, what are we waitin' on then?!"

We each had a Four and with those head crushers that's all you really need. Derek drove because he's not really a drinker; just likes to get high and have a good time. We all hopped in the Altima and I asked Ellie, "So where's this party at, anyway? Is there gonna be a lot of girls there, you think?"

Von chimed in from the backseat beside me, "There better be. I'm ready to get some bitches."

I always hated calling girls bitches, but it seems like that's how everybody likes to talk. I don't know. I guess when it comes to girls and finding the one; I don't want to start everything off with treatin' her like garbage. I want a true queen; somebody I can take over the world with; a true ride or die. A real love story doesn't start off sour like that. I don't know, though. I guess calling them bitches is just the cool thing to say nowadays. Lord knows, some chicks really know how to act like one.

Ellie laughed at Von, "You ain't gonna get any, anyway. You don't ever get any play."

She was right. He never did, but I didn't either, so I wasn't one to talk. Derek, on the other hand, was a man whore. He damn near got girls everywhere he went. Must've been because he has a six-pack, but who knows? I ain't gonna lie. I wish I had game like him. Honestly, it made me look up to him.

Derek turned the wheel and asked Ellie, "So, where's this party at, anyway? You never said."

Ellie sparked up a port and replied, "It's goin' down on Sharon Avenue."

When we pulled up, cars were lined up and down the block and you could hear Waka Flocka's song "No Hands" bumpin' threw the walls of the house. There were people everywhere.

Derek took a smooth puff off the blunt and said, "You ready to do the damn thing, bubbies?"

I wasn't sure. Even though I had a good buzz going on I still wasn't ready for the crowd. I'm fine when I'm around people that I know, but when it comes to being around a bunch of folks that I don't, I tend to withdrawal a little and follow Derek's lead. On top of that, I didn't have a good feeling about it. There was just something in the air. I wasn't sure if it was paranoia getting' the best of me or what. There was just something dark out there. I pushed the feeling down and ignored it. I had to for my friends; there was no other choice. *No backing out now.*

The front yard was packed and, as heads turned towards us; the anxiety demons came stampeding in. A couple of guys near an old rusted out grill hollered what's up to D, so we walked over to clap 'em up real quick. I'd seen them around town before, but I didn't really know them like that. All I knew was everyone called them Lee and Jay and you never saw one without the other. I didn't know much about Lee, but Jay, on the other hand, he was sort of famous for the sawed-off shotgun he had. Folks would say he'd polish that thing multiple times a day, but I never heard of him using it.

We didn't spend to much time in the front yard, though, and when we opened the door, of course Derek had to make his presence known. He let out a howling noise like he was the big bad wolf, ready to blow the whole house down. Of course there were a couple of girls he knew there already eyeing him down and coming his way. But as far as I go, I was practically unnoticed. *A walking husk, within the dusk. Stranger to all, beyond the wall.*

I didn't know a soul there. That was the thing. I grew up in this town and I felt like I should have known everyone, but in a way, I was just a ghost floating through the crowd, seen but unseen. *Noticed, but not memorable in any way.*

The house was a wreck already. There were beer bottles, loko cans, solo cups, you name it, littered everywhere. Some spilled, half full, or still to be open. *Gonna grab me a fresh one; a swig or two, perhaps a few.*

Every seat already had someone getting it in with a chick's tongue in their mouth; getting' quite hot and heavy, too. I sighed to myself and thought, *It sure would be great to be loved by somebody. To truly feel someone's touch and have that knowing when you look in their eyes; that they love you, too.*

I looked about to see if I could spot me a pretty girl in the crowd, even if I never had the courage to talk to one. Before I could though, Derek bumped into me with a four and said, "You ready to get your drink on or what?"

Von snapped, "Damn, what about me? I'm standin' here, too."

D clicked his tongue.

"I got one for you too, man. Damn. Just chill, ight?"

Derek handed me a four, and Von angrily snatched his. He took a gulp immediately. I did, too. Half of the can was gone in one swig. I really needed it. My nerves were on high alert.

Ellie disappeared as soon as we walked in, and there was no hope of finding her. Not in that crowd. *I'm lying. It really wasn't that bad.*

Derek cracked up and hollered, "God damn, you tryin' to get fucked all the way up tonight!"

I knew if I had enough to drink in me I'd be ok. *Drown. Swallow yourself up in the ecstasy of it all. The loss, the losing of oneself. All matter of frailty is put upon the shelf.*

I could barely hear D over all the loud music. I yelled, "D-damn, right! Hey, man, y-you wanna go in the k-kitchen or somethin'? I can't hear shit in h-here."

Really, I just wanted to have an excuse to get out of the thick of the crowd. Even if nobody acknowledged me, it still felt like all eyes were on me—or at least someone's. I could still feel the darkness in the air. It was an overbearing feeling that weigh heavily on me. *Down to Davey Jones, my boy. Become weightless in the water,* the voice in my head said. I took another chug and instantly I felt as settled as a newborn babe. *There you go. The numbness is settling in.*

97

I felt a sigh of relief wash over me once we escaped from the crowd. It wasn't loud in the kitchen noise wise, but it damn sure was smell wise. I panned the room with a red devilish glare as I began to settle back into myself. The four bubbled, the sweet "I don't care" feeling quicker than I thought it would within a matter of minutes. The crowd in the other room didn't seem to matter as much as it did before, and I could feel the liquor possessing me as a sly smile peeled across my face. *There you are, Mr. Hyde,* I thought.

Here I am, the voice in my head said. *Go ahead and light up the town. I'm gonna always be around.*

The thought of trouble enticed me even more when I looked to my left and spotted this chick building a gravity bong and prepping it all for lift off. I walked up behind her and said, "Hey, how you doin'? Are you buildin' what I think you are?"

She spun around, and I recognized her immediately. It was Paul's cousin Shanna. Her face lit up as she gave me a hug and said, "What are you doin' here? I haven't seen you in forever."

My, how great it is to be acknowledged by somebody that's a woman. I felt even more at ease with her around. Honestly, I was sort of checkin' her out with the little shorts she had on and all, but I didn't want to go there because she was Paul's cousin. I counted her as a cousin too, really, even though we're not actually blood related. Still, I couldn't cross that barrier. *We weren't in West Virginia after all.*

I lit up in delight as I embraced her. I replied, "I know it's been awhile, right? Me and my boy D just dropped in to see what ya'll had goin' on around here."

She looked over at Derek and ran over to give him a hug, too. Apparently, they had a history together, which wasn't a surprise, because Derek was pretty much a pimp, anyway.

Shanna put her other hand on her hip and said, "How come you never texted me back the other day?"

Derek lied his ass off. He replied, grinning, "What you talkin' about? You didn't text me the other day."

Shanna snapped her neck to the side and flirted, "You're lying. Well, if you can't tell me the truth, I guess I'll just have to count you out then."

I was rather perplexed as she walked back to the gravity bong. *What does she mean? Like he can't have her or he can't hit the gravity bong?* I was so confused as my thoughts rambled. I busted out laughing like a dumbass. Assuming she meant the weed I chuckled, "You can't have any, man. Guess more for me then. You gonna let me hit it right, Shanna?"

Shanna looked up at me, jaw agape, and then placed her hands back on her hips. I thought, *Damn, standing firm tonight aren't we?* She got stern with me when she said, "What the fuck are you talkin' about? We're cousins dumbass."

I shook my head and dropped my face into my palms, laughing. *Clawing away at the skin I'm in. A fresh face filled full of sin.*

I tried to look at her, but I couldn't. I fell against the wall to prop myself up. I rambled, "No, no, no."

My laughing carried on, "No, that's not what I mean. I meant the weed, man, the weed, like more weed for me and you then."

Shanna cackled hysterically over the gravity bong like a gremlin.

"Oh, that's what you meant. Well, of course you can hit it, cuzzo."

I stood ready to aim and fire like a soldier on the front line. *A call to duty.*

I asked Shanna, "Bet, you can't out smoke me, though. No, no, no I'm the best there is, ya see. You can't outdo me."

Derek answered to the call as quick as I did. I looked around to see if I could find Von, but he was gone. *More for us, I guess.*

D hollered, "Shit, I out smoke you all the time! You already past the level and we ain't even left gravity behind yet."

Shanna accepted my challenge, though.

"Don't think because you beat me a couple of times racin' when we were little you can get me. Those were bikes, but this right here is a rocket."

I pondered upon it. The gravity bong was a gleaming spectacle of architectural magnificence. The five gallon bucket was filled full of clear crystalline water that dazzled and waved the jeweled ice cubes that lay within the midst of smoking ripples. It was all crowned with a six letter word that was cut off right at the bottom—Sprite. *Here it goes*, I thought. *It's time to get right.*

I addressed the remaining members of the launch team, "Why don't we step it up a notch? I think after every hit, each one of us picks up a four and chugs it until the next person lets out their smoke. What do ya'll think?"

Shanna shook her head and said, "Nah, that's fucked up. What are you tryin' to do to kill me?"

Derek busted out laughing as he headed towards the fridge to grab a few more fours.

He handed me one and turned to Shanna and raised his eyebrows, grinning.

"You down or what?"

Shanna shook her head and threw her hands up in the air, "Fuck it, guys, I guess."

I cracked my four open and took a preliminary sip, "Alright, Major Tom, time to prep for liftoff."

Suddenly, Tony popped into the kitchen and asked, "Major who?"

It shocked me to see him there. I figured he'd be hanging out with Kayla all night. Derek threw his arms up in the air and yelled, "What's with it, bubbies?! I didn't know you'd be here."

Tony dapped him up and replied, "Shit, I heard it was goin' down over here tonight."

I cut in, "You didn't bring Kayla with you?"

Tony pushed his eyebrows down and shook his head. "Hell nah, I told her I got shit to do. Why you worried about Kayla, anyway?"

I shrugged my shoulders and replied, "I don't know. I was just askin' I guess. You tryin' to lift off, man?"

Tony clapped his hands and rubbed his palms together, "You already know I'm wit it."

He turned to the living room and yelled, "Ey, Deonta, come here, man!"

Deonta, I thought. I didn't really care for him too much, either.

Back in the day, when we had class together, he used to always make jokes about me in front of everyone. They were meant to make me feel lower, inferior even, and it worked. I hated feeling that way, but I never let loose and knocked his teeth out like I wanted to. I've always preferred to be someone's friend, rather than their enemy, but when it comes to Deonta, I don't know. There's just something off about him.

Derek liked him too, which sucked even more because that meant I'd have to be the fake kind of friendly to keep everything cool so we could all have a good time. Derek didn't waste anytime in clappin' hands with him. He yelled, "Oh shit! I didn't know you were here! You got away from the baby momma tonight?"

Deonta cracked a smile and replied, "You know I don't give a fuck about that bitch. I just drop in to see my little girl, hit it, and bounce. I ain't tryin' to play house and all that shit."

I couldn't understand why anybody liked him, but I guess him and Tony were pretty tight growing up. Deonta pulled his hat off and pointed towards me, "Ey, I ain't seen you in a minute, Eminem! What you been up to?"

Keep it cordial, I thought to myself. *He's friends with your friends, so keep it cool.* I ignored the Eminem jab he threw and reluctantly replied, "Not shit really, man. Just hangin' out."

Deonta nodded his head with a slick grin on his face and replied, "You ain't gettin' beat up playin' ball no more?"

He elbowed Tony and laughed, "Em, got elbowed in the teeth one time and cried like a little bitch. He couldn't stand his own for nothin'."

I could feel the rage inside kindle like a stack of logs; the liquor had me boiling. I wanted to rip his head off right then and there, but then Shanna cut in and said, "Are we gonna smoke or what guys?!"

I didn't have a clue where Ellie or Von were and Derek didn't either, so unfortunately, they missed out. Either way, it sounded like a plan to me. Thank god Shanna let me have the first hit. I needed to calm down, anyway.

When the cauldron bubbled and the steam rumbled, I felt myself ascending like an angel upon clover laden wings, flying towards the branches of the treetops to come face to face with the Cheshire cat. When I finally let up, the smoke rolled out of me like a creeping snake that expanded itself into a translucent picture across the room that was as dazzling as Van Gogh's most magnificent masterpiece.

Alice, we are getting quite lost aren't we, I thought to myself as I slammed the bitter taste of the four down my throat. The burning liquid chased the billowing cloud in my lungs all the way down. All I could muster afterwards was a good old-fashioned belch against the wall. I was hurtin', but floatin' at the same time. *It felt; oh so good.*

Shanna, on the other hand, damn near filled her whole body up with smoke. She was a little gal, too. She was only around 4'11, if that, so I knew that smoke had to have her feelin' crisscrossed worse than applesauce. *It was that good, good, for sure.*

Derek took his hit like a champ and chugged his whole four in one go around. Tony and Deonta didn't do too bad themselves. After a few go arounds, my anxiety was extinct and my other half started to take over. It's easier being a careless clown once I get enough to drink in me. My hat doesn't say joker on it for nothin' after all.

I posted myself up like Superman and spoke in my well-mannered, dignified voice, "Well, folks, it looks like we have gotten ourselves into quite the predicament."

Everybody busted out laughing. Thankfully, Deonta didn't throw any more jabs and acted more friendly. For the most part, anyway. He busted out, "Man, you gotta cut it with that Mr. Rogers sounding shit. You gonna have me dyin' over here."

It did make me feel good to make everyone laugh, even him. It felt better making myself a joke rather than someone else. *I was taking my power back*

As everyone was still losing it within the haze, I noticed Shanna wasn't really laughing along. She had her head hung low and her hand on her stomach. I scrambled over to her across the debris of empty beer cans. I clasped my hands on both of her shoulders and said, "Oh, my god, darling, are you going to be ok? Do you need a hug?!"

Shanna just shook her head and rumbled low in her throat, "No—no—I think—I think I'm gonna be sick."

She bolted immediately towards the bathroom. I chased after her, working my way through the crowd screaming, "Oh my everyone! We have an emergency! Please clear the way! I'm a doctor! This is serious business, folks!"

An unknown close by said, "Who the fuck is that guy?"

The best around, that's who, I thought to myself. Shanna slammed the bathroom door closed and locked it. I placed my ear up to the door. My devilish grin ran from ear to ear. She was throwing up, that's for sure—a lot. I placed my palm against the door—trying to console her from afar. I spoke through the wood, "Shanna—honey—are you ok?"

All I could hear was a constant reoccurring gurgling noise from behind the door. I kept on and knocked, "Shanna—would you like a wet towel perhaps, sweetheart?"

Still no answer, just the gurgling. With that, I threw myself onto the ground and stuck my lips under the door and said, "I fuckin' told you Shanna. I told ya you couldn't out smoke me."

I finished off gloating with my 1940s mobster guy voice, "You messed with the wrong one; ya see. I'm the best in town, myah."

You're goin' quite mad, ya see.

My *myah* was followed with a blah. She didn't say a thing after she came out. She was ready to get home, so she left in an ambulance a few blocks away, some say. Tony and Deonta didn't stay too much longer, either. Which sort of sucked because I liked partying with them, even Deonta. As long as they both could keep it cool and not make any jokes about me they were alright guys. I still didn't know where the hell Ellie was, though.

I looked around the room rapidly as I thought, *oh lord, we have lost a brother, or rather, sister in arms.* Surprisingly, she was right in the living room with everyone else. She was talking with someone and, for some reason, there was something familiar about the guy.

I stumbled over to Ellie to see who it was. I couldn't believe my eyes. It never clicked in my head that I knew the guy the party was for, after all. I knew him well, but it had been forever; it was Shawn.

CHAPTER VII:

MY SUMMER VACATION

The sun sat high, and the wind was cool, when Shawn walked out of Lucasville Prison; he was full, but kind of cold.

The day he was arrested four years ago was a hot, blistering summer afternoon. He had nothing but a tank top and shorts on. Nothing too flashy for a guy that got busted, nailed, and hit with the second degree. Shawn bit his lip. He was searching for his ride. His boys didn't seem to be there, but then he spotted them; both a pair. Bread and Butter pulled up with style in a glittering red '82 Chevy Malibu.

Shawn spread his arms out and smiled.

"Aaayyyoohh! I thought ya'll done forgot about me!"

Butter hopped out of the passenger side first, and held his arms out, too. He was a skinny dude; Mr. Pretty boy some folks like to say. He always has to look fresh and the guy never wore the same outfit twice that just wasn't his style. He was too clean for it.

Bread, on the other hand, was a little slower, a lot bigger than his brother Butter. He wasn't as stylish as him, but always kept a fitted hat on just like his twin. They always liked to match when they were kids, but Bread just couldn't keep up with him.

Butter kind of put you in the mind of the rapper Sticky Fingaz, and he kind of talked like him, too. He ran up to Shawn first and gave him a hug.

"Damn, boy, your cuts lookin' rough. They ain't know how to use clippas in there or what?"

Shawn embraced him, too, and patted him on the back.

"Damn, Butta, don't do me like that. They can't get it right up in there. Nothin' but cold food and brittle socks. Know what I'm sayin'," Shawn laughed.

Butter broke out laughing hysterically, but then Bread came up and gave Shawn a hug, too.

Bread laughed, "Don't tell me it was that bad. The food was cold? Ey, ya booty hole didn't go pop, pop in there, did it?"

Shawn shoved him off and said, "Man, stall out on that shit. You know, ain't no muthafucka finna bend me over. I don't play."

They all laughed and walked towards the car.

Butter was to the rear door first and said, "Ey, you can ride shotgun today, but just this once. I gotta give you at least a little treat since you finally free and all."

Shawn hooked his hand on the passenger door and yanked it open.

"That it? Just shotgun then?"

Bread climbed into the driver's seat and said, "Nah, that ain't it. Far from it; wait till you see what Chan done worked up."

Shawn grinned when he closed the door.

"Good, I'm ready to see what the fund done bought."

Bread grinned back as he pulled the car into drive.

"You're gonna love the new operation; it's gotta lot of potential."

The engine rumbled as Bread flicked the key. The tires squealed, and they were off. The red Malibu swung out of the parking lot and they made the turn towards I-71. Shawn took one last look at the prison that held him in the never ending days before. I ain't never goin' back, he thought to himself. *I'll fry bacon before I do that.*

Shawn didn't care to look at the place anymore. He turned towards Bread and said, "So where Chan stay at now, anyway? Where the setup?"

Bread was busy lighting up a black-n-mild, and he rolled the window down to let the breeze in.

"It ain't too far from home. There's too much traffic up in Columbus and you know how the north side be sometimes. We moved to a more quiet area, less noticeable. You remember Black Run? It's about twenty minutes outside the 'Ville."

Shawn shook his head and said, "Nah, I've never heard of it. Is it close to Newark?"

Bread replied, "More in between Newark and Zanesville, like Nashport? You remember where that is right?"

Shawn grinned, and peered into the side mirror, eyes burning, and chiseling away at the reflection, thinking of her.

He cleared his throat and replied, "Yeah, I know where it is. I used to have a girl that lived out there. You remember her Butta?"

Butter busted out laughing in the backseat, "Hell yeah! Little shorty that be wearin' the skirts lookin' all high class and shit?"

Shawn grinned, "Yeah, that's the one."

Butter jerked his elbow out in excitement.

"Damn! I had my eyes on her, too, but you beat me to it. Shit, you was in love with that girl. What ever happened to it ain't no fun if the homies can't have none, huh?"

Shawn grinned, "Cause it ain't. You gotta keep a prize like that all to yourself."

Butter replied, "So it's like that then? Ey, whatever happened to her, anyway?"

Shawn glanced out if the window at the passing traffic whizzing behind and frowned a little.

"She fell more in love with the needle. Last time I saw her was at a K up there around Newark somewhere. I barely recognized her."

"Damn," Butter said, "that a shame. Somebody done served her up then?"

Shawn's gaze stayed locked in on the traffic.

"Nah, it wasn't like that. Bitch took a pinch out of the stash and just wouldn't quit."

"You fuck her up, dawg?"

Shawn shook his head; eyes still fixed, remembering how pretty she once was.

"Nah, I just let her go."

The ride didn't seem to take long at all. Shawn was caught in catching up the entire way to Chan's. Once they were off the interstate, he could finally take in the green. The glimpse of the Ohio valley reminded him that he was alive again. *Reborn, just like the morning star.*

Bread turned the tires towards a dirt road and the Malibu bounced as they went down a narrow incline.

Bread said, "Man, we shoulda stopped and got somethin' to eat while we was on the road. I'm getting' hungry."

Butter slapped the back of his seat and said, "You always hungry! Lucky you ain't been to jail; probably start eatin' muthafuckas like a hyena and shit."

Shawn muffled his laugh into his fist. Bread replied, "Man, quit. I'll snap yo skinny ass like a twig. You ain't never took me down."

Butter bounced forward in the back seat, closer to Bread's ear.

"Yeah 'till I point a harpoon gun at ya fat ass."

Butter held his fist up like he was holding a spear in the back and swung forward playfully. The car bounced further down the road and Shawn could spot a little white house coming up closer.

Bread replied, "You better hide ya ass in some steal, comin' at me like that."

He looked over his shoulder at his brother and smiled, "See you ain't stupid."

Butter crossed his arms and mashed his eyebrows down across his forehead sternly.

"Whatever, fuck you, bro."

Bread pulled the gearshift up into park in front of the little white house and looked over at Shawn.

"Well, this is it."

Shawn didn't say anything at first. He was pondering upon the accessibility of the location. Not too far from two towns and it was hidden on a private drive; nowhere near what they had in Pike County, but there was potential. After all, I-70 runs from East to West, easy access to a lot of major cities. The 'Ville was just a hop off the jetline; a skip of the rock. Inconspicuous and—*Perfect.*

They all climbed out of the car and shut the doors. Dirt shuffled under their shoes and blew away in the wind as they made their approach.

Shawn noticed foil glittering across the basement windows, and it made his mind run.

No outside light, it's sealed tight. No heat-seeking birds flyin' around; gotta watch that electric bill, though.

Bread knocked on the door, and it didn't take Chan long to open it. He was a stoner all the way. A Chinese guy in a bathrobe with long hair and mutton chops stood there in the doorway, startled with excitement. He went for the blunt in his mouth and slowly tucked it away between his index and middle finger.

He threw his hand up, and Shawn caught it.

"Man," Chan exclaimed, "you got big, man. Lookin' super muscley there, my dude; right on."

Shawn smiled, and said, "What's wit it, my boy? You got good news?"

Chan chuckled and threw his pointer fingers up in the air.

"Oooh do I ?! Wait till you see this shit bro, it's gonna blow your lid off, man!"

He held the blunt out to Shawn and said, "You wanna try?"

Shawn waved his hand out.

"Nah, no thanks. I ain't tryin' to smoke like that no more."

Butter stood behind Shawn and gasped silently; jerking his head up and down fast. He pushed through him and Bread, then said, "Ey, Chan, I don't know what's wrong with him, but you always know I'm down."

Chan smirked and replied, "Hell yeah, that's my boy."

He handed Butter the blunt, then said, "You guys want to come in now or what?"

They all followed, and the door closed.

The place wasn't too tidy and anybody could tell Chan wasn't too keen on cleaning a thing up. Dust was everywhere, almost as if nobody had been there in years. It looked more like a storage house.

Shawn asked, "So, Chan, you the only grower? Who all has been here? Who got access?"

He turned around and replied, "Yeah, it's just me that doctor's the plants, man. And the only people that know about this place is standing here right now."

Shawn nodded grimly; still speculative of everything and everyone. He had to stay on his toes.

They continued to follow Chan towards the basement door. He reached for the nob, then turned around and smiled.

"You're gonna love this, bro. It's like Wonderland down there."

The steps creaked as they made their way down. *The smell was intoxicating*. That was the funny thing. You couldn't smell a thing upstairs. They'd found a way to seal the smell off and contain it. *Genius*.

Chan spread his arms out and said, "Welcome to the garden of Eden."

Shawn's jaw fell and his eyes danced around everywhere. There was a line of plants on the left propped up on a long wooden bench that ran down around ten feet long. They were all tight together and their branches were tied up across a screen of some sort. From the top you couldn't even see the roots in the soil, you'd have to bend down close to really catch an eye at them. Long fluorescent bulbs hung overhead on each side. They were blinding. Shawn could tell Chan learned a lot while he was inside. On the right was where the real magic was happening; *hydro*. These plants weren't as tight as the soil grown crop and they were massive compared to the others. The black tanks they grew from made a low hum. *Merry Christmas*. Shawn was in shock.

"Damn, Chan, this too many plants to be all you."
Chan smiled.

"Bread and Butter help me manage 'em, but they don't have the science down quite yet."

Chan wiped his brow as if sweat was there, but there wasn't. He laughed, "Took a lot of work setting it all up, but here it is."

For once, Shawn was tongue tied. He didn't have a clue what to say. Then he thought of the math. He knew the amount of ounces a soil plant could grow, around four to six if you're lucky, indoors, but with the hydro, he didn't have a clue. He pointed towards his right and said, "How much is the yield on each of these?"

Chan put his hands on his hips like Superman, and replied, "Around fifteen to sixteen for now, but I think I can push them for seventeen, eventually."

Shawn thought out loud, grinning, "Okay. Let's say fifteen times three hundred, wholesale, shit that's like forty-five hundred per plant."

Damn, that's over a hundred gees just on the right, Shawn thought to himself

Butter chimed in, "Mista human calculator over here, and shit, look at that. You got it down, my boy."

Bread shook his head and laughed.

Shawn grinned, "How often is the harvest?"

"Around three months, but we use regeneration with some of the plants, too. Sometimes it works, sometimes it doesn't, but with regeneration it cuts down the turnaround to about a month."

Shawn didn't gasp outward, but he did inside. He couldn't let his emotions show too much, he knew better than that. *Trust will only take you so far with anybody.*

"I'm not sure what to say, Chan. I'm impressed. You've really came a long way with this shit."

Shawn glared at Bread, then asked, "So ya'll harvested and dried, yet? What we working with? How much we have to move right now? We gotta a deadline; our benefactors expect their cut within the month."

Bread exhaled slowly, looked towards the ground for a second, then back at Shawn.

"Shit, we got a lot ready to go, but that's the bad news. These muthafuckas, they be wearin' black and blue.

They hit a couple of our houses. I mean, we were cuttin', too, and they done hit the powder room. The connect won't even fuck with us no more. We had just enough to break even so they wouldn't kill us."

Shawn's teeth clenched, and the devil glared through his eyes.

"So what you sayin'? We got all this, and we broke?"

Bread replied, "We dead in Columbus, bruh. We ain't got no soldiers no more. They either dead, or got locked up, just like you."

Butter snapped and wailed his arms around.

"Fuck those muthafuckas in black and blue. Who they think they are? Crips? Man, them niggas a joke, bro. I'll pull up on the block and spray all dem bomblacades."

Butter laughed, "Ya'll didn't know I was with the Rasta shit did you? I mean—"

Shawn yelled, "Ey! This shit ain't no joke and talk is cheap."

He gave Butter a stern glare. Butter might've been crazy, but he wasn't wild enough to mess with Shawn; to his face, that is.

He asked Bread, "What's the plan? How we gonna move? I'm only askin' you because ya'll done dropped the ball while I was inside."

He stomped his foot, pointed towards the ground, and yelled, "It don't matter how many plants, houses, or how much we can grow! Ya'll can't even move it!"

Chan re-lit his blunt and didn't say a word. He wasn't on the streets, he just grew. That was all Bread and Butter.

Bread was tough, but Shawn made him stutter, "T-that's w-why we goin' back home. Word is, it's dry right now. Ain't nothin', but low grade mids floatin' around."

Butter chimed in, "Yeah, we givin' back to the community and doin' it a favor."

Shawn was still pissed, but his temper had cooled. He'd learned a lot of patience during his time in Lucasville. Many got checked, but lived to see another day. *Save one.*

"One town ain't gonna be enough. We the same distance from two. I want both. Butta you know some of them boys in Newark, right?"

Butter nodded, "Yeah, we can get us a little squad up there."

Shawn snapped, "I don't fuck with nothin' little."

His eyes burned viciously for a moment. *I need a network. I ain't got time for games. La Sombra will be waiting.*

"Don't worry about your connect, I have my own. He drop us, so what, we do it likewise. I'm expectin' a call from you know who—the benefactor. We gotta get the deck in order. Bread you the diplomat. I want you to hit the streets and find out who's who and what's what around here. We gotta get the ball rollin' now before we lose even more ground."

Bread asked, "You wanna hit it, tonight?"

Shawn replied, "Nah, I still want you on the burner, though, settin' shit up."

Bread replied, "Okay, then, good. There's a welcome home party lined up for you in the 'Ville. Gonna be a lot of folks happy to see you tonight, man."

Shawn clapped up hands with Bread and said, "Ok, then. That's right. I'm back."

Butter asked, "What am I chopped liver over here?"

Shawn grinned, then clapped up Butter, "Nah, you one of the strongest soldiers I've ever known. We got this."

Butter joked, "Shit, I do, but you don't. We gotta get you some fresh gear. Bread's got your cut stashed in the closet over there. You ready to pull out?"

You just wait, Shawn grinned back, and nodded, "Let's do it."

115

CHAPTER VIII:

TEARZ

When I got my first bike, grandma and grandpa told me that there were two sides to Luck Avenue. The good side, and the bad side. We lived on the good side, they assured me, but I was never allowed to go up the hill and down.

"That's where all those thugs hang out," Grandma said, "and don't ever go around that store, Ritchey's; that place is bad news."

It had been closed down and abandoned for years by the time I made my way down there. It's hard to go up the hill, but it's easy to go down; *a quick fall.* That's where Shawn was from, and he was a lot older than me.

It didn't seem real. He looked a lot different from the last time I saw him, but it was still the same guy. At least I tried to tell myself that. In his face I could see the kid I used to know, but there was something else there—in his eyes, that is. They were dark, but his smile was friendly as ever.

I stuttered, "Sh-shawn?"

At first he wasn't sure who I was either; it had been awhile. His eyes studied me for a moment, then he gave me a big hug. *Mad love.*

Shawn hollered, "Oh shit! If it ain't the little boy who just turned two!"

He laughed, "God damn; you got big! It's been too long. You back in town for good, now, man or what?"

I stood there, dumbfounded. After all these years, we'd ran into each other just like that—at *the snap of a finger.* It's funny how the universe does that; like it's all sort of planned out.

Unfortunately, by some haphazard chance, I bumped into a girl along the way and made her spill a drink all over herself. It soaked her in liquor and Kool Aid. I felt absolutely terrible about it.

The girl screamed, "Really?! You made me spill my cup all over myself!"

Shawn dashed an annoyed glance at her and said, "What do you want a trophy? Go get yourself a towel or somethin', bitch. We're talkin' here."

At the moment, I didn't feel bad for the girl at all. It's like along with the rest of my weaknesses, empathy had gone out of the window as well. *I sure do like this reformed version of myself, I must say.* The girl simply stormed off and the party went on.

Ellie hollered over all the noise, "You know, Shawn? You didn't say anything about that along the way."

Apparently, somebody had turned the music up because The Joker's "We Do it For Fun Pt. 1" was blaring steadily across the room. I could barely hear a thing.

I screamed, "Yeah! Yeah, I do! We're boys. We go way back!"

Shawn tapped Ellie and muttered something. Then he waved for me to follow him out of the crowd. So we walked outside for a smoke. I lit up one of the "ready-to-go" blunts Derek had rolled up earlier and offered it to Shawn. He leaned up against the bricks, waving his hand, and said, "Nah, I don't fuck with that."

I was surprised. I replied, "What? You don't smoke? What's up with that?

Shawn grinned and lit up a black, "Nah, I try to keep my mind straight these days."

Then, he laughed, "You know what they say, though? Remember the rules, right?"

"Never get high on your own supply," I replied with a smirk, "You still with it, like that, man? I mean, you still got it?"

Shawn winced and sucked his teeth, "Man, what's with all the questions? I just got out. Shit, out here actin' like the police and everything. What's been good with it, though? How you been, man?"

I shrugged my shoulders and replied, "Okay, I guess. I mean, y'know, it gets kind of boring around here. There ain't much to do. What about you, though? I know you gotta be glad to be out."

Shawn took a drag and replied, "Shit, I heard that. Just out here tryin' to make it; know what I mean? Just tryin' to get this money."

I nodded and danced my head around nervously; *not sure why*. There was that feeling in the air again. *Something dark and ominous.*

Shawn tapped me on the arm with his elbow and asked, "You good, man?"

Dazed and confused, I replied, "Y-yeah, I'm g-good."

I tried to collect myself before I said more, but Shawn beat me to the punch. He laughed, "If you say so. Hey, you still got that stutter. That shit used to be funny. You'd always do it when you was nervous."

I laughed, too. *Calm, collected, and cool.* I brushed the feeling off the best I could. I still shivered, though.

"Y-yeah, I g-guess, I l-lose myself sometimes."

Then I let out a deep exhale, smoke crawling through the air, "Ahhh—I'd lose my head if it wasn't attached."

Shawn yelled, "Simon Phoenix! Oh shit!"

I cackled, "John Spartan, is that you?!"

Shawn made a gun with his fingers and pointed it at me.

"Bad day, blondie."

We both cracked up. "Demolition Man" was both our favorite movie when we were kids. I've always been one for the hero, but the bad guy is always so much more interesting. *Edgy, to the point, and often chaotic.* The bad guy gets things done. He's what gives meaning to the whole story.

I rattled, "Damn, I ain't seen that movie in a while! Around when I last saw you, probably."

Suddenly, a hefty guy in a red cap and a cape-like shirt to match opened the back door and said, "Ey, Shawn, we gotta ride. You good to go?"

Shawn took a hit off his black and turned his head. "It's that time?"

Red Capper nodded, "Yeah, it's time to ride."

Hefty shuffled right back in as if he were in a hurry.

Shawn stood there still and took another hit.

"Ey, man. You got a phone? Go ahead and put my number in there and get at me sometime. We gonna get back up."

I smiled and nodded my head. It was great to have my old friend back. He'd always seemed like an older brother, y'know, him bein' six years older and all. I took his number down right away and called him so he could have mine. Then Shawn dabbed me up and said, "Ight, then. I'll get at you later."

He walked back inside at that, and I soon followed.

When I got back in, the party wasn't as full as it was, but it was still lit. Lil Wayne's new song "Gonorrhea" was bumpin' across the speakers. Derek wasn't anywhere in sight, but I spotted Von makin' out on the couch with a fat chick. I smiled and thought to myself, *The fellas ain't gonna let you live this one down, buddy.* They never would either. I know because it happened to me.

Don't get me wrong, I love fat girls; the pretty ones, especially. They're a lot more kind and tender-hearted than the Barbie dolls. They're not shallow, and most of them accept you for who you are. Fat, skinny, or whatever, either way, I can't stand the boujee actin' type. Makes me sicker than anything, in fact.

Ellie wasn't hard to find again, though. I guess I was just too high to notice at first, but from the looks of it, she already had a girl on lock for the night.

I figured I'd offer Ellie a smoke or something at least, since she missed our lift off earlier into the nether regions of space. I ruffled my way through the crowd towards Ellie and the pretty girl she was talkin' with. I asked, "Ey, what are you doin'? You seen D around?"

Ellie smiled at me and turned to the brunette on her right. She had her hand cuddled in both of her palms and pulled it up to her mouth to kiss it. Then she replied, "Nah, I ain't seen him. I was just talkin' to Miss Fine here." She paused and looked into the girl's eyes.

"You gotta lot of interesting things to say, girl."

It seemed like Ellie was losing herself a bit, but then she snapped out of it.

"She's got a friend, too. Where'd your friend go? What's her name again?"

The girl danced her fingers through her hair playfully and replied, "Her names Jules, you forgot that quick?"

Ellie burst out, "Jules! Yeah, that's her name. Hey, look! There she goes right there."

It was as if it all happened in slow motion. *Two blasts from the past in one night.* I turned my head toward the crowd and felt my heart speed up in a rumbling pattern as a petite dark-haired girl with blonde highlights waded her way through the crowd towards us. I knew exactly who Jules was. How could I ever forget?

I felt knocked off balance in the ring of a roaring crowd for a moment. I couldn't believe that she was at the party. I mean, she wasn't even from the 'Ville, I met her when I was going to school out in Valley, but there she was, looking as fine as ever, with a few drinks huddled between her elbows.

Jules lit up and yelled, "What are you doing here?! I haven't seen you since you changed schools."

My heart was pounding and I could feel myself blushing. I replied, "I could ask you the same. What are you doin' in town?"

Jules handed Miss Fine and Ellie their drinks and took a sip of her own. She replied, "My girl Alicia told me about this party and I figured I'd come down and see what's happenin'. I thought you lived here."

She paused, giggled, and rambled, "You look smoked the fuck out already."

Boy, is she right, I thought to myself. *A blind and jibbering man fumbling my way through the fog.* Jules was the only girl that I didn't feel nervous talking to. Of course, it wasn't that way at first. I nearly jumped out of the school bus window when she opened her mouth to talk to me. I cleared my throat and replied, "Well, damn, my feelings are so hurt. You didn't grab me a drink?"

It sure is a joy when Mr. Hyde puts his hat on; he's such a smooth talker. Jules giggled and gave my arm a shove when she replied, "I didn't know you were here or I would've got you one. For all I know you're holding out on me, anyway. You got any smoke?"

I ran my fingers across the bill of my hat and replied with a grin, "Why of course I do, mam. You tryin' to go a round or what?"

Suddenly, there was a crack that rolled like lightning through the air before she could answer and the front door ruptured open with a boom. A few guys in all black and blue came storming in. The leader of the pack walked to the center of the room. He was tall, and lean; his crazy eyes looked mean. One looked left while the other eye pointed straight, slightly cocked to the right. I didn't have a clue who he was looking at, but I sure hoped it wasn't me. My nerves raced everywhere.

The guy folded his hands in front of him. Poised up and ready to go. All he said was, "Where he at?"

The phrase, "Where was who," had to have been juggling in everyone's minds. All went silent. The man in black and blue unfolded his hands; swaying from left to right, with a watch glittering on his wrist.

"Ya'll can't hear?! Nobody can talk?! Where the fuck is that, nigga, Shawn at?!"

He looked around at everyone. The whole party halted, and if there were crickets outside, they were silent, too. The man in black and blue nodded his head grimly.

"Ight, then. Maybe this will get y'all's attention."

Before anyone knew it, a Smith & Wesson was already out of his jacket and in the blink of an eye, it was in the air. Then he fired; *shoot for the sky.*

"Let that be a message! Tell Shawn, Rondo is lookin' for 'em!"

More bangs with bullets rang out, and everyone panicked.

I scrambled around and grabbed Jules by the shoulders. I shouted, "We gotta get out of here!"

I tried to be cool, but I was high. I'll admit it. I was in a bit of a panic.

My eyes darted around, looking to get a head start on an escape, then I spotted a way.

"Look, there's a side door right over there!"

122

Jules shouted, "What about you?!"

I was paralyzed in fear. Ellie and Von were already gone, but Derek— I wasn't sure where Derek was. I wasn't frozen in my tracks anymore and my feet didn't have a problem running for the door. Only my mind weighed me down. *The adrenaline washed over my buzz.*

I figured Derek had to be outside with Ellie, but when I got to the Altima, Ellie was the only one standing there and Von—well, he was gunnin' it down the street like a track star. I screamed, "Hey, Von!"

Onward through the night, he ran, disappearing past the street lights, and vanishing behind the crest of the hill.

"Von!"

It was a lost cause. He was gone. I shook my head.

"Damn, man," then I diverted towards Ellie and yelled, "Where's Derek at?!"

Ellie scrambled around, panicked, and just said she didn't know. Then I heard Derek yell. He was still inside. I looked to Ellie first and then to Jules, and said, "You and your friend need to get out of here. I'll hit you up later on, ok?"

Jules nodded her head. I didn't wait for anymore of a response. I ran back towards the house, but then I halted at the tip of the hill. *Watching.*

Rondo had a hold of Derek, and his goons weren't that far behind him.

He squeezed a fist into Derek's collar and snapped something I couldn't make out.

D was blank. He didn't say a thing. He went void. Rondo lifted the gun and put it to Derek's head; pressing it further into his temple.

"Don't make me blow your head off over some shoes, now," I finally heard Rondo say.

D's eyebrows twitched, and he gulped. Slowly, but surely, he began to slip his shoes off; *toes grinding away at the heel.*

Rondo grinned, then snickered, "Don't go pissin' yourself. Nice-n-easy."

After the shoes were off, Rondo let Derek go, but he still had the gun pointed at him. Derek backed away through the front doorway slowly. He kept his eyes steadily fixed on the pistol. He didn't look scared. That was the strange thing about it. He looked—*menacing,* if there's any word I could use to describe it. Almost like if he had the gun, he would've shot Rondo dead on the spot.

Suddenly, Derek stopped. I wasn't sure why. Did he have a death wish I didn't know about? I wasn't sure, but obviously Derek didn't care. He stare at Rondo, not moving a muscle, then he looked him dead in the face and said, "You ain't seen the last of me."

Rondo and his goons laughed in the doorway. He waved his arms around, gun still in hand, and said, "Oh, it's like that? Tag your it? Just like little kids."

Rondo's eyes gleamed, and he grinned. Then he puckered his lips and went, "Pow."

The gun in his hand bounced up as if it really went off, but lucky for Derek, it didn't. It was all a game to Rondo.

He cackled, and waved his arms around, and done a bow.

"I yield for your sake today."

Rondo licked his lips and one of his eyes dashed to the left, then he grinned again at Derek.

"I'm feeling—merciful. I don't wanna kill you, man. Just get the fuck outta here."

Laughter ripped through the air from the doorway. They humiliated Derek.

I ran down the hill, meeting him halfway. I reached for his arm, but Derek pulled away.

"Come on, man, we gotta get outta here!"

We ran together back to the Altima. As soon as everyone got in, I gunned it down the road. The tires squealed away from the sirens. I wiped the sweat from my forehead and pounded my hand against the steering wheel. I yelled, "What were you thinking, man?! That guy could've shot you!"

Derek screamed back, "Well, where were you at anyway?! Ya'll just left me in there. We supposed to have each others back, man!"

I waved my hands over the steering wheel. *Aggravated and afraid.*

"I thought you were already out, man. I thought you were at the car."

He had the look of the devil in his eyes. I've seen him mad before, but never like that. His glare was burning. Derek shook his head and settled in his seat, "Nah. I was tryin' to make sure ya'll made it out."

Ellie cut in, "D, it wasn't even like that. When we knew you were still in there, we were comin' to back you up."

Derek stare straight out into the oncoming street lights and didn't say a thing at first until he finally broke the silence. It's like a different side of him came out that night when he said, "It don't even matter, though. One day, ain't nobody gonna be able to punk me like that. One day, I'm gonna be the nigga to run from."

CHAPTER IX:

THINGS DONE CHANGED

The night shadowed everything, and it was dark. The river flow, and the crickets chirped. Shawn leaned back on his bronzed brown Chevy Chevelle and took a hit off a cigar; staring out past the canal. A voice spoke low, in a deep tone on the other end of the burner. Shawn stood still, attentive, listening with the phone held to his ear.

La Sombra whispered on the other line, "My associates speak of few pleasantries; estoy decepcionada. Remember our bargain, el corredor; a favor for a favor, we want the ball returned."

"I got you, señor; the deadline will be met," Shawn replied evenly.

"Careful, el corredor; we don't allow any weak links within our chain. Every move is being watched," La Sombra whispered.

The line clicked on the other end, and all went silent for a moment. Shawn began to itch, but he tried not to let it show. *We gotta make this thing work.*

The sound of a trunk slamming shut echoed close by, and Bread came up to stand by his side.

"Deal's done, we got it all set," Bread said.

Shawn exhaled, thick lairs of smoke, and replied, "Good, we needed that line solid. Now that we have it, we gotta channel to move through, but still. That shit ain't gonna be enough."

Shawn blew the extra layers of ashes from the ember of his black, and continued, "We gotta make this thing work, Bread; these Viento muthafuckas don't play."

"How you get into it with 'em anyway," Bread asked.

"I took an opportunity and did a job for 'em on the inside. That got me in; they backed the grow house and put us back on. I did what had to be done," Shawn replied.

"Yeah, but now we owe 'em," Bread coughed.

"We got it, though. We're on a ladder of opportunity. The Vientos be on some franchise type shit. They like the bank; they'll front, you do good, it builds your credit with 'em, and the ball keeps rollin'. I got plans, man. I'm tryin' to make it flood out here."

Bread laughed, and his belly jiggled, "Man, look where we at? This little bit a town ain't nothin'. We gotta make it back to the big city; that's where the real money's at. Shit, the food's way better up there."

Shawn's glare flashed menacingly for a moment, Bread didn't even notice.

"Wrong," Shawn snapped, "that ain't where it's at. You gotta deal with more competition, more drama—that shits bad for business. It's sort of like—"

Shawn paused, gazed out past the traffic, narrowing his eyes, lost in thought, then he continued, "Think about it. You wanna sell burgers, and you're a startup; are you gonna sit your stand right next to everybody else that's done been there or are you gonna move to a town that ain't got one yet or if they do, the shop is rundown. Renovate, and replace, my boy, straight like that."

Bread nodded, scratching his chin.

"Oh okay, I think I get it. We like the clean-up crew."

"Exactly," Shawn grinned, "but there's more to it than that. You know me, I'm methodical; I'm on some art of war type shit, like Genghis Khan. He didn't start out attacking kingdoms, he started with villages because they're easy, they ripe for the pickin'. That's how you stockpile your resources, that's how you gain that influence."

"Then we attack the big city," Bread cut in.

Shawn smiled, and nodded, "You got it; that's how real empires are made. You build slow, make it a siege, get the towns around the capital, then you say hi to big man. See what I'm sayin'?"

"Yuh," Bread replied, "don't forget about the snake bitin' the tail, though. You might be movin', but somethin's always headed for your ass. How you know these Vientos are straight?"

"Because they are," Shawn uttered, "they move like the wind; that's what Viento means in Spanish, wind. They never break their code. That shit is law. As long as we move quiet, and silent, don't make any waves, we'll be straight with 'em."

Shawn paused, assessing and measuring his words to get his point across.

"They don't like spectacles, it's bad for business, and brings heat. You can't fuck with the man's army unless you got one to match it. That's what El Jefe Sin Nombre's all about; he tryin' to build a new world."

"El Jefe Sin Nombre," Bread interjected, "that sounds like some cartel shit. What they doin' in Ohio? This ain't Florida."

"They're everywhere; that's why they call their lieutenants, La Sombra, that means shadow. The entire organization follows the code; nobody has a name. That's what Sin Nombre means; man with no name."

"But they Cartel, though. I done heard how them muthafuckas act. They be usin' that hot sauce and gasoline."

128

Shawn laughed, "It ain't like that—it's straight. We just gotta stay off the front lines, sit back, and get this money. It'll all take care of itself. We gonna be fed."

Bread checked his watch, and replied, "You right about that. I stay hungry out here."

Shawn laughed and elbowed Bread in the side.

"You got that take it all mentality. That's why I fuck with you Bread and we've always been tight like that. You loyal."

"That's just how I be," Bread replied, then paused, and took a drag. All went silent, save the river, then he asked Shawn, "Say, man, who was that kid you was talkin' to earlier?"

"Who? The white kid in the Joker hat," Shawn asked.

"Yeah," Butter replied, "seem like ya'll go back. That kid young, though, how you know him?"

"He's just a kid I used to look after; y'know, make sure nobody fuck with 'em," Shawn replied, smiling at first, then his cheeks fell as he remembered the day he met the kid with the purple billed hat.

Bread asked, "Oh, yeah? I didn't know you were Batman for little kids and shit back in the day."

Bread studied the blunt in his hand, nodding, then said, "Very honorable."

Shawn tssked through his teeth, and said, "Man, you trippin' it ain't even like that. The kid was getting' beat up one day, and I helped 'em out. That's it."

Shawn laughed to himself, and shook his head, "He did used to hold the baggies, though. I couldn't go around the house. His mama was crazy, but when I'd catch 'em poppin' in and out doin' trades. I could tell he had himself a little groove. He was always movin', always had to have a new game; somethin' to sell. That's why I caught up to him one day, and made 'em a proposition."

Bread puffed his blunt and said, "For real? Ya'll were like black man and Andy or somethin'?"

Shawn's face wrinkled in agitation, and he waved his hand in the air.

"Man, you startin' to sound like Butta now. Cut it out with that shit," Shawn snapped, paused, then continued, "Nah. The kid was cool, though. He was loyal. I started 'em off with holdin' bags, while I sell, then he moved. Up to some farm or somethin', I was still hookin' 'em up, though. He was doin' alright, but then his mama found his stash, and the kid disappeared off the map. He didn't say a word, though. I knew, because if he did—man—his mama woulda done had the swat team on my ass."

"Damn," Bread replied, "he your little sidekick then. You thinkin' about cuttin' 'em in?"

Shawn shrugged his shoulders and shook his head.

"Shit, I might. Ain't like I need, too. We rounding' up plenty of soldiers, but I'll probably give 'em a little weight, see how he do."

Shawn winced and looked around as he studied the scene; rolling the tip of his cigar around in between his teeth. Butter was never on time.

"Where this fool at, anyway? Shit, he was supposed to be here like half an hour ago."

Bread blew out some cold air, and shivered, then replied, "He probably with a girl or somethin'. Y'know, how it goes."

Bread continued, chuckling, "Mama call him a baby makin' muthafucka. She said if he have one more kid, she's gonna fix him herself."

"True that. Ya'll's mama is crazy as fuck," Shawn laughed, "Remember when she chased Butta down the street with a frying pan? Man, I thought he was done for sure."

Bread smiled, remembering, "Yeah, that fool had to hide in a trash can to get away. I was walking down the alley lookin' for him, and he popped the lid up on me like—"

Bread imitated his brother in the moment. His eyes bulged, and his neck went to actin' shifty. He busted a gut, and continued, "He said, 'Is momma gone yet?' Oh man, that shit was funny. He got his ass tore up when we got back home."

Shawn grinned, nodded, then exhaled, "The good old days. I miss mama Evette. I gotta stop by and see her sometime."

Bread nodded in agreement, "You should."

Then, suddenly, a phone rang. It was Shawn's. His ringtone mimicked the sound an old-fashioned rotary phone would make. It reminded him of the good old days; the time when he was a kid. Shawn flipped open his burner and answered, "Yo, what's with it, my boy? We was just talkin' about you."

Butter snapped on the other end, "Ey, bruh, peep the shit I just heard. You remember that party ya'll were at earlier?"

Shawn nodded, "Yeah, yeah. What's up?"

Butter replied, "Well, some foul shit went down after ya'll dipped. Word is, this fool Rondo bum rushed the joint, and was askin' bout you. Said, he lookin' for you, actin' all wild and shit shootin' shots in the air like he Billy the Kid up in this muthafucka. He—"

"Say, what? You say his name's Rondo," Shawn snapped on the other end.

He jerked his back away from the Chevelle and took a few steps forward; piercing his gaze toward the still waters that lie in the canal.

Butter replied, "Yeah, that's what he call himself. Mista Rendezvous, or whatever. You know 'em?"

Shawn's gaze pierced deeper into the muddy water; the moon reflected and glittered overhead. He licked the corner of his lip and answered, "Yeah, I know who he is."

Butter snapped, "Well, he don't know us. I don't care who he think he is. I got that six for his ass. You already know my fingers are always itchy."

Shawn stare dead into the water still.

"Yeah, yeah, bet. You know we gotta answer that shit. A call's gotta be paid."

Butter replied, "And I'm the payphone, my bruddha. We gonna ride or what?"

Shawn tilted his gaze from the canal upwards towards the rushing, dark waters of the river. He blew smoke out of his nostrils and stare out intently.

"Not yet. We gotta hit the streets and gain some intel first. I wanna hit 'em where it really hurts."

Butter rambled back, "Oh, yeah? A bullet don't hurt? Man, fuck all that shit. We need to snatch dude up right now. Why we gotta do all this plannin' and shit?"

The waters rushed ahead, and a train rumbled; screeching in the distance and blowing its horn. *Because you idiot,* Shawn thought to himself, *it's all about the chase. It's all about the game.*

Shawn replied sharply, "Because we ain't gonna act like some wild cowboys out here, we're better than that. "

Shawn paused; twirling a black and mild around in his fingers; *thinking methodically.*

"Nah, we gonna light the brush first, then watch it all burn. I wanna take it all, and he's got just what I want."

Butter tssked through his teeth and replied, "Man, why's he after you, anyway? How you know him? You steal his candy or somethin'?"

"I knew his brother inside. Don't worry bout it. It's just bad blood."

Shawn licked his lips, and looked sideways towards the moon. Then he continued, "Like I said, we're gonna hit 'em where it hurts. I want his entire organization mapped out. We gonna find out who's runnin' with 'em. We gonna learn where they rest at. I want to know where they eat, who they fuckin', I wanna know it all, and most importantly, I wanna know where he's droppin' the loot."

Butter replied, "Damn, he got it like that?"

"Yeah, he does. He took over his brother's organization while he was on the inside. I—knew him."

"Oh yeah," Butter replied, "he's ruthless enough to take food out of his own brother's mouth like that?"

"Nah, he had, too."

"Why?"

Shawn hissed into the phone, "Because I killed him."

CHAPTER X:

MIND PLAYIN TRICKS

Derek was still distant when I dropped him off back at Ellie's. He didn't say much of anything. I offered him a pair of my shoes because I have a few, but he said he was good. I don't care I'll probably give him some, anyway. It's the least that I can do, plus ever since we became best friends, I told him what's mine is his, anyway. I don't mind sharin' that's how it's supposed to be.

He didn't say much to Ellie either. She asked me if I was alright before she got out. Honestly, I was and I think she was, too. It wasn't because I'm used to having somebody waving a gun around, but that's just how things go sometimes. Zanesville, to me, is the town of mystery, you never know what to expect next. "Stay on your toes," I suppose, is how it goes; especially around here.

I knew I had to call Shawn, though. There was a man named Rondo wearing black and blue, *a fiend in the queue,* searching for him with his crew. It was weird dialing him up since we hadn't really talked in so long, but I had to tell him what was going on. The line rang and rang, but there wasn't an answer at all.

I gritted my teeth and banged the steering wheel. *Fuck.* A text message would have to do.

Give me a call as soon as you get a chance.

That's all I sent. I couldn't say no more. You gotta be careful when it comes to phones, especially when it comes to stuff like that.

I was still worried about Derek. He's cool and lighthearted most of the time, probably because we're always high, but when it comes to him feeling like somebody got one over on him, he would turn into someone else. I've never seen him retaliate against anybody, not even throwing hands, but I don't know how to explain it, he was just different. I was stuck with that feeling, of a complete shift, the whole way home. All I could do was hope; sometimes that's the best you can do.

Honestly, though, I was too tired to worry about anything or anybody at this point. Even though I was still pretty buzzed, I managed to drive straight as an arrow towards home or at least it seemed that way.

Before I pulled into the driveway, I cut my lights off and everything turned pitch black at the snap of a finger. I didn't want to risk waking mom up. We didn't live out of town completely, just enough to where we didn't have any neighbors or street lights blaring down around at every corner. You could actually see the stars out there. I've always been a stargazer, to tell you the truth.

When I look at the stars, I feel so amazed by the vastness of it all. All those lights just stretch out so far and they really have no limit at all. They're unboxed, free to shine, and from the looks of it, they never run out of time. They're never alone in the shadows. I guess that's why they call the folks in Hollywood stars, because they're just like that. Everyone looks up to them and they want to shine, too. If everyone else doesn't, I know I at least do.

I've had to play different characters for a while now. It's like being the sweet guy doesn't get you anywhere at all anymore. Nobody respects that. You gotta be tough and be down to do what you gotta do. When I was little, kids would always try to beat me up because they knew they could get away with it. They'd pour drinks out on my lunch, trip me in the hallway, and they'd even try to take my shoes. I was better off being the clown. I was always a target when I kept my head down and tried to be—*the nice guy.* My first fight told me a lot about myself.

It all started with a typical day in class. The teacher asked us all what we wanted to be when we grew up and we had to give our answer in front of everyone. I hate being front and center.

Some kids said a firefighter, another said a doctor, one even said a fisher, but nobody said a cop. Truth is, I don't think any of us knew what we truly wanted to do. It's all so up in the air and in a small town like mine, you just don't care. Ain't no time for dreamin'. You live and die here. That's it.

That's the attitude most folks have, but not me. I don't know what I want to do, but honestly, I sort of get stuck on a feeling like I always do. Something true. Feelin' good. Laughing. *Oh, laughing would be good.*

When it was my turn to get in front of class, all I could come up with was, "I just want to make other people happy."

The teacher sat at her desk poised up, and responded, "Well—that's not really a profession, young man. What do you want to do? Why do you want to make other people happy?"

I stood there frozen. *It's not a profession, it's not something to do, but it's a needle in the dark stuck between the two. Something out there somewhere, yes it's—*

The entire class stared at me. The wind blew sharply through the windows. I pulled my sweat jacket closer together at the collar to bite the chill. *I always feel cold. Ever since daddy. Ever since he left me.*

I knew I had to say something. I stuttered, "I d-don't know what I w-wanna do, but I guess—I guess I just want to make other people h-happy 'cause I know w-what it's like to be very s-sad."

I nodded my head and I could feel the tears coming, but I couldn't let them through. *Stop that. You're just trying to get people to feel sorry for you.* I swallowed, still nodding away. Then, I smiled as big as I could because at the moment that's all I could do. *Beat those tears down, boy, nobody can tell the truth. You're broken inside, another lost youth. There ain't no point in being true because nobody out there will appreciate you.*

The bell rang as I stood there frozen in a grin. *Seven years old, not nearly ten; there's something inside of him, throw it to the wind.*

Later on that day in the hallway, a kid tried to make a joke out of me and all the other kids were laughing. I just stood there in the hallway with my shoulders heaving away at the rhythm of each deep breath. *Tick tock, tick tock at the click of the clock; maybe soon, death will knock.* All I could do was stare at the ground and wish for a better place. *A happy home, a safe space.*

I was afraid and humiliated. Smiling wouldn't save me, and there was no hiding. I thought to myself, *But why? Why me? Why does everyone treat me this way? I'm always nice to everyone, but none of them are good to me. I get beat up here and there's no peace at home. I'm scared; I'm just so tired of being afraid all the time.*

I stood in the hallway just like that until this kid pushed me up against the wall. He screamed, "Come on! Make us happy, make us laugh!"

The kid made a boo hoo noise and laughed in my face. *They're laughing,* I thought, *they're all going to laugh at you.*

I jerked my head up, and everything froze. It got silent for a moment, but I could feel it. I saw—*him*. Waltzing his way up the hallway in a dusty black coat and a large, purple brimmed hat. He wears dark leather finger gloves to cover up his battered hands, too. Flipping the coin away with the watch. The old crow was there; the man in the hat. *Always wearing a grin, always making a joke of things.* He terrifies me sometimes, but—it's hard to explain. He feels familiar, almost as if he's the only one that can truly understand me. *A friend. Yes, a friend; I like friends. A big brother coming to back everything up.*

The man in the hat whispered in my ear, *Just let go, brew in the fear.*

He flipped the coin, and I caught it. At that moment, I lost myself. I tackled the boy and put him on the ground. I didn't punch him, though. No, I couldn't. *My fists won't hit hard enough.* I wanted to hurt him because he hurt me; *cut me very deeply in fact.* That's why I moved quick, I had to get him—*he deserved it.*

I wrestled my way up from the ground as he still struggled, then I kicked him across the jaw. I'll admit, it felt good. *Finally, I'm not misunderstood,* but then I felt guilty. I shuddered, thinking to myself, *but I didn't want to hurt you. I really didn't, but I—*

Then the man in the hat said, *But he hurt you. Oh yes, he would've done bad things to you if you would have let him. Off with the baddies, ain't that what we always say?*

I let go, and I kicked the boy more; gritting my teeth with tears burning in the corner of my eyes. *Why did you have to do it? Why? I didn't want to, but I'm glad that I did, glad that I am. Am I the victim? No, you're mine.*

I was raving mad, unraveling away. The tears stung my cheeks. I felt possessed and I could feel the man in the hat there still; creeping close by in the shadows, encouraging me evermore with his words, *It feels good, doesn't it?*

Nobody's laughing now. Look at them all; they're afraid. Better to be a terror of your own, than to be a victim to another's. You feel safe now, don't you? It's good to feel safe.

The terrible voice in my head made me feel like the bad guy and all I've ever wanted to be was a hero. Just like in all the stories I used to read. I never wanted to be a villain, but the world has a way of making you into one. Whenever I do something bad, I just remind myself that one day it won't have to be that way, but until that day comes, I'll be who I have to be.

All of those thoughts went with the stars. *Bad and ill, but sometimes that's all you got.*

I was done with my star-gazing, though. I was out of weed, and I was more than ready to be knocked out in my bed. The last thing I wanted to do was wake my mom up. I knew she'd be ready for some school talk as soon as I poked my head through the door. Luckily, she was probably asleep, but I wouldn't have minded if Jim was up. His car was in the driveway, after all, and he was always a pretty cool guy to talk to. When he came on the scene, I wasn't too sure about him at first. After a while, though, I guess he kind of won me over, especially when he taught me how to drive.

On the days he'd come over, I couldn't help but smile when he'd pulled in. I'd catch him before he could even go inside. I'd run up to him and say, "Hey man, what's up? You wanna go ridin' today?"

He'd always be down for it and he'd even let me have one of his swisher cigars, too. We'd cruise around town, practically puffin' away. I knew I was doing alright when I heard him say, "Your getting' pretty good at this, son, I'm proud of you."

He tapped me on the shoulder and smiled right after. For a moment, I felt a lot of warmth and acceptance from it, but suddenly it made me want to cry. I didn't just sayin'. *Stop that. You're just trying to get people to feel sorry for you.*

I swallowed my tears away and smiled back at him. I said, "Thanks, man. I've really been trying to get the hang of it."

Then I snapped my fingers and said, "Smooth operator, right?"

"Smooth operator," Jim replied with a grin.

I'd never let anybody know because it would be acting too sweet, but I love having him around. Not just because of how cool he is, but it feels like I have a dad again in a way and it's helping me heal.

Jim brought faith back to my heart when it comes to people. Most of the folks from the outside world, outside of my family, have been cruel to me, some very cruel, *heartless even.* Truth is, there aren't really any good people out there; not all the way, anyway. We're all a little of both. Good and bad or for some, it's just bad meets evil. I don't know. All I know is, he's one of the few people I've met that seems like they don't have any bad in them at all.

I knew I had to be as alert as an eel when I went to unlock the front door. I pressed my arm up against the door and slowly turned the handle for it to open. The house was pitch black and nobody was up—thank god. I slithered like a burglar down the dark hallway towards my room. The worst part about it was that mom's room was right across from mine, but she damn near snores like Popeye and that was echoing all over the place, so I knew I was in the clear and how amazing it felt once I approached my bed. I threw off my Joker hat, took a deep breath and exhaled, "Finally, time for some rest."

I closed my eyes, spread out my arms, and leaped onto the mattress—or at least attempted to. Instead of the softness from a pillow top, my forehead knocked and bounced off a mountain it felt like. I saw a white flash through my eyelids and felt a rush of blood run down my face right away. I screamed and moaned, "What the fuck was that?!"

I clenched my forehead in my hands and writhed all over the mattress. I was ready to be knocked out, but not in that way. *The damn windowsill,* I thought, but then I knew what had to come next. The one thing I didn't want to do. I had to wake up mom.

I rolled my way off the mattress as I tried to regain my composure after the bang. I stumbled through the dark towards the chair in my room to lift myself back up. There it was—*the dreaded green mile.* Before I made the walk of shame, though, I flipped my light on to assess the damage.

When I let my hand drop it looked kind of cool to be honest. I looked like a bloodstained warrior in my imagination, but in reality, I looked more like a mangy wolf with blood in my teeth. The gash looked horrible. It wasn't that big, but I'm anemic, so when I injure myself, I bleed a hell of a lot. It's definitely going to need stitches, I thought to myself. It was time for the moment of dread whether I liked it or not.

I slowly shuffled my feet across the hall and knocked on my mom's door as gracefully as I could. If I had to wake her, best to be gentle about it.

The snoring stopped immediately. Mom's voice drew out as if she were coming back from the dead. She yelled, "What?! What?!"

I opened the door and edged my head slightly into the room; my forehead clasped in my palm. I told her calmly, "Mom, I—I think I messed myself up pretty bad."

Both her and Jim set up in the bed. Mom asked, "What did you do?"

I opened the door to let the light from the hallway shine in. I definitely didn't want to flip the bedroom light on after all. I've caught Jim walking around naked before and I really didn't want to take a chance on shining a spotlight on that again. Mom gasped when she saw the blood, "How did that happen?!"

I gave her the rundown on it all and Jim told mom that she needed to get me to the hospital because the gash definitely looked like it needed stitches—that's for sure. Mom threw some clothes on really quick, and we loaded up in her old handy dandy PT Cruiser to head towards the hospital. Along the way, mom asked, "Hey, do you think you'd be ok if I stop and get some coffee?"

I thought to myself, *Sure. Don't mind me. My blood hasn't soaked through the rag completely yet.* I just looked over at her and told her it was whatever. It was sort of funny to tell ya the truth. Good thing I didn't get shot earlier. If mom would've had to drive me to the hospital over that, I would've died in Tim Horton's drive thru.

After she got some coffee, she looked over at me and said, "So, let me ask you somethin'."

I rolled my eyes and bounced my head back against the headrest and replied, "What, mom?"

"Have you been drinking tonight? I know you have, so it ain't gonna do you no good to lie. You've been doin' more than that, too."

I clenched the blood-soaked rag tighter on my forehead from the annoyance of it all. I swung my head towards mom and said, "Do we really have to do this right now? I mean, look at me, mom."

Mom slid her hands across the steering wheel as she turned back on to Maple Avenue and said, "Well, I get that, but since you're here, we might as well talk about it."

She cast one of those aggressive looks of hers at me and pointed her finger, "I'm not gonna sit back and watch you ruin your life. I'm just not gonna do it. You walked out-of-school today and I know you're not going to do the online classes that you said you're goin' too. You can't bullshit me as much as you think you can. You're not gonna just run around and get fucked up all the time while you're under my roof. I'll just tell ya that right now!"

I knew it was coming and at all times for it to happen; it had to be while I had blood literally pouring out of my forehead.

I took a deep breath and replied, "But mom, I really am gonna do the online classes. I don't know why you think I'm not going to and if you wanna know the truth, yeah; I was drinkin' tonight, but that was it, I swear. I just wanna have fun, mom. All you guys had your fun. I mean, I want to have funny stories to tell, too, like all you guys."

Mom passed under a green light and said, "Why can't you just go to school? I mean, you only have less than a year left." She shrugged her shoulders and shook her head, "You ain't gonna put the spotlight on me either. That ain't gonna work. Yeah, I might've had fun, but look where I'm workin', in a steel mill. You think that's where I really wanna be? I want to see you do better and from what you're doin' right now, you're just fuckin' it all up. You're smart, just like your dad was. Don't you wanna make something out of that?"

I'd love to be just like him, but I'll never be good enough. I'll never be able to measure up for any of them.

I stare at the glare from the streetlights as it bounced its way across the windshield.

"I just don't fit in there, mom. All of my old friends moved on without me and I feel like I don't really have a place there anymore. It makes me feel like an outsider bein' there. All I want to do is just get this school stuff over with so I can start doin' what I wanna do. Can't you trust me? I'll do the online classes, mom, I promise."

Mom exhaled and shook her head. For a moment she didn't say a thing until she broke the silence, "You better not be bullshittin' me. I'm tellin' ya. You better not drop out."

I clenched the rag tighter to my forehead.

"I won't, mom, I promise."

I had to get over ten stitches in my head at the hospital. It was the first time I've ever had to get sewn up for anything. Although, I did get staples in my knee once before from actin' stupid on a dirt bike. I wasn't being crazy on it or anything, I just couldn't get the damn thing to slow down, so I jumped off. I didn't realize the foot peg split me open until Paul's dad, Ray, pulled back the torn fabric above my knee. Mom sure was mad over that one.

I meant what I told her about doing the online classes, though. After getting some sleep later on in the day. I caught back up to mom before she had to go in on night shift and showed her paperwork for online classes to assure her I wasn't playing games—sort of. I just wasn't going to worry about signing up right away. I could tell I'd cooled her down on the subject when she said, "Well, okay. Just make sure your set up for them on Monday."

I wasn't sure how to ask her, but it had been on my mind for quite some time, so I asked, "Hey, mom. I was wondering if I c-could—if I could have my dad's letters now that he sent you in boot camp so I can read them."

Mom paused as she was getting her papers ready at the kitchen counter. She looked up at me and said, "I'll give them to you someday; I promise. Just give me time to read them again. One last time."

I wanted to plead more for them, so I could be with his words again, but I knew not to. *I'm already a disappointment for a son.* I could at least let her have that with no trouble; let her read them in peace. One last time.

I've always wanted a true love story of my own. I just don't see any hope of getting one. It's easy relating to folks when I'm playing characters, but it's not when I'm the real

144

me. People just don't align and they don't understand. They don't think in the same language that I do. They say there is different dimensions to everything, including thought. I'm not on an above level by any means, just a different one. Still, to find that one. That girl for me, to be true, there's no other world that I'd rather be. It would be to die for, honestly.

Jules. I instantly felt an edge of excitement in the air.

I still couldn't believe I ran back into her—or Shawn, for that matter. I didn't even have a chance to get her number again in my new phone. Rondo fucked that up. So I figured since I was on the computer anyway, I'd look her up on Facebook.

Me and Jules have never been a thing, but I've had a really big crush on her ever since we met. She had the cutest sounding laugh, especially when we would hit the gas mask. She was funny, daring, and didn't care, just like me. We'd went out on a date once, but that turned into a disaster. I try not to think about it too much, honestly. We figured we'd just be friends after the whole fiasco—well really, that's what she wanted, not what I preferred, but I figured if I held out long enough she'd give in.

I typed in her name, and there she was. Her relationship status is what I noticed first. Single, and the green light was on. *My, how lucky I am. Time to give it another go.*

I wasn't sure what to type at first. *Should I charge in like a bull guns ablazin' and ask her out again? Or should I play it smooth, like a high-five guy, and take the slow road?* I figured I'd take the slow road. I didn't want to seem desperate, even though I was. Virginity is awfully shameful. *A dirty little secret.*

I messaged her, *Hey there you make it home ok from the other night? Sent.* I could feel the butterflies rippling away, driving me crazy, as I beamed at the green light under her picture. Suddenly, it disappeared. She must've just gotten off line. Either that or my message made her jump ship. *Don't think yourself to death on it,* I told myself, *she'll reply eventually.*

I tried texting Derek, but no reply; Von, on the other hand, was good to hang, but he didn't have any money. Suddenly, I'm not sure why. I didn't feel like doing much of anything. Crickets hummed outside the window. Silence, along with the peace fell across my shoulders. I closed my eyes and breathed in deeply.

Ahhhh, I kind of miss this feeling.

I sat there for a moment, relaxed and secure, then my eyes opened. The first thing I saw were the stacks of books that were laid against my bedroom wall. They were right next to the large, ancient looking chest my grandmother had given me.

It feels like forever since I picked one of those things up and flipped through the pages.

I'd spent most of my life reading. It was my first escape. My favorite book of them all was the Bible. *Back then anyways; before I discovered the truth behind it all.*

I always used the one my dad had written a prayer for salvation in. The spine of it was still a little chewed up from a puppy I had once. The little rascal had nearly torn it to pieces. I'm not even sure how he got to it because it always sat atop my dresser, but nevertheless, it didn't matter. By some sheer amount of luck or divine will, that book had saved itself. I didn't know where it was for quite a while until I found it under the same dresser stowed away safely. I was so glad I didn't lose that, too. His hands touched that same leather after all. My father that is.

We both would go to Cornerstone church every Sunday, and I loved being there as much as he did. I remember the place had a calming presence, and the sanctuary was huge. I'd be holding my father's hand the whole way walking in. He'd always move fast and take big strides. I remember looking up at him and smiling. I felt so proud just to be there, walking alongside of him. It took everything I had to keep up with him, but he was there and I was, too.

We'd sit up all night sometimes when he'd have me on the weekends, and he'd teach me about the word from his own Bible. He had his favorite verses highlighted throughout many of its pages. He loved the stories in the Old Testament, just like I did, and he said when he read the words he could go there, back to the long distant place of the ancient lands. It was like a big movie in my head, too, and the farthest times always felt close to home, but not quite it. There was something further back from way before that always called to me. From the way he would talk, I think that same place called to him, too. *Home.* It all felt so real in my dreams.

The people, they were beautiful; they shone magnificently. Spiraling towers of brilliance shimmered past the clouds across the island, and a giant bird soared above in the heavens. A *vabzir, the child could mirror the sight in their eyes.* Then there was another place in my dreams and I was there, too.

The bitter cold bit the boy's neck and blew through his cloak. Hawk feathers hung from his sleeve, dancing in the wind; he shivered from the chill. He stare up at the giant ice wall, and shuddered. It made him feel so insignificant. Steps crunched upon the ice behind him, then a hand fell softly upon his shoulder. It was his father.

"Come, Ahnzerah, our journey isn't complete."

The wind whooshed. The little boy turned around, and nodded, "Okay, papa. I'm ready to get out of here anyway; this place is scary."

Then a flash.

The same little boy in the ice was running within a golden grove. Leaves were falling and swirling everywhere. *It was my special place.* His father stood in the pines with him, and his armor shone brightly. The boy hopped into his arms and gasped excitedly, "Papa! You're back!"

He patted his shoulder. "I told you I'd be."

Then came the clash of swords, the fall, and a shout, "Ahnatarkis!"

The ancient philosopher of creeds crashed into the waves beneath the waterfall and was lost. *Zep Tepi; the world is at an end. The king is dead.*

Then, there was the awakening; a rebirth.

"I have to find my son."

"Then you must travel," the lady of the well declared, "there is no saving your kingdom. The time of our world is at an end, the serpents are dancing near. Find your son, and make your escape to the gate which lies in the West upon my sister Mara's oasis. That with whom you seek abideth there; the one true king, the River Master. He is the gatekeeper."

She handed him an amulet of nine stones. *Five on the lamen, four on the chain. Wanderer in the Wilderness, what is thy bane?*

Suddenly, a creak came from the hallway bringing me out of my thoughts and back to my room. There were three knocks on the wall, then I could hear shuffling across the carpet.

"Paul, is that you?" I asked shivering. Not a noise at all. The house was void and absent. I got up slowly, hairs standing up on my neck, and edged my way towards the door. The atmosphere felt like a vacuum wilting away at my energy. I yawned because I was suddenly growing tired, but the fear kept me awake. I stuck my head out past the door frame and peered down the dark, empty hallway. Moonlight ebbed through the blinds of the kitchen window. Everything was still, until another creak came, then a fumbling. Goosebumps ran up my back and down my arms. I slammed my door shut before I could even think, and hopped under my covers as if they were the only shield that could protect me. *I hate the dark, but I'm afraid to turn the light back on.*

Fear was losing it's grip on me, and I was beginning to spiral away. It was like I'd taken a bunch of NyQuil, but I knew I hadn't. *So strange,* I thought as I nodded again. *Falling and peeling away from the world into another dream.*

Wind rushed, and brick chimneys blew smoke into the atmosphere. The moon lit up the night sky; it was full. I could see the clock tower upon the courthouse in the distance. It looked like I was in downtown Zanesville, but it wasn't what it looked like today. It seemed—*older.* Had to be because the cars that were parked along the walk definitely weren't modern. They looked like the kind you'd see in the 1930s.

A soft whistle roared through the blowing wind; it sounded like that of a sparrow, but then it came sharp. A train rumbled, brakes screeched across metal tracks, and the town disappeared. *Everything faded to black.*

My feet lie within a shadowed puddle, and the sharp whistle of the sparrow came again. Fog waded across the shallow waters and I spun around continuously, trying to find the source of the mysterious sound.

Suddenly, I saw a little boy in the distance. He had his back to me, and I couldn't see his face. He had old patched up trousers on, and suspenders that pulled up across a long white shirt. His dark brown arms were visible below his rolled up his sleeves. A flat cap rested upon his head, and the sharp whistle came again. I rushed towards him. The water splashed under my feet as I ran, but with each step, he moved further away. I yelled after him, asking him who he was, but he wouldn't answer. There was only the sharp whistle of the sparrow hissing from his lips.

A flash came, and the boy was in front of me all of a sudden. I could see his face now. He couldn't have been older than ten. There was something familiar about him, especially his eyes. They had a certain glow of innocence to them, but panic brewed in them. His lips moved quickly as a constant whispering chatter flowed from his mouth. Then the sparrow's whistle came again. This time, it nearly split my eardrums.

"They're coming," the boy said.

Then another flash.

"They're coming," he yelled.

Then, I saw him back on the same rooftop I first found myself in. The sound came again. Then the boy screamed, "They're coming, Jack! They're coming!"

Everything went black again, and the boy blew away with the dust of the wind. Strobing light ran along with a tick, and a shadowed figure in a long dark coat appeared walking towards me. He had a fedora on, waltzing close, ever near. Then came the smile and the grin under his purple brim. He was upon me before I knew it, and he snatched me up by the collar. His hand crept towards me as the light strobed still. His fingers stabbed into my chest and I screamed. Cackling enveloped my soul, and I jerked awake in my bed, howling.

Screaming in the dark; the scars make their mark.

CHAPTER XI:

DEVILS PIE

A brick house in Putnam loomed in the shadows, mixed within the rest; the clouds were gray that day. Chipped away arches propped up the sinking roof, and a dog in the distance howled out a woof. The door swung open, and the man stepped in, he was ready to get it, even at nine between ten.

"So ya'll ready, right?" Shawn barked. He was standing there in a crisp, cool red sport jacket. His jeans hung low, and a watch flicked on his wrist. He rubbed his nose and shuffled his shoulders. Somebody in the room, between the four out of five, rocked their head and said, "Yeah, let's get it."

Shawn clapped his hands, rubbing them together, and grinned, "Let's get it then."

He paused, rolled his shoulders, and said, "Okay, then. Now we've all done did this shit before, but this time it's gonna be different. We ain't here to make no noise. We just tryin' to blend in."

The five nodded their heads, hands in their red hoodie pockets. Butter was smacking his lips eating a taco; Bread was eyeing his hands like hungry a savage. Shawn continued, "Now this is how it's gonna go. Lil Reese, you're the doorman."

A young dark kid in a dew rag nodded his head in acceptance. He was quiet, the silent type. Shawn went on.

"The peep hole is your best friend; always keep your eyes on the door, know who's gettin' in. We gonna use passwords, mix it up, make it whatever, but switch it up every week. We can't risk any fools getting' the drop on us. We gotta keep things tight and roll like a company; policy is law. If they can't follow—"

Shawn cut a slice with his hand across his throat.

"Then, they done. We ain't tryin' to catch no bodies, though. We ain't no ghetto superstars. I mean, look at us; we in a half country ass town that's rundown, it ain't like that, but choose your men wisely because if they can't make the cut, it's gotta be out with 'em. Extra mouths that ain't in just breath more wind; best to keep the air in the bubble, if you know what I mean. If you float on the outside folks gotta be popped—that's it."

A voice with a hat chattered in his ear. Shawn got excited, and bit the corner of his lip. His eyes flared.

"We only usin' the back door; the front ain't gonna be in use, customers use the alley, ain't none of it out in the open. Three knocks after the throw, this a shop. This ain't no nickel and dime house; they come to us, ten middlemen to a house each, no more, no less. Bout an ounce or over we can rock with that, and the kids, the youngstas, get to know a few of 'em, they the eyes. Throw 'em a little somethin' and make 'em feel cool. Front 'em, use 'em, do whatever, but make sure they keep those eyes open. If they sleep— canceled. Knock 'em off the roll. There's plenty of missin' around here, anyway."

Butter snapped his neck, and lettuce jiggled out of his mouth. He was eating another taco; Bread's mouth salivated.

Butter rambled, "What you talkin' about killin' kids for? Ain't that gonna draw more attention?"

152

Shawn craned his neck to the side and looked at Butter sideways; his eyes burned menacingly.

"That's why ya'll better be selective; I don't wanna dump no trash. We need to get it on lock and keep everything tight. I know ya'll got this. We that five man red G man crew."

Everybody nodded their heads; Bread was in the kitchen starting the microwave.

Butter yelled, "Ey! What you doin'?! I was savin' that other one for later."

Bread couldn't wait another second. He pulled the taco out of the microwave and shoved it in his mouth. Butter gasped.

"Why you gotta steal my food like that for? Why didn't you just buy one?"

Bread mashed his lips together. They were goin' crunch, crunch, and he said. "I just ate before we got to the drive thru, though."

Butter snapped, "You always eatin', muthafucka, you don't ever stop."

The taco was gone; Bread licked his fingers.

"Yeah, I do."

"Will ya'll shut the fuck up," Shawn snapped.

Bread and Butter both jerked their necks towards him. They weren't afraid; they were about that business. They wanted to hear more. Shawn was like another brother to them. That's the only reason why he could get away with talkin' to them like that.

Shawn's glare burned, and he continued, "The Vientos came through, too. Once they get the first cut, we get that increase, a shipment gonna be comin' in."

Shawn paused for a moment and studied the faces in the room, then he continued, "Now ya'll might not be cool with it, but we gotta roll with the flow. We getting' some of that cheap, cheap, but there's a lot of it; ya'll know what I'm talkin' about, it's that pineapple number 8. It drives muthafuckas wild, and they love it. That's how we really get it in. This shit runs about thirty a k, but we gonna cut it, too. With this type of product, fools be hangin' there head to the side half asleep, but their legs still runnin'. Regular heroin ain't cuttin' it no more. Folks want it both ways. They want that up and down."

Shawn took a breath and studied the room. Everyone was still quiet, but nobody objected, so he continued, "Get ya bitches into that spice, too. They can bake it, muthafuckas love that shit. Buy a little herb, get a bottle of acetone, sprinkle a little AM-22 you know what in it, and spray it on there. Put it in the oven, let the acetone evaporate, and there ya go. Shit, you could spike any kind of herb like that with damn near anything."

Kane chimed in, "Imagine if somebody did that with some acid or some shit; that would fuck somebody up."

Lil Reese jerked, and shook, "Nah, that would be terrible to do to someone. Don't say that."

Kane replied, "But you could do it with any drug, like the RCs and designer drugs in Europe."

"Exactly," Shawn continued, "If the line runs smooth, we get more, we get that upgrade towards that white ice, igloo bricks, but we gotta spread out, divide up, get your own people, make your own crews, they got crews, you know the deal. We on that takeover; the breaks over."

The ruler's back.

Butter laughed, "Shit, the blueprint."

He went on and started spittin' lines to Jay Z's "The Takeover."

Shawn smiled and clapped his hands, "That's right. That's the word right there."

Then he continued, "We smugglin' differently, too. Once the supply builds, we'll be shippin'. Stuffin' couches and old love seats, and off with it. Find a white boy that can dress nice to drive the truck; the cops ain't never gonna pull that fool over. We gonna be big; we finna explode."

Lil Reese felt talkative; more than usual, he asked, "What about the internet, though? You could set up a black market through a Tor browser in the dark web and sell just about anything. You don't even have to see any customers. No traps, no nothin'; just click and boom."

Shawn clapped his hands together in an applause and laughed, "Damn, Lil Reese! You a genius. I didn't know you was good with that computer shit."

"Yeah," Lil Reese nodded, "you can just be the middle man online and search out your supply. Find it, order it, then jack up the price on your own page. You could do that with four wheelers; literally everything. It's how to run an online shop."

I might have to kill this motherfucker, Shawn thought to himself. *He's a threat.* He was about to reply, but Butter interrupted him. He chimed in, "Shit, I love rippin' up old love seats; you gotta know how to cut right. Never across, start at the corner, and under, but don't take all the stuffing out."

Butter got excited and rambled further he was high.

"It's gotta at least still look like a couch. That's why you gotta hide the cut. If the truck did get searched, they ain't really gonna fuck with all that. We got those heavy duty vacuum sealed under the cotton. A dog can smell it, but a pig can't. You—"

Bread interrupted, "Man, we know. You talkin' to much. That Henny gettin' ahold of you already."

Butter laughed, "Shit, that's my juice."

Then he took another sip.

Shawn nodded his head methodically, his shadow fell behind him.

"Yeah," he nodded his head, "we finna take the whole pie."

"What about Rondo, though?" Butter licked his lips after taking another swig. He shook a little on the kitchen counter, wavering a little, then continued, "what we finna do about him?"

Shawn burned a stare at the challenge. He didn't even want to talk about it, it was a part of the code, but he did anyway.

"That's already handled, bruh. El Sombra gave the word. Susurros is coming."

"Who's that," Bread asked.

"You don't wanna know," Shawn replied, "she as dark as night; and she has bright blue eyes. She like a ghost; you can't see her."

Butter humped his hips forward off the counter, "She sound fine."

Shawn didn't take it lightly; he knew and heard the stories about her from Jericho in prison.

"Nah," Shawn shook his head, "don't even think of that. You'll be gone, bruh."

Butter laughed, and the rest of the five man red G man crew stared at him. He was being disrespectful.

"She's a bitch, though. Fuck her. We're men. She ain't any harder. Who the fuck is Susurros anyway?" Butter rambled.

"Whispers, that's what Susurros means," Shawn replied quickly, "that's Sin Nombre's daughter. You don't fuck with her."

"Okay, okay," most of them nodded, save one; all except Butter.

"She's the devil."

"You fuckin' right," Shawn replied, "don't ever fuck with Susurros."

That means Whispers, you don't talk about her, she can't speak herself anymore; after her throat was cut, that is. She survived the attempt on Sin Nombre's life and saved her father. He is the King of the Underworld. He held her after it happened.

"I got ya baby girl; I got ya," he whispered to her, as she was bleeding out in his lap.

"We gonna fix it; we got this."

"Pa pa," Whispers gasped.

Antonio Sin Nombre held his daughter still as he handed her a needle, weaved with some thick thread to sew her neck back up with.

Her bloody hand shook towards it, in confusion.

"Pa pa," she gasped as she spit blood, "h-help me."

He wouldn't sew her neck up for her. He placed the needle in her quivering hand and held it still.

"I am the hand that guides," Sin Nombre said, "and you are the hand that sews."

It was all a matter of strength to him.

"We are a strong people, Whispers," Sin Nombre told her as tears ran down her cheek. There was no emotion in him, not even towards his daughter.

"I am the guide, and you are the sewer."

CHAPTER XII:

STEP INTO A WORLD

"Just another manic Monday," I screamed to myself, as The Bangles blared through the car's speakers. At first I tried to deny the song; I couldn't listen to it, didn't want to hear it, but the tune had a catch to it and it made me feel crazy. After the first chorus; it had me. I was lost to it, hotboxin' it in my ride. Suddenly, I had become disgusted with myself, paranoid even, and stopped singing along at the mashing down of my eyebrows. I turned the nob down and looked around; *is anybody watching me,* I wondered. *The damn detectives won't get a picture of me dancing and singing along to a song.* I rolled my window down and smoke billowed out.

For a moment I had forgotten I was in Wal Mart's parking lot, waiting for Shawn to arrive. He'd texted me back this morning around 2pm, and I was glad, too, because I couldn't find a thing to do.

I hadn't slept in over twenty-four hours; not since the terrible dream. *Not since the night terrors.* Usually if you drink and smoke enough, you don't dream at all, but I had to be sure. I'd copped some Adderall to keep me awake, but could it happen again? Would I still dream? I sure *hope not,* I thought to myself, *I can still feel the shadow's fingers in my chest.*

Suddenly, a figure appeared at my window, and I jumped back. It was Shawn. He laughed, "Ey, you alright? You comin' or what?"

I clenched the filter of my smoke with my teeth, grinning, and nodded my head quickly, as I cut the engine off and swung open the door.

"Where's your ride at," I asked. I didn't see him pull up.

Shawn laughed, "You didn't hear me revvin' up when I was comin' through? I figured that would get your attention for sure."

But it didn't. I was lost in the maze already. I shrugged my shoulders and shook my head, about to speak, but Shawn had cut me off.

"You can't miss it, it's right over there."

Confused, I looked around, still not knowing, still blind, but then I heard the jingle of some keys and seconds later the rumble of an engine. The hair's on the back of my neck stood up. As soon as I turned around, glinting bronze flashed across my irises and I gasped. She was a beauty, a genuine wonder, straight out of time. Shawn smiled behind the wheel of a 1970 Chevy Chevelle. *Marvelous.*

Shawn revved up the engine again and rolled down his window; I'd never seen him so happy.

"Ey, you ready to ride or what?"

I was speechless, and the question made no sense. Of course, I had to ride; the classics were my favorite.

I opened the door with ease and slid across the smooth leather bench seat.

"Damn, man. How long have you had this," I asked, grinning from ear to ear.

Shawn smiled, "You like it?"

My chin fell, gawking all around the ride in amazement.

"Do I like it? I love it!"

Shawn laughed as he pulled the car into gear and backed out of the parking spot.

"I knew you would."

We spun out of the lot, and the tail spun a little.

I howled, "Damn! She's full of fire, man, this ride's gotta lot of soul."

Shawn grinned, "You ain't seen shit yet."

We gunned it through the yellow light, past Captain D's, and hopped on Bell Street, Shawn cranked the nob on the radio and winked. Lloyd Banks "Beamer, Benz, or Bentley" blasted in my eardrums.

"Oh shit," I shouted and held on for dear life. It was a dream come true; I'd always wanted to take a ride in a classic car. I hadn't since my dad's Ford Torino.

The system pounded, and the engine purred as we flipped a right onto West Taylor, past the church. The engine rumbled as we flew past, startling an old man clicking his cane across the sidewalk. I hung out of the window with a mean mug, and yelled, "Boooo!"

Not sure why, it was stupid. Shawn grabbed the back of my sweater and pulled me back in the window.

He snapped, "Ey, man, don't be actin' all retarded and shit hangin' out the window like that. That ain't cool."

I nodded my head and sunk into my seat; clasping my hands together in my lap, determined to behave.

"Sorry. I guess I'm just excited that's all. This car is awesome, man."

Shawn laughed, "It's all good, man. I'm glad you like it."

He pressed the peddle down further. *We were gettin' it.* Suddenly, Shawn eased on the brakes, and turned down the radio.

"Fuck, there they go, the pigs."

A cop sat down the road on the left, parked at Maple Hill Park. We scoped him first. I took a deep breath and shook my head. I brushed my fingers across the bill of my hat and grinded my teeth.

"I hate the coppas; they always gotta swing around and ruin a good time."

Shawn laughed, "Ey, what's up with the New York accent? You practice doin' voices now or somethin'?"

My eyes shuffled left to right, and I grinned to myself; taking another sip of rose out of the cup I'd brought with me.

"Uhhh, I mean, yeah, I guess. I like doin' voices. It's like I get to be another character for a minute."

Shawn nodded, smiled, and replied, "That ain't too bad. Maybe you could be an actor or somethin' someday. They say a lot of 'em end up goin' crazy, though. They just get good at hiding it."

I shrugged my shoulders.

"Who knows, man?"

I didn't care. I wanted to know more about the ride.

I continued, lost in another thought, "This car is pretty nice, though. When did you get it?"

"A few years back. Some guy had it for sale for a while and old dude about junked it, but I wasn't havin' that. I bought it, clean, title and all."

Shawn tapped and rubbed the dash with his fingers, a little dust swirled across the windshield.

"It still needs a little work, especially on the outside, but at least it runs now. That shit was like a dream come true when I finally got it to fire."

"I bet it was," I said, "you ever think about takin' it on a road trip or somethin' once you get it all done? That would be amazing."

Shawn smiled and his eyes flicked towards the right as we passed Center Drive; no cars were coming. We drove onward keeping the course straight and took the bend on to Adams Lane.

"Damn, right. That would be, though."

Shawn chuckled and scratched his cheek.

"You still tryin' to make it out to California someday? What was that place you used to talk about goin? Twenty-five, thirty-nine—"

I interrupted,"29 Palms. It's in California."

Shawn nodded, "Yeah that's the place. Man, I bet Cali's got some fine ass bitches. Nothin' but blonde heads, lookin' all pretty upped, layin' out on the sand."

Shawn paused; smiled at the thought and then jeered excitedly, "Or what about Vegas?! Damn. Think about rollin' up in there and winnin' it all; the whole show. Just walk out of there in a tailored suit, briefcase in the knuckles. Just like that, livin' like a million bucks."

"It sure would be nice," I exhaled deeply, thinking; lost in the thought.

"I ain't to much of a gambler, though. I mean if I went to Vegas, I'd probably end up like that dude Doug on the roof from that one movie, "The Hangover" or somethin'."

Shawn laughed, "Shit, dealin' with Vegas you gotta be on a mission, my boy, keep it straight, it ain't all about catchin' a buzz. Better to be a stacker than a spender."

Wind blew through the trees and the bare branches rattled from above. The Chevelle's engine rumbled and startled the crows beyond the corner. I shimmied around with the bill of my hat and shifted it lower, then asked, "You ever think we'll get it like that, though? You know like really make it and be able to do stuff like that?"

Shawn shrugged his shoulders and played with the wheel.

"I don't know, man. In this type of world, you gotta go with the risk. You ain't gonna get anywhere workin' and breakin' your back at some lame ass job makin' pennies on the dollar. When you got what you want figured out, you gotta gun it and go for it. That's the way it's always been, like Jesse James and all them, way back when."

I grinned, "You're sure right about that. I always hated the thought of it. You know just getting' stuck like that. No hopes, no dreams, just hittin' the clock blowin around like some kind of tumbleweed. That shit is scary to me. I'd rather die today than live the rest of my life like that."

"Same. These muthafuckas out here that fall into the image, the trap, it's sad, man. I mean, it seems like everybody all around, especially here, they all give up on the dream before they even get started on it. They say in their head 'I'll save, I'll save' but fuck all that savin' and rollin' up pennies shit. I ain't tryin' to see it all after my eyes grow tired, and it's all a blur. I want it now. That's why I ain't gotta choice, I gotta get it. That nine to five don't get you anywhere."

Shawn shook his head, I could tell he was getting irritated just thinking about it.

"I know what you mean. I just don't know how, y'know? To get it, to get there, y'know what I mean? I wish I could snap my fingers and just be where I've always wanted to be."

I drew in the cool air deeply and stare out of the window.

Dark clouds were rolling in, the shadows were spreading; I exhaled. Thinking about it all, looking past the stars. *If I could just get there, somewhere. Happy sure would be a nice start; an actual smile.*

"It don't work like that, though," Shawn muttered, "you gotta make a plan and roll with it. Sometimes it don't pan out, but you gotta at least keep on tryin'. When we was kids you used to always talk about it, destiny. You gotta pick yours, believe in it, and just go for it, where you're meant to be, it'll come. In the meantime, you just gotta enjoy the process."

"What process," I asked.

Shawn bit his lip and grinned.

"What you mean? They built the system for slaves, you can't get anywhere like that; pushin' a broom and all that shit. You gotta make your own way; carve your own path through the jungle, know what I mean?"

"How do you do it?"

Shawn laughed and his eyes danced across the dash, the sun was falling.

"You already know how I do. It ain't easy, but it's faster and it's fun. Folks respect you more too because you got the balls to do what they're afraid to do."

I bit my lip, and grinned, "Hmmm, what's that?"

I was acting goofy to be honest.

Shawn flicked a narrowed glance my way and shoved his eyebrows down, before returning his gaze towards the road.

"What I gotta do? Spell it out for you? You just gotta be a taker. You see somethin' you want, you gotta get it because if you don't somebody else will. Just gotta be smart about it that's all; know how to cover your tracks. You catchin' my drift now?"

I took another sip of rose and shivered. *I was back in it.*

"Yeah, I guess so. I mean, I feel like that's what I've been doin', though, and it really ain't been workin' out."

Shawn laughed, "That's because you're not leadin'. To worried about followin', worried about everybody else."

Shawn paused and cut his eyes at the yellow lines running towards us and cleaned the corners of his mouth.

"Now don't get me wrong, havin' a little crew that shit is cool and all, but somebody has to keep their eye on the ball. You gotta be that guy. Its human nature. Assert yourself, be strong, show no weakness, and all the pawns fall across the board on their own."

164

"I know what you mean. I don't know, though, all I really do is sell CD's and fake ass moonshine nowadays; that's it. I ain't got no connect for anything else really, so I don't worry about it too much."

Shawn shook his head and grinned.

"Still not listenin'? You're wrong about not havin' a connect, too."

"Really, how's that?"

Shawn smiled, "You got me."

I wasn't sure. It all made me a tad nervous. The man in the hat was grinning in the side mirror, but I couldn't feel the same on my face.

"So what are ya sayin'? You tryin' to front me somethin'? I ain't got no bread or nothin' like that."

Shawn nodded, "I got you. I'll start you off with a little and see how you do. If you do good, there's more."

I grinned to myself. My mind ran wild with fantasy. New suit, fast cars, a big mansion house, me sittin' at a desk like Tony Montana; powders all over my face. My heart gets torn apart by a lady named Virginia, and she's just broken off our engagement. I'm running down a marble staircase chasing after her. She swings open the door, I fall to my knees in the rain and yell, "No, Virginia, No!"

Thunder cracks, and there's the sound of a cork squeaking out of a bottle. Then a chug, and a needle to the toe. My friends find me the next day passed out on the mahogany carpet. Puke is on my vest, and a little intervention ensues; I agree to go to rehab.

It is there where I fall in love with a lady doctor; she seduces me, and we have twenty two children together, and we all get old. I have grown weary and tired. The nights sitting up in my library in a turtleneck puffing away on my cob pipe have paid off. I have discovered the secret to existence and I have become the wisest man in the world. I stand upon a mountain, and gaze at the setting sun. I smile and say to myself, "It was worth it, it was all worth it. It is—"

Suddenly, Shawn shook me back, too. He nearly startled me to death.

"You listening, man? What you thinkin'?"

I cleared my throat.

"My bad, man. I was just thinkin' that's all, but I can't do that, man. I mean, you was just talkin' about pawns and all."

Shawn's eyes grew big, and he smiled again, nodding at the words.

"Y'see, that's how I know you'll do good. I could always see you goin' somewhere, but yeah. A pawn, but don't think of it that way. We all start as pawns somewhere. Just gotta keep your eyes on the king."

"Like Rondo, you mean," I slipped.

Shawn's mug fell clean. There wasn't an expression on it. The air grew tense.

"Fuck that fool. He ain't shit."

Shawn shook his head and glanced out the window as we sat at the red light; ready to turn on 146.

"Nah," Shawn muttered, "he ain't no king; more like a rook, and I—I am the bishop. I always got my eyes on the king."

Shawn licked his lips and laughed, "But Rondo, he's gonna get his, best believe that."

Shawn nodded and cut his eyes.

"Best believe. He's gonna be answered; yeah."

Shawn sucked his teeth and made a clicking noise, then glanced over at me. I kept my eyes fixed on my left hand again. *It's getting grey.*

"So you down or what?"

My head jerked up, startled.

"With you frontin' me, you mean?"

Shawn nodded.

I shrugged my shoulders, and replied, "I mean, yeah, I guess so. Can I at least try it first?"

Shawn's mug grew stern.

"Never get high on your own supply, man. That's one of the number one rules."

I was a goner, then.

"But I smoke, though. I mean, if it weren't for beer, smokes, and weed I'd probably just evaporate into thin air. I can't survive without it."

Shawn snapped, "Man, if you're just gonna smoke it all. I ain't gonna front you none then."

I frowned, and my lower lip fell out; puddles glittered in my eyes. *No, it's free weed. I can't let it slip through my fingers. I wanna smoke it, but I'll sell some, too.* I grinned to myself, *Yes. I'm gonna be a drug dealer, but I'll be a nice guy about, and give people deals like wally world.* People will give me high fives everywhere I go, and I'll give 'em the finger snap, and scream, 'Oh yeah, you got it, buddy. Then, toss 'em a bag.' They'll catch it and I'll give 'em a wink, and a point—Alright!

"Get out of your thoughts," a voice snapped.

I fumbled to reply, "No, man. It's cool, I'm not gonna smoke it all. Pinky swear, cross my heart, and hope to die."

Shawn laughed under his breath.

"Man, you're a fool; stop playin'. I ain't to worried about it, really. All I'm givin' you is an ounce, but don't fuck up. "

"I won't, I promise," I eagerly replied with a grin.

Shawn continued, "Because if you do, if you smoke it or sell it, whatever, I'm still gonna need my money."

"I got you, man. Don't worry about it."

Shawn's eyes flicked hot for a minute as he glared at the road, then he muttered.

"You better, because if you don't. I'll kill ya."

167

I laughed, "Come on, man? Over a hundred somethin' dollars?"

Shawn patted the wheel and laughed, "You gonna get it, though. Test it, do whatever, but really try to move it. The faster you sell, the more you'll get."

I nodded my head coolly, while taking another sip.

"Yeah, lets do the damn thing."

We dapped up just as the red light turned green. Shawn gunned the Chevelle threw the light and flicked the dial up. Kanye West's "Mercy" blared across the speakers.

I looked in the rearview mirror at myself as the wind blew past my cheeks. Only it wasn't me there, it was him, the man in the hat. Eyes shaded by shadow, clicking his tongue behind a cracking grin. I shuddered. He was there, but then wasn't. Gone, but I was going somewhere. I just didn't know where.

CHAPTER XIII:

KNUCKLEHEADS

Shawn ditched me at Dillon State Park for a few while he made a run to get the weed. I tried to go with him, but I guess, he didn't trust me enough to know where his stash was. *That figures.* I was glad when he delivered. The swing set was getting boring. He was all about business when he stepped out of his ride..

"Y'see, normally, I don't do this type of thing. Takin' a chance like this sometimes it costs a lot, but with you, I got a good feeling about this because nobody knows you. They think they do, but they don't, they ain't got a clue. You're the ghost, man. They don't see you."

I stood by the trunk of my car and took a hit off my cigar. I could see where he was coming from; Shawn was right. *Play it cool, be smooth, nobody can see you.*

"Shit, I'm gonna be honest with you, man," I muttered, "I ain't sure if I even have the clientele for this. I mean, I don't even know people like that around here anymore."

Shawn hung his head to the left and lifted an eyebrow up.

"What you mean you don't know people like that? You ain't got no friends?"

I exhaled deeply, then said, "I mean, yeah, I do, but it's just a couple of people, really. Not enough to make a lot of cash off of."

Shawn crossed his arms and grinned, his eyes began to sparkle methodically.

"And these friends of yours, don't they know people? I scoped you before you even saw me at the party. You know people, they know people, that's your crew."

"So they sell it? That's what you're sayin'?"

Shawn winked and clapped his hands.

"Exactly. See you're getting' it now."

I took another hit off my cigar and let the smoke roll around in my mouth. *Be the ghost; seen, but unseen.*

I nodded my head and said, "Okay, I got you."

We dapped up hands over the trunk and I shut the lid, concealing the red duffel bag.

"It's only an ounce, but I got faith in you. Move this and I'll have more for you."

Shawn tapped his fingers on the trunk, *click, click, click.*

My keys jingled in my pocket as I pulled them out.

"Okay, I'm bein' honest now, I ain't makin' any promises. I'm not sure if I can move it for you, but I'll try."

Shawn put his hand on my shoulder and said, "Have faith. If you can't find nothin' to believe in, at least believe in yourself."

I shifted the bill on my hat, pulling it lower, and more to the side; *twisted upon the brim.*

"Okay," I muttered, "I got you."

We each pulled out after that. He went his way; I went mine. It was time to check the time. *Eight thirty-ish.* The sun had already left.

I picked my phone up and hit speed dial for Derek. The phone rang a few times, then he picked up.

"Wassup, what's with it, bubbies?"

"Not shit, really, man. You home right now?"

Derek huffed into the phone, "Yeah, bored as a muthafucka, too. What you about to get into?"

I grinned, there was a yellow light ahead, but I sped up and kept going, had to keep the wheels rollin'.

I happily hummed a little to clear my throat.

"Nothin'. I got a surprise for you, though, somethin' to show you."

Derek barked into the phone excitedly, "Really what is it?"

I tapped my fingers across the steering wheel, grinning still, clicking my tongue behind my teeth; letting the suspense build, then I said, "You'll see soon enough. I'm bout to pull up."

"Okay see ya in a few, then."

"Ight, bet."

Click.

When I pulled into the alley behind Derek's house the rocky pavement crumpled under my tires and I put the car in park. Derek was already outside smoking a cigar and tapping away at the keyboard on his phone. I honked my horn to get his attention. He jerked his head up and hopped off the porch, and ran toward the car. I guess he found an extra pair of shoes.

"Hey, man, you can't be out here honkin' like that. You're gonna wake my stepdad up."

My eyes flicked from left to right under the shadow of the bill of my hat, and I grinned.

"S-sorry. My mistake."

Derek nodded his head and fixed his fitted cap.

"It's all good. So what you got to show me?"

I jingled the keys in my hand.

"Let me pop the trunk for ya, real quick."

I didn't care to waste another second. I threw the lid open and revealed the red duffel bag.

"Well, what's in it?"

Derek's confusion grew, he didn't have a clue. I bit my lip and grinned again. My cheeks hurt I was doing it so much. I unzipped the bag and if he couldn't smell it before, we both sure could then.

Derek gasped, "Damn! How'd you get all that?"

Then he got giddy and clapped his hands. He rubbed them together and nodded excitedly.

"It's about to be a fun night."

I put two fingers up and waved them as I shook my head.

"Nah, no, we can't smoke it all, that's not what it's for."

Derek barked, "What you mean, man? We just gonna look at it or what?"

I shook my head again.

"Uh uh, nope. We're gonna sell it."

Derek's smile fell, and he put his hand on his chin.

"For real? You wanna sell it?"

I got flustered.

"Well, yeah, I mean, we can do it. Why not? We go to plenty of parties, we know people that smoke."

Derek stood there for a moment. Paused and poised, thinking; measuring it all out while he gazed inside the trunk. He didn't act the way I thought he would, and I wasn't sure; *no not sure at all anymore*, but then he smiled and muttered, "You tried it out, yet?"

"Nah, not yet," I replied.

Derek clapped his hands together and grinned, "We gotta at least try it out. I mean, how we gonna sell it if we don't even know if it's good or not?"

"I don't know, man," I replied, "if we do, we can only smoke one blunt of it. I got this shit fronted to me, so it ain't like it's free or nothin' like that."

Derek mashed his brow down and asked, "Who fronted it to you?"

"Don't worry about that. I trust you and all, but I gave him my word I wouldn't say nothin'. He don't want his business out there like that."

Derek nodded, understanding, and stare back at the bag in the trunk.

"Okay, then. We gonna at least smoke some, though?"

I grinned, "Fuck it, let's do it."

Derek rolled a rillo up fast in the car and we sat behind his house with the radio on low. Kendrick Lamar's "The Recipe" hummed through the speakers; I broke out coughing, "Fuck, that shit hits hard."

Derek laughed, "That it do. What's this shit called anyway?"

Perplexed, I replied, "What do you, mean? It's weed."

Derek took a hit and lost himself in a coughing fit.

"I know that, but like, what's it called? Old dude, didn't tell you?"

I shrugged my shoulders, "Nah, weed is weed, man. You ain't gotta call it nothin'."

Derek clicked his tongue on his teeth, "Man, we gotta name it somethin'. Pop is pop, but there's different kinds. Mountain Dew, Pepsi, whatever. When people go to buy it, they already know what they want before they even get to the store, they gotta taste for it. Know what I mean? We gotta have a brand name, so people know what to ask for."

I nodded my head.

"Yeah, yeah, yeah, I know what ya mean. Like High five, cloud nine, or somethin' like that, right?"

Derek's glance narrowed, and he laughed.

"High five, what? Man, hell nah. What about Gorilla in the mist? Or somethin' like that?"

I shook my head fast and said, "No, man. That's way too long. You gotta take a deep breath before you say that. What about the jolly green giant?"

Derek craned his neck back in disgust and didn't say a word.

I tried more to convince him.

"Man, don't be like that. You ain't never heard the tune?"

I had to press further. I danced around in a cartoon waltz, and sang in a sing songy voice, "Here he comes, it's the Jolly Green Giant, spreading joy to all! He's the one you want to see, the place you gotta be. Here's the Jolly Green Giant!"

I ended with my arms spread out in the air, smiling, and paused just like that, Derek busted out laughing, "Don't ever do that again, bro, or we can't hang out no more. We gotta take this seriously. We gotta have a name."

I had another one.

"What about Peter Pan? Like Never Never land?"

Derek snapped back, "Man, hell nah."

"Yeah, like roll up the Peter, and put it in your mouth, that's easy to say."

I gasped in shock at myself, "Oh god, no. That one is terrible."

We couldn't agree on a name. It seemed like we went back and forth for hours, ages even, but in reality, it was only fifteen minutes. Derek was frustrated already, I could tell, but nevertheless he sent the text out that we got it, and it was good; *yes, very good indeed.*

Nobody hit us up at first, so we smoked another one to figure it out while we waited. Nobody seemed to care. I thought it would all be simple and the wheels would be rollin' nonstop, but that's not the way it went. We cruised around for a while, but I was losing my patience with it.

I smacked the wheel, sloshed in a stupor.

"Man, this is so stupid. You'd think people would be all over it. I mean, is it just us, man? I mean, do folks not really like us or what?"

Derek clicked his tongue through his teeth; chillin' back in his seat.

"It's only been a few hours, bro. Why ain't you sent the word out? I mean, I texted who I know. Why's it all gotta be on me?"

I cut my eyebrows low, and snapped, "What's that supposed to mean? I pretty much got it for us, and I figured you bein' mister popular and all. We could get rid of it fast."

Derek shook his head as we cruised along under the railroad pass entering Putnam.

"It don't work like that. It ain't just gonna pop off like that. This shit ain't the movies, bro. What you think we was just gonna be rollin' around with duffel bags of cash right at the get go like Scarface or somethin'? Just like that?"

I hit the blunt again and said, "Well, yeah, pretty much. I mean, I thought everybody around here liked to smoke, so it would be easy. This is stupid."

I passed Derek the blunt, and I could tell he was in a daze. He didn't care to much, but I was worried. I didn't want to look stupid and disappoint Shawn.

Derek laughed, "Man, it ain't stupid, you are. You got the shit fronted to you and expect me to sell it. That ain't right. I'm just along for the ride. It's your shit, you try sellin' it."

I gritted my teeth in frustration, and slammed on the brakes in the middle of the road. I didn't care.

"I don't know anybody," I snapped, "just you, Von, and fuckin' Tony, really. He's an asshole, so I don't even like to count him, so really just two. I can't ever get ahold of

Von these days, not after the other night. I guess his ass has been peekin' through the blinds all paranoid and everything. I don't know what he's been doin'. So really, like in reality, there's just you, man. That's about it. I figured we could get this money together, that's all, but it's like nobody wants to hit us back."

A car laid on its horn behind us, and it blared, sending the dogs to barking' in the distance.

I screamed out of the window towards the rear, "Yeah, yeah, yeah! Fuck you, asshole! Why don't you just go around?! We're havin' a meetin' here!"

Derek mashed his hand in his sweater pocket and leaned up. He muttered, "Man, you're trippin' you're gonna get us killed out here."

I took note, but I didn't say anything. *What's in his sweater pocket?*

I saw their car door swing open in the rearview mirror, and a fat guy emerged. He was super fast for a chubby fella, and I was sure as all get out that he was going to rip me right out of my seat. His hand was nearly right on the handle, but I hit the lock button on the side just in time. I shuddered; his mug looked mean. He fumbled with the door handle, but it wouldn't release. His hands were slippery, I could tell. Maybe someone had caked them with French fry grease or something.

Mr. Macho man yelled, "I'll fix you, ya skinny little crackhead lookin' bastard!"

But he couldn't get in; I was safe, and I knew it. I let loose, grinning' and howling' behind the window. I nailed my foot on the gas and rolled the window down an inch or two and yelled, "Myah, you'll never catch me, buddy. I'm the bad guy! See?!"

The engine purred and my tire went over a strange minor bump in the road, but it didn't surprise me much. The roads are in terrible condition around these parts, especially in Putnam. Some roads aren't even paved, and some still bear the same old red brick from back in the day. I love those type of roads.

I glanced in the rearview mirror, watching the road roll away. The big guy hopped around, holding his foot. *Thank god for the distance, it saved us.*

Derek looked at me like I was mad.

"You gotta chill, bro. I'm pretty sure you just ran over that guy's foot."

Uh oh, that must've been the bump, I thought to myself. *That makes me feel bad.*

"Well, uhhh, I didn't really mean, too. I mean, did you see that guy? He was about to kick our asses."

Derek rolled his eyes.

"You gotta stop trippin'. I mean, we do got like an ounce in the trunk. Are you tryin' to go to jail?"

Of course, I wasn't; jail terrified me. For a moment all I could picture was my own sad mug behind the bars; strapped up in a jumper laden with black and white stripes. It all looked like some sort of cartoon in the image, only there wasn't anything funny about it because my weird cellie was creepin' up behind me. I shuddered at the thought as I made a turn towards Woodlawn. I'm too much of a pretty boy to go down like that.

I gulped, simmering down at the thought of it.

"I don't know, man. Maybe this was a bad idea. I mean, I just wanted us to look cool and for everybody to like us. It's not about the money for me; more about the girls, really. Nobody's interested in me. I wish I was more like you, honestly. You ain't got a problem in that department."

Derek took one last hit and threw the roach out; I downed the rest of what was in my cup. I was getting stressed.

Derek replied, "Man, you just try too hard and you think too much. It ain't difficult; you're the one who makes it that way. I mean, what happened to old girl from the other night?"

As my face melted, I lost any trace of a smile.

"She never responded back to me. I sent her a message and the green light bleeped off."

Derek replied, "Oh shit, she left you on read?"

"Pretty much," I replied, slumped over and sad; *what a waste.*

"It is what it is, though," I continued, "I'm basically the most unwanted guy on planet Earth."

Derek replied, "You just give up too easily, man. She didn't reply, so what? Add another chick and hit 'em up."

I can't; I'm too scared, I thought to myself, but I gave him the answer that he wanted. I shrugged my shoulders and agreed, then the phone rang. I barked excitedly, "Is it a sale?! Oh boy! I'm so excited!"

Derek shook his head, and chuckled, "You're a trip, man. It ain't even my phone, it's yours."

Mine? Nobody ever hits my line. I hit answer without even checking who it was.

"Ey, what ya'll getting' into?"

It was Von.

"Dude," I frantically replied back, "you're alive. I've been trying to get ahold of you, but you ain't been pickin' up."

Von replied, "When that crazy dude started shootin' the other night, I lost my phone. I ain't gonna lie. That shit had me scared."

The crack in his voice almost made me laugh because Von was known to be a tough guy.

Bang, bang, ain't a knock you want to hear. I wrestled the waves down, and I replied, "Yeah, that shit was pretty fucked, man."

I didn't really want to talk about it because Derek was near, so I changed the subject. I didn't want to see him come undone or unsettled. There was something different about his tone; less joyful and more on the watch. He didn't want to get caught slippin' again. I could tell.

"So you wanna smoke?" I asked Von.

"Shit, I'm down. I can't watch Jeopardy with grandma no more. I feel like I'm back in a cage, man. She never wants me to leave."

"Just be a meanie head about it and tell her to fuck off. I mean, that's pretty much what I'd do."

That's a lie. I wouldn't. I'm too sweet of a guy for that, but still; *ya gotta get out sometimes.*

"Man," Von tssked on the other line, "I ain't gonna do that. I'll just climb out the window. She's about to fall asleep, anyway."

Awww. He didn't want to admit it, but he loved his grandma. He couldn't do anything to hurt her feelings. He knew that he was her best friend.

"Hokey, dokey, buddy," my voice chimed back, "see ya soon."

Then the line went click.

Kid Cudi's "Wildin Cuz I'm Young" drummed through the speakers, and there me and Derek were cruising along on Cliffwood. I was rockin' with my shades on.

We'd just passed Putnam Hill, and a heroin addict shivering on a bench. *Gee whiz.* Why heroin, though? Why even try the hard stuff? It steals souls. Everyone knows where it gets you, but some still do. They're so lost, they don't even care. I don't ever want to be like that, but I admit sometimes it worries me.

I shook my head and drove onward, taking a puff, and bobbing my head. Then came the swift shuffle and grab for the door handle. I slammed on the brakes.

"Hey! Hey! Hey! What the frickin' f is going on back there?!" I wailed.

I only said it like that because the smoke had me feeling a little introspective. Sort of had me thinking I need to clean up my act a little. *I have too much of a dirty mouth.*

Derek's hand went into his sweater pocket again. *What's he got there?*

The rear passenger door swung open quickly and shut. Von hopped in the back seat, heaving, out of breath.

Derek barked, "Damn, man, what's with you runnin' all the time? You can't be comin' up like that, bro."

His arm relaxed; I noticed, but I didn't want to ask.

Von heaved, "I thought ya'll saw me. I mean, this muthafucka looked right at me."

I didn't notice.

I replied, "Yeah, dude, but you can't be doin' all that. Why you movin' so fast for?"

"Cause I'm ready to go," Von simply stated.

"Still, though, that shit had me scared, but I don't know, anyway, you wanna buy any smoke?"

"I ain't got any money," Von replied, "I'm broke."

Derek rolled his eyes. *Of course.*

"Man, you ain't never got any money. You ever gonna be able to put in?"

"I've been puttin' in," Von yelled, "fuck you mean?!"

Derek's fingers tapped his knees as he gazed out of the window at the passing houses on Pine Street, shaking his head.

"You know you ain't, bro. Not this time, not last time, not even before that. You always broke, man."

Von snapped from the back, "Yeah, but when I got money, I always get ya'll."

"He is right about that," I chimed in as I turned the wheel. We were just cruisin'. "On My Level" bopped within the interior.

I looked into the rearview mirror, and smiled, then said, "You wanna smoke, man?"

We rode around and burned down another one. We sat chillin' in the parking lot of Merrick Park, and hot boxed there, too.

"Damn," Von took a drag, and coughed, "where'd ya'll get this?"

I smiled, and rambled, "It's from a dude I know. He's pretty cool, and he's got the hookup, man, for sure, for sure. Y'know, anybody that would buy some?"

Von shrugged his shoulders and shook his head.

"Nah, not really, but D probably does. You ain't sold none yet?"

Derek tssked through his lips, and replied, "Man, I don't know why ya'll are trippin'. It's only been like an hour since I hit everybody up."

Wow, it seems like a lifetime has passed since then. We've done so much.

I turned back towards Putnam and hated it slightly because I had to go with the thought that was nagging in my head, it was just sort of the path. I told Derek, "Hey, man, call Tony."

For some reason, I knew he played a big part in what was happening. I don't know. I could just feel it. I heard the line buzz under the music in my ears, and Derek answered, Tony was down, so we headed there.

When we pulled up, Tony was just coolin' it, sittin' in a chair on the lawn, by the stoop. I was singing "Day-O" by Harry Belafonte, under my breath when I parked. I was ripped, I'll admit. Songs from grandpa's radio pop up in my head all the time. I grew up listening to it. That's why I love music so much.

Tony jumped up and wailed, "Eyyy! Who done killed my kid, bruddha?"

I did, ya punk bitch, I thought to myself as I got out. Jiminy cricket, I didn't like Tony, but I realized he was a part of the board. *Perhaps he knows a few folks*, I thought to myself. Derek clapped him up first, me and Von followed.

"What's been goin' on with ya'll? I ain't seen ya in a minute."

"It's only been a day or so, man," I retorted, but Derek ran over my response.

"Man, some fuck shit happened at that party the other night."

"For real? What happened?" Tony replied.

Derek chattered back, "These guys—they. These muthafuckas ran up in the joint, and one of 'em put a gun to my head. This fool done stole my shoes and everything, man. How you think that makes me feel? He got me, and I gotta get him back; I just got to."

He clutched the inside of his sweater pocket again. But I still didn't have the courage to ask. *He's got a gun; he has, too.* A voice chattered in the shadows, *Good. No more knucklin' around. Let's get down to business.* I fumbled in my thoughts. *Guns are bad, real bad.* I can't have one, I lose my temper too much. I know I never would, but still, if threatened, especially if it were to protect someone I loved, I'd do it; *skip a dance, that is.*

Tony yammered back, "I heard about that, man. Yo, that shit was fucked up. You good?"

Derek shoved his shoulders up quick in his grey sweater, and said, "Yeah, it's all good. I just wanted to let you know what's goin' down. Keep a lookout for 'em."

Tony clapped him up, and said, "I got ya, bubbies. What they look like?"

Derek pulled at the end of his sweater and stood firm. Me and Von were just dazed out and lost staring away at the bushes. We didn't care to talk, only listen. *The crows they're everywhere again. Every year when he's near, they're here. It's so weird. I keep seeing them. They're getting so close. I'm—*

182

Derek got tense and cracked his knuckles, then said with a mean stare, "All of 'em were wearin' black and blue, like they a gang or somethin'."

Derek paused in thought, then glared at Tony, and continued, "Hey, didn't Kayla say somethin' about you hangin' out with dudes like that?"

Tony gulped, "Nah, I mean my cousins are twins and shit, they be doin' stuff like that, but I don't know no gang or nothin' like that."

Derek looked unnerved, out of it even, then he replied, "Okay, then. I just thought I'd ask. I'm just tryin' to add this shit up 'cause I'm gonna get 'em. You can believe that."

Tony nodded and clapped him up again. They did the hands.

"I got ya, bruh," Tony smiled and said, "we like brothers. Anybody come at you, I'm right there, don't even trip."

Then he changed the subject and asked if we had any smoke. *How peculiar.* Of course we were tryin' to get up though, so we told him what was what, and rolled up some.

Tony coughed and said, "God damn! That shit is that lit, lit, I love it."

He was toasted, all of us were. Von just sat in the yard in meditation; he wasn't even in this world.

Derek laughed, "Yeah, we got the hookup and we're tryin' to sell it. You know anybody that wants any?"

Tony nodded, "Yeah, I can send the word out and all, but what I get out of it?"

I naturally chimed in, "You can smoke."

Tony shrugged his shoulders, "Works for me, let me send the owls out."

I jerked up from the brick wall behind him and Derek's chairs. Von was drooling' with a stare. I rattled onward with a smile, but their glance was bare.

183

"Oh shit! Do you like Harry Potter?"

Tony wrinkled up his mug and replied, "Man, hell nah. I ain't never watch that shit."

Knowing that he did. *Yes, he saw all of them.*

"Geez, man, you really gotta check 'em out. There like the best movies ever."

"Man, I ain't watchin that shit. I do football, not quidditch."

"See," I yelled, "you do like it! You even know the sport the wizards play!"

Tony waved his hand in front of his face, shook his head, and said, "Nah, stop playin' I don't like it."

Then he switched the subject, saying to Derek, "You know ya'll ain't gonna make any real money this way, right? You gotta hit them licks; that's what it's really about. That's—
"

Perplexed, I quickly interrupted, "What's that? What's a lick?"

Derek looked at Tony, and they both laughed. Von bounced his head up and smiled, not having a clue what was happening. He could barely open his eyes.

"What's a lick? You don't know," Tony snapped.

I shook my head and said, "No, I don't know what a lick is."

"Ya'll got any ice cream," Von asked in his half stupored slumber.

"Man, shut up," Tony snapped. Von's head just fell; he didn't even try to argue. Tony turned to me and said, "A lick is robbin' a muthafucka, fool. Just think about it; they do the legwork, make the money, you wait for the right time, then you tax. You get all the money and dope. One hit, a grand here, a grand there; that's that fast money. That's what the real wolves be on."

Derek shook his head, "Nah, that's fucked up, though. I ain't out to do anybody like that."

Tony jerked up in his chair and rattled excitedly, "But that's the name of the game. Everybody does it. You ain't really in it if you ain't with it."

I shook my head, and retorted, "No, that's not cool. You gotta have a code. You can't get by with doing somebody like that without it coming back to you."

Tony tssked, "Man, ya'll a trip. You ain't gonna make no money then."

Derek's phone buzzed, and he grinned from ear to ear.

"Wrong, the owls are flyin' back in."

CHAPTER XIV:

JUST A FRIEND

Business started kickin' a little; a gram here, a twenty there, the bubble grew and before I knew it, we sold the whole ounce. Of course, we probably smoked half of it, but we still managed to make enough to break even so we could pay Shawn back his money. *Thank god.*

I knew he wouldn't hurt me. I mean, we grew up together, and of course he didn't have the heart to do that, but still, there was something evil in his eyes when he said, "You better because if you don't; I'll kill ya."

At first, I laughed it off to quell the edge, but the feeling still lingered in the air. *He meant it, he really did.*

When we linked up again for the drop, Shawn clapped his hands together smoothly, and smiled, "See, I told ya you have a knack for it."

A black n mild wagged around in my mouth when I replied, "Yeah, I guess. It ain't a whole lot of money, though. I feel like I'm just makin' enough to smoke for free. I don't see the point behind the risk."

Shawn replied, "You ain't pushed enough weight yet. I mean, what you think? After one little ounce, you'd be ballin'?"

I shrugged my shoulders and played with my hat.

"I mean, yeah, I guess. At least have enough to buy some shoes or somethin'."

Shawn tilted his chin up and grinned.

"So what you sayin'? You wanna roll the dice and go bigger?"

"Hell yeah, I do. It's sort of fun, actually. You meet a lot of interesting people, and the best part is they pretty much always end up smokin' what they bought with us. Y'know, if there cool and all."

Shawn crossed his arms across his chest and swayed, staring at me in a studying manner.

"Okay, then. You right, you right, but you gotta be careful, y'know; always be on the lookout. When there's movement in the water, the hounds come sniffin'; they'll get ya if you ain't payin' attention. Catch my drift?"

"Yeah," I nodded, "I guess. We're careful about it, though. It's only folks that Derek knows."

Shawn ran his hands down his face and laughed, "Come on, man. Stop playin' stupid. You know how muthafuckas are out here. You saw it and I did, too. You gotta keep your eye out, it's always gotta be on the ball. It's cool and all to smoke a little, don't get me wrong, but you gotta keep a balance with it. Get numb, and still have fun. Just don't be dumb."

"I get ya," I nodded, "I know. It's just easier for me to not assess the situation openly. I feel like once you put something in words, you speak it into existence. You've brought it within the mists of reality. It's best not to give speech to a bad thought."

Shawn threw his fist into his hand, and it clapped. He winced a smile and jumped.

"See, that's that shit right there! Why ain't you on that type of focus all the time? Why you always play dumb?"

I stood frozen.

"Because. People expect more out of intelligent people, and I don't want the pressure. I ain't on the guys' level, but look at Steve Jobs. That dude doesn't get any peace and quiet. The whole world is literally consulting him in a way. There's no way I could deal with that. I'm pretty much a recluse. I hide all the time, even in public. The cloak can be pretty handy sometimes, y'know?"

Shawn nodded proudly. I'd lifted the shroud. He tapped me on the shoulder and said, "You got it. You're ready. I'm finna front you a QP."

I asked eagerly, "Really? What's that?"

Time to put the cloak back on. *It's more fun this way.*

Shawn's keys began jingling as he laughed and went for the trunk.

"Stop playin'."

I really didn't know what it was.

"It's a quarter pound, but this a magic strain; it's called Blue Lotus. This shit had my boy Chan lit, and he smokes a lot."

"For real," I said eagerly, and excited.

"Yeah, for real. You got it. I believe in you. You got that red duffel bag?"

I didn't hesitate to grab it out of the car. I eagerly unzipped it, and handed it to Shawn.

It took a good chunk of the bag up.

I gasped, "Wow, man. Holy shit! That much?!"

"Yeah," Shawn replied cooly, "like I said, you got it, right?"

I nodded my head quickly, "Yeah, I got it."
He'll kill you if you don't.

We clapped up hands over the trunk, and Shawn said, "Bet."

We went off.

When I got home, I was glad to be in the clear; nobody was out and about in the house yet. *Awesome. I can just go to my room and chill.*

I walked down the hall, opened the door, shut it, and flopped in my recliner. *Finally, time to relax.* It had been a busy few days, and I hadn't slept much at all. I didn't want to take a risk on anymore nightmares still. Truth is, I was exhausted, but I had to keep it moving.

It didn't take me long to grow restless. *I gotta do something; I gotta move; I gotta occupy myself.* My eyes danced across the room and stopped on the dresser. *My laptop; I'll just mess around online.* Of course, the first thing I checked was my Facebook, and guess what? I had a message. I blushed and smiled real big. *Nobody ever messages me. Who could it be?* It was Jules, she messaged.

I guess. I didn't go home, though, I'm still at my friend's house here in Zanesville.

It was a response to what I sent her a couple of days before. It took her a while to reply, but it didn't matter. She did.

I jumped up from my chair and nearly sent the laptop crashing into the ceiling. She was still in town. I sat back down and readjusted myself to begin typing again.

Really? You're still in town? What are you doing tonight?

The bubbles danced under my message for what felt like an eternity, but then her reply finally came.

Bored actually. Do you got any smoke?

My mind shrieked in excitement. My fingers hit the keys rapidly in reply.

Of course, you know me. You tryin' to hang out or what?

Jules responded much quicker than before.

Yeah, you should definitely come over. Can you get some liquor, too? And some smokes? My friend is almost out.

Absolutely, I thought to myself, *whatever it takes for you to hang out with me.* I told her I would right on the spot.

Big Daddy Kane's "Ain't No Half Steppin'" played as I got ready. I tried outfit after outfit, but none seemed to be the one. I almost cracked my head open again when I was fittin' on some fresh jeans, but they wouldn't do either. Finally, I settled on something.

Yeah, this seems right, I thought as I studied my attire in the mirror. There were white fifty's and graffiti marks all over my black G-Unit shirt, and for my pants, each leg was a different color, too. The left was black; the right was white.

I grinned in the mirror and was pleased with myself.

"Damn, I look good," I said as I fixed my collar and threw on some Bod cologne. I'd been wearing the same brand since eighth grade. Unbeknownst to me at the time, years later I would come to hate that cologne. If you're a grown man that wears Bod, there's just no hope for you. I'm sorry.

I did the finger snap and winked in the mirror, grinning.

"Damn, I look just like Harvey Dent," I said to myself. *Two face.*

I texted Derek, and we settled it. When I closed my bedroom door, I could hear mom out in the kitchen; banging around, cleaning up dishes. She was always hard at work.

I walked down the hallway towards all the noise and said, "Hey, mom, what's up?"

Mom was rubbing away at the plates and Jim was sitting on a stool at the countertop bar with his papers and all; shuffling through, always moving and typing away on his laptop. He was cleaned up for the day and ready for the task.

Jim yanked his head up from the counter with a smile and said, "Hey there, son. You're finally joining the rest of us. Did you get some good sleep?"

Normally, with anyone else, I'd think he was being a smartass, but with Jim, he didn't have a negative bone in his body. He's just that nice; that welcoming, something I'm not that used to. That's why he seems so special to me.

I threw my elbows on the counter and clasped my hands together, then smiled.

"Yeah, I guess so. It was sort of a long night. How you doin'? What's with all the papers?"

Jim shuffled through them more; eyes dancing across each page.

"Just some work stuff, that's all."

Jim put his papers down and fixed his glasses. Then he said, "Do you got any plans for tonight? Your mom and I came up with a really good idea for dinner. How's pizza sound? I got some movies, too. I think we all might like."

Jim's hand darted towards some Redbox movies on the counter and he snatched them up quickly; gazing at each title.

"I got the movie Drive, Real Steel, and Dream House. The dream house one is supposed to be scary, "Jim looked at mom and smiled, then continued, "I know your mom likes the scary ones so I picked that one up, too."

"Oh, you got, Drive?! That's probably one of my favorite movies. It's really good."

It was, too, down to the soundtrack and everything. I love the song that plays in the intro. When I hear it, I imagine being a famous guy, a real star; in the spotlight for some reason, I don't know. I just see it all there; *there's something about you,* folks would say and in my vision everyone loves me. I'm a champion for the people; a real smooth operator, just like Ryan Gosling in the movie.

Jim replied, "You already saw it, though?"

"I mean, yeah, but I could watch it over and over again and it would never bother me. I—"

Mom laughed, "You used to do that all the time when you were a little boy, too."

It was nice to see my mom smiling. She usually looks tired and irritated most of the time. I know why, too; I'm not stupid. Everything has always been on her. With me and my brother, she had to carry the weight all on her own. Sometimes I'll watch her and remember when she was younger, when it was just her and me. I love my brother, but I sure do miss those days.

After her and my dad split up, we moved in with Aunt Louise and Uncle Stallone. All they had was a little bedroom upstairs that was hardly big enough to turn around in, but we made it our own. At night time my mom would hold me in her arms real tight, almost like she never wanted to let me go, but she was always the first one asleep. I'd give her a kiss on the cheek while she was snoring and say, "I love you, mommy."

I'd smile and stare at her for a while, just like that. *My mommy is a princess, just like in the stories,* I'd think to myself, *maybe daddy will come by and give her a kiss, too, just like Prince Charming and she'll wake back up.* Only that time was past and they weren't together anymore.

I wasn't sure what was going on; I was only three. All I knew was I didn't have to share her with anybody anymore. When she met Paul's dad, those times were over. My father knew. I can remember seeing it in his face, *their time was over, too.*

A dish slipped out of mom's hands and she snapped, "Dammit!"

She gasped, rolled her eyes, and shook her head.

"I almost thought I broke it."

Jim smiled at mom and fixed his glasses as he looked back to me.

"So, are you hanging out with us tonight? It looks like you might already have plans."

I nodded, "Yeah, I do. I was gonna meet up with a few friends here in a minute. We'll probably just hang out and play video games, but y'know—"

Mom interjected, "Did you sign up for the online classes, yet? You better not be putting it off because if you're plannin' on droppin' out, you ain't gonna be stayin' here. You'll be flippin' burgers at the golden arches, if that's the plan."

I gritted my teeth and shook my head.

"Yeah, I did, mom. Just stop worryin' about it, ok? I'm not gonna drop out of school. I just gotta do what feels right for me, that's all."

Mom looked up from the dishes and arched her eyebrows. She had the sinister look there. It's funny and scary at the same time. If I ever push her buttons too much, I just run. *I'm the fastest man in the world, y'see, she's never been able to catch me.*

Mom said, "Ok, then. Just make sure you get it done. You're a big man now that makes all of his own choices, so go ahead and do it if you say you are."

Jim interjected, "Renae, he'll get it done. Don't worry about it; he's smart enough to know right from wrong."

Mom pressed her lips together hard as her head hung towards the dishes.

"Okay, then. We'll see."

There was an awkward silence after that, but when Jim began shuffling through his papers again. The tension in the air had swept away. *Flip, flip, flip.* Jim gazed along, then he said, "Well, I wish you didn't have plans, but I understand if you do."

Suddenly, he placed his papers back down and smiled. Then he said, "Would you like to go golfing with me next Saturday? Everything should be open and I think it would be good for us to have some quality time together; just you and me. How does that sound?"

I'd never been golfing before, but I could already imagine how it would go.

"Get in the hole, you stupid ball! The hole is your home! Go back to your home!"

Just like Happy Gilmore. There would probably be a lot of dammits bouncing around the course, but a day out with Jim sounded great, no matter what we would be doing.

"Yeah, that sounds pretty cool. I'm down with it," I said. Then I clapped up hands with 'em and did the finger gun thing. I taught him how to do it, just like us kids.

Jim laughed, "I like that handshake. The finger gun at the end is pretty cool."

"Yeah, it's the best. You should do that at work. I bet the folks on your shift would like it a lot."

Jim replied, "Not likely. A boss isn't supposed to fraternize like that. When you're a leader, you have to keep it professional."

Damn, right. Jim has a way of coming up with the best one liners.

After I got done chatting it up with mostly Jim, and Mom, I stomped down the steps towards the game room, where I knew Paul would already be. He was in the thick of it, a complete mess. The boy has seen some things on Call of Duty, that's for sure. When the last footstep fell on the concrete at the bottom of the steps, I heard him scream, "Fuck, man! You were supposed to cover me, dumbass. Camper's clipped me right on the side! I'm not playing with you guys anymore!"

I heard the PlayStation controller clatter against the ground, and Paul was yelling still. When I walked in and peered into the doorway, he stopped. Startled, he said, "Shit, bub, I didn't know you was there."

His eyes danced two and fro, from corner to corner, then he said, "You alright and everything?"

"Yeah, I'm alright. You good? It looks like you're getting' your ass kicked. "

Paul waved his hand and threw off his headset.

"No, I'm not! It's just these guys I'm playin' with. Jeremybluebird187 just keeps clippin' my ass. It's not fair! There's a tournament tonight, though, and I got a plan to get 'em."

"What you gonna do?" I smiled.

Paul shrugged his shoulders and fell back on the couch.

"I just got one, that's all. What you about to get into?"

I waved my hand.

"Shit, bout to go hang out with Derek and them, y'know, probably go to a party or somethin'."

Paul jerked up from the couch.

"Can I come? I'll forget about the tournament tonight. I wanna have fun, too."

I leaned against the doorway; sinking within, and said, "No, I don't think so. Mom and Jim will know what's up and they're already bent 'cause I'm not gonna be here to do movie night again."

Paul looked so down; disappointed even. He looked towards the gray floor, at the concrete, and said, "Okay. You wanna pick me up later, though? We could have fun then."

I figured I wouldn't. I didn't want to corrupt him. I couldn't play games with Paul.

"Nah, I probably won't be back, but we can go to the movies or somethin' tomorrow night if you want."

Paul exhaled, "But there's school the next day and I'll have to go to bed early. Movies aren't a whole lot of fun anymore anyway."

I tapped my fingers across the door panel.

"They are with me, though."

Paul reached for his headset and controller simultaneously.

"Whatever you say. What about next weekend, Friday or somethin' maybe?"

My arm fell, and I shoved my hands back into my pockets.

"Maybe. We'll see, man. Keep it cool, alright?"

I was ready to go. Paul replied, "Okay, bub. Be careful tonight, okay?"

I laughed, "What are you, mom now? Be careful? I'll be fine, man. Just chill."

Paul threw his headset back on and began tapping away at the buttons on the controller again. *Lost to the world.*

"Okay, bub. I'll see you later on."

It was set. Another night was on.

On the ride to pick up Derek, I wondered what type of mood he'd be in; he'd been off lately. *Always on the watch.*

When I saw him, he looked fine; cast off under the dark, shaded by the tree in the night. An ember burned, and then it turned. Derek stuffed his hands in his sweater pocket and walked up to the car.

He grinned when he slid in, clapping his hands together, then he said, "What's with it, bubbies? What we getting' into?"

All I could do was match his smile; I guess we were two clowns in the car from the way we looked. I pulled the car out of park and the headlights danced across the red brick alleyway. I replied, "What you think? I got a couple of girls lined up for us tonight. We're gonna go hang out with them."

Derek chuckled, "I know I'm still in shock over it all. My boy's turnin' into a player, after all."

Damn right, I thought to myself as I wiggled the bill of my hat around in the rearview.

We pulled up to this certain store of ours we found to get some booze for the night. Derek was pretty cool with the guy at the register, and we damn near had access to anything we wanted, like we were adults already. As long as we had the money for it, that is. They charged us a little extra for being underage.

Derek was ecstatic, as always, when he hopped in the car with a couple bags of fours and a giant bottle of Smirnoff vodka. Not my first choice, but girls love somethin' with a little flavor to it. At least Jules did anyway.

When we pulled up to her friend's house, the two girls were eagerly waiting outside for us under the willow wisps of cigarette smoke that had collected itself under the hanging roof of the porch. Derek glanced over at me and said, "So which one's yours?"

I blushed and smiled, "The little blonde sitting over there to the left. She's pretty, ain't she?"

Derek darted his look quickly back to the porch, then back to me.

"You tellin' me I'm gonna have to keep, big girl over there occupied?"

She was slightly larger than the average girl, but she looked pretty in the face. I've actually found myself attracted to quite a few big girls myself, to tell you the truth. There's just something that seems so warm and welcoming about a girl with a little more to her; as if you could just fall into their arms drunk and say to yourself, *It feels so warm here. I like the way this feels. I like you. I really do.* I have to admit it happened to me a time or two. I never allowed it to go any further than that, though. I want to save myself for the one. I'm a man with morals, after all.

I replied, "So what if she's a bigger girl? Ain't nothin' wrong with that. Chicks like that are better for you, anyway; they're a lot nicer."

Derek replied, "Okay, let's switch, then."

"Stop bein' so shallow, man. She's pretty," I shrugged my shoulders and said.

"Whatever, man. Says you."

When we got out of the car, Jules jumped up out of her lawn chair and ran towards me. She gave me a surprise hug and hopped back immediately. *Very quickly,* then she asked, "So did you bring the stuff?"

I jingled the grocery bags full of fours in my hands and replied, "Hell yeah, I got it right here."

Jules studied Derek up and down immediately. I could tell she was into him right away. Most girls were. He was tall, and pretty shredded for a thin guy. Meanwhile, I was just standing there, a gangly, sick looking geek drooling all over her. I have to admit, I was jealous of the way she looked at him. I'd never had a girl look at me like that before. Jules burst out, "Is this your friend?! What do you got right there? Is that Smirnoff watermelon?!"

Derek nodded his head and replied, "Yeah, you tryin' to get a shot?"

Jules ripped the bottle from his hand immediately and took a swig. She wrinkled her face up to the side and said, "Wheeww, that's my favorite. Hey, you care if my friend Sarah has a shot, too?"

I reassessed my presence and replied, "Well, yeah, what do you think? That's what we got it for."

Such a fool; your bein' used. I ignored the voice. I couldn't listen to it. I laughed instead.

"We might as well pass it around."

Jules was acting super wired up for some reason. I mean, she always had an upbeat and outgoing personality, but this was different—like she done some meth or speed or somethin'. Jules took the bottle and hit it again. *Gee whiz,* I thought to myself, *she sure is a drinker.* She yelled, "So what are you guys standin' there for?! Are you comin' in or what?"

Sarah, on the other hand, was quiet; nervous even. She didn't say much, but she had a certain type of kindness to her eyes that you don't find in much people. She was pretty, and her brown hair was sort of shiny, with a slight reddish tinge to it. I have to admit when we met eyes, I blushed, and put my head down. Then, we followed them towards the door. Jules skipped ahead, and Derek said under his breath, "What the fuck are we doin', bro? This bitch is crazy."

I shook it off, and replied, "Yeah, I know, but that's why I like her. It's like Joker and Harley Quinn, y'know?"

Jules stood in the doorway and yelled, "Get in here, buddy!"

Oh boy, she just called me buddy. What a bummer, I thought to myself. Derek elbowed me on the arm and said, "Yeah, get in there, buddy!"

He continued; shaking his head, "You're in the friend zone all the way, man. This shit ain't no good."

I knew it, too, but I didn't care. *He's jealous that's all, just waltz on in.*

When we got inside, the living room was quite open. It was merged in with the kitchen and everything; almost like the house was one big room. The counter tops were shiny, and the floor was a bit of a mess, but it smelled like pumpkins so I sort of liked it. The one light on in the room was a corner lamp. The rest of the room was dark except for the TV. There was some guy lounging in a recliner with his headset playing "Call of Duty." It looked like he hadn't had a shower in days.

After we shut the door behind us, the dude turned a set of bulging, bloodshot eyes towards us as he tilted his headset away to say, hey. He didn't make anytime for conversation.

Jules and Sarah were chillin' on a worn out leather couch that sat opposite of the front door. Jules packed the cigarettes I got her faster than the roadrunner and had a square lit up in no time. She said, "Well, are you guys just gonna stand there or are you gonna get comfortable?"

She flicked her eyes towards Derek and said, "Hey, what's your name again? You can sit between me and Sarah if you want to."

Derek didn't smile and I could tell he was a tad unsettled by the tornado wrecked environment we were in. He replied, "My name's Derek, but, nah, I'm good. I'm just gonna chill right here."

He sat down at a stool near the kitchen bar. Jules cast a wide smirk at me and patted her hand on the spot between her and Sarah. She said, "Well, what are you waitin' on? We got some catchin' up to do!"

Derek was grinning then. He sat there with his arms crossed, looking as closed off as ever, but I felt completely open. I didn't mind. The closer I could get to Jules, the better.

I sunk down into the sofa and smelled a sweet aroma coming from one of them, or perhaps both. I blushed at Jules and asked, "What are you wearin'?"

Jules' eyes dilated and popped at me. She bounced back and replied, "A pink tank top, a bra underneath, and some bootie shorts! What's it look like?!"

The guy in the chair tilted his headset back and calmly said, "Hey, Jules, I can hear you over the game. Can you, like, not yell, please?"

Jules smiled and nodded her head. When the guy turned back towards the TV, she mashed her lips and threw a middle finger up at him. The dude tilted his head set back again and asked, "Did you say something?"

Jules shook her head to and fro, then replied, "Uh uh, nothing at all."

I pointed to the guy and mouthed the words, "Who is that?"

Jules waved her hand at him and replied, "Nobody really. You can talk as loud as you want."

Sarah blushed on the other side, giggling, and said, "That's my older brother, Jeremy. Don't worry about him."

Jules laughed, too. I looked over at Derek and he was texting away on his phone, attempting to set up an escape plan, I assumed.

We needed to liven things up a little, I thought, so I asked, "Ya'll wanna play some quarters with this bottle or what?"

Everybody was down and we definitely needed a change of pace; things were beginning to get awkward after all. My cheeks flushed, I was smiling away, and doin' pretty good for a change. Derek was up, though. He held the quarter between his thumb and middle finger as he counted, "One, two, three!"

He popped the quarter right in the glass. Jules jumped up in the air and screamed, "Oh my god, you got it again!"

She bounced over to Derek and tried to give him a hug, but he pressed his hand up, shaking his head and said, "Stop playin'."

Then he cast an evil grin at Sarah and continued, "Your up! You gonna drink or what?!"

Dammit was written all across her face. She slammed the shot glass back and winced with fury. The girl definitely knew how to party.

Jeremy flipped around in his chair and yelled, "Guys! I'm tryin' to play a game here! Ok? Just—just keep it down a little. Ok?"

Sarah snapped a finger at him, and said, "You don't run things here, Jeremy. You're not daddy around here; you don't tell me and my friends what to do."

Jeremy replied, "Look, guys, all I'm saying is, you're not the only ones here. This is an important battle for my clan. We've been working towards this moment for weeks."

Jules arched her neck out and bobbed her head like a chicken as she said, "Well, would you like a shot?"

Jeremy rolled his eyes and flipped back on his headset. He was dedicated to that game like he was married to the thing or somethin'. I mean, I sort of got it and I didn't. I thought to myself, *There's a party goin' on, bro. Why are you worried about the game?*

I couldn't get it, but I was up. I flipped the quarter and missed the glass. Jules shouted, "You fuckin' suck, man! Pick that glass up and take it! Take it like a real man!"

I had no other choice but to do what she demanded.

I couldn't look weak in front of the girls, after all. Jeremy shouted behind me, "Fuck! Pavman60! Fuck! That little kid got me! Weeks! Fucking weeks down the drain."

I heard Paul laugh on the TV screen, and his army guy tea bagged Jeremy's defeated shell. That made it even worse; he had to rub it in. *See? Some brothers do have things in common.* I smiled proudly. *You got 'em, buddy, you really did. I sure do miss you, kid.*

Jeremy threw his headset at the TV and cracked the screen. Sarah stomped towards him and pointed her finger, "Mom is gonna kill you! You're so stupid!"

Jules smacked her hands on her cheeks like the "Home Alone" kid as Derek cackled in the background. Jules ran over to Jeremy, skipped over the coffee table, and threw her fist into his chest and yelled, "Yeah! Stupid! You're stupid!"

Jeremy tossed his controller in the chair and hung his head, "No, I'm not. You guys—you guys just don't understand. My dream is to be a streamer—like with a webcam and everything, y'know? People make real money with YouTube videos."

Jules poked her finger into his chest and shouted, "Well, it ain't gonna be you! Is it?! Is it?!"

Poor Jeremy tried to back away to escape, but he tripped over his own chair and ended up on the carpet. Jules clutched her stomach and gasped; laughing over him. She pointed and said, "How could you—could you trip like that? See?! Stupid!"

The whole scene threw me off. I thought to myself, *This isn't the Jules that I remember. This isn't the same girl,* but I knew there was good in her. I saw it. She was just drunk, that was all. *Remember that night when she cried in your arms?* You held her, and she told you. She told you of it, and she let herself go. You understood it. She did, too.

Jeremy brought himself back up and straightened up his shirt. He looked like he was on the verge of tears. He replied, "I already lost. You guys—you guys don't know how much time I put into that. I'm just—I'm just going to go back to my room."

Sarah even looked like she felt sorry for him and honestly, I did too. It had to be all the shots Jules took. That's why she was acting the way she was. She was a good girl at heart and I knew that. I couldn't deny it. I always believed in her.

Derek flicked open his phone and said, Hey, man, we gotta make a run real quick. You tryin' to split?"

I turned to Derek and replied, "Where we gotta go?"

Jules exclaimed, "Yeah! Where you goin'?!"

Derek replied, "I forgot the shells. We gotta ride to get some rillos. We'll be back real quick."

Jules exclaimed, "You mean you got weed?!"

Oh, that's right. We got a whole QP; it seemed to have slipped my mind. I've literally been riding around with it all day. Luckily, mom didn't pop the trunk. She would've been pretty mad.

I replied, "I mean, yeah we do; we sorta have a lot, actually. We've just been playin' quarters—"

Derek tapped my arm, and said, "You mean, you re-upped and didn't tell me?"

I shrugged my shoulders, and replied, "I mean, yeah, I met with the guy today. I just forgot to tell you, I guess."

Jules jumped up and pointed her finger in my face. *You're getting on my nerves,* I thought to myself, then she snapped, "You've been holdin' out on me! There's a gas station right up the road. We can just walk; we don't have to ride."

Jules bounced up and down.

"I need to stretch my legs, anyway."

She ran over to me and snatched my hand and said, "Come on, we gonna go get some shells or what?!"

It felt so warm for her hand to be over mine. *It's not cold anymore.* I melted within her grasp, and replied, "Sure, let's go, then."

The dark edge was looming, and the hairs suddenly stood up on the back of my neck. The feeling alone made me want to stop in my tracks and jerk my hand away immediately, but I didn't. I was stuck.

Tssk, tssk, tssk, the man in the hat clicked his tongue. He continued onward in a sing-songy tune. *Everybody plays the fool. What a tool.*

I ignored the voice and continued onward. He was there, then wasn't.

Derek kept looking at me like I was crazy the whole way there. Suddenly, Jules snapped, "If this bitch doesn't leave me alone, I'm gonna have to beat her ass!"

Sarah's eyes danced nervously around on the ground, and she stuttered, "W-what's goin' on now?"

Jules snapped and threw her hands up in the air.

204

"It's fuckin' Nay Nay again; she just doesn't know when to quit."

"Really her again?"

The two of them went back and forth about it the whole way there. I couldn't believe Jules was acting the way that she was. I mean, she was really coming off like a lunatic or somethin'. She's always been the type of girl to stand up for herself, but somehow it was all different. *More lethal.*

They all piled in the Starfire when we got there, but my cigar was still lit, so I didn't go in. A *chill to the skin; always cold within.*

Suddenly, a strange man appeared from the other side of a pump, and he sort of looked like the school janitor. The one who tried to talk to me right before I left school on my last day. *Where will thee go?*

He didn't look like a janitor anymore, though. He was very clean cut, perhaps too fancy for this end of town, but his grey suit and manicured silver beard did make him look quite distinguished.

"Hello," the man said with a rather familiar smile. He had a soft and calm countenance.

"Uhhhh, hi," I replied; quite confused, and a little startled. There was something odd about his presence. *Where did he come from?*

The Grey Man just stood there and studied me. Not in a weird way or anything, but his eyes glowed with a certain level of understanding that I knew was way past my own. He scared me to tell you the truth. Even though I knew in my heart he was a friend; *an unknown one.*

Perplexed past comprehension, I asked him, "Wh-what d-do you want?"

He coughed to clear his throat and pointed at my still burning cigar.

"You should probably put that thing out, y'know, one wrong flick, and you could blow yourself up."

He was right. I did have the thing literally burning right by an open gas cap, and I didn't even realize it. My attention was solely on him, and the air seemed odd. It felt like the world was literally on pause all around. Cars weren't even passing, everything had grown void.

I jumped back and put my cigar out quickly under the bottom of my shoe, making sure no stray embers got away.

"That's better," the Grey Man continued, "now you're a lot better off."

"Who are you? What do you want?" I asked again.

The Grey Man folded his hands behind his back and replied evenly, "To talk; that's all."

I was stuck. Terrified and confused by the old man's presence. I couldn't move. He had me locked in. For whatever reason, I'll never know.

My words came as natural as water, almost like I'd spoken them all before. I asked, "About what?"

The Grey Man replied, "About you. About him."

I gulped. *He knew. He knows. He can't possibly know what I—what he did.* I choked, then replied, "H-him? What do you know a-about him?"

Somehow, I knew that he knew; about him, the man in the hat. He could give me answers. That's why he was there; *give a little context to what lies unknown.*

The Grey Man edged closer, and said, "You know what you did was wrong. Back then, you let him in. Don't do it again. Don't let the man in the hat win."

I froze. The wind gripped my pores and shook me to the core. I dropped my cigar; frightened from afar.

"H-how? How d-do you know? You can s-see it; him don't you?"

"Everyone can sense it; him in you. Him and you. The hour is growing near, y'know? The caw of the crow, he's around; he's there. Beware on old Hallows Eve; I've seen it go many ways."

Why so cryptic?

His words didn't make any sense to my mind, but they spoke to my soul. I stammered, "But why?"

Suddenly, something I couldn't control manifested, and spoke through my lips, and the pitch of my voice changed.

"Who are you anyway?" I croaked.

The Grey Man lifted his head so his eyes could stare into mine.

"You see, that's him. The anger, the hatred, the thirst for vengeance. It's all him and all of you. He saw it and I do, too. That's why he came. That's why he followed you—"

I didn't want to hear anymore; the presence of the shadow was weighing me down. *I can't hold it.*

I snapped, "You're a fool; that's what you are. Look at you. You think you're wise, but you're just another old man. You don't know me. You don't know a thing."

The Grey Man's eyes grew deeper. A well for each side; dark and light are what reside inside.

He replied, "I was there. He wasn't that much of a boy, should've been a man, by then, but the child within still resided in. I was there when he got the hat. I'm the one that gave it to him."

The man's face grew grim, then he continued, "A new start he said, and I saw the path go towards both ends. I should have saved him, but I didn't know when. Freedom of choice can be such a sin."

My eyes narrowed at the Grey Man. *He saw what was within.* The man in the hat he knew where he'd been. I was about to ask a question, but Jules stepped right in.

She hopped around the corner with a grin, and shouted, "Where have you been?!"

It all caught me off guard. There she was and the Grey Man—he was gone; blown away by the wind. I had no idea where he went. His words rang like a bell, but I stuffed them within. Not caring when I'd go to decipher them again.

I threw my hands up to respond, but behind me a girl screamed, "Hey, bitch! I told you I was gonna find your ass!"

I jerked my head towards the voice and a tanned brunette with burgundy highlights came marching up in her apple bottom jeans, y'know, and the boots with the fur.

Sarah shivered and shimmied closer to me.

Jules hollered in response, "What are you even doing here? Are you following me?"

The brunette stopped about seven feet away and responded, "No, you know what I'm doing here. You fucked my man, Dandy. He was so pretty, and you stole him, you bitch! Remember him? I'm sure it's hard to keep track of everybody you've been with."

That hit me harder than it did Jules. *She's nothing but a crazy whore, y'see, gonna amount to nothing,* a voice whispered.

The thought of her being a hoe and sleeping around made me feel sick inside. She wasn't like that before. She was pretty much a loner chick. *No, that's not her. She's a good girl,* I thought to myself; only because I couldn't allow myself to think about something else. My eyes fell on Sarah, and her eyes danced nervously into mine. She wasn't a fighter either, just like me. *There's something familiar in your eyes; I like you;* I thought to myself, but I beat the feeling down, and turned my gaze back towards the charade.

Jules stomped closer towards the girl in fury. She screamed, "You don't know shit about me! Maybe if you wasn't such a dead fuck, he would've stuck around."

Jules snapped her finger and grinned.

"Somebody had to show pretty little Dandy some love."

A couple of dudes from a nearby gas pump shouted, "Oh, shit!"

The girl lurched at Jules and snatched her up by the hair. Jules wailed and clawed at the girl's hand to free herself. The girl punched her in the face and twirled Jules around.

Jules dug her nails deep into the girl's hand and you could see her skin break. The girl ripped her claws away and screamed. Jules smacked her in the face, but the girl was keeping her pace. She threw a left hand into Jules' stomach and my heart began to race. She knocked the air clean out of her.

Jules fumbled on the ground and the girl went to kick her, but then the store clerk guy came rushing out and screamed, "What are you doing by my shop? Huh?! Jew, need to get out of here before I call the cops, mayne!"

I scrambled to help Jules out because we had to leave. I helped her up, and we rushed away. The girl scurried back to her car and screamed, "I'll see you again! You don't have to worry about that!"

The store clerk was still there in a hot temper. He kept shouting, but we were out of there. He didn't have to worry about that.

Jules looked hurt, and I felt bad for her; y'know, for getting her ass kicked like that, and all.

"Who the fuck was that, the Nay Nay girl?"

"No," Jules shook her head, "that was Brittany, but Nay Nay is a fuckin' bitch, too."

"Really? What's she after you for?"

Jules brushed herself off, and replied, "She thinks I stole her, man."

"Damn," Derek barked, "you stole that bitches, man, too?"

Jules shook her head rapidly in defense, "No, she just thinks I did. I really didn't, though, honest. I'm not a whore."

Kind of sounds like you are, I thought to myself, but I beat the rumblings down. *It's not to judge, I guess.*

After a while, I figured it would be a shame to make Jules walk all that way, so I had her climb up on my shoulders so I could carry her. She wasn't apprehensive about it at all, which really made me feel good. She laughed and said, "Oh, you wanna be my Prince Charming and carry me to the house? Ain't you sweet."

At first, it felt good because Jules had her thighs straddled against my cheeks and her hands on my head, but as the walk carried on, I could feel myself buckling down like a broken down mule. *We're getting closer. The door is just a few steps away;* I kept telling myself, but my legs were beginning to give out and my back screeched for relief. I couldn't put her down because I didn't want to look weak. We nearly made it to the door with only a few steps away, but then there it was. *Boom, slip, pow.* My foot landed in a hole. I threw Jules off my shoulders into the yard to save her from the impact, but then my head went. *Crack.*

I wailed, "Oh fuck! Oh god! Not again!"

Damn near hit my head in the same spot. My hat flew off, and my stitches busted open.

Sarah screamed at all the blood, and Derek yelled, "Damn! You fucked up, bro!"

"Oh, my god! Oh my god," I screamed, panicked, and clenching my forehead. Tears ran down my cheeks with the pounding pain and blood. I wasn't trying to cry, but y'know—I did. Jules simply cackled on the ground.

"Frankenstein," Jules pointed, and wailed.

The ringing in my ears started again; and I was losing sense, but then Sarah came to my rescue and lifted me up.

"Oh no! You busted your stitches open! Geez, you're bleeding everywhere! Come inside; I'll get you a rag."

Jules still lie on the ground laughing. Derek was, too, but he still asked if I was okay.

"Yo, you good, man?"

"Yeah, I'm good," I heaved upwards as Sarah held my hand and pulled me up. She led me inside with her hand on my back. Believe it or not, Jules was still laughing. Derek dialed away on his phone behind us as we walked inside and closed the door.

I fell on the couch.

"Ahhhh, geez, that hurt."

Sarah rushed for a closet and pulled a towel out, then ran over to me and pressed it on my forehead. The pressure felt nice.

"You're gonna have to go to the hospital; you split your head wide open."

"I'm not going back to the hospital," I snapped, "all I need is bubblegum and some tape. I don't care. I'm not going back."

Sarah giggled, "That ain't gonna work. It won't heal right. Don't you care about yourself?"

She patted my forehead repeatedly with the towel, tenderly soothing me. It made me feel good.

I replied, "I mean, yeah, I do. I just have a different way of doing things, that's all."

"To bad. I don't have some butterfly band aids that might do the trick," Sarah responded, but then she stopped everything and said, "wait a minute. I think I might have a couple left in my room. Wait here, I'll go get them real quick."

She's so nice, I thought to myself. *She's not really my type, if I even have one, but she makes me feel warm, and I can tell she's caring. Not like Jules, no, not like her at all. How are they even friends?*

Sarah rushed back in, and handed me a couple band aids, and I took them. My hand pressed down on the gash with the towel, and I winced, "Thanks, you're a lifesaver. I really didn't want to use tape and bubblegum, but I would have, y'know? I don't care. I do what I have to do."

Sarah laughed, and her eyes glittered.

"Your nuts. Then you'd really look like Frankenstein."

She's so casy to talk to, too.

I smiled through the pain and replied, "It would be about, right. I feel like the living dead sometimes."

The man in the hat whispered, *It's because we are; we are. You and I, Prince of Fools, combined, but separate, tools. Ghost, and host together, we are the living and walking dead.*

The whisper wisped away like so many others. I was so used to it; it didn't even matter to me. It was just another thing, but there he was. *Always there, always watching, but why, why me?* I didn't know, couldn't find the time to figure it out, but when I did—

Derek burst through the door.

"Ey, man, you good? I'm ready to go on a blunt cruise."

I rolled my eyes with the towel pressed on my head, and said, "Yeah, sure. Don't mind me. I'm just bleedin' to death over here."

Derek replied, "Man, you can't still be bleedin'? There's no way."

I patted the towel on my forehead and gazed at the blood streaked across the white fabric.

Not as bad as I thought. I shrugged my shoulders and said, "Never mind. I think I'm good."

I wiped the blood away, and slapped on the band aids, then threw my cap back on.

"Fuck it, I'm ready to go," I jumped up.

Sarah smiled at me. I turned my head to hide the blush.

"Thanks again, Sarah, for helping me," I said, peering at the ground at first, but then I lifted my head up to meet her eyes, and smiled, then said, "it really means a lot."

Sarah blushed, and giggled, "Oh, it's no problem. You needed somebody."

"Yeah, I did," I gazed back at her in reply, hot-cheeked.

"You comin' to smoke?"

"Yeah, sure," she eagerly replied.

We went outside, and Jules was out there barking on the phone at somebody. *Always into some drama.* I didn't care. I clicked the trunk open on the car and waved for the others to follow. Jules still wasn't paying attention, but Sarah and Derek were. I unzipped the red duffel bag, and announced, "There we go folks. Pure beautiful Blue Lotus from Egypt. Isn't it magnificent? I still have yet to try it."

Derek gasped, Damn, man! That shit is purple as fuck."

"I know," I proudly smiled, "it's a true wonder of the world. Ready to give it a go?"

Derek nodded calm, and coolly, "Yeah, let's get lit."

CHAPTER XV:

JUMP AROUND

"Make It Rain" by Travis Porter reverberated seamlessly across the speakers, and there we were, the four of us, still together. We were rollin' down West Main Street feelin' cool. Jules stole my hoodie and sunglasses; she was hanging out of the rear window flashing gang signs to everybody we passed. I don't recall telling her she could have any of my gear, but she just sort of claimed them, I guess, and she always wanted me to buy her stuff. It all kind of reminded me of a talk that Cliff Huxtable and his son Theo had on "The Cosby Show."

In the episode, Cliff is trying to explain how money works to Theo, so he hands him a stack of cash. He goes through the different things you need money for, and each time he takes another dollar away. Towards the end, Theo still has a lot of money left, but then Cliff asks, "Do you plan on having a girlfriend?"

Theo nods his head, "Of course."

Then Cliff snatches the rest of his money away and says something like, "See? That's how money works."

The laughing box of a fake crowd cuts on afterwards, and the lesson was pretty much over. That's the thing, though. For kids that don't have a dad, we get a lot of our lessons from the dads on TV, and Cliff was one of those guys for me. Cliff Huxtable wouldn't ever do anything wrong. *No, not a thing at all.*

We spun a corner towards Ridge Avenue, and Jules maintained mean mugging everybody while a big fat blunt hung out of her mouth.

"Holy smokes, guys; that's some really good sativa," I rambled.

Derek went to snapping his fingers and acting goofy in the shotgun seat. I sort of wanted to sit by Jules, but I had to be doing something. I was focused and ready to do the job. The Adderall she gave me had me grinding my teeth.

"Y-y-yeah," I snapped in a high growl.

We'd been everywhere the past two days. I still hadn't slept. You could call it a little bender, I guess, y'know, like the fancy folks say.

Derek couldn't believe we were fronted that much and really, I didn't either. *Is Shawn stupid or crazy? Why would he give me this much? He must have a lot. If so, good. I like the taste of it.* Everybody we came across did, too.

The first kids we pitched to were doing kick flips off the ramps at the skate park down in Putnam. They were pretty cool, and I loved their wireless speaker. While Derek gave 'em the salesman talk, and all that, I posted up beside the thumping beat; polishing my kicks up, and whatnot. Hopsin's "Nollie Tre Flip" tune was playing and I started rockin' to the beat. I lit up another rillo just to match the occasion. By this time I'd gotten my shades back so I was feeling quite debonair. The skater kids were so blown by the time we packed up they didn't even notice their speaker was missing when we left.

We hung out around the north end and smoked with the kids from up that way, too. Most of them are rich kids. They were pretty cool to tell you the truth. Most just wanted to escape mommy and daddy like the rest of us.

"Wow, this hits really good," a guy named Dave nodded as he took a puff, "I can pass my exams with flying colors now, man."

A smoke alarm went off; the house went up in flames, fire trucks honked in the distance. All of us stood outside, gazing out at the billowing smoke ascending into the beyond.

"Fuck," Dave said with his hands folded over the top of his head, "this ain't good, man."

"No, it ain't," I replied; startled and dumbfounded.

Derek snapped excitedly, "Damn, man; how did this shit happen, anyway? I mean, we was all just chillin' in the living room."

Sarah chimed in, "Well, I smelled smoke first, and Jules—"

"Yeah, I was takin' a piss, and I knew somethin' was goin' on. That's why I hollered for you guys to get up and get the fuck out."

She paused, then came to a realization, smiling, "I saved all of you guys."

You look guilty, though, I thought to myself. She pointed us all down, but we quickly turned away, back towards the fire as the front of the home peeled off and crumbled.

Dave whimpered, and cried, "My parents are gonna kill me, but—Oh! Oh, no!"

"What?" we nearly all asked simultaneously.

Dave panicked, "My girlfriend Amanda's birthday present was in there! Oh, man, dude! I gotta get her a new one. Can you give me a ride to Wally World? I can get her a bear there or something."

I swung my fist up, smiling, and said, "Sure you got it, pal. What are friends for?!"

The radio kicked on when we hopped in my ride, and Y 107.3 was playing.

"Get in the trunk, Dave. We ain't got room anywhere else, man. We're gonna go get your Amanda a birthday present."

"It's Not Unusual," clapped across my eardrums, and Tom Jones' melodious voice swam across the speakers. I kicked up the volume.

"Nobody touch the fuckin' nob, alright?! I love this song!"

We charged through the doors of Wal Mart, and it was a mess; *pure mayhem.*

Dave told us, "Okay, we gotta go in and make it quick. Her plane leaves in a few hours and I might not ever see her again. This gift is my last hope. I—"

"Dude," I interrupted, "this is crazy, man. I feel like I'm in a fuckin' movie right now or somethin'. What's goin' on?"

"Mission, find the best bear for Amanda is what's goin' on! You all in?" Dave asked.

We all huddled together, bumped knuckles, and hollered, "Find the best bear!"

Our hands flung up in the air at the same time, and before I knew it I was in a wheelchair speeding around corners. Derek was running behind me, pushing me along. Meanwhile, Jules was darting around the women's clothing section and shoving bras, panties, and who knows whatever else into her purse. Sarah reluctantly followed, but didn't steal a thing. We were whooshing along, following after Dave. He was ripped off that Blue Lotus; we all were.

"Wheeee! This is a lot of fun!"

I made the sound effects of an engine, and everything. Derek raced along, and stopped near a corner. We were about to switch back off.

"Okay, my turn now. I—"

"Hey," a staff member hollered, "you don't need that! It's supposed to be a tool for disabled people! It's not a toy."

Derek and I froze.

"S-sorry," I stammered, "we didn't mean anything by it. We just got back home from college."

"College?" the old man snapped, "what the fuck does that have to do with you speeding" around in a wheelchair? Somebody might need that right now, y'know? But they can't get in here to shop because you have it."

"Well, we're really sorry," I responded, "you can have it back."

"No harm, no foul," the old man took the wheelchair and nodded. He started to walk away, but then he turned around and asked, "what college do you boys go to?"

"Steadmanshirehearst academy, sir," I replied quickly; not knowing a word that was coming out of my mouth. *Old folks like to be called, sir.*

The old guy smiled, but was confused, "Steadman's Shire Hearst Academy? Where abouts is that?"

"Up in Green Hills, Colorado; it's a real fancy place," I replied sharply.

The old man gave us a nod and walked off.

Suddenly, Dave hollered across the store, "I found it! I found the best bear!"

We rushed off to Amanda's and Dave bestowed her his gift. She sort of just threw it to the side in an 'oh well' type of fashion. Dave jumped up with glee when she told him they had canceled her flight. He asked her why.

"I don't fuckin' know, Dave, just chill out, alright?"

Amanda took a big burn from her cigarette, and the smoke danced. We were huddled in her living room, just hanging out. We got a beer out of it, plus Amanda seemed cool. She was an older girl, and she had a kid. Her little boy

218

popped out of a corner, made a gun out of his fingers and pointed it towards me giggling, then shouted, "Bang!"

I played along; shuffling my elbows quickly.

"Bang! Bang!"

I took cover behind the couch, too.

"Bang, bang!"

Roll across the carpet.

"Bang, bang, bang!"

"Hey," Amanda hollered, "don't be getting' him all riled up! Go to your room Aaron!"

Aaron howled like a dinosaur and slammed his bedroom door shut.

Amanda asked us, "So you guys got good weed? Care if I have a sample?"

"Sure, let's roll up."

Derek got the rolling papers ready, and we smoked. The whole time Jules was eyeing Dave, but he had a woman. She was right in front of her; I didn't get it. *I mean, why not me? Why do I have to be so ugly?* It didn't make any sense. I mean, I'm easy to get along with. Give me french fries and a ferris wheel, I'm a pretty happy guy, but my thoughts still rambled. It didn't even register to Amanda. Sarah laughed at something Derek had said that went right past me; I was in a daze.

"But yeah," Derek leaned forward across the coffee table and told Amanda, "if you wanna buy wholesale we gonna have to do two forty an ounce, I mean, this shit's rare. It ain't no dirt ass mids."

Amanda nodded, "Yeah, I think we can work something out. It's the best I've had in years."

Suddenly, a click from a BB gun went off, the TV crinkled and cracked.

"Aaron! I'm gonna tear your ass up!"

Amanda charged into the bedroom and gave him a crack. My fingers tapped across my knees. *Oh, geez, ready to go, please.*

Derek put a lot of people on, and they loved it, but the best part about it was, they'd always smoke what they bought with us. *Hell yeah.*

We were kickin' it with everybody. Of course mostly our own, y'know, folks around town, the kids of the pines, but we also fucked with folks in Maysville, Crooksville, McConellsville, Newark, and we even went out to Valley. Jules had to pick up a few things, and we stopped by my friend Beauregard's house. We smoked down with them; his mom, his sister Jenny, and her boyfriend Julian were there, too. His mom Malerie passed me the blunt and laughed, "That makes you a little giggly. I like it."

I drummed my hands on my knees, and chattered, "I know, right? It's got me speedin' like crazy. I feel like I can reach mystic worlds, y'know, like things fit together a lot better with this type of focus."

Jules blurted out, "That's not the weed, that's the speed."

She wouldn't even sit by me. She was too focused on gettin' at Beauregard, and before him she tried to cozy up to Derek again, but he still wasn't havin' it. He didn't even try to sit down this go around. He stood propped up on the wall, puffin' away, standin' tall. I don't think he liked Jules too much, but he was still cordial and friendly. Sarah, on the other hand, didn't mind sitting next to me. It felt sort of good, in fact, but I was still hung up on Jules a little. It seemed like she was interested in everybody but me. *Why? What's wrong with me?* I thought to myself. *I guess it's just the chase.*

Perhaps you're better off. Yes, better off indeed, a voice whispered.

I looked over at Sarah; she just sat there, sort of spaced out, and quiet. I think the environment was a lot for her to take in. *Maybe we do have a few things in common.*

Beauregard reiterated what I said earlier and added to it. He was more interested in that.

"Dude, mystic worlds, man. That's got me thinking. Have you ever, like, looked into quantum theory?"

I sat back on the couch and grinned. *Of course, I have.* Before I actually came out of my shell, that's all I'd do; read and study. I was following a whisper, a call, perhaps a message. It tugs away at my soul--memories of a lost world in the days of old. Images, shouts, colors, and places jumbled into my mind at a rapid pace that I couldn't follow, but then there it was again--*the amulet of nine stones.*

Julian snapped his finger, and said, "Dude, what were you going to say?"

I shook. Sarah giggled, and Jules snorted. Jenny laughed, too. They pretty much all did. Jules jumped up, and rattled in my face, "You're fuckin' spacin' out, man. You're whiggin' out, dude."

Hell, I laughed, too.

"I know, I know, but, uh, I guess, I was saying, when it comes to quantum theory, anything that could possibly happen, has happened, just on a separate paradigm, plane, reality, whatever you want to call it; it exists there, somewhere, and that's pretty much the source of déjà vu. It's the feeling of crossing timelines or parallel events rubbing together. The tetrahedron cube of reality bursts asunder, and everything is divided. It's like everything is true, but all is nothing."

Julian nodded, and grumbled, "Dude, that's fuckin' deep, man."

"That's not even the tip of the iceberg," I replied.

Everybody burst out laughing, and Jenny yelled, "Let's smoke another one!"

"Fuck, yeah."

"Alright, alright."

"Myah! Pass the joint, wise guy! See?!"

We jumped around everywhere; physically and mentally. We even ended up in some crazy guy's trailer. He had chickens under shopping carts, which was weird. Half of the building was literally gone. *Perhaps, a car crashed into it, and this guy never got around to fixing it,* I thought to myself, but I wasn't sure. The dude was definitely giving the girl's uncomfortable looks, though. *What kind of friends do you have, Derek?*

Jules didn't mind sitting by me now, but there was still her friend. I blushed at the thought of her. I knew I had a crush.

Harold sat in his chair, and belched, then picked up the conversation. He was getting' lit off that Blue Lotus, too.

"So what kind of customers do ya'll got? I mean, how do ya do business?"

Harold had been rambling for hours it seemed like, and nobody else could get a word in.

He continued on, "Because I'm tellin' ya ain't no better customers than your people. Your family, brothers, sisters, cousins, uncles, kids, grandma—whatever. If they really love you they'll never call the law on ya. They might shoot ya or pinch your bag every once in awhile, but my son knows better than that. He's been buying pot off me for goin' on around ten years now, and the little feller just turned seventeen, but my second cousin Sue Bob let me tell ya about her. She's the finest stripper the Foxhole has ever done seen, and out of all my cousins, third ones, and all; she's the best piece of ass I've ever had, boy, I'll tell ya what."

At that point we were all pretty lost, shocked even, but thankfully Derek's phone rang, interrupting it all. He answered, listened, then said, "For real? There's a Halloween party goin' down?"

He paused, then continued, "Shit, bet. We'll be there in a few."

I didn't even know it was Halloween. *That's why all the crows lie across the fields. I can feel him near. It's his time of year.*

Derek gave me the directions, and we headed for the party. Apparently, it was in a cornfield. *Cool and ominous all at the same time.*

We stopped at a gas station that sold liquor on the way there; *it was time to drink.*

I parked at the pump, and we all got out.

Jules ran up to me and hugged my arm.

"Can you buy me a pack of smokes, please?"

She was all giggly and smiley. It made me feel warm inside when she was like that, but it never lasted long. After she got what she wanted, she'd usually run off and go on the hunt again. I knew what it was. I wasn't stupid, but that's just how most folks are. *They bleed you dry and steal your time.* Everyone you come into contact with uses you for something; *good or bad.*

"Sure, I can," I replied.

I walked; smiling with her arm in mine. She pulled away and jumped up in excitement.

"You're the bestest friend ever."

Yay. Friends.

I choked and swallowed.

Sarah hollered, "Hey, no fair! What about me?"

Jules uttered back, "Oh, you're my girl. Don't worry. I mean, I know me and Jeremy broke up, but we can still be friends and have fun."

She dated Sarah's brother? That dude?

I couldn't believe it. I went to ask more, but suddenly an older lady around forty somethin' rushed us.

Derek jerked his hand in his hoodie pocket, but he simmered down quick; processing the sudden unexpected.

She held up a printed out missing poster and asked us, "Have you seen this boy? His name is Boston Reynolds. He's been missing for two weeks now."

Jules clutched at my arm and looked up at me. I looked down at her. *It feels so nice to be close to somebody.* Then, I looked behind me. *Sarah;* she was blushing.

"Have you seen this, kid?" I asked them.

They all edged closer and looked.

Sarah shook her head, no, and Derek said, "Nah, I ain't seen him."

"I haven't either," I looked back at her and replied. I stared at the held up picture. *That kid looks cool,* I thought to myself. *It's a shame he's missing. I wonder what happened to him?*

The lady dropped the picture and gazed at the cement, then began sobbing and crying. I felt so bad for her.

"Hey, don't—"

A sharp wail screeched out of her, and as if by instinct or whatever, I walked up to her, and put my hand on her shoulder.

"Hey, it's okay. Don't cry. I'm sure you'll find him, and he'll be alright."

I did the best that I could to console her. I slipped the paper out of her hands and patted her again as I gazed at Boston's picture. *Perhaps this is how I turn my life around. I'm going to be a detective, and solve missing person cases. Yeah, yeah, yeah, that's who I'm gonna be; a true hero.* There was even a reward at the bottom. *Two thousand dollars, last seen in Putnam.* It said more than that, but that's all I got out of it.

"What do ya say I keep this picture so me and my friends can help you look for 'em? I actually do stuff like this all the time."

224

It was true, I'd found somebody's cat once. It was caught in a tree, and I helped it down. When I got to the bottom, though, the little fiend clenched its nails into my leg and screeched; *it was a little demon.* I swung my leg around screaming and sent the beast scurrying off into the road. The owner saw the whole thing and ran down the walk smiling and hollered. "Jingles!"

A diesel truck fired up the road and crunched the thing to smithereens within seconds right in front of us. The kitty was reduced to a flat red pool of hair. The owner gasped, and screamed, "No! Mr. Jingles!"

He halted his jog and burned his gaze at me from across the street; then pointed his finger, and screamed, "It's all your fault! You scared him off into the road!"

I panicked.

"N-no, I didn't! I swear I didn't! That truck came out of nowhere, man!"

"You're a monster," he panted, and screamed, "a monster!"

"No, I'm not," I whined, heaving and fleeing the scene. *I'm really not. I can't believe it happened to another one; every time I try to do good everything goes bad. So very bad.*

The memory of it all scarred me, and my consciousness returned to the present. *To the woman and the missing boy.* The lady looked up at me and asked, "You'd do that?"

"Do what?" I asked; perplexed.

"Help me find my son; you'd do that?"

"Oh yeah," I nodded, "I definitely can. We're actually headed to a Halloween party right now. I'll show the picture around and ask folks around there if anybody has seen him."

The lady hugged me suddenly, and it took me off guard.

225

"Thank you. It really means a lot."

It made me feel good.

I took the picture, folded it in my pocket, and the lady thanked me again. Then she left in her minivan.

Derek said, "Wow, it feels like ever since we started smokin' this Blue Lotus, crazy shit has been happenin'. We really gonna look for the kid?"

"Yeah, sure," I nodded, "why not?"

Jules jumped up, and shouted, "We're detectives now!"

"Yeah, like the hardy kids or somethin'," I laughed. Sarah kept blushing at me. I looked nervously away and darted for the gas station door.

We clamored inside, all at the same time. From the jump, I knew it was a bad idea. The store clerk was eyeing us down. He looked gray. *There's something strange about him,* I thought to myself. His cheeks appeared sunken, and his eyes had a yellowish hue. It was a dark day to begin with, but for some reason, the shadows seemed thicker in the store; almost as if we were standing in a large crowd, but no one was around. *Odd. There's no cars driving by either. It's as if we're cut off from the world; fallen into a gap, a tear within reality.*

I wasn't sure what to do, but we were there and I figured I'd give it a go and try to buy some smokes first before we got our hopes up for alcohol. The cashier's menacing eyes tore through me. I'm pretty sure he was a member of the Chilean mob or somethin' like that. I took a deep breath and asked him for a pack of Newport one-hundreds. He got me on the spot, just like I thought he would.

"I.D.," he asked coldly.

"I a-ain't got it on me, but I swear I'm old enough, honest."

"No, I.D. No sale."

I shuddered.

"Come on, man, don't be like that. I—"

The clerk's eyes bulged, outlining the ghoulish looking wrinkles on his face. He slammed his fist on the counter, and yelled, "No, I.D., no buy!"

The girls laughed by the shelves and coolers. Derek was looking for a bag of chips in the aisle behind me; he had the munchies.

"You good, man," Derek looked towards the counter and asked. He was staring at the store clerk, with his hand in his sweater pocket still. He still hadn't said a thing about having a gun. It was like his personal little secret; *a litany for the shadows.*

Tears welled up in my eyes, and I turned around. I panicked, clenching my teeth as my nails dug through the air while I talked with my hands.

"No, I'm not," my eyebrows flew up, "I'm all over the place. I just want a beer and a smoke. I'm gonna die without it."

I flipped back around to face the cashier; shoes squeaking on the tile.

"You're a thief of joy, mister. I'm out of here."

A grin crept up on his face, and he stood frozen, staring at me; the air grew void. *Strange, it feels like there's another presence contrary to his own sitting behind that gaze of his. I can see it. I can feel it. Something or someone else is affecting him.*

The cashier was still motionless, save for the grin. It was still present. *Very unsettling.* Derek saw it, too.

"Yo, what the fuck? This dude done broke like a robot or somethin' up there. He ain't even breathin'."

"Get out," the cashier suddenly grumbled. It was deep, grave, and dry.

"O-okay, man. We're leavin'. Just—"

"Get out!"

The cashier howled, and I rushed for the door.

"Bail out, bail out!"

The others followed. Derek first, he threw a bag of chips at the counter. The cashier went to barking and acting crazy. Jules followed next and mooned him with her left cheek. I didn't miss it; I'll admit. *Wow, a star tattoo that's really cool. It's like a target.* She giggled and shot out of the door; the cashier rambled more behind the counter, shaking his fist. Sarah, on the other hand, didn't do a thing but run.

We all hopped in the ride and snatched the doors closed quickly. The store clerk emerged next, wild-eyed and vicious; wielding a dangerous mop. I flicked the key, switched to drive, and took off. The tires squealed, and we darted out into the road; someone went to blaring their horn. To the left, a car sped towards us, and Derek screamed like a girl. It missed us by an inch.

"Gee whiz, man, did you see that shit?! Man, people really need to watch where there going."

That scream, though.

"Damn, bro, I thought we were dead," Derek shook still.

Jules giggled, "Oh my gosh, dude! You need to learn to drive."

Adjusting the rearview mirror, I pointed it at Jules and laughed, "What do you mean? I'm an expert, really."

Jules shook her head and giggled under her breath, "Ummm, no you're not."

"How would you know?" I asked.

Jules shrugged her shoulders.

"Because I've seen you in gym class. You're not really good at anything," Jules laughed.

My smile fell, and I gulped. *That was harsh, and it cut like a knife.*

Derek put his hand down and gazed at the CD book.

"Okay, then."

His eyes bulged, and he awkwardly tried to occupy himself with a search in the music library.

Sarah wrinkled up her face in disgust; shooting Jules a dark look. She didn't even notice. I could see her gazing at me in the rearview mirror. There was so much sympathy in her eyes.

Sarah said, "Well, I know I sure did learn a lot from you today; listening to the way you talk to people."

I blushed and tapped my fingers subtly against the wheel. Jules turned her head and burned a hard look at Sarah; she looked jealous.

"Really? You mean about the quantum stuff and all that?" I replied. Finally, somebody is interested in what I have to say.

"Yeah, that stuff was cool," Sarah replied, "your passion really comes out when you talk about it."

"It does, though," Derek agreed as he flipped through the CD book.

"You need to be a preacher or somethin', like some new gospel type of shit; bring 'em the word."

I laughed, "Come on, man. I ain't no deliverer of good news; that ain't me. Plus, any type of new spiritual movement ends up bein' a cult; like some drink the Kool Aid type of shit, and the priest starts fuckin' everybody's wives. It happens all the time."

Jules burst out laughing, mimicking distress, "Oh, come, father! Take me!"

Sarah giggled, and Derek just let it blow over his shoulder. I laughed for good measure to entertain her, but I didn't really find it funny; *sort of corny, actually.*

"It's like that, though," I flipped the blinker and continued, "honestly, I think the best model for being a spiritual teacher is to hide things in plain sight; it's there, and it's not. Sort of like, 'those who have ears, let them here.' If I wanted to be a teacher, I'd be like Enoch, before the flood, y'know, pop in and pop out every once in a while, but pretty much stay away from everybody. That's the only way you can really do away with the common idol worship that happens between teacher and student. Like the AA (not the alcoholics, but the order) or some sort of society like that. I don't know. Many preach in public to gain admiration, sages seek solace in the one, and deliver their messages periodically, by word or in tomes."

What shall thee be? Priest or prophet?

Derek kept flipping through the pages.

"I don't have a clue what you're talking about, man. You lost me."

"Yeah, I know. I get carried away sometimes, I guess."

Sarah started to speak, and Jules snapped her neck at her again; she didn't care. Sarah kept on with what she wanted to say.

"You should really write a book; I think you'd be a good writer, and the things you say and talk about, it makes you think, it really does."

Sarah paused for a moment, staring out of the window; I did, too. *She wants to say something.* The crows pecked with their beaks across everything. *It's all blanketed in shadow,* I thought to myself, but right before Jules began to speak, Sarah broke the silence.

"These birds are everywhere this time of year," she muttered, "they make everything seem so dark."

"Hey, it's Halloween, ain't it," I eagerly chimed back, "we need 'em. I sort of like 'em, to be honest."

I smiled to myself, and Derek popped in a mix; only the CD player wouldn't take it. The sound switched to the radio, and there was static. I banged on the dash to fix it, and it stopped; the CD skipped, and Gucci Mane popped off.

"Okay, well, that was weird," I uttered.

"Hell yeah, it was," Derek said, slapping the CD book closed.

Jules laughed in the back and called my ride a hooptie.

Covering up my shame, I laughed, "It's the ghosts, man, I'm tellin' ya. Something' is goin' on today."

"No, there ain't. It's just the smoke," Derek denied.

I chattered back, "Maybe, who knows, but—"

Suddenly, Jules cut me off, by hollering, "Who wants drinks?!"

She pulled a couple of thin bottles of Captain Morgan she'd kyped off the shelf back at the store.

Derek gasped excitedly, "Shit, you got one for me?!"

Jules perked up, and gave him the stare, and handed him one, slowly; teasing him a little.

"Of course, I didn't forget about you."

They all unscrewed their caps, and my lap were empty.

I snapped over my shoulder, "Where's mine?"

Jules shrugged, and took a chug, then said, "Sorry, I didn't have time to grab you one. You pissed the guy off."

My eyes narrowed, my voice shifted, and rattled on its own.

"Ok, then. Well, I guess me and you are sharin' then, because if you don't let me have one, I ain't givin' you no more smoke."

I reached my hand back and demanded it.

"So give it up."

She reluctantly handed me the bottle.

Crossing her arms, she opposed, but then she smiled. I took a swig.

"That one's yours, anyway. I was just messin' with ya."

She leaned up between the seats and kissed me behind the ear.

"That was kind of sexy."

That's all it takes, I thought to myself. *I don't even feel like I'm the one that said it.*

You didn't, the man in the hat chattered. *It feels good doesn't it? For me to take control? You know you love it; y'know you like the taste of it. It's so sweet.*

I shimmied around with the bill of my hat and made it straight; shadowing my eyes. Then I rambled onward. It was nearly uncontrollable.

"I'm turnin' into a new man," I muttered to myself.

A grin seared across my face. My throat croaked, then I shivered and swallowed. Something heavy was weighing down on the back of my neck, and I couldn't control my thoughts.

Suddenly, my words didn't feel like my own. I'm not sure if it was from fatigue, hunger, smoking all day, or being nearly buzzed drunk, but it lowered my defenses on all levels, and I felt like I was losing control. *Another influence is taking over. I'm no longer myself.*

My neck twisted towards Derek in the passenger seat, and my eyes fell upon his sweater pocket.

"You don't have to hide it, y'know," I told him, "I know you got a piece on you."

Derek looked surprised at first, but he wasn't stupid. He knew that I knew the whole time. Neither of us wanted to say anything about it, though. We both chose to ignore the elephant in the room.

"Let me see it," I said.

He reluctantly handed me the gun, and Jules shouted excitedly in the back when the sunlight glinted across the barrel.

"I wanna see it next," she said; Sarah looked uneasy.

The CD player switched to the next song, and the beat cranked up to M.I.A's "Paper Planes."

"Ewww," I licked the corners of my lips, and grinned, "I like this song."

I rolled down the window when the chorus came. I was feeling it. *Pure and utter bliss as the wind blows.*

I stuck my arm out into the cool breeze, pointing the gun up in the air, and pulled the trigger.

Bang. Then another bang, bang.

I cackled as the wind blew in my face.

Derek yelled, "You're crazy, bro! You're gonna get the po po on our ass. Give me the gun back!"

I gave it back with little to no reluctance; still laughing—*always laughing.*

"Ahhh, come on, pal. Ya gotta give in and let go every once in a while."

Then came a flash of some distant memory that wasn't my own. A dark Studebaker from the 1930s raced down a dirt road that ran through a thick line of trees and it was giving chase to another vehicle in front of it. Clouds of dust billowed behind each set of wheels, "Willow Weep for Me" hummed across the radio. An old Tommy gun hung out of the passenger side window. Bullets thundered ahead from its barrel and terrible cackling ripped through the air. Then, I saw him, he was holding the gun, the man in the hat. He licked his lips and bit them into a sneer. Everything went black, but the thundering bullets and cackling continued.

"I can't see! I can't see," I screamed. I pulled off to the side of the road, or at least hoped that I did. I heard the gravel crumple beneath the tires. I rubbed my eyes, but I was still blind.

Panicking, Derek asked, "What's goin' on? Are you alright?!"

The girls pretty much said the same. I threw open the driver side door to catch some air, rubbing my eyes still, and said, "I d-don't know, b-but you gotta drive to the party. I—I'm n-not feelin' too good."

"You still wanna go?" Derek asked. All I could do was nod my head. My vision returned to a faint blur. I could see enough to make my way towards the passenger side. I fell into the seat as Derek took the wheel. Cold sweat was pouring out of me. I could feel it, and I shivered. Derek pulled off, and I rested my head back.

Easy, easy. I'm here to help. Just play the puppet for a few, and I'll handle things.

No, you can't. A thought of my own broke through.

Ahhh, but you're wrong there; you're full of it, spirits that is. Why do you think they call the hard liquor that? You drown yourself until you stumble. Defenseless and helpless as a babe; you fall for it every time. Don't forget who your caretaker is, now. I've always been there. Ever since the day. Why you, remember, don't you? Recall what we did? The little deal we made. Why don't you recall? The deathly fall off the log?

CHAPTER XVI:

RUNNIN' UP THAT HILL

Everything went black, and the hollow abyss swallowed me up. I could feel myself falling into the ever familiar limitless nothing. Weightless and untethered from the confines of the natural, physical world; I fell into another. I landed in a dark hallway; the air was chilly, and the stabbing ether made my soul tingle with an ebbing vibration. There I found myself; in a chasm within the void.

I lifted myself up from a puddle. There was nothing around, save for my reflection that lie within the shadows upon the ground.

The puddle grew and turned into a pool. Colors swirled, and the picture shifted. The sun was bright, and I saw myself in the pretty place again; within the golden grove, my special place that was now lost to me. *I've been locked out. I don't ever think I'll make my way back.*

I was a little boy again, sitting in my father's lap. The memory played like an echo. I'd always wonder to myself, *Is this place heaven? The golden grove from my dreams. I've never been certain, but it sure does feel like it.*

I gripped his warm hand, smiled, then I looked up, and told him, "I want to go on a real adventure someday. Do you think I ever will? Will you go with me if I do, daddy?"

He smiled and gripped my free hand back.

"Of course I will. I'll follow you wherever you go."

I pulled my hands away and hugged his shoulders.

"Promise? You think we'll really make it? Go on a real adventure someday, I mean?"

He kissed me on the cheek and said, "We will if we truly believe we can. You can go anywhere. Always remember, through the Lord you can do anything."

"I will, daddy, I will."

The waters rippled, and the image fluttered away. My father's words turned to whispers, and I could barely make them out. *The hollow hole swallowed everything up again.*

"I'll love you always and forever, don't ever forget that."

The white stallion falls. Sunken within the swamp. The boy becomes lost; through the mud, in the dark he digs.

The pool shook and rippled once again. I could hear a little boy crying, he was lost within a dark forest. The sharp limbs of ancient trees whistled above his head, and the sweeping wind cut across his chapped cheeks.

I saw myself, still as a kid, huddled under a large oak tree. I lay my face upon my knees and I was sobbing.

"He got rid of them. Chip Hazard and Archer are gone. They were my favorite toys."

I wiped my face dry, and continued, "They were my only friends."

I remember that day; I tried to run away. I'd come home from my grandmas, and a bunch of my stuff was gone. I shifted through the toy box and tried to find them, but they were missing.

"Where are they?" I balled my fists up and screamed.

"Don't yell at me," my stepfather pointed his finger and hollered.

I didn't care. My dad bought me those toys, and they were one of the few things I had left of him. They were there with me that night; when his last words were spoken. *Screaming in the dark, the scars make their mark.* My little sister screamed, too. I shuffled my way across the carpet toward her and sat by her pack-n-play with my toys. I didn't know what to do, but Chip Hazard and Archer would protect us.

I'd always kept them close since that night. Two years had passed, and now they were lost to me too. It was partially my fault. I should have never left them behind.

"You knew they were my favorite," I wailed, "you knew it and you got rid of them! Y-y-you d-did it to hurt me!"

My stepfather gritted his teeth and snapped, "You're a spoiled little brat. You had too many toys, anyway. What you're looking for in that box is gone; we donated it all to the Salvation Army."

My eyes felt hot, and I shook. Then I cried, "You could have gotten rid of everything; I don't care! But not those two! You knew they were my favorite! You knew!"

He charged towards me with his hands out and tried to grab me.

I threw my hands up and crunched down; he had that look. He was going to smack me or take out his belt. I screamed, "No! No! No!"

My feet moved faster than my thoughts and I ran.

"Don't run away from me!"

I fumbled out of the door, crying; I didn't know where I was going. All I could see were the woods. *I can be safe there.*

My stepfather's yelling dwindled as I made some distance.

"You better run! And when you come back you're in for it!"

I ran as far as I could until I made it to the oak tree. I came undone for so long my face had swelled. Then I heard a whisper. *Wanderer, where art thou? Wanderer in the Wilderness, where hath thou been?*

Then, the whisper turned into a soft tune; a woman began to sing.

The words weren't in English, they were in a strange language; *it felt all too familiar, like the words from the book. Forgive my veiled words they hail from a language before. A magician's song that opens a gate to a door.*

"Ils umd iadpil tia ils umd."

The words of the tune carried through the wind as it blew through the trees. It was so soothing. The soft beat of drums followed.

"Mirc aqlo erm oma ils umd."

The words came again, and I followed them.

"Loholo mirc nonca, Ahnzerah, ils umd."

The leaves crumpled underfoot, and I followed the words of the beautiful melody, until I heard the sound of rushing water, running its way down the creek.

"Iadoias, galsagen, gahoachma."

The words flowed again, and I came to a log that lay across the waters. It stretched all the way to the other side of the creek.

"Ils umd, Ahnzerah, ils umd."

I heard all the words again; *such a soothing tune.* It reminded me of the before place from my dreams. It was the same language the people there spoke.

I climbed onto the log and tried to balance myself as I crossed, but there was a scream suddenly, an ear-piercing screech. It startled me, and my foot slipped on the moss. I fell into the rushing creek and struggled. The water was high from all the rain. I still didn't know how to swim.

My eyes popped open under the galloping stream as I struggled and fought for air. I could still see the trees, but everything was wavy; running along in dancing colors under the rushing water. I panicked and I couldn't reach the surface, but then I saw a man. He was wearing a wide-brimmed hat in the distance. He stood tall, straight and narrow along the bank, and I fluttered my hands in the water towards him; hoping he would help me. *Closer and closer; I was almost there, but not quite yet. I need some air.*

The man in the hat kneeled down slowly and propped his elbows upon his knees. His hands hung between his legs, but I still couldn't see his face. It was dark, hidden below the wide brim of his purple hat. He was watching me drown.

I lifted my head above the water for a few seconds, just to plead.

"Help me," I screamed.

The man in the hat stretched his fingers out slowly above the flow, but he didn't reach down. I snatched at his hand and grabbed it. Then he lifted me up.

The water splashed everywhere, and I gasped for air. My shoulders heaved. I huffed in and out until I made myself a believer. *I am still alive.*

I turned my head slowly towards the man in the hat as the water dripped from my hair. He was grinning; I couldn't see his eyes still.

"Decided to go for a swim today, eh?"

I shook my head and said, "No, mister, honest. I hate the water. Y'know, since I can't swim and all."

The man in the hat bit his lip, and the left corner of his mouth edged back.

"Say, what are you doin' all the way out in the woods playin' by yourself, anyway?"

I blinked my eyes fast, and water trickled down my chin. The dry leaves on the ground began to soak beneath me.

I stuttered, "I j-just—I d-don't know. I just got s-scared that's all. Did you hear that scream?"

The man in the hat ignored my question, then asked, "Scared enough to come all the way out into these dark desolate woods all by yourself?"

My eyes widened, and I nodded.

"Y-yeah. I'm u-used to scary things, though, e-especially at home."

The man in the hat's grin widened.

"What kind of scary things? What's got you so shook up?"

I didn't want to say, but the ghosts. I've been accustomed to dealing with familiar spirits all of my life, but I had never talked with one. After the night my father died, only then the bad ones came. I lost my innocence. Evil was a true thing and I discovered that the world wasn't a good place after all. It was like a bite of the apple, a rite of passage. Even the people you love have the capacity to maim your life forever. *But isn't that love? Doesn't it all result in pain; from one form to another?*

I was afraid of this man in a hat before me, but I thought he might be able to help me with the tormentors that scared me at night. *The creepers in the shadows.*

I shivered from the chill, and my shoulders quivered. The man in the hat was eagerly awaiting my reply. I stuttered, "W-well—wait. P-promise you won't laugh or t-think I'm dumb."

The man in the hat did just that. He laughed; cackled even, then grumbled, "Well, you don't have to worry yourself. I already got that out of the way."

Then his grin melted away, and his tone changed. He still made it sound soft, but his teeth began to clench, and his eyes were still hidden beneath the shadow of his purple brim.

"Go on. Out with it," the man in the hat snapped.

240

I gulped, "W-well, ya see, mister. I see ghosts sometimes, really scary ones. Not all the time, but usually at night. They're really mean and bad. Sometimes it feels like they wanna hurt me."

The man in the hat hummed and nodded slowly.

"Mmmm, you got some baddies on your hands, then. Don't you?"

I nodded back fast, and replied, "Some really, really big baddies. They're the worst."

I didn't want to say the words, but I had to ask. There was something different about him; this man in the hat.

I stuttered, "A-are y-you a ghost, too?"

The man in the hat's lips peeled back and the corners of his mouth nearly touched the tips of his ears.

"It depends. Are we friends? I can only be honest with a friend; someone I can trust. Know what I mean?"

Cold chills ran up my arms and the goosebumps bit. I gulped hard to knock my stutter back, but I couldn't help the condition.

"Y-yeah, w-we're friends. Gotta be, I guess. I mean, you saved me."

The man in the hat edged closer, and I could see the yellow flash in his green eyes. They mirrored the chasing gaze of a wolf.

"Then, we are, and I am," he crooned.

The man in the hat frowned, and his voice softened into a sing-songy tune. He pressed the back of his hand against his forehead and tilted back. It was all an act of terrible theater.

"I've been dead for a while now. It makes me so very sad. Sometimes I feel like I don't have any friends at all."

I smiled at him and said, "Well, you don't have to be sad anymore, mister, because now I'm your friend. You're a good ghost, I can tell. You wouldn't have helped me if you weren't."

The man in the hat jerked his head forward and gave my shoulder a quick tap.

"Ya got that right. Say, you mind if I come home with you? It sure does get lonely in these cold, dark woods."

I was more than happy to have a new friend. I jumped up and grabbed his hand.

"I guess so. It could be like a sleepover!"

The man in the hat's eyes widened, and he grinned down at me as he stood up; with his hand in mine. We began strolling back towards home away from the rushing creek behind us, and I asked him, "Say, mister, what's your name, anyway?"

The leaves shuffled under our feet and he swung our arms back and forth between us.

"I'm just a man in a hat, kid. Pleased to meet ya."

The sun shone through the trees, bleeding across the shuffling leaves that twirled around our ankles. The light was settling and the day was beginning to retire into twilight.

"Hey, since you're a ghost, can you help me keep the baddies away?"

The shadow replied, "I sure can. I'll keep all the baddies away."

"Down with the baddies," I proclaimed.

The specter's voice lowered and grumbled, "Down with 'em all."

Then came the mirror. *You are me and I am you.* Over and over again repeatedly. *You are me and I am you.* From that moment on, I recognized the man in the hat as my shadow. All of us have one, but this story goes beyond mere psychology. We became tethered through the familiarity.

Inside I knew that he had always been there because of the fear. He is my pain, my sadness, and my sorrow. *I can* now taste the vengeful hunger of the wolf upon my tongue. He is my hate, my anger, and my wrath. *I love thee shadow show me the path.*

"We're the same; you and I," my shadow whispered. I was no longer a little boy, but another lost youth; a teenager who had dropped out of school. The man in the hat coaxed me further.

"You see me in your head; I live in your nightmares, and I whisper in your ear. Terrible deeds that must be done. My, how the chaos can be so much fun."

"Lead the way," I uttered back in the dark, shallow puddle. I didn't know what I was saying. Mist lie all around and the vacuum took an echoing breath; I heaved in the hollow air.

"W-where w-where am I?"

"Come on, we've been here before," a voice echoed, and steps stomped; splashing in the puddle.

"You rarely remember, but we often meet, y'know?"

The voice echoed near, and dark boots became clear. A figure; a man in a long dark coat and a wide-brimmed purple hat slowly emerged from the thickening fog.

"I slip more into you like a glove every time."

The man in the hat's white teeth shone under the shadow of his dark brim, and he continued, "Why do you still hang on, huh? What good has it really done you?"

I know you. It was always you. You're always near, you keep my head unclear.

The man in the hat laughed, "Stop it, you fool, I can hear your thoughts, y'know? We share the same mind."

"What happened?"

I snapped further, "How did I get here?"

"You drowned yourself again, boy. Remember the old Hallows' Eve party you were goin' to? You're a walking husk right now."

The man in the hat pulled his coat tighter, and smiled, "Don't worry. I'm pulling some strings and making sure everything stays level."

"What did you do?" I snapped.

"Nothing, relax," the shadow ushered in a wave.

"I'm never committed to doing anything too far out of character. I just plant the seed, and, y'know, speak what's really on your mind."

"I've lost friends because of you," I shouted back. My voice echoed in the vast void.

"Oh yeah? Who really needs 'em, they were weak; they couldn't handle the steam, but you—oh you; you just don't have the strength to take the world by storm. You have so much raw potential that you don't use, even refuse it, yes you do."

The edge of his dark cloak flapped, and he gritted a grin.

"Shameful. That's what you outta be. We could be so much if you'd just let me lead the way. I can get you back to that heaven; that special place, just like I promised."

"You tricked me," I shouted back; *digging in the well, I find myself in hell, seeing through the eyes of the little boy I wish I could tell.*

"I didn't trick you," the man in the hat whispered back, then he raised his voice into a rattle.

"We are bound now; shadow and host."

"But w-why—why me," I stuttered, then gulped, "you used me."

"Those spirits plagued you," my shadow replied.

"And you wanted rid of them. I did what I said, didn't I? Remember how you felt forsaken? Oh, well, you remember that, you think of it every day. The screams in the dark, they made their mark on you."

"But you weren't around then," my voice shook.

"Before I lost him—my father, I didn't see any of you, but after—why did you and your shadow men come after?"

"Your cries lie unheeded; the guardians forsook you. Your familiars in the time before even abandoned you. You became the lost son. We smelled your grief—like hounds after blood. All of us, even them, the ones that were harvested. Oh, what a little magician you were. You were like a lighthouse, boy."

Remembering it all I stuttered, "Y-you—you, w-what you did to them, though. That was t-terrible. It was horrifying."

The man in the hat clenched his teeth.

"They serve a better purpose now; harvested in the mind of the hive."

His yellow eyes burned under the brim, and he grinned.

"You're so very wrong, though," the man in the hat continued.

"About all of this; I've always been near. Even before the death of your papa. You know it, but you deny it. Haven't you ever wondered what connects us? Why we're really such a match? You saw it when you read that letter. He had it, too—a scar carved in the blood; an old curse of the crow."

The figure of his form dwindled away into the mist; and his voice echoed into a whisper, chattering across my mind before I could implore for more.

"I believe our time is up. See you in our next session, and oh—enjoy the treat. I'm certain you'll love it."

CHAPTER XVII:

WHEN DOVES CRY

My nostrils burned, and I dug my knuckles under the tip of my nose. Sniffling and shaking, I came back to, and hollered, "Whoa! What was that?!"

Chuckles echoed within the confines of the bathroom, and Jules giggled on my shoulder. They spread out lines of white powder on the edge of the sink. I gasped and smacked the tip of my nose, and dusty stuff brushed into my palm.

"Did I just do cocaine?" I wailed.

Everyone laughed again. I began to panic.

"Calm down," this kid with a key around his neck said. He was holdin' the bag, *an eight ball in fact.*

"It's good, right?" he asked.

"Damn right it's good," Jules cut in giggling.

What if they laced it, my thoughts raced. My eyes darted and teetered across the faces in the bathroom. *I don't trust any of you. Not a—where's Derek and Sarah?*

Jules bounced off my shoulder and over to the guy with the blow. She ran her fingers down his forearm and he grinned. Jules' eyes danced from his lips to his waist.

"Can I have some more?"

The kid with the key handed her a card to edge another line up with. Jules snatched it right away and rolled a crinkled dollar bill up. She snorted the coke up quick. *Everything is happening so fast,* I thought to myself.

The kid with the key walked up behind Jules and smacked her on the right cheek, and gripped. Jules still leaning against the sink; blushed, and she grinned at the grab as she arched her back.

"That's the last free one; you gotta pay for the next one," the kid muttered.

What is happening right now? my thoughts chattered. Laughter from the others in the room reverberated and rung across my eardrums; a loud piercing sound came scratching away at my soul. I nearly went to shove the kid off her, but Jules didn't want to be saved. She turned around and hugged his neck; biting her lip.

"Don't worry. I'll pay you all the way up."

They kissed each other, and she fell into his arms. The other girls in the room looked back and forth at each other, slowly preparing to make their exit. The guys that were in the bathroom simmered a little, and stare like hungry dogs. I stood stiff and shaking in shock. *It's like waking up in a nightmare. Everything is so sudden.*

"What are you doin', Jules," I chattered; confused and displaced.

The kid with the key let her go, and she slid away slightly, still hanging on to his arm.

"What?"

She asked, "What's the problem? We're just havin' fun."

"Y-y-you—you—"

The kid with the key smiled, and said, "Oh yeah, I forgot this is your, dude, right?"

My eyes darted back between him and Jules both; the air grew thick and the room felt tense. *I have to escape.*

Jules laughed, "He's not my man; we're just friends."

"You," I snapped, but choked again, "you—"

My eyes burned, and they felt hot; seeing her in his arms made me sick. *I can't take it. I can't take it in here anymore.*

I rushed to the door and swung it open, ushering myself out into the hall. I was in somebody's house. Who knows who's; kids shuffled and music blared from downstairs. Pacing quickly, my eyes darted for the steps.

Jules hollered after me, "Hey, where are you goin'?!"

I stumbled against the wall. My legs felt like rubber. I nearly fell down the flight. Jules darted out of the room and chased after me.

"Hey, come back!"

I reached the bottom of the steps and caught myself on the slip. A red solo cup teetered away; empty on the ground. Jules caught me by the arm, and pulled at me, asking again, "Where are you going?"

I jerked my arm away. *The ringing, the scratching in my ears. It just won't quit.*

"What was all that about?" I snapped, still stumbling in confusion.

"What?" Jules edged closer to me; staring back intently into my eyes.

"I was just playing around. The guy has free blow. I wasn't going to do anything with him. Besides, why does it matter? We're not together."

"I just," I stuttered," I just—"

Then I paused for a moment. *I can't process all of this right now,* I thought to myself, but still I continued.

"I just don't like seeing people like that. I could feel everyone in the room. All those guys wanted to take advantage of you. It was terrible. A—"

Jules hushed me, shhh-ing softly as she edged closer. I shivered when her cold hands landed softly under my elbows; it made me tingle.

"Just calm down. I came here with you, okay?"

I didn't breathe a word. The cocaine had me feeling numb. I became frozen in my thoughts. *She just doesn't know. She doesn't have to flaunt herself for other guys; she doesn't have to let them take advantage of her, it's okay. I want to help her, as a friend, or whatever. Being her boyfriend would be cool. She's nuts, I'm nuts, but—*

Jules interrupted the spiraling and caught me in the moment.

"I know you want me. That's why you get upset when other guys flirt with me, huh?"

I gulped, and shivered; her grip tightened on my arms. I couldn't answer her. *I love the way this powder makes me feel, but this is the worst time for it. Say something; you gotta say something.*

"Come on," Jules swayed closer, playing with the edge of my jacket.

"You know you want me."

Don't worry, a voice whispered, *just let go a little; follow me.* I felt a wave roll within. Starting from between the eyes, it rolled backward. Cold chills shivered down my spine. Suddenly, my arm began to move, but consciously I still felt glued. I was a passenger in my own vehicle. My arm wrapped around Jules' waist, and I said in a low hum, "Yeah, I do."

"Come here," she pulled and whispered.

Her hand slipped into mine, and she led me back up the steps and down the hall. I shivered behind her and followed. Everything felt so cold. A dancing dude in a shimmery jacket brushed past us in his shades and he hollered, "Oh shit, somebody fittin' to get fucked!"

He snapped his fingers, dancing backward, and hollered, "Hell yeah, my boy!"

Jules giggled and tightened her grip on my hand. She swung open a bedroom door, and deep savage moans erupted. She let the plank fall back quickly.

"Already occupied," she turned with a smile, and her eyes glittered back at me. *This can't be happening, this can't be happening.* My thoughts paced and my heart raced. The next door she tried, the room was empty. *I'm not sure I can do this,* I thought repeatedly, on and on.

We walked into the room and it had a cinnamon smell to it. The space was pretty bland, but it had a big TV so I figured it had to be the parent's room of the house or somethin'. The bed was big, though. It had a soft plush red magenta cover on it and posts edged upward towards the ceiling in each corner. I guess the posts were made like that to tie somebody up on or something, but I'm not sure. I mean, what else would they be used for? *I don't trust her enough for all of that, but—*

No, no, no, another thought interrupted. *It would be amazing, but you can't let it happen. She'll leave you here if you do.*

Jules pushed me towards the edge of the bed, and danced in front of me, then rubbed her hands just below my navel.

She hummed, "Come on."

Then, she pulled me in closer, and began kissing on my neck. I shivered, and my eyes rolled.

"You like that?"

"Y-y-yeah, I do," I stuttered, and smiled. Jules did, too, smile, that is. Then, she brought me in for a kiss; it was my first. Her lips were soft, and it caught me up in a trance; swept and curved into a whirl. *It feels so good.* Things got heavier, and she got excited. She was squeezing me hard, her nails dug into my arms. I shivered and heaved. *It feels so good, but I'm so scared.*

Her pants were already off and she went to undoing mine; my jeans fell with a thud. She kissed viciously at my neck more, and reached her hand down, pulling at me, but nothing was happening. I just wasn't getting there. She tried and tried, and tried, but nothing would work. I just couldn't get into it. *I'm so ashamed of myself. Even when I get the chance; I still can't make love.* Eventually, Jules shoved me back onto the edge of the bed, and she was pissed. She threw her hands up in the air and said, "What the fuck is wrong with you?! Huh?!"

My feet shuffled nervously, and my belt buckle jingled across the carpet. I rushed to pull my pants up to cover up the shame. I shivered, struggling, eyes growing heavy. *I'm not even a man,* I thought to myself. *I am nothing.*

Jules snapped, and threw her hands up in the air, rambling, "So you don't want to fuck me then? Well, you don't want anybody else to fuck me. So, what are we doing here?"

"I—I d-don't know," I stuttered, "I just—"

Pausing, I swallowed. I couldn't even look at her; I felt so powerless.

Jules stood still grinning at me, looking me up and down, then giggled, "You know what? You're the one with the issue. There's plenty of other boys around here that don't have that problem."

She edged toward the closed door, still grinning and giggling.

"Good luck with your problem, handsome."

She blew me a kiss, and busted out laughing, then swung the door open, and rushed back into the hallway. I stood stuck, frozen in self pity, my eyes grew hot. My teeth tore into the edge of my lip and I shivered. I even sniveled. *What a waste you are. When it comes down to it, you're not good for a thing. Y'know it and you see it. Come on, you're useless by yourself. You're—*

Tears ran down my cheeks and I wiped them away quickly. I jerked the hood up on my jacket and rushed out of the room. I had to get away from everybody. I ran down the hall past the same dancing guy again; I guess he was just going up the hallway, doing it repeatedly.

He snapped his fingers again at me, and pointed, "My boy! Oh shit! Was it good?"

I flung away my glare quickly in shame as I burned past the corner searching for the steps; *they were right to the left. I have to get out of here.*

Lil Jon reverberated across the walls; and colors danced from a bulb that was propped up on the kitchen island. I brushed past the beer bong players and didn't make eye contact with any of them; the floor assured that. I rushed to the door. Somebody hollered, "Hey, somebody change this shit. This song is boring!"

"Yeah! Yeah! Yeah!"

I slipped past quickly, jerked the door open, and rushed outside. The bitter cold bit my wet cheeks, and I shivered on the porch; gazing out, searching. *I don't have my keys. Where are Sarah and Derek?*

I stumbled off the porch and across the yard; head turning, searching—hoping to find a familiar face. Voices chattered all around, and I didn't know a soul. Walking along, I threw a glance at everyone, it probably appeared pleading, but I was antsy. *I just want to escape. Nobody looks friendly. We're here, in this night together, but there's always the great wall between me and the rest. I can read the glow, but I can't reach them. They're too apprehensive.*

My eyes popped open in shock, and a wave of major relief fell over me—sort of. Rambling among a couple of girls to the left, right by the cornfield, was Tony's girlfriend, Kayla. I rushed over to her immediately.

"I don't care! Where is he?! He always does this to me!" Kayla screamed.

One of her friends swung back her braids and wiggled her neck.

"Uh, uh, y'see, you the one that lets that fool get by with the shit. If I was you, I woulda done left his ass. Tony a motherfuckin' bitch, anyway."

Another girl cackled hysterically, "Girl, you're crazy."

"He is, though," Braids continued, "I could beat that fool's ass. He ain't shit, for real."

Kayla sobbed, "But I love him, though. I—"

"Hey, you seen Derek around or anything?"

I didn't mean to interrupt; I could tell she was upset, but my own anxiety swept across whatever type of restraint I had.

Kayla jerked her neck towards me, and tears bubbled in her eyes. Her gaze widened, and she snapped, "You mean you didn't go with them? Him and Tony took off in your car."

"What?!"

My eyes popped in panic, and my nails dug into my palm.

"They did, what?" I continued.

Kayla's chin danced repeatedly as she nodded.

"Yeah, they did! They took off and went somewhere. Did they tell you where?"

I shook my head. *There's no way for me to know. But what are they doing in my car while I'm here?* It all sort of pissed me off, really. *How could Derek do this to me,* I wondered to myself. *I got a quarter pound in that trunk, and he just ripped me off.*

My knuckles cracked, and my neck craned. I could feel the fury, and the man in the hat chattering rapidly. Wind blew through the dark starless sky and shook the corn stalks. *I can hear his cackling in the wind.* The crows cawed.

"Well, did they tell you where?"

Startled, I finally answered, shrugging my shoulders, "Honestly, I don't have a clue what's going on. I guess I blacked out, so maybe I let them take the car, but yeah, I don't know. Doesn't sound like something I would do."

Kayla hunched over and shivered. Her head shook, then she stomped her foot into the mud.

"I'm tired of him doing this to me," she snapped.

"Mmhmm," Braids chimed in, "you need to slap him the fuck up in front of everybody and embarrass his ass. That's what you need to do."

"Can you call Derek, please?" Kayla asked me.

"Yeah, sure, I was about to anyway."

I patted my pockets, but they were empty, and all the money I had was in the car. *Why would they take it?*

I wasn't even mad, just confused. It just didn't match up. *Did Derek really betray me?*

You'll see where things go soon enough, the man in the hat chattered.

I switched to a song in my head to muffle him up again; only thing is, it was getting harder to do that. It's like the barrier, the veil between us was growing thinner, and I was changing. *I'm not the same person. I can't feel the same light anymore.*

"I can't find my phone," I gave up and said. *The bedroom. Oh no. It probably fell out of my pants; the shame.*

Braids threw her hand on her hip, and cast a stern gaze my way, evaluating me.

"Well, did you leave it in the house? It's gotta be somewhere."

"Probably. I mean—"

Pausing, the madness of my anger settled, and a wave of grief washed over me. *I wasn't ready. She came at me too fast, but the embarrassment, though. What if she tells everybody? I'll never be able to show my face out in public again.*

"Well, you gonna go get it or what?" Braids snapped.

Startled, and a tad threatened, I nodded my head fast and headed back towards the house. Kayla stare after me, distraught and heartbroken. I really felt bad for her. I mean, Tony pretty much is an asshole, but I couldn't get over my own sorrow. I knew that I was a fool, and I was sinking, but I didn't even care. I let go, and fumbled my way back in the door. The beer pong game was still goin' on.

I rushed up the steps quickly. I didn't want to run back into Jules. I couldn't face her again. I made a beeline for the room and shuffled around the bed until I found my phone lying there; *just below* the *edge.*

I felt relieved for a mere second, but the shame flooded back. My eyes grew heavy as I stare at the carpet. *I'll never know love in this life; I can't even have sex.* It's as hopeless as a person could ever feel. *I'll never know what it feels like to share a connection with anybody.*

I walked back through the doorway, and tried to run for the steps, but the kid in the shimmery jacket sort of blocked me. He looked very disheveled, his sunglasses were twisted, and he wasn't dancing anymore. Gazing at me emptily, he hung his head quickly in shame, and went for the steps. There was moaning in the distance. It was coming from the bathroom.

I'm not sure why, but a foot stepped forward, and then another, edging closer to the bathroom door. The panting and moaning grew louder. It sounded like a pack. My fingers shook towards the edge of the door. I didn't want to look, but I had to. I had to know.

They were all naked. Jules was in there; with all of those guys. She shook her hair around smiling and licked her lips. A smack came, and another one stepped in front of her. I shuddered and fell back from the door. *No, no, no, no, no.*

I gasped and groaned; hot tears fell onto my cheeks, and I whimpered. *That's terrible, that's so horrible. There's so many of them.* I couldn't believe it or even fathom it. I shuffled quickly down the hallway. My heart was beating so fast. I ran down the steps and grew short of breath, and had to catch myself at the bottom. Everything was spinning.

But why would she do that? Why? I clutched my ears to stop the ringing and thought the same words repeatedly. *Why?*

People asked if I was okay, but they might as well have been speaking a foreign language. I just wasn't there. I saw a bottle of Black Velvet and slid it off the counter. I shuffled towards the door, dazed and in shock.

"Hey is that yours?" somebody yelled, but I didn't even answer.

I leaned my elbow into the door, and stomped wearily out onto the porch, and down the steps. The screen door slammed behind me. Kayla and her friends were waiting outside.

"Well? You get ahold of 'em?"

Braids was on me right away.

I stopped, frozen, without an answer; stuck and scarred by the scene in the bathroom. *I don't think that will ever leave me. That wasn't love, that was, that was—terrible,* I thought to myself.

My eyes welled up, and I shook. Braid's gaze heightened, and the other girls looked confused. My heart skipped a beat, and I threw my hand over my mouth, shaking my head. *No, no, no, no, no.* The tears fell again, and my throat croaked.

"Oh my god," I muttered.

Kayla came closer to me, looking confused, but concerned as well.

"What's wrong?"

I panted and came undone.

"Oh, no, no, no, no," I shivered and sobbed. *But she was a good girl; she really was.*

I scratched and clawed at my face.

"What's the matter?" Kayla's tone deepened; and she snapped, "where the fuck is Derek and Tony? Something happen?"

I shook my head, and stuttered, "N-no, n-no, nothing h-happened. I just want to go home, okay? Can you take me home? Please?"

"But where are they?" Braids snapped.

I threw my hands up in the air, and cried, "I don't know, okay?! I'll call them in a minute, alright! I just want to go home!"

I heeded closer to Kayla quickly and begged her.

"Please! Please! Just take me home, Kayla, please! I'll give you money. I'll find Derek and Tony; it's whatever, just please get me out of here."

She agreed. When we got to their cars, Kayla told the other girls to follow her for backup. Braids was reluctant, but Kayla wanted to ride with me alone so she could calm me down, and figure out where my car was exactly.

I hopped in, and we started down a dark gravel road. The rocks crumpled under, and the ride shook.

Kayla asked, "Are you okay? What's got you so upset?"

I couldn't stop seeing it. *I'm just gonna drown it.* I unscrewed the cap off the Black Velvet bottle and took a giant gulp. *The liquor warmed and cradled me.*

"You gonna talk to me?" Kayla asked again. I swallowed, the tears fell again, and I groaned; shivering.

"I—I—I d-don't know why I'm here."

"What do you mean?" Kayla asked.

"This place," I took another swig, and continued, "t-this place is terrible. E-everybody—"

I shook and gulped again.

"Everybody's just so horrible. I—I d-don't want to be in this place anymore," I moaned and shivered more.

"Hey don't say that," Kayla darted a sad look at me, and continued, "what do you mean you don't want to be here anymore?"

"I d-don't belong h-here. I just w-wanna go home, but home doesn't even feel like home. It's like I'm a glitch in the system and I'm not a part of this puzzle. I don't want to be. People hurt and destroy each other s-so much," I cried. It was like Kayla wasn't even there and I was talking to myself.

"T-they do terrible things, and it's like all the pretty things—"

My voice shook, and groaned, "A-all the p-pretty things—all of it. It all gets ruined! It all gets so ruined."

It's true in a way. You can't come out on the other end unblemished; this is the world of scars. It's like for anything good you have to pay your price in pain. The world holds no sympathy for the innocent.

"You're wrong, y'know," Kayla replied, "This place isn't terrible. You're a good person, I'm a good person, my friends are, the world is filled with great things. It's just all about how you look at it."

Shaking my head, I said, "You're wrong, it's not good. This place is evil. I think we're livin' in hell and this place is a prison, but you are right about one thing."

"What's that," Kayla asked.

"You're a good person. It's people like you that give me hope."

Kayla gave me an apprehensive look and I caught it immediately.

"No, it's not like that. I see you as a friend. Don't worry, but I still remember what you did for me. You helped me more than you know."

"What are you talking about?" Kayla asked.

"When we were kids, we were in the same class, kindergarten, I think. It was raining out that day, and we had recess inside, in the classroom, remember? You came and sat by me in the corner at the window. I was watching the rain fall, thinking of my father. It was a sad day, and you helped me, just by being there and talking. It meant the world to me."

Kayla craned her neck, thinking, and said, "Hmmm, I don't remember that, but I'm glad I could help."

"You still are," I told her.

My hand wiped my tears away, and I smiled.

"Maybe if we all worked on helping each other in a selfless way, things would be different. The whole world could change."

I nearly got lost in my thoughts again. A message was knocking, but it wasn't ready to reveal itself. Something was coming; I could feel it—*the crossroads.*

Kayla turned the wheel off the gravel and onto the blacktop.

"You ready to find out where they are now?"

We found out where Derek and Tony were, but I can't even recall the name of the place.

There was an after-hours joint located off or around West Main in town, or maybe Newark, Columbus even. I was lost. I'd drowned myself, and the bottle was nearing the bottom. I slurred into the phone, "I told you to take the car?"

"Yeah, you did," Derek repeated, "we tried to get you to go, but you wanted to stay with that crazy ass chick you was with. You need to leave that girl alone, bro; that bitch is for the streets."

I gulped, eyes feeling hot again. *That was so terrible.*

Derek barked into the phone, startling me. Music blared in the background, and I could hear Tony rambling, too.

"Well, you gotta ride? It's lit up in here. You should come."

I replied, sloshing my head into my palm, exhausted, but still holding on; fading in and out.

"What about the weed, man? What about—"

I paused in thought, then continued, "What about that Sarah chick? Is she with you guys?"

"Nah," Derek responded, "her and that Jules chick got into it bad. She called for a ride and she left. That girl look like she loves you. You outta get at her."

I shook my head, thinking, *What's the use? I can't do anything, anyway. Useless, I'm so useless.*

I muttered into the phone, "No, I can't."

Derek asked, "Why not? She's pretty and she got a big ass on her. What's wrong with her?"

The proper question would be what's wrong with you, the voice whispered.

"I can't because she's fat. That's pretty much why. That'll just give everyone more reasons to laugh at me."

My how the shallow muddle themselves through the judgements and statutes of society. What a waste.

Kayla gasped and got a surprised look on her face.

"I can't believe you just said that," she muttered.

"Whatever you say," Derek replied on the other end of the line, "you gotta ride here or what? I'll come get you, but I got a dime I'm tryin' to get at right now. Tony got one, too."

"I'm in the car," I slurred, "Kayla's bringin' me. See ya soon."

"No, don't—"

I hung up the phone before he could say anything else. I didn't care what they were doing. *Who cares if Tony gets caught? He deserves it anyway,* I thought to myself.

As soon as I got off the phone, Kayla got on to me about my little comment. *How terrible of me.*

"Why would you say something like that? It doesn't pay to be shallow, you know. Maybe that's why you can't find anyone."

My head stare out at the empty blackness of the dark country road leading towards wherever the directions took us. It was all void. The colors in the sky had disappeared; the stars weren't even there anymore. *I don't care about any of it. I just want to go home.*

"I ain't gonna hook you up with any of my friends; if you think about women like that. You—"

"It's not me that thinks that way, though," I interrupted, "it's everyone else. I just don't want anybody laughing at me."

"People don't care as much as you think, y'know," Kayla snapped, "it's not like everyone is awaiting a news flyer about you. Most of the time, people are so wrapped up in their own lives they don't even notice anything else around them, and if somebody laughs, who cares? Go with what makes you happy; that's all that matters."

But I can't, I thought to myself. *I can't even make love; I'm crippled.*

"I-I'm okay. I t-think I'm just better off alone, anyway. Maybe that's the way it's supposed to be."

Kayla went on and on, but her voice drowned out. My eyelids fell, and I trailed off to sleep in another empty dream. The wheels carried us onwards towards the after hours spot; the rest of me was lost.

CHAPTER XVIII:

SHOOK ONES

Colors flashed, and vapor crept around, enveloping the air. Most of the smog originated from the smoke machine near the DJ's booth. Fat Joe's "Ha Ha (Slow Down)" was beating across the speakers and the people were lost in a haze. The crowd danced, and nearly everyone was dressed up; it was still Halloween night after all.

Butter waltzed through the door with his two-man crew following him, Stretch and his boy, Cuts. They were both wild, and down for anything, too.

Butter lit up a square and took a puff. His white teeth shone a bright blue from the neon colored lights that pervaded the entrance. Turning back towards his boys, he said, "Shit, between the three of us we finna fuck every hoe up in here."

Cuts snickered wildly. He was short and put you in the mind of a gremlin; a pretty crazy dude. His tall white tee jiggled around his dark jeans. Stretch rocked his shoulders and roared when Waka Flocka's "Grove St. Party" came on. That dude was solid, he was damn near built to look like top flight security—sort of like Terry Crews. He nodded seriously, and uttered, "Yeah, we on the hunt."

Derek and Tony were at the other end of the spot, and they had a couple of chicks pressed up against one of the many glowing walls. It was the paint, it seemed like everybody had a can. Bright neon green paint still dripped and ran from the spray. The place was a basically a Halloween glow rave. It was lit pretty much. Tony held his "tonight" closely, and his voice muffled into her neck. "Damn, girl, you smell good."

Derek attempted to pass Tony the blunt as his chick played around with his waistline. Not everybody appreciates someone getting action, however, especially if it's with their girl. Some guy decked out in a Jordan jump suit that matched the neon vibe emerged viciously out of the crowd, and barked, "Hey, what are you doin' with my girl, bruh?"

Tony lifted his lips from the girl's neck slowly and looked at Derek, confused.

"This fool talkin' to us?"

Derek didn't know either, but he still had the gun.

Neon Jordan hollered again.

"Shut the fuck up, or you can get it, too. Nah, I was talkin' to your boy right here."

His eyes darted menacingly toward Derek, and then to the girl next to him.

"Ey, Melanie, what's up?"

The girl looked scared, her name must have been Melanie, I presume, but she didn't jump at her boyfriend's bark. She merely gasped and leaned closer towards Derek for him to protect her.

Neon Jordan kept running his mouth as his eyes pierced towards his girlfriend and Derek.

"What you doin'? You tryna get somebody poked?"

Derek gripped the handle of the pistol that he had hid in his waistline. Neon Jordan—the boyfriend; noticed, but he didn't trip. He wasn't alone either. Little did Derek know the man he was looking for was just on the other side of the spot.

Lil Wayne's "6 Foot, 7 foot" pounded across the speakers and the ground shook. The crowd went crazy. People were whistling and hollering everywhere. Rondo cackled and slammed his fist onto the bar, and hollered, "That's right! Give me that change! I told you that fool would drop the ball!"

He was with his people, just like Derek and Butter, but none of them knew of each other. *No, not yet.*

Kayla swung into the parking lot of the joint, and my head bopped; bouncing off the window.

I groaned, shaking myself from the slumber; and slurred, "A-are w-we there yet? I-is this the place?"

I looked around and nothing made sense. *I just want to get my car and go home.* The thought quickly changed when I licked my lips and felt the cottonmouth. *I need another drink.*

Kayla jingled her keys out of the ignition quickly, and snatched at the door handle.

"Yeah, we're here," she eagerly said, "you goin' in or you just gonna chill?"

My head thumped, as I wiped my eyes, nodding.

"Y-yeah, I might a-as well, I guess."

Car doors slammed behind us, and Braids marched towards us through the gravel with her right fist balled up. She was on a mission.

Back inside the spot, The Game's "Drug Test" dropped on the beat, and rumbled across the walls. Flashing lights matched the rhythm, and beamed across the crazed crowd.

Butter nudged Stretch on the arm; and pointed towards the bar.

"That who I think it is, bruh?"

Stretch peeped where Butter was pointing, and saw Rondo sittin' up there with his crew. There were two others with him; a clean cut dude with shades, and a tall guy in blue sweats with braids.

"Yeah, Mr. Rendezvous," Stretch replied. He was eager to check somebody.

Butter edged his chin down; staring menacingly at Rondo. Dim blue lights flashed across his face as he nodded. His mug still remained partially shaded.

"I ain't gonna stay quiet no more. Fuck what Shawn said. That fool's getting' soft," Butter snapped.

Cuts cackled, and squealed, "Yeah, we finna go poke, poke, on 'em."

The tempo of the atmosphere was rising, and tension pervaded around every corner of the unbeknownst party goers. People were getting up on that molly, and the place was turning into a real rave. *A slip on the tongue; a drop on the other side.* The floor was getting slippery. Things were growing heated for Derek and Tony too.

"So what it is, homie? What you doin' with my girl," Neon Jordan barked at Derek.

Tony pushed his girl off and marched forward. *So much for love.*

"What's good? You got a problem," Tony snapped.

Derek clutched at the gun that was now in his hoodie pocket ready to go. Derek said evenly, "We ain't lookin' for no problems, bro. Take your girl back."

Tony pressed it on further, though. *Of course he would.*

"Nah, fuck that. He ain't gonna get us. You got a problem, then step," Tony shouted at Neon Jordan. His people weren't having it, though. They edged closer to back up their friend. Derek pulled for the pistol. Meanwhile, I was just arriving. I was clueless to everything that was brewing.

Smoke swirled around everyone's ankles; and I stumbled through the crowd making my way past the entrance. Some crazy fiend met me right away, and charged. I jumped back, and slipped on the wet floor. Stale spilled beer covered me all over. It matched my demeanor, I guess. I got sprayed down without any mercy, and everything about me glowed. My attacker slipped back into the crowd, howling in laughter. I didn't even care. I lifted myself up from the soiled floor with a groan.

Just give me something to drink, I thought to myself. I felt so weary, and drained. *One more and I'm goin' home.* Then someone bumped into my shoulder hard, and hollered, "Watch it, kid!"

I cowered a little, and shuffled my hands wearily in front of myself.

"S-sorry, I didn't m-mean to."

The guy just stormed off. Thank god, he didn't press me further; I would've gotten beat up.

My tired eyes swung across the leering, overwhelming crowd and searched for the bar. *I can't find it.* Then, the grinning man appeared again, but only through the flicker of a second. He was there, then not; *there, then not.* My jaw fell, and I felt stuck there, unable to move. It's like my mind had my legs locked.

I studied the crowd onward, spinning around, stuck in the middle, but then suddenly my fluttering and confused glare halted on the blue glow of an all white sweater. The face was ebony dark under the hood; and her demeanor was void. Despite her gear, all you could see were the whites of her eyes.

The girl's hands were tucked tightly within her front hoodie pocket. A headphone cord ran down from her ears, and bounced across her chest.

She was slipping through the crowd slowly, like a flowing creek, there, but unnoticed; like a ghost, if you will. The girl was coming towards me, and I shuddered at her nearing approach. There was something about her that was terrifying, but I couldn't move. The figure's aura felt like a vacuum. It drowned out everything else nearby. My eyes grew larger as she came closer and my mouth hung open from the fear. I shivered as she passed and my shoulders slumped; I almost couldn't breathe.

She has a scar running across her throat, I thought to myself. My eyes wandered across the floor. *But her eyes—she has bright blue eyes.*

"Whispers," a voice muttered in my ear, "that's what they call her."

I turned my eyes to follow her; I was going off gut instinct. *There she is; she's headed for the bar. Right for—wait. That guy looks familiar.*

There was a pause, and the focus shifted. Butter and his crew was prepping up to make a move.

Butter zipped up his dark sweat outfit and shimmied the brim of his red hat lower to hide his eyes. Cuts handed him the blade.

"Go get 'em, go get 'em, Brady," Cuts snickered.

Stretch flexed up and nodded in agreement.

"Yeah, we got your back. Go get that fool."

"Monster" by Kanye West screeched across the club's speakers, and the bulbs strobed. The club was full of freaks. Goblins, ghouls, Martians, even; you name it. The void was there. *Oh yes, it was there.*

Derek pulled his gun out on the other end of the spot, and the angry boyfriend, Neon Jordan, threw his hands up, pleading for mercy.

"Ey, bro, it's cool. It's cool; we don't want any problems."

Everyone shuddered and screamed nearby; only Derek wasn't aiming for the boyfriend. He'd spotted Rondo getting up from the bar and his eyes followed his target. He was headed towards the DJ's booth. Rondo disappeared behind somebody, blocking Derek's aim. He was still wearing the shoes that he stole.

Derek threw Neon Jordan a mean glance and tucked the gun back into his hoodie pocket, and marched towards Rondo. *I'm gonna get my shoes back,* he thought to himself.

The girl in the white hoodie, Whispers, was drawing closer to Rondo as well, and she had her switchblade ready; she was prepared to eliminate the disturbance.

Whispers brushed further past all of the swaying shoulders towards Rondo in the crowd, menacingly eyeing him with an empty stare. *Let the rivers flow.* Whispers got her blade ready, but suddenly someone bumped into her; knocking her concentration off. It was Butter.

"Watch out," Butter snapped, and Whispers threw him a mean glance. She held the blade tighter and clenched her teeth behind her lips. Butter brushed past her towards Rondo.

Screaming came from the other end and the club started to clear, a kid in a Chicago Bulls hat, shoved a gun into his sweater pocket, heading towards his target, but turned away. Everybody had made Derek and saw the gun. The crowd was beginning to panic and clear.

In the midst of it all, I shuffled around and felt something overwhelming in the air—*death; it's in the smoke,* I thought to myself, but then I spotted Derek and Tony heading for the entrance. Tony turned around behind Derek, and waved, then laughed. It was towards somebody, but I couldn't piece it all together. Then I finally noticed Rondo was there, too. *We have to get out of here,* I thought in a panic. *Somebody is going to die.*

Rondo was wading through the crowd. The girl in the white hoodie, Whispers, snuck towards him, but a guy in all black with a red hat bumped into her, it was Butter. He was aiming for Rondo, too.

Butter crept up on him, and snapped, "What's good?"

Then he swung the blade towards Rondo's chest. Everyone that was near saw it, and they screamed. The crowd began to shuffle towards the door, and disperse; the music paused, and the overhead lights flicked on. Everything turned into a spotlight. The dark girl in the white hoodie disappeared. Rondo lunged away from the swing; disheveled and confused. He didn't even reach for his piece; he began to run.

Butter bounced up, and barked, "Catch you along the riverside, fool!"

The crowd roared for safety. Rondo ran towards the back with his crew, the guy in shades, and a dude with braids. Both of them were in black and blue, too. Butter and his crew tried to rush them further through the back, but witnesses began to emerge. Folks were staring at him; everyone saw his face. Butter flagged for Cuts and Stretch to follow him through the front and run out. They had to make way for an escape. I had already made mine. I was a goner. *But the girl, Whispers, the voice called her. Who was she? Where'd she go? It was like she was of the wind; she simply disappeared.*

Everyone moved towards their cars in a shuffle. Braids screamed in the parking lot at Tony.

"There he goes!"

Tony halted and pointed to his chest.

"Who me?!"

Kayla climbed out of her ride. I guess she didn't even go in. *She tricked me into doing all the dirty work for her,* I thought to myself.

"Yeah, you," Braids yelled.

"What I do?" Tony threw up his arms and asked.

Kayla marched towards him, with her fists swinging at her side, and screamed, "Why did you leave?! Who were you with?"

Tony rambled back, "I wasn't with nobody, you trippin'."

"Yes, you was, I saw you," Kayla barked; she was up in his face. Tears glistened on her cheeks. I just noticed she'd been crying. I guess she did go into the club. *How wrong of me to assume.*

Braids shuffled quickly towards him with her fingers cracking into her palms.

"Boy, you a dog! You don't deserve her!"

Derek and I glanced at each other, confused, both of our minds were shuffled; we stood by the car and watched the scene. *Finally, my car, a way home,* I thought to myself.

Tony glared into Kayla's wet eyes sternly after he burned a glance at Braids, and said, "Bitch you best get out my face or we gonna have some problems."

Kayla shivered, and whimpered, "But why?! I gave you my all and you treat me like a dog! You—"

Tony smacked her across the face, and Kayla's jaw swung. He hit her hard, too. I shuddered and gasped. *What did he just do? Why would he do that?* My skin boiled, and my teeth clenched.

Kayla gasped at the swing and fell back. Braids lunged for him.

She swung a right into Tony's jaw and then slammed a left into his stomach. Tony bent down, gasping for air. Braids knocked the breath out of him.

"Yeah, bitch! I'll show you not to hit a woman," Braids wailed, then she pulled Tony's shirt over his head and kneed him in the face; his nose began bleeding. Tony threw his hands up to catch the blood, but Braids shoved him down; Tony fell. The rest of the girls in Kayla's crew hopped in too. It was a beat down. They pretty much jumped him.

"Damn," Derek yelled as we both watched. Tony groaned, and Kayla cried. Then she lunged in to, dispersing the mob, and snatched Tony's chain off his neck. He whimpered on the ground.

"Yeah, bitch, I bought this for you," she snapped in his face, then continued, "and I'm takin' it back and givin' it to a real man."

She annunciated it; the word real. Then she continued, "You should've never taken advantage of my love and everything that I gave. You can be with yourself now."

She got up and spit on his chest. Tony lay on the ground, moaning and bruised.

"K-k-kayla d-don't leave me," Tony stuttered and shivered.

She backed away towards her car.

"It's over, bitch," Kayla hollered.

Tony cried on the ground.

"N-n-no, n-no, no—pleeaasse."

Braids kicked him in the stomach one last time.

"Yeah! You had a queen!"

She spit on him, too. They covered Tony with blood and cooties.

He groaned, "Don't leave me, Kayla!"

All she did was slam her door. The rest of them did, too; but there we were still left, barely anybody else was left in the parking lot. I definitely hated Tony at this point, but I still had a heart. Derek helped him up. I just lit up a smoke; trying to hide my grin.

Tony groaned and fell into the back seat, not saying a word. Derek glanced over at me. He had that empty look, too. Things were getting dark; *yes, very dark indeed.*

I sat low in the passenger seat as Derek drove. None of us dared saying a word, but we all felt it. *There's something, something in the air. The cauldron is beginning to bubble in Hell's Kitchen. I don't belong here,* I thought to myself as I stare out of the window into the empty night.

I just want to go home and be with my mom.

CHAPTER XIX:

DEVILS

The engine of a '70 Chevelle revved, and Rick Ross's "I'm Not a Star" beat across the speakers. Shawn's fingers wrung tightly against the steering wheel and his brow clenched. Oncoming headlights blinked into his irises over and over again as he gunned it down the road; thinking of the call that he'd just received from Butter.

"Now don't get all angry," Butter rattled across the line, "but we saw Rondo at this after hours' joint; and I almost had 'em, but—"

Shawn's eyes lit like flames, and his nostrils flared; as he bit the corner of his lip. Teeth clenched, he snapped, "You did what?! I told you I had it. I told you it was under control."

Butter snapped back, "But you didn't have it. The more ol' dude gets to walk around and throw shade on our names; the more we look like fools. What about respect? What happened to checkin' muthafuckas when they need it?"

Shawn shook his head as he mashed his foot viciously into the pedal; the engine roared. Everything ahead was spinning.

"That ain't the principle we're ridin' on; I told you that. How many people saw you? Huh? You think about that?"

"Shit, I definitely made a statement; that's all that matters," Butter replied nonchalantly, "that fool look like a Space Jam character or somethin' in person; he's a clown, but I bet he ain't laughing now because we got the drop on one of his boys."

"You did what?" Shawn snapped.

"Yeah," Butter replied, "somebody gotta be out here handling business. We peeped one of his boys from the club at the pump, waited for 'em to go in, and Cuts climbed in the fool's backseat. Y'know, on the low, low ducked down in the floorboard. We—"

"You sayin' I ain't out here handling business," Shawn muttered evenly; steaming mad.

"We got 'em, that's all that matters," Butter replied smoothly; but there was challenge in his tone.

"I got 'em in the stash right now. He tied up out back in the garage. You should roll through. It'll be fun. Meet 'em, talk to him a little. It's time we take it to these fools where it hurts."

It wasn't soon after they ended the call. *Too many lines are being crossed.* Shawn tempered and controlled himself. *Now just isn't the time; but I've waited long enough. Time to get a handle on things,* Shawn thought to himself.

Branches crunched, and the gravel rumbled. The gear shift squeaked as Shawn put the Chevelle in park.

He cut the engine off and popped open the door. It was time to put somebody on the floor. Bread stood outside of the garage behind the grow house; puffing on a black and mild. He blew smoke as Shawn approached, and said, "He's in there right now. You know Butta he ain't got no patience. Told him to wait."

Bread shrugged, "But you know him."

Shawn hung his head, and his eyes burned towards the crumpled leaves on the ground. He scratched, clawed, and rubbed the back of his scalp. Butter's shouts, muffled beyond the walls, Shawn jerked open the garage door.

There was panting, and Butter shouted, "You know it, right?! Where the stash at?! Where's the money?!"

Butter lifted a baseball bat above his head and swung it down hard; cracking the wood upon the beaten man's knee. He screamed, shouted, and heaved heavily; braids shook across his shoulders and spit dribbled from his lips.

The man spit blood out, and snapped, "J already told you. I ain't tellin' ya'll shit!"

Butter's mug grew tense as he clenched his teeth. His fingers flexed on the handle of the bat, and he charged towards the man again, but Shawn held his hand out and stopped him.

"That's enough, man. He's talkin'. Let's try to spit it up with 'em. Y'know, a little good old-fashioned reason."

Butter jerked back excited, smiling, and said, "There's my brotha. That's the old Shawn right there."

Shawn threw him a quick glance and tempered himself quickly. He stepped over the bag that had been over the man's head, and knelt down in front of him, clapping his hands and peering into his eyes.

"Okay, so we about to chat it up," Shawn smirked. "I'm gonna talk and you are, too."

The man spit at Shawn.

"Fuck you; I ain't tellin' you shit."

Not all of it, but a little spittle landed on Shawn's cheek and it irked him; *just a few drops.*

He wiped it clean, slow and nodded as he studied the spit on his hand.

"Okay, okay. That's one. You owe me one."

Shawn stood up and turned towards Butter.

"We got any pliers up in here?"

Shawn had to take his anger out on someone. He couldn't strike where he wanted to yet. *No, it's just not the right time.*

Butter grinned and nodded his head fast; rushing towards the toolbox in the corner. He dug through the top drawer, muttering to himself.

The bloody man in the chair shouted, "Ya'll ain't getting' nothin'! You think ya'll can scare me?! Man, ya'll fools ain't about shit. Let me one of this chair and see what happens; go 'head, let me loose."

Shawn knelt towards the man as he heaved in the chair and grinned, not saying a word, never even blinking.

The man tried to compose himself, but he shivered when Butter held up the pliers and hollered, "Got 'em. Catch!"

He threw Shawn the tool, and they missed his hands. They shot and clonked right into the man's face instead. He stomped his feet like a kid and shouted, "Damn, man! Come on!"

Shawn reached down by the chair to pick up the pliers, and the man swung in the chair towards him; attempting to tip it over. He heaved when it bounced back on all four legs.

"Come on, man! Fuck!"

His heaving and panting grew heavier as Shawn circled his way in front of him; snapping the pliers.

"Butta, hold his head back. We gotta make 'em still."

The man in the chair heaved heavier and heavier. Spittle dribbled on his chin, and snot ran out of his nose.

"Man, ya'll ain't shit! I'm Breezy! Ya'll can't see me!"

Butter slammed his head back in the chair. The door opened and closed; Bread came in.

Butter laughed, "Just in time, my kid, bruddha. We about to make this hummingbird sing."

He rubbed Breezy's forehead from behind, as he whimpered, and said, "Yeah, you gonna talk, you gonna talk."

Shawn stood straight with his head hanging to the left as he stare at the already tortured man. He attempted to plead, "Man—"

Shawn was on him before he could say more. He packed the pliers into his fist and pounded his knuckles into the wailing man's face; the meat from Breezy's jaw squished as Shawn lost it.

"Shut the fuck up! It ain't time to talk! I say when! I say how it goes!"

The man groaned and cried, "Man, don't do this to me, man! Please!"

Shawn shook his head as he glared into his pleading eyes. He didn't blink once.

"I can't," Shawn grunted, "you owe me one."

He charged towards Breezy's mouth with the pliers, and clamped onto a bottom tooth on the left side, and yanked, then pulled. Breezy screamed and struggled. Bread rushed over to hold him down; wrapping his arm around his neck and pressing his weight down on his shoulders. The tooth didn't come out right away. Shawn yanked harder again, and the man squealed. It came with the second pull. Shawn brought the pliers closer to his gaze and studied the bloody tooth.

"Now we're square. Now I got one."

Butter smacked Breezy on the cheek from behind his chair and snapped, "You gonna talk now? Huh? Where the stash at?"

Breezy whimpered and cried; shaking his head towards the ground.

The garage door flew open again, and Chan was standing there. His face looked horrified.

"What are you guys doing here? You can't do this; not here."

He rushed in and his hands shook. Bread, Butter, and Shawn stood still with Breezy sobbing in the chair between them.

Chan held his hands out in front of his face in shock, and his brow wrinkled nervously.

"What is this? You guys brought him here? Why?"

Bread answered, "Cause it's peaceful and quiet out here; nobody's around."

Chan gripped the sides of his head and said, "You guys can't do this shit. You brought him here where the stash is? What if he tells somebody?"

Butter snapped as Shawn, and Bread stared.

"Man, how would he know our stash is here? We didn't tell him, but you just did."

Chan put his hand over his mouth and gasped. Then he made a croaking vomiting noise in his throat.

Shawn twirled the pliers in his fingers and said, "Chan, you ain't built for this side of things. Go back to the house. We got this handled."

Chan nodded his head quick, and rushed back outside, past the door. It clinked shut. Breezy was still crying with his head hung towards the floor. Shawn turned back and stared him down.

"Now, you tryin' to talk? You heard my man over here. Where the stash at?"

Breezy shook, slobbered, and cried, "Man, if I tell you; ya'll gonna let me go, right?"

Shawn hushed smoothly, "Yeah, man. Just tell us where it's at, and we good."

Breezy's head tilted towards the side, blood was running from his mouth and staining his lips. He gave a weary nod and said, "Okay, okay. I'll talk. I'll tell you."

Breezy huffed and shook his head.

"I ain't sure how much or what, but Rondo makes a run once a week to some old dude's house; he live out in the middle of nowhere. He always go there after he makes the pickup from Big Smurf."

Breezy gave them further specifics on the location, and once he was done, he pleaded again.

"Ya'll gonna let me go now, right?"

Shawn glared at him and nodded.

"Sure."

Then, Shawn's gaze burned on Butter, and he nodded again, then said, "We gonna keep this fool on ice. He might know more."

He cut a gaze across the bleeding man, and continued,"Yeah. Throw the bag back on his head and let 'em soak."

Shawn kneeled down and whispered in the man's ear, "You best not be lyin' cause if you are—"

Shawn licked his lips, and grumbled, "Nah, never mind. Just wait and see."

Breezy hollered again as Bread went to throw the bag back over his head.

"Don't do me like this! I told ya'll what you wanted!"

Shawn cracked him across the jaw again and yelled, "Shut up!"

Then, he looked at Butter and said, "Tape his mouth shut and if he makes any more noise," Shawn threw him the pliers, "take some more teeth."

Breezy jerked around and hollered. Butter rolled the duck tape around his mouth and rotated it a few times, passing the back of his neck in circles, then he ripped the roll clean. Breezy's menacing glare disappeared under the hood again. He bounced and struggled still as the three men walked out of the garage; shutting the light off behind them.

Once they were back outside; Shawn broke it down.

"I want to keep an eye on the place first. We know where Rondo picks up from and where he takes it to; now we just gotta get the schedule of the runs down. We know where the dinner table is, but I wanna figure out what's goin' on in the kitchen. I—"

Butter interrupted, "We got all we need, bruh. Fuck all that plannin' shit. We rush in, and just hit the fool. It's that simple."

Shawn's glare grew void, and fire burned in his eyes. His gaze could pierce through souls when he got like that. *Getting' to bold,* he thought to himself; *I don't like that.*

Cold air blew from Shawn's nose, and he said, "We ain't doin' it like that because we ain't no wild cowboys out here, kid. We secret agent men."

CHAPTER XX:

PAIN

When I awoke, my head was pounding; everything was a blur. *Where am I?* I was in a daze. The sun shone through the windows; the dust dancing within the light came into view first, blurry, then it was firm. I was in bed, surrounded by my own room. *Thank god, I made it home,* I thought to myself.

My head thumped, and I flopped back down into the mattress, groaning. I didn't even care to go over what had happened the night before. *I'm done with it all,* I thought to myself. *I'm gonna sell the rest of the bud off, get back in school, and go off to the Marines. Yeah,* my thoughts continued as I smiled. *I can be a hero, just like my dad.*

Muffled shouting vibrated through my bedroom walls, and my skin crawled. It sounded like Mom. *Oh man; I hope I didn't stumble in and piss on the floor again. The dog's not around to blame anymore.* Footsteps marched down the hallway and the door swung open. It was her. *Oh, geez.*

She stood in the doorway, silent, all that could be heard was the steaming sound of her breathing; her shoulders were heaving.

"Well, what do you have to say for yourself," Mom snapped.

I was tongue tied, afraid, and most importantly, annoyed. I huffed, then exhaled slowly as I pulled the covers up and ran my hand down the side of my face. My eyes winced closed, and the pounding in my head began again. I cringed with agitation.

"Say about what, mom," I grunted. "I was safe last night; look, I made it back fine."

Mom jerked her finger up and snapped, "You haven't been home in days. Days! You wouldn't answer my calls and when you finally did, I heard you and your friends on the phone."

She charged into the room, stopped at the foot of the bed, and screamed, "You've done it all, huh?! You think that's somethin' to brag about?!"

I rubbed my eyes, rolled closer to the wall, and groaned into my pillow.

"Mom, you're over exaggerating. I was just home yesterday. I don't know what the big deal is."

"What's the big deal?" Mom snapped, then she jerked the covers off. The chill raddled my spine, and my knees crumpled closer to my chest. My eyes felt like they were partially glued shut. I could barely open them all the way. All I wanted to do was sleep; *sink downward into the great escape.*

"Geez, mom, what are you doing? What if I was like naked or somethin'? That woulda been pretty weird."

Mom clenched her teeth and snatched ahold of me. Her nails dug into my skin, dragging me closer to the edge.

"Get up, right now! I'm tired of you acting like this! You think you're so smart! You think it's funny to run around town with a bunch of bums, getting' drunk and all highed up all the time! Well, I'm not havin' it! I'm not putting up with it anymore!"

I wiggled around and pushed her away as quick as I could. Then, I shouted, "Get off of me! Why are you actin' all crazy?! All I'm doin' is hangin' out with my friends and havin' fun! I'm tired of this room, mom! I'm sick of being shut up like a prisoner!"

I fumbled angrily through my blanket and bed sheet. My fuse was lit; I was tired of it.

I stood at the edge of the bed shaking. My eyes dug and narrowed.

"Everything was always fine, when I kept to myself. It's always great when I keep the door shut."

I bit my lip hard, and waved my arms around towards the books lying in the room, then continued. My eyes watered.

"I'm sick of it! As long as I stay out of the way and keep up the perfect picture for everybody, it's all good! Oh, look at my son, he likes to read so much, and look at him, he's gonna be so smart! That's all for you, mom! Not for me! You don't care about what I want! You don't care about me at all! I let you ruin high school for me because I always listened and done what you told me to do, but I'm sick of it, mom! I'm so tired of all of this! It's been video games, movies, books, my own little world for years, mom, for years," I pleaded; then I gasped.

"All I wanna do is have friends, mom. That's all. I just wanna have fun. All you guys did it, you have stories, but me, I don't got any stories. I don't have anything to tell at all."

For a minute, Mom seemed to cool, and she almost looked as if she were sorry for snapping on me like that, but her face was simmering red still and her voice remained sharp.

"So you think it's fine to find you're fun in drugs," she replied cooly, her lips wrinkled, and mashed together tightly.

"I heard you on the phone. I don't know where you were, but I heard it. You said you like doing it all."

Her head nodded softly, and she said, "Anything goes. Cocaine, pills, weed, whatever. That's what you said; the other night. I don't think you meant to call me, your phone was probably in your pocket, but I heard. I thought I raised you better than that. I just thought you knew."

I laughed; *I couldn't help myself.*

"Mom, I'm not on everything. I've never done stuff like that. Sure, weed every once in a while"—lies—"but that's it, honest."

My eyes darted towards the left next, then I looked back at Mom quickly.

"Well, and drinkin', too, but pretty much everybody does that. I mean, there ain't nothin' wrong with drinking in my opinion. I mean—"

Mom shook her head, and her nostrils flared. Then she charged at me again.

"You just think it's funny! You just think everything is a joke!"

She nearly had me by inches. I dodged her and ran out of the room. My heart beat pounded in my head, and the hallway spun.

Mom screamed, "Get your ass back here!"

I felt terrified; I'm not going to lie. I nearly screamed like a T-Rex from Jurassic Park as I ran down the hallway.

I fell against the wall and stumbled into the kitchen. The tile felt cold enough to freeze my feet, and I shuffled towards the other side of the corner, behind the island in the kitchen.

I screamed, "Mom, what are you doin'?! Why are you actin' all psycho for?!"

She stopped closing in on me at this point. There was about a six-foot distance between us, which made me feel a hell of a lot safer. Mom snapped and nodded her head. Then she rushed towards the other end of the counter. There was no sense in running. I didn't feel like it

284

anymore. She jammed her finger in my face and screamed, "You need to make a choice! If you're living here, you're going to live by my fucking rules!"

She threw her hand back and screamed.

"You're going to respect me!"

I heard the crack first, then I felt it. My cheek burned hot. She smacked me. It stung, and it made my eyes shoot towards the ground in shame. Her hand didn't just bring my grief towards the surface, it brought my hate along with it. The cauldron bubbled. I could either find a way to cool it down or turn up the heat. Saying I'm sorry would've been admitting she was right, and I knew what happened at the party wasn't my fault that night. *No, she's wrong,* I thought. *She always thinks the worst of me.*

Mom stuck her finger in my face again and screamed, "Your lucky Jim isn't here because if he—"

When I looked up from the floor I didn't feel grief, fear, or the tears anymore, all that was left was rage. The light of my soul pierced and evaporated; all that remained was the hollow feeling. The anger, the spite, the darkness. A grin tore across my face to chase away the sadness. My eyes cut, and I spoke smoothly, "If he what? If he was here, to what?"

Tears began to well up in her eyes. She stammered, "If he was—"

My head shook, and the grin dug deeper. I replied softly, "If he were to what, Mom? If he were rough me up a little? If he was here to tear me down? What would you do, huh?"

My flesh ran cold, my hair stood up, and a gray shadow moved across my skin. *Something else was settling in,* the tempest shook.

I bit my lip, and the corners of my mouth edged back.

"What would you do?"

A tear dropped and ran down her cheek. She swallowed and began crying. Her voice grew strained.

"I've given you everything. I work like a man every day, so you and your brother can have all that you need, and you treat me like shit."

"You're so ungrateful," she grumbled.

I hated it when she went there. I didn't want to face the fact that I owed her a thing, but I did. I owed her for it all, and so much more. I was blind to emotions. The switch had shut off, and I didn't feel a thing. My skin went cold, and the void drowned me. I bit the tip of my tongue, and my face rattled. Then, I hissed, "Yeah, I owe you so much, Mom. Where were you when I really needed you?"

My mom cried, and her voice grew muffled and strained.

"I had to go to work! Why can't you understand that? I wish I could've stayed at home, and a basket of money fell on the doorstep every day, but that ain't how it works. Everything I did, I did for you and your brother."

My eyes grew heavy because I knew her words were true. *I can't stand to see her cry,* I thought to myself, but I wasn't trying to hear it. My back stood firm, but my eyes still burned.

"So, is that why you left my dad? Was that for me? Or was that for you?"

Mom shook her head and cried more.

"You don't know everything that you think. All you want to listen to is what your grandma tells you up in Dillon Hills. There was another side to him that you didn't know, but I did. He was great, b-but he could be treacherous. If I wouldn't have left I wouldn't be here. I did what I had to do."

My tears ran before I even gave them notice. My rage fumed, and I snapped, "You're not going to ruin him for me! He never laid a hand on me, not one finger! I never even saw him get mad, Mom! You're lying. I know you are! You're lying to make yourself look better."

Mom's voice grew strained again.

"He changed. Afterwards, I truly believe he did. Whatever he found in God, it really spoke to him. I know he was a changed man; I know it."

I couldn't even process what she was saying. I was so mad. I wiped the tears from my cheeks and gritted my teeth.

"Yeah, he was so bad and terrible, says you. What about the next one, though, Mom? Huh? He was so much better. It's fine if I get my ass beat as long as yours is fine."

I turned my back to her and began to storm off. I made it to the other end of the island, and paused, then I turned back around. Mom's eyes were swollen from crying. I didn't notice before, but she looked that way because that's what she had been doing for days. I couldn't feel anything. She had crossed the line and tried to ruin my dad for me; that's how I saw it, anyway. *All I have left of him are great memories, and you want to steal that away, too,* I thought to myself. All I wanted to do was hurt her, even though the words on my lips weren't true.

"I love my dad with all of my heart, and you want to steal that away from me. Everything turned out great for you. Everybody drug him through the mud and treated him like shit, but, y'know, it's all good; everything turned out so wonderful for all of you. That's what makes me so sick. I saw it for myself. Everybody loves him so much now, but when he was here, he was everybody's doormat. Everybody's fuckin' dog."

I licked the corner of my mouth with my tongue and shook my head; eyes shifting, grinning with a groaned giggle.

"I guess that's how it goes. Nobody truly loves you until after you die."

My teeth clenched, and my eyes seared with fire.

"If you wouldn't have left him, he'd still be alive."

Mom gasped, and her mouth went agape; she groaned, "Just get out. If you hate me that much, just leave."

I put my head down and turned my back to her; marching back towards my room.

"Fine, I will."

I rushed with fury into my closet and began throwing whatever I could into a red duffel bag. When I yanked a pair of Jordans off the hanging shelf, a heap of books landed on me, followed by a picture. Those hardbacks that I collected over the years felt like stones crashing down, but the picture was what I was most worried about. It cracked when I heard it fall. I flipped it over and saw the face of my father. My eyes welled up with tears, and my hands shook as I picked up the photo. It had been so long since I had the courage to look at his face.

I ran my fingers slowly across the dust on the glass. Tears fell upon it. *I don't think I'll ever be able to make you proud; I don't know how. Things always felt right when you were around, but now they don't. They haven't since you left.* I could feel myself coming undone. It scares me when that happens because it makes me feel vulnerable; *everything hurts now.*

Suddenly, I heard someone rush into my room. I juggled the duffel bag open to shove my father's picture in it under my clothes. I jerked my hand up to wipe the tears from my face right before I saw Paul standing in the middle of my room. He must've been in the basement playing his game and heard us arguing. It was clear that he was both scared and worried. He said, "What are you doing, man? You're not leaving, are you? Why is Mom crying?"

My heart hardened again. I pushed past him, then snapped, "I didn't do anything to her. She's just acting crazy, like always. I can't take this shit anymore, man. I'm gettin' out of here. Ya'll can be the picture perfect family without me."

Paul grabbed my arm and pleaded with me more.

"Come on, man, you can't go! Where are you gonna stay? Mom will calm down eventually, you'll see. Just stay here with me. You're my big brother. It wouldn't be the same around here without you."

I was beginning to feel vulnerable again and I couldn't have that. I had to be strong, and I wasn't about to let Paul see me cry.

"I can't take it anymore, man. She's always on my ass about somethin'. I just need to breathe, man, y'know? You act like I'm leavin' the state or somethin'. I'll still be here around town."

A wind of anguish poured across Paul's face. I looked away from him because if he cried, that would make me cry too. He replied, "Please, just stay. I don't want you to leave."

He reached his hand out to grab my arm, but I jerked it away.

"Just stop, man! I'm not gonna stay here; I can't deal with mom anymore. Even if I did good all the time, she'd still find a problem with something."

He was going to cry, and I was about to with him. I didn't want to leave, but I had, too. *It's just the way things gotta be.*

I pushed his shoulder and mimicked a laugh to cheer him up.

"Come on, man. We'll get to hang again together soon."

There it was; he was crying. He didn't even try to say anything back. He knew my mind was made up. *Don't look at him; you can't. He's just trying to make someone feel sorry for him.*

I snatched up the duffel bag and charged past him.

Paul whimpered, "Please—just stay—just—"

I felt terrible for him. I knew he loved me, and I knew he didn't want me to go, but I had to.

I pulled him in for a hug. His tears fell across my shirt and he hugged me back. I wanted to cry with him, but I couldn't. I've never shown the side of me that actually cares about things, not even to those I love. I couldn't even do that with Paul, and I loved him more than anyone else in my life. I patted him on the back and forced myself to smile.

"Stop all that cryin', man. I'll be around here for you. We just won't live in the same place anymore. We're brothers and it's ride or die no matter where we are in the world. You gonna believe in that or what?"

Paul lifted his head and looked me in the eyes, then he replied, "But bub—where—where are you gonna go?"

I pulled out of our hug and threw the strap of the duffel bag across my shoulder.

"I'll figure it out, man. Don't worry about me. Look, I'll tell ya what, whenever you miss me, just come to my room, it's pretty much yours now, ok?"

Paul nodded his head and wiped his tears away. He sniffled, "O-okay. Just call me soon, ok?"

I patted him on the shoulder and said, "Ok, man, I'll see you soon."

He kept nodding with his head down as I walked out of the room. My feet stomped down the hallway, and behind me, Paul cried even more.

I hated to leave him standing there like that, but there was nothing I could do for him. When it comes to the hard things, you gotta deal with that on your own. That's one thing that I know. It's the only constant thing that all people have shown. In the depths, you're all by yourself.

Mom was still in the kitchen, and I didn't dare to look at her. All I wanted to feel was the knob, but when I turned, her words stopped me in my tracks.

"You're a monster."

My chin dropped, and I felt shame. I grew envious, hungry for the void. *I really need a drink.*

I didn't look up. I threw open the door and muttered, "No, I'm not."

Then, I rushed to my car. I threw my red duffel bag in the passenger seat and cranked the ignition; the engine purred. For a moment, I paused. My hand was still on the gearshift, headed towards reverse, and I began to doubt myself.

Is this really the right thing? Should I really do this? If I do, everything is going to change.

I looked to my left and saw one side of my face reflecting back at me. I saw myself. I was sad, and the corner of my mouth hung low. *You can't go back, you can never go back; if only time worked that way.*

When I turned to my right, an immediate shock overwhelmed me. I gasped. There was another man in the rearview mirror sitting in the driver's seat smiling back at me from under the dark shadow of his wide purple brimmed hat.

"Oh, but you can," he snapped. His voice grew hollow and hoarse.

"Oh yes. You can always go back."

I jumped back in my seat. The air was being sucked out of me, and I felt dizzy.

I shook my head and gritted my teeth.

"No, no, no."

I snatched the gearshift into reverse and hit the gas. I spun a circle and my tires squealed out of the driveway. The day grew dark.

CHAPTER XXI:
THE CHOICE IS YOURS

Much, much better. When I put the straw to my mouth and the sweet taste of the red splashed across my tongue, the numbing effect was coming back. *How very wonderful.* I tried to get ahold of Derek, but he wasn't picking up and I really didn't care to call anyone else. I was buzzin' and havin' fun all by my lonesome.

Big L's "Fed Up Wit the Bullshit", blared through the speakers, rattling my ride, and I was getting' into it. The light turned red. I hit the brakes, but I wasn't stoppin'. I reasserted myself and fixed my shades, and got my nasty mean mug goin' on as I sung along; jutting my fingers out in jabs towards the windshield.

Yeah, nobody wants to mess with me. I'll poke somebody's fuckin' eye out. Two finger punch, just like karate kid, I thought to myself.

I kept bobbin' my head and rockin' my shoulders, feelin' myself; getting' mean. *Yeah, I'm tough.*

My head swayed to the right, and I jumped back immediately. A stone cold glare was fixed on my every move in the lane next to me. I shuddered.

The older gentleman was in a Prius, minivan, or somethin' like that, and his gaze didn't move. He looked extremely confused; like he had come into contact with some unknown creature. Honestly, I felt the same. The single stashed folks always scare me; they stay creepin' up the block.

It made it even more awkward with both of our windows down. Big L was still blaring. I turned the stereo down to a low hum, and took a sip out of my cup, stared back, then said, "Uh, sorry, man. I sincerely hope that my music didn't disturb you."

The man said nothing. His mustache didn't even twitch. He still stared.

I jerked my head to check the light quickly; still red. *I'm about to run this thing. This dude gives me the creeps.*

"Why do you keep starin' at me?" I asked.

Still nothing; not a move. I gulped.

"Please don't look me at me," I pleaded.

The man looked mad. I could tell he didn't like me; *no not at all.* The light was stuck on red.

"Come on, man. What's your problem?"

My head flicked to the left; the light was still frozen. The man still stared; he looked furious. *Was it the music?*

I shook my head fast repeatedly, and hollered, "Don't look at me! Don't look at me!"

The opposing light was turning yellow; red was about to become green. My knuckles tightened on the steering wheel. I madly shook my head around and screamed at the man as I stomped on the gas.

"I'm ugly! Don't look at me! Don't look at me!"

The engine revved, and I gunned it through the light, heaving repeatedly. I pulled a smoke out of the pack and lit it up nervously as I gazed in the rearview mirror. The man's car hadn't moved an inch. I shook my head.

"Geez, what was wrong with that guy?" I muttered to myself. There was no hope of figuring it out. He may still be at the same traffic light today. Wondering, pondering upon unknown things lost upon the youth. He didn't seem to have a clue.

293

I cruised around for a time, bumping away again, until I noticed what road I was on. I was daydreaming so hard I didn't even realize I was going down Luck Avenue and coming up on my grandma's house. Grandpa waved at me from the porch. *Damn it, he saw me.* I didn't have any choice. I had to stop by. *It would hurt his feelings if I don't say hi,* I thought to myself.

I didn't care too much, really. I just hoped mom hadn't called and told grandma anything yet about me packing all my stuff up and leaving. I really didn't want to hear anybody's mouth about it. *I'm an adult. I can make my own choices. Nobody has a say in what I do, but me.*

It was always a very heartwarming place to be, grandma's home that is. Her and grandpa lived in a little white house on the corner of Indiana and Luck. From the front sidewalk to the little red shed in the back, some of the best memories I had as a kid took place there. Grandpa would always be tending to his garden of tomatoes and he even had a bunch of flowers, too, that he made sure he took care of every day. There was this little bell in the back that stood up on a pole and whenever I'd feel mischievous and want to set grandma off, I'd ring it and you could hear her scream through the walls of the house.

"Stop it god dammit!"

She did daycare back in the day too and there were always other kids there to play with. One time, this little fat girl fell into grandpa's tomatoes and was rolling around in them. She couldn't get back up because she was too heavy, so she just rolled down the line squashing them all. Grandpa said, "Oh no, that little girl is ruining all of my tomatoes!"

Grandma yelled, "Hawke Alexander, help her out of there!"

I tried to, but I couldn't. I yelled, "I can't! I can't! She's too heavy! Maybe we can pull her out with some jump ropes or something?!"

Luckily, Uncle Shua was there to save the day. Good times. Grandma's house was always the place to be.

Jay-Z and Kanye's "Otis" drummed across the speakers as I pulled up; the brakes squealed a little. Grandpa waved again and hollered something, but I couldn't hear him over the music. I wanted to impress him with the song. It was his type of music; *a part of the introduction.*

I hollered back, "Ey, grandpa! You like this song?!"

Grandpa fixed his ball cap in the front, nodded, and smiled. He had his shades on. *Good, he approves.* I smiled back to myself.

When I got out, I could hear grandpa's radio playing tunes in the wind as I approached the porch. That old song "Groovin" by the Young Rascals was playing and grandpa was chillin' in the same spot he was always in.

When he saw me he said, "Hey, Hawke! How you doin'?"

I walked up the steps and said, "Oh, I'm doin' alright, I guess, just cruisin' around town, really. What have you been up to?"

Grandpa yawned, pointed his finger, and said, "Not much. I'm just trying to sell that lawnmower over there. It's a pretty day out, ain't it?"

I sat down in a chair next to him and replied, "Yeah, it's a nice day out for a change."

I pointed to the can of beer he had sitting on the table and asked, "What are you drinkin' on over there?"

He smiled, picked it up, and said, "That's Pabst Blue Ribbon you've never had it before?"

I shook my head and said, "No, I ain't ever had it. Is it really good?"

Grandpa took a sip of his beer. He didn't drink much. He replied, "It's the best."

The best, hmmm, seems I've been missing out, then.
I replied excitedly, "Really?! You care if I have some? I mean, if not it's ok, but umm, yeah, can I try it?"

Grandpa smiled and said, "Yeah, sure. There's some in the refrigerator if you wanna grab one."

I nodded my head, scooted my chair out, and said, "Okay, I'll go get one then. You want another one?"

Grandpa replied, "Yeah, sure."

I jerked open the front door and the first thing I saw was Robert De Niro strangling somebody and screaming, "Where's my money, huh?! Where's my money you fuckin' mut?!"

Grandma exclaimed, "Oh my god!"

The screen door slammed. I walked in and asked, "What are you watchin' in here?"

It startled her, and she shook in the recliner. She flipped her head around at me and said, "Oh! I didn't know you were here."

She turned back towards the TV and continued, "Just Goodfellas. Look at 'em Hawke, there sick in the head!"

I grinned and said, "Yeah, I guess so, it's a good one, though."

Grandma asked, "Did you have a good day in school today, honey?"

Thank god she didn't know a thing. Grandma can chew you out worse than mom if she really wants to. There was this one time I was riding in the car with her, well honestly it happened all the time, she tends to get road rage, but anyway, somebody cut her off or something and she slammed on her brakes, punched the horn and screamed out of her window all sort of obscene things. She done let the devil loose. She was tough, and I'm sure that's one of the reasons grandpa loved her so much. She could handle things on her own. *Independence.*

There was even this one time we were ridin' along, and Grandma was venting off some steam, and was all worked up. She said, "I'm tellin' you, Hawke; they do. Everywhere I go, men still try to get after me. They're sick—all of 'em. The—"

Suddenly, the car in the next lane slowed down next to us, and this older Chinese guy was looking at grandma smiling, and started wagging his tongue around at her. It even looked like he gave her the eyebrows. It shocked me. *Damn, she wasn't exaggerating.*

Grandma jumped back and screamed in the driver's seat.

"Get the fuck out of here, you sick bastard!"

I busted out laughing; I thought I was gonna die.

"Y'see, Hawke, y'see," Grandma pounded her fist on the wheel and drove on.

"They're all sick everywhere!"

That wasn't the worst, but she'd snap on you if you pressed her buttons too much. Never me, though, because I'm pretty much her favorite and she loves me more than everyone else.

I replied, "Yeah, it was great. I'm just ready to get it all over with, y'know?"

Grandma asked me, "Have you been getting good grades?"

Oh boy, I sure hate lying. I responded, "Yeah they're pretty good, A's and B's, you know me."

Grandma looked at me and gave me such a warm smile. It made me feel really bad for lying to her, but I didn't have much of a choice in the matter. I'd rather make her happy with a lie than sad with the truth. She said, "You always were really smart, just like your dad."

Then she turned back to the TV and continued, "You need to be careful at that school, though. There's a lot of no good kids running around up there. Did you hear

297

about what happened to that lady down in Putnam the other day?"

I really just wanted to grab a beer to tell you the truth. I didn't mind talking to her, but my buzz was starting to wear off and it felt like a tragedy. I shook my head and replied, "No, what happened?"

Grandma said, "Well, they found a woman dead over there in her apartment. They say a couple of people broke in there and raped and killed her. Ain't that awful?"

Grandma shook her head and continued, "They think it was over that settlement money. She got back for a wreck she got in, but people are nuts out there."

She continued on, "This place is turning out bad, BAD. I don't know what's happening to this town. Oh, Hawke, it used to be so beautiful around here when I was a little girl. Now it's starting to turn into a ghost town. Every year they tear more of it down, and they don't put nothin' else up."

It's almost as if the land is reclaiming itself. This used to be a holy place. They found Israelite artifacts in the mounds all the way up past Black Hand Gorge, and there were also the giants. Dr. Everhart found one in an ancient sarcophagus just outside of Zanesville. It was of enormous dimensions with Egyptian hieroglyphs embroidered upon it. They brought offerings from distant lands to these woods in the Ohio Valley. It was the seat of an ancient empire, but when the settlers came, John McIntire, and his bunch, it was Chief White Eye's town. It was—

"Just make sure you stay safe and out of trouble," Grandma said; interrupting the thoughts I had concerning the research I'd done on the land.

It's because of the curse the man in the hat put on this place; there on the bridge. The old crow cawed.

I had to escape, so I replied, "Yeah, that's terrible. I gotta go to the bathroom really quick. I'll be right back."

I rushed away in full on pretend mode. I opened and closed the door so she could hear it, then I stood in there and stare at the faucet for one hundred and twenty seconds. I know because I counted, and jerked the door open to get grandpa a beer. Grandma yelled, "Wash your hands!"

I muttered under my breath, "Geez, I hate it when she does that."

I turned the faucet on and stare at it for a few, then turned it off, and shut the door. Grandma yelled, "Uh, uh! Don't just let the water run! You need to wash 'em now! You can't walk around with filthy hands!"

I balled my fists up and clenched my teeth. Then, I started shadow boxing the wall. It really got on my nerves when she did that. Grandma yelled again, "Go on! Get in there!"

I threw my hands up in the air, made a grimace, then finally gave in to her demands. I took a deep breath and let it out after I turned the faucet off. I raised my voice and said, "There I got 'em washed now."

She didn't say anything back, so that meant the coast was clear. I grabbed grandpa and I a cold beer and made my way back towards the living room, but Grandma caught me right in my tracks and said, "Uh, uh, what are you doing with those?"

My eyes bulged, and my mouth dropped. I replied, "I'm just getting' grandpa a beer I mean—"

Grandma interjected, "Well, why do you have two of them, then?"

I stalled, shrugged my shoulders, and replied, "Grandpa said I could have one, so I got one."

She blinked her eyes hard, pointed her finger at me, and snapped, "Uh, uh, he's nuts. That's why he's been takin' more naps during the day; it's from the beer. You can't have one of those, you're not old enough."

I pleaded, "But it's just one, I mean—"

Grandma shook her head and said, "Nope. Put it back."

I turned around with my head hung low, slumped my shoulders, and made my way back towards the fridge. She had me, caught me red-handed. *Or so she thinks.* I perked up with a smile.

I opened the fridge up quickly and shut it. Then, creeped towards the back door with both beers in hand still and opened it very gently so she couldn't hear the noise. Then, the same with the screen door. I placed one outside quickly and crept back inside.

I rushed through the kitchen and back into the living room. Grandma asked, "What were you doing?"

I shrugged my shoulders and replied, "Put the beer back like you asked. I'm gonna go ahead and give grandpa his now. I'll be back in a minute."

She let me off with an ok. *Thank god.* You see, she adds up things quite well, and it takes an expert to get anything past her. That's how I became a master schemer. I'm the best of them all, in fact. Getting things past Grandma growing up was like a training camp for that.

When I walked back outside, "The Book of Love" by the Monotones was playing across grandpa's radio and he smiled when I handed him his beer. He looked at me and asked, "Where's yours at?"

I leaned in close to him and replied in a hushed tone, "Grandma said I couldn't have one."

He winced as he took a sip of his and muttered, "What?"

I nodded my head and said, "Yeah, but I hid it on the back porch so she won't know, though."

He pointed his beer towards the backyard with a smile and replied in a low tone, "Well, go get it then."

I rushed off with an "ok" and ran back to retrieve it. When I got back on the porch with grandpa, I stuck the beer under my jacket to muffle the sound of the can cracking open because there was already one crack on the porch from when grandpa opened his, so two cracks meant somebody else had one, which would lead to me. It wasn't that big of a deal, but I knew neither one of us wanted her to go off or anything, so we just kept it cool on the sneak, sneak.

When I brought that first Blue Ribbon to the tip of my lips, I didn't know what to expect. *It's on. Blue Ribbon Bravery.*

I thought to myself, *My, where have you been all my life?*

It was so lovely because it wasn't a "paint your nails" type of beer like Bud Light or Michelob Ultra. It was hard, but smooth. It made you want to flex up a little while you're blowing off some steam. It was a man's beer, plain and simple. *I ain't no boy no more.*

I smiled and said, "Damn, that's good. You've been holdin' out on me this whole time."

Grandpa laughed and replied, "We'd always drink this when we played cards. It's goes good with Euchre."

A car passed by and grandpa waved away. He damn near knew everybody in town just about, but then another ride started pulling up. It was Uncle Shua stopping by.

He got out and then his little girl Gabby did, too. She came rushing over with her arms spread out and yelled, "Papaw!"

He chuckled, caught her in his arms, and said, "Did you have a good day at school?"

Study cheerfully. That's what he'd always say when he dropped us off for school.

Gabby nodded her head and said, "Yeah, we drew a lot of pictures at school today. I drew one for you, too, papaw."

I didn't see what she drew; she handed grandpa the picture.

"That's really pretty, thank you," he replied.

She looked at me next and gave me an icy glare, not saying a word. All I did was scrunch my face up like I was a monster in reply. Uncle Shua walked up on the porch and laughed, "Come on, don't scare her, man. What ya'll up, too?"

I took another sip of my beer and replied, "I'm not that bad of a guy. I don't know why she's so scared of me."

Then I looked to Gabby again, teasing her and laughed. I answered Uncle Shua, and said, "Not shit really, though, just chillin'."

Grandma yelled for Uncle Shua inside.

Super senses. How could she have known? Uncle Shua yelled, "Hold on, I'll be there in a minute!"

He shook his head and said, "Damn, I just got here, man."

Grandpa chuckled a little under his breath and said, "She wants those boxes down in the basement moved out to the shed.

Grandpa waved his hand and declared, "Don't worry about it right now."

Gabby went inside to show grandma her pictures, too, and Uncle Shua sat down and asked me, "So what's been up, man? I haven't seen you in a minute."

That was the thing. Uncle Shua and I used to always hang out. Hell, I spent more time with him at his place on Grove Road than I did with my own friends, and he was the best—still is, in fact.

I shook my head, took a sip of beer, and replied, "Not shit, man. Just running around town and partyin' that's about it."

Uncle Shua grinned and laughed, "You been getting' any pusssyyy?"

Grandpa chuckled at that. I blushed in embarrassment and replied, "I mean, I've been tryin' too."

Don't think of the embarrassment; you're not limp.

Uncle Shua shook his head and replied, "I've been hearing about the same girl for years now, man. You gotta strike while the iron is hot. Just give 'em—"

Suddenly, Grandpa yelled at a group of girls walking down the street. He hollered, "Hey!"

The leader of the pack was a pretty blonde, there was a brunette, and two chicks that had braids, one even had dice in them. They all stopped and stared at us; they were them Pine Street girls—*beware, they are very deadly.* Grandpa pointed at me and hollered, "He wants to talk to you!"

The blonde wrinkled her face up and twisted her neck. I guess I was the most hideous and disgusting creature on planet Earth.

The girl hollered back, "Sorry, I don't fuck white boys."

Rejection, the story of my life. It stung. Grandpa's black, so I think he figured he could win me some points. He hollered back, "But he's my grandson!"

The girl wrinkled her face up again, and shook her head, then marched off. The rest followed. Uncle Shua busted out laughing, and Grandpa shook his head, then smiled at me, "What's wrong with 'em, Hawke?"

"I don't have a clue, man. I guess she's a racist," I replied. It didn't make any sense. I mean, she was white, but it was whatever. *I'll just drown myself in this beer and snivel to myself.*

The three of us sat on the porch conversatin' for a little while about different things. The town, the world, and of course I got more advice from them about girls. I needed all the help I could get. I kept looking into grandpa's eyes, though, while we were talking. More than I ever had before.

There was something there that I hadn't noticed before. I kept thinking about the little boy from the dream I had. The one with the flat cap, patched up trousers, and rolled up sleeves.

"There coming," he said, "they're coming, Jack, they're coming."

Then came the whistle of the sparrow. *Is it, or was it grandpa,* I wondered. *Grandma said he's been napping more. Did he find me unconsciously in a dream?*

Uncle Shua eventually went inside for a moment to use the bathroom, and me and grandpa were alone, so I asked him, "Hey, do you have any pictures, grandpa? Like of you when you were a little kid?"

He just shook his head and grew void.

"No, I don't have any."

But why? I wondered to myself. *Everybody else does. Grandma even has pictures of her when she was little. How come grandpa doesn't?*

"Why are you asking about that? Grandpa said.

I didn't know how to tell him, but I knew I had to; about the dream, that is.

"I don't know, grandpa. I've been having some weird dreams lately. I—I think—I don't know. I just saw this little boy with a flat cap on and patched up trousers in a dream and he had the same eyes you have. He kept saying, 'they're coming, Jack, they're coming', but I don't know who Jack is, and who the little boy was. None of it makes any sense, and I c-can't figure it out. It's the ghosts that's what it is. I told you about the boy I seen hanging in the house on Stewart Street. It wasn't him. He was pale with dark hair, but this kid was—"

Grandpa interrupted quickly, "Ghosts aren't real. Don't talk about them. It's best to leave the dead alone. There isn't anything they can do for you."

I replied quickly, seeking an answer.

"But I saw it, grandpa, I saw it. The little boy with the flat cap, and he was whistling a warning to a man named Jack. Who's Jack? It doesn't make any sense, and then there's this man in a purple hat that always talks to me. He's been around for awhile, from the olden days even. You lived back then. Did you ever know a man that wore a wide brimmed purple hat?"

Grandpa sat frozen in his chair; it seemed like he wasn't even breathing. His eyes pierced more than they ever had before.

"You don't know what you're talking about," he said, "that's impossible. That man is dead."

"So you know then," I replied eagerly, "Jack. Is that the name of the man in the hat?"

Grandpa wasn't rocking in his chair anymore, he just sat still. It almost looked like he hated me for bringing it up. All he said to me was, "Don't ever follow any ghosts, Hawke. They'll lead you straight to your death."

Suddenly, Uncle Shua came back out, so we stopped talking about it and switched the subject. Grandpa began staring at me in a different kind of way. Worried, but his eyes held belief. *He's gotta find his own way; he'll make it through.*

Aunt Jane stopped by, too; that was Uncle Shua's wife. She's always had a wild and spontaneous personality. She's definitely never afraid to speak her mind and what I've always respected about her is that she's always been honest. She's one of my favorite people out there in fact. A true original.

With all of us there, it turned out to be a great day. It made me forget about everything that had happened with mom earlier and, of course, the conversation with grandpa. I didn't get any answers.

It was all okay, though, with me and them, until Grandma came out and said, "Well, I just talked to your mother."

I shuddered, *she knew.* Grandma blinked hard, pointed her finger, and snapped, "She said you haven't been going to school and she told me about what you did today. I'm gonna tell you something, mister, you need to apologize to your mother, and you need to start going back to school. You're to smart to throw your life down the drain."

Uncle Shua followed next, "Come on, man, you gotta go to school."

I shoved my chair out from under me before they even finished and started to march off; edging towards the old Irish goodbye. Grandpa said, "That's none of our business. He's a man now."

At least someone understands, I thought. Grandma screamed after me, "I'm not going to let you throw your life away! I'm not doing it!"

I swiveled my feet around on the sidewalk and yelled, "I'm so tired of everyone trying to tell me what to do all the time! What about what I want?! What about how I feel?!"

I shook my head, gritting my teeth and yelled, "You guys will never understand!"

Uncle Shua hollered, "Hey, hey, calm down, man!"

I screamed back, "Whatever! Everyone always takes mom's side! I don't need you guys! I don't need anybody!"

I clicked for my car to unlock, stomped towards the driver's door, and jerked it open. Grandma screamed, "Get 'em! Somebody get 'em!"

But nobody moved. They knew my mind was made up. I cranked the car, stomped on the pedal, and I was off. I beat my fist against the dash in fury and wailed. I jerked my Styrofoam cup of red out of the console to take a sip, but it was empty. I threw the cup out of the window in a rage.

Nobody cares about what I want. Nobody does.

The only place I figured I could go next was my other grandma's house, my dad's mom. She'd be happy to see me, I figured. Only thing about being out there is, I'd have to be completely sober. My dad's side of the family are the religious type and they don't believe in stuff like that, they think it's evil. *Well, if that's the case, then I'm the worst, an absolute devil.*

Staying with family in general, I wouldn't be able to be completely neutralized most of the time in the way I liked, but I didn't have a choice. I had to find somewhere to go.

When I pulled into the driveway and heard the gravel under my tires, I felt safe. It was always a wonderful feeling going out to grandmas, but by being there, there was no running away from the thought of my father. It was right in my face. I loved hearing grandma talk about him, but when the stories were over and the day would end, I'd be stuck by myself, rolling every detail of each tale around in my head, trying to piece together who he actually was. I never got a chance to actually know him. I was only six years old when I lost him.

Grandma lived in this enormous house that she designed herself. It was just the way she dreamt it to be, and it was beautiful. I sort of missed the way it used to look, though; before the renovations, that is. Mom always said she did that, so she wouldn't have to look around and remember, but I don't know. I can still feel him there, no matter what. He grew up there, after all. I can still see it all in the home movies.

I had a big smile on my face when I sped up the walk towards the door to give it a knock. I tried for a time, but nobody answered. I rang the bell a few times, still nothing. I ran over to the garage to see if the cars were in there. They were, but there wasn't any answer. *They have to be home,* I thought, *but why won't anyone answer? Is it because—they don't want me around? Is it because they don't want to deal with me?*

I was already a mess over having two falling outs in one day. I didn't know what to think, but I accepted the obvious. They were home, but they wouldn't let me in. I hung my head and made my way back down the walk towards my car in defeat.

My aunt Mary lived right down the road; she was my dad's sister. I knew I couldn't go there either. I wasn't allowed in there home.

After I got expelled from school for drugs, a couple of years back, they figured I was a bad influence on their kids and they didn't want me to spoil them. *You're a bad seed, a bad seed indeed.*

It hurt me terribly because everyone promised me that they'd be there for me after my dad died, but that wasn't the case. My cousins James and Joy were the best friends that I ever had as a kid. *We wandered in the wilderness together.*

The last time I showed up at their home my aunt cried.

She hugged me, and tears were pouring down her cheeks. She cried, "I'm sorry. I'm so sorry, but you can't be here."

I shuddered, and asked, "But why?"

"Because of my husband," she said, "you can't be here. I'm so sorry."

I felt the lump in my throat and I choked, "B-but I—I w-wanted to see y-you. I miss you a lot. I, uh—"

"You can't be here," she said again.

My eyes felt heavy, but I couldn't let myself cry. I used most of my tears up a long time ago.

"Okay, I'll go then. I j-just w-wanted to say hi."

I rushed for the steps and before I knew it my shoes were back in the driveway. It sounded like she said she loved me, but I didn't stay to find out. I didn't want to bother where I wasn't welcome.

I didn't want to process where I failed and how I wasn't welcome. *You'll never fill his shoes. You'll never love Jesus enough for them to love you, too.*

It wasn't the truth, but I felt like I had lost everyone all in one day; except one.

I dialed up Derek. The phone rang and rang, then he answered.

"Ey, what's happenin'?"

My fingers tapped across the steering wheel.

"Nothin' much. What are you doin'?"

Derek replied, "Not shit, we're all just chillin' over at Ellie's right now. You tryin' to come through?"

I nodded fast on the other end, "Yeah, yeah, I'll be there."

I couldn't talk anymore. I felt distant and withdrawn; lost to myself. *I have nowhere to go, but I can't be alone. The silence will take me. It's always there; swallowing away at my soul. The empty place forever lies hungry; a devourer lying within the hole.*

CHAPTER XXII:

KNOW THE LEDGE

I didn't care to tell anybody what happened; that was my business. All I needed to say was that I needed a place to stay, and it was cool. I'd been on my own for a few weeks by this point. All by choice, might I add. Thanksgiving day had passed solo in Mickie D's parking lot with about two large fries, a milkshake, and three McDoubles. I starved myself for five days prior to the meal, so I pretty much already paid the price, and I was guilt free with every bite. It was one of the best meals I've ever had in fact. The heaviness brought some warmth to the growing chill in the air. Winter was well on it's way.

As far as business went, we carried on at the same level, at the same pace, just nickel and dimin' every day. Eventually, it all rolled into the same routine. We were moving, but nothing was changing or improving; we were stuck and a hope for some real money seemed like a long shot, that's until I got an idea.

"We need to move this bud quicker; like go wholesale or somethin' like that," I told Derek. We were strolling towards the store to pick up more shells. Snowflakes were fluttering down, and melting upon our shoulders. It may have been dark and cold, but I didn't have a chance in driving, and Derek refused. He was damn near twisted off them xans, too.

"How are we gonna do that? We don't know anybody. That'll buy that much," Derek replied. He took a hit as we walked along, blowing smoke, and laughed, "I mean, I don't know anybody that'll buy that much. Ain't nobody hittin' your phone back. You ain't made a sale yet."

I hated when he said that. He was only teasing, but I took it to heart. *I just wanna be good at somethin'. I can't even earn my own keep.*

I took a breath of fresh air, and my head felt swimmy; I was in the void.

"I might know somebody we can make a deal with."

"For real?"

I pulled some menthols out and lit up.

"Yeah. This dude's cool. We go back and used to party all the time. I'll hit 'em up and see what's goin' on."

The only person I could think of offhand was my dude, Julian, that I knew from Newark. He was sort of like a Juggalo dude, y'know, with the chains on the pants and all, and they all love I.C.P. Most of 'em are crazy, but they're cool. They love drugs and Faygo; they gotta have it. They love the green. *But they haven't smoked the Lotus yet,* I thought to myself.

Julian wasn't big in the game or anything, but for all I knew, he could've needed a re-up. I didn't really want to go there, but considering things weren't really moving, I wanted to up the ante; *place a little bet.* I figured I didn't have a choice.

I clicked on Julian's name in my phone and puffed away as we walked; all in a rhythmic pattern. The phone rang in my ear.

Julian answered, "Yo, what's up? I wasn't expectin' you to call."

When it comes to buying or selling, you always got to be careful when it comes to phones. Not that I was being tapped or anything; it's just sort of the code. I replied, "Not shit, really. What you up to?"

Julian replied, "Nothin', really. I'm in Cincinnati right now, meetin' up with some fam," he laughed and continued, "I'm fuckin' fried already out here, man."

I wasn't expecting this; *already dead in the water. I'm so sick of it.*

"Shit, man, I didn't know you were in Cincinnati. I got somethin' you might be interested in."

Slipknot blared in the background. He was definitely at a party, but then the noise ceased when he replied, "For real? If you're talkin' about what I think you are, how much?"

I hated talking business over the phone, but at this point, I didn't have a choice. I replied, "A couple of ounces. This shit is the loudest I've ever seen, man. It's that Blue Lotus. When you gonna be back in town?"

Julian replied, "I ain't gonna be back in town for another week. What's the deal, though? How much?"

I couldn't wait a whole week, that would be too long. *I gotta get things movin' somehow. I need to make some cash; that's my only hope of escaping this town.*

My eyes cut and we passed a street sign. *Pine Street.* The Starfire lie just down the road. Derek swung a glance my way and chuckled as his fingers tapped at the keyboard on his phone.

I cut the silence and said, "How's two fifty a pack sound? I can't wait no week, though. It'll be gone by the time you get back."

Julian coughed into the phone. He was burnt already, I could definitely tell. He replied, "Damn, that's a little high, but if it's as loud as you say, I could get one of my boys to meet you somewhere. You remember Brian, right?"

I muttered, "Yeah, yeah, I remember him. He seems alright."

I didn't like Brian too much because he was shady, but at the same time I didn't care. *I just need to save up enough to run away from all of this. But where? Where will I go?* My mind wouldn't stop running.

Julian replied, "Ight, just give me a few and I'll get ahold of 'em, my dude."

We both hung up at that. Derek glanced over at me as we strolled past the PAL gym on the left.

"You good, man?"

No, I'm not, I wanted to say, but I couldn't. I was too numb to care.

"Yeah, I'm okay," I replied. My gut had a bad feeling about the whole thing, but I didn't want to tell Derek that; *I need this.*

"Brian's alright. I just ain't seen him in a while, that's all. I hope everything goes good with it."

Derek laughed, "Man, this ain't a movie or some fake ass story; this shit is real. Ain't nobody gonna do nothin'. We can do the damn thing tomorrow."

Derek's feet stomped, and his laces bounced. He looked to me grinning, and said, "It's out in the country, right?"

He looked ahead, smiling as he rolled his head around playfully.

"I love the country. It's fuckin' beautiful out there."

It didn't take long for everything to get hazy yet again. The sound of a grinding bottle cap twisting off sounded, and I turned around in my stupor, towards the sound; it was the next day. *Or is it? What day is it?*

I didn't have a clue, but I did when I felt the buzz and the text hit my phone. It was Brian. We set the deal. We got up and drove out to the sticks to make it happen.

Something about it all felt off, and I tried to ignore the knots in my stomach when we pulled to the side of the agreed upon shady back road. *It gives me the creeps out here,* I thought to myself as the engine hummed and the heater blew.

The sun was still up, but darkness was encroaching upon the horizon. I drove and figured Derek could handle the deal when Brian pulled up, but for some reason, he wasn't on time. That was the first red flag.

Derek tapped his fingers across the bag on his lap and said, "Damn, where the fuck this dude at? You sure we got the right time?"

I looked out the window and behind me for some oncoming headlights. Still nothing. I replied, "Yeah, I mean he should be here any time. I don't know where he's at."

Derek shuffled around in the passenger seat. He could feel something off about it all, too.

"Man, I don't like this shit. Somethin' feels funny with it."

I replied, "I know, man, I know. Let's just stick with the deal, though."

I need to be done; I'm so ready to be done with all of this. My thoughts raced.

A dance with death, a voice chattered.

I could feel it; I knew, but I didn't care. *Something is about to happen; the pit is coming, the god awful abyss.*

My eyes darted towards the road, the mirror, and my fingers tapped across the wheel repeatedly. *Come on, come on;* I even began humming to myself. Derek looked at me like I was some sort of nut.

"Man, the humming shit is making it worse."

"I know, I know, man. I—"

Then came the headlights ahead. I tapped Derek on the shoulder and pointed.

314

"Look! There he probably is. It might just be the woods or somethin'. That's why things feel weird; it's creepy around here, anyway."

There's something out there; something out there in them woods.

The car halted, parking in front of us. It was a Ford Taurus or something like that; the beige and plain type of ride. Brian hopped out of the passenger seat, all jittery. The scene already felt off.

He flipped his greasy hair around, grinning, and tugging at his ICP hoodie. He walked up and his chains clanked along the driver's side of my car and he hunched down at the window.

"What's goin' on, man? I heard you got the good shit?"

"Yeah, we got it."

Derek handed me the packs. They landed in my lap.

"That's all of it," Brian asked, nodding fast.

His fingers tapped on the edge of the open window, and his other hand danced around in his hoodie pocket. *Perhaps it's the cash.* I nodded, and my hands automatically went to doin' the trade, but instead of cash, Brian was holding a gun.

"It's cool, man! It's cool," I yelled, throwing my hands up. Derek jerked back in his seat. *Where's the gun? He doesn't have it, he—*

Brian snatched for the product and scooped it up through the window out of my lap, still pointing the pistol, laughing. Then came the squirt, and a splash; water danced down my cheek. Derek gasped; Brian cackled and rushed back towards his car. Apparently, his girl was the getaway driver.

"Nice doin' business with ya," Brian hollered, and hopped back in. A freezing sensation overcame me. *Did he just—did he?* He robbed us with a squirt gun.

The wheels rolled in front of us, gravel kicked, and they took off.

"That motherfucker," I snapped and pounded the dash. Then jerked at the gear. *Now we're in—drive.*

Pulling out, we kicked rocks, and they flew behind the tires as I spun around to give chase; we nearly got lost in the ditch.

"What just happened, bro? What are we doin'," Derek hollered over the sound of the grumbling tires. The shadows of the trees ran across my car's silver hood. *Over two and a half rpms; I'm goin' past the third. I'm gonna get them.*

The engine revved louder, and the radio whirred. Static scrambled across the speakers, and a song came on. It was Kim Wilde's "Kids In America."

Derek looked shocked and shaken on the side. I couldn't say a word; all I could feel was the menace. I slammed my fist into the dash. The beat kicked off in the song as the wheels spun and the tail end swung out. The man in the hat grinned at me through my reflection in the rearview; *we were dancin' with the devil.*

The red taillights were growing closer ahead, and I bite my lip; my eyes burned as my grip tightened on the wheel. Dust blew past my windows as gravel kicked and clanged underneath.

Derek hollered, "What are we doin', man?! Ey! We're startin' to slide. We're startin' too—"

Realigning the wheel faster than a reflex, I hollered, "Just chill, man, okay?! I got this! I'm an operator, alright?!"

I bit my lip, knuckles growing white from the grip. We spun around a corner, edging closer. Clouds blew from each set of tires, ours and theirs. The engines roared, my cheeks burned, and I glared past the wheel; focused and determined. *We're gaining on them.*

The nose of the car edged towards their rusted rear, and I had the mind to play bumper to bumper with them for a tap and a tad; *yeah we're aiming for a crash—and the cash.*

The engine of the Ford Taurus squealed ahead, and they sped up, climbing towards the curve. My foot mashed on the pedal.

"I wish they would just crash and roll down the hill," I snapped; gritting my teeth, pressing over sixty. *Not too fast; not to—*

They hit the corner and obviously didn't have a clue it was coming. Their tail end spun outward, and the car rolled down the dead man's curve. *See ya, wouldn't want to be ya,* a voice chattered. We slowed down, and both of us gasped together at a halt.

The sound of crinkling and crashing metal rolled away as their car flip-flopped further down the hill. Derek looked at me. I did the same. There were no words for it. I pressed the gas pedal back down towards the smoke rising faintly through the limbs of the bare, broken trees. It's too cold for this.

Derek started whiggin' out, and ranting the same phrase over and over again.

"What just happened? What just happened? What did we do? What did we do?"

I wanted to speak, but I couldn't. All I could do was wade through the dead, brittle grass towards the crash. When I saw the wreck for myself; I shuddered. *What did we just do? I didn't really mean what I said. Am I speaking things into existence again?*

The car was completely flipped over on its roof; the headlights were still on. If it weren't for the trees, they would've never stopped rolling. Brian was hanging halfway out of the passenger side and his girl was dangling upside down from the driver's side seat belt. Broken glass was scattered everywhere. I clenched my hands into my hair, standing there wild-eyed trying to process it all. *Are they still alive? What if they're dead? I never wanted anybody to get hurt.* My mind rambled and rambled on. Derek shuffled up quick behind me. He looked a mess just like I did, only he didn't stop in his tracks like me. He ran right up to Brian hanging out of the car.

I yelled, "Is he ok?! Are they ok, man?!"

Derek didn't answer, but the man in the hat did. *Who cares if they're ok? Would they care if that was you? Why, of course not, y'see, they'd find it funny. They'd all just laugh at you.* The man in the hat's words possessed my mind. My nerves hardened and my fist clenched up. I could feel him near; *watching, always watching.*

I looked towards the woods and caught the faint outline of the man in his hat, grinning from ear to ear. His cackling shrieked through the air and he spoke again, *Come on, you don't have to pretend with me. I know you much better than you think. You only act concerned because you think you're supposed, too. Dig a little deeper.*

He was right. I could feel hate swimming there as I stare down at the broken boy in the shattered glass. The man in the hat sauntered along the edge of the trees. *Ah, there it is, you found it. It stings at first, but if you let it in, it isn't too bad, now is it?*

Derek scrambled around the car; broken glass crunched under nearly every step. He hollered, "What are you doin', man?! What are we gonna do?!"

I didn't answer him right away; I couldn't. All I could do was watch the blood from Brian's forehead drip off his nose and into the dirt. *Right where he belongs, right at home,* the man in the hat said. *Looks like we won't have to put an old dog down today after all.*

I couldn't feel a thing. I wasn't sad, glad, or mad. I was in the midst of the untempered hollow. The man in the hat said, *Ah, luxurious, let it go with the breeze; it's time for the crows to feast.*

Derek yelled again, "You hearin' me, bro?!"

My mind snapped back to the moment, freeing my frozen consciousness. There weren't any more thoughts. The only thought was survival. *Always have yourself, because nobody else will.*

I ran over and scrambled through the broken glass with Derek. He found our weed on his side, but I found something else on mine; a black duffel bag. I snatched it up and unzipped the thing. I yelled, "Hey, Derek, come here!"

There was a little bit of cash; *a little chunk for gas,* I guess, and from the looks of it, maybe an ounce or more of some purple rock. I can usually look at weed and spot the weight pretty well, but when it came to crystal; I didn't have a clue. It was a lot, that's all I knew. *It appears we aren't the first ones Brian pulled the squirt gun trick on.* Derek gasped, "Shit, I'm kind of glad the deal went bad now."

I have enough to run away with now; I can finally leave. Derek paused for a moment and looked back towards the flipped over car.

"So, what are we gonna do about them?"

They were still alive and breathing, you could tell that. Timing was imperative, though, and there wasn't any time to think. Sink or swim were the options and Brian chose to put on the cement; that's it, that was on him. I let go of the need to do the right thing. He had the cash to make the deal smooth, and he chose not to because he saw us as punks to get one over on. All I did was shake my head and bagged up the product. I looked at Derek and declared, "There's nothing we can do. If we call 911, we're fucked, and I know I don't want to go to jail."

I shrugged my shoulders and looked back at the wreckage. I could feel the remorse, the guilt, the sadness working its way up, but I knocked it back down in the dirt with the injured folk. I took a deep breath and said, "Somebody will drive along and find them. They'll get to the hospital—yeah—they'll be ok."

I threw the duffel bag's strap over my shoulder and began walking back to the car. Derek followed along behind me and didn't breathe a word. Before we got to the car, I could hear what sounded like a girl coughing and scream, "He-he-help! Somebody help me!"

I slammed my door and cranked the car. I looked over towards the crows cawing over head across the dusk, and muttered under my breath, "Help yourself, bitch."

CHAPTER XXIII:

THE GRAVEYARD

A hammer went click on a Luger, and the clang of a trunk slammed on a bronzed brown '70 Chevelle. Shawn and Butter were gearing up to break the bank on Rondo. They'd been watching the spot for weeks; timing all the runs. They had the schedule locked down and the sweetest part about it all was that the whole stash was practically unguarded. The only thing between them and the lick was a tired old man. Little did they know this old man didn't play no nick knack patty whack, give a dog a bone, and he sent more than a few bodies rollin' home.

Aldon passed across the carpet in his slippers and coughed as he hunched over. The grandfather clock rung in the corner, and the hour had just struck midnight.

Crickets chirped through the paned glass of the kitchen window. Aldon's dark weathered fingers stretched toward the cupboard door. *I need a glass of whiskey.* They were at it again, the terrors in the night. He could still hear the echo of a dream.

Bullets rattled, and screams rang in his ears. Long dead faces lie in the mud, and then there was the road; *the gauntlet.* We couldn't do anything to save them during the retreat. They ran right back over their cold, lifeless bodies in those trucks. *Like a mashed pebble in the mud.*

He heard their bones crunch again, and he winced. Aldon pulled at the Wild Turkey and poured himself a glass. He took a sip quick, and let his eyes shut at last. *I need some rest.*

The whiskey swished, and Aldon shuffled past the kitchen table, towards his chair; the light was burning there.

He sat down in his dark, blue shaded recliner. Glass clattered on the end table. Aldon groaned. *There goes that throb in my back again.* His legs felt stiff, he pulled one up slow, and propped his ankle up on his knee. The grandfather clock ticked further, and the hands shuffled slow. *Second by second; tick tock tick.* Aldon spotted a scab that he started to pick.

He heard a creak in the hall, and his eyes shuffled toward the wall. Then, back towards the whiskey on the end table. He stare at the still liquid. His gaze fazed out, and he blinked; remembering the photo album that lie right by his seat. Aldon reached to pick it up.

His wrinkled hands rubbed across it's smooth surface, and he pulled open the cover. *Georgia.* He smiled at the sight of his pretty wife. *You're so fine, I'll love you until the day I die.*

Flashes of their life together ran through his mind backward all the way towards their first date. It was at the drive-in theater; a kiss on the cheek from him to be modest, and Georgia taking his lips. *You're the only woman I could ever love*, he thought, then laughed to himself. Thinking of the memories he had made at the same drive-in with all of his old friends; out there past East Pike. He chuckled again to himself. *Old Geno, and Eddie, them two were a trip.*

He smiled to himself as he turned the pages; remembering all the times he helped Geno and Eddie Legs sneak into the drive-in so they didn't have to pay to get in. They climbed in the trunk of the Pontiac and he drove on through. "Speedo" blared across the car's radio, and passing horns blew.

Aldon tapped his buddy on the shoulder as he got out. They were both grinning ear to ear.

"We got 'em again, ya'll, didn't we Geno?"

Geno snickered behind his teeth, smiling big, and Eddie Legs climbed out next after him.

"We sho did," Eddie laughed.

People were moving everywhere. Some towards the popcorn stand, others towards a back seat. Geno grinned and studied the crowd. He was trying to figure out where a pretty girl could be found. *Those were the days.*

Aldon continued to turn the pages until he landed on a picture that made him freeze. There they were, the Furious Five. Private Bradley, the military photographer, took it during one of their campaigns out in the jungles of Korea. Life was hard, but there they were. All camouflaged, helmet straps dangling by there cheeks, and rifles loaded at their feet.

Aldon was on the far left. *I was so young.* The smile of his youth glinted back at him in the photograph. *If I could just go back.*

To his right was DeMarco Jones; standing tall, with a cigar in his mouth. He was so light he could pass for white; his father was Italian and his mother was one of the prettiest lady singers in New Orleans at one time. She named him DeMarco because his father didn't want to give him his name. DeMarco, that means son of Marco, in Italian. *He had us during the war, but damn everything that came afterward,* Aldon thought to himself.

In the middle was Geno, and he was standing firm; holding his rifle close as it dangled in his arms. Further to the right was Eddie, his arm hung across Geno's shoulder, and he stood tall with a handsome smile. *Nothing could ever bring Eddie down.* Aldon smiled to himself; *you were one of the good ones Eddie*—they all were. His smile crept back down his cheeks. He heard the screams in the jungle again.

"I got ya, Eddie! I got ya!"

Boots thundered in the mud, and bullets whistled through the air past their ears. A grenade exploded in the distance.

"I'm in the hole, Gene! I'm in the hole," Eddie screamed.

"Help me cover him, Anthony! Help me cover him," Geno pleaded and hollered.

Aldon's eyes moved further across the picture to the right. There he was— Anthony "The Gun" Lenard. Aldon remembered the blood. Drops of red ran across the record as it spun. The Chantel's sung, "I Love You So."

I can't say whether or not you got what you deserved, Aldon thought to himself.

Suddenly, he heard tires crumple in gravel, slow and still, then a squeak. Somebody had parked their car down the driveway. Aldon closed the album. *Somebody's outside.* His fingers reached for the blinds.

Butter chattered in the passenger seat as him and Shawn pulled up to the old man's house. Bread stayed back to keep an eye on Breezy.

"Shit, we spend more time in the country than we do the city these days," Butter muttered.

"We gonna be corn-fed like a muthafucka before it's all over with if we don't watch out," he continued.

Shawn threw him an annoyed glance, and asked, "What's that even supposed to mean?"

Butter shook his head and shrugged his shoulders.

"I don't even know."

"You're retarded, man. Cut that shit out and throw the mask on. We gotta get this shit through," Shawn snapped.

Shawn parked the Chevelle midway down the driveway, and tied a black bandana across his face. Butter threw a ski mask on. They got the guns locked and ready, then crept toward the door. The gravel crumpled under their feet until they reached the grass, where the shadows were cast. A light flickered off behind the blinds. They halted.

Butter muttered, "Shit, the old man must be awake."

Suddenly, barking erupted in the air; from which direction neither knew, but soon, within seconds, a Rottweiler emerged charging at them both beyond the midnight shade of the trees. Shots rang out towards the dog and it whimpered; crumpling towards the ground.

"Damn," Shawn hollered; and panted, shuffling closer to the fallen guard dog.

"Okay then, Mr. Silent, looks like your way done went completely out the window," Butter stood up straight and snapped. Shawn was still heaving hard; he could handle any man but the beasts; he just didn't like them. He edged closer towards the dog, then another bang; he sent a kill shot to the poor thing's head.

"Damn, man," Butter hollered, "you think the muthafuckas dead now?!"

Shawn caught his breath and nodded cooly.

"Yeah, it's dead."

The silence didn't last long. Another shot fired; only not towards the dog. A crack came from the porch, and a shell hitting the deck made a clonking sound, followed by a click.

"Come get it," Aldon hollered, "I see you out there."

Another shot rang past their heads, and they both ran towards the shed for cover.

"Damn, this old man don't play," Butter rambled; Shawn began to sweat. He gritted his teeth and fired a few shots of his own back. They sang across the moonlight.

Aldon ran for cover behind the front door frame. He couldn't move as fast as he used to.

The pain in his knees stung, and he winced to himself. His legs were growing shaky; he needed to prop himself up on something. *I might be old, but I'm still one of the best shots there ever was.* He tightened the muscles in his legs, settling the shake, and reaffirming his stance. His eyes burned with fury; and he rang out another shot. The shell rattled at his feet, and the barrel cocked. Aldon fired a couple more.

"You best get out of here," he yelled, "this is my home!"

Shawn didn't care, nor did he say a word. He was in the mode.

"Ey," he whispered to Butter as the bullets fired, "you distract the old man, and I'll creep around back. That's where the dog came from; I bet the senile muthafucka left the door unlocked."

Butter winked, and smiled, "He's wide open, then."

He peeked around the shed and fired; shots rang out towards the door. Butter cackled, "Ey, you got some country fried steak with some gravy in there, old man?"

Aldon fired again from the door, and didn't holler back a word; he was running out of breath. He tightened his grip on the gun, wincing, and reloading again. Shawn ran for the back door.

Butter yelled, "Ight, old man! All we wants is the money and we good; we outta here! We ain't tryin' to hurt ya. You can go back to, y'know, to your newspapers and all that, and we done. Ight?"

Several more shots fired out of the house towards Butter; one went through the wood. A shell clicked and kicked; there was a slide coming from the barrel. The door creaked behind, and a hammer clicked. It was Shawn. His arm swung, and he hit the old man in the back of the head

326

with his gun. Aldon fell onto the carpet. A signal was whistled; Butter heard it and rushed in. Shawn went for the old man's rifle, but he had already shaken off the blow. This old man was tough.

Aldon gripped his gun with both hands and knocked Shawn in the face with the barrel. Gripping his nose, he fell back; grunting. Butter saw Aldon fumbling in the dark to get back up, and tackled him before he had time to point his gun. The rifle flung across the kitchen tile. Aldon gasped, and groaned; the fall was hard.

Butter sat up on the old man and rammed his knuckles into his face. Aldon wrestled with his wrists, but he just didn't have the strength he used to. Butter hit him a few more times. Aldon gasped and groaned.

Shawn pulled Butter off of him and said, "Enough. We need him alive so he can tell us where the money is."

Butter got up and dusted himself off. Then kicked Aldon again.

"You lucky this time," Butter spit.

Aldon groaned, "What money?"

"Where's the light?" Shawn snapped, "It's dark in here."

The old man pointed towards the switch on the wall. Butter stomped across the carpet and flicked the light on. He turned his gaze to Shawn and clutched his shoulder, wincing.

"Damn, this shit hurt."

It wasn't bleeding bad, more of a grazed wound, but still it burned. Shawn held his gun out and pointed it at Aldon. The old man struggled to catch his breath.

"Where the money at," Shawn asked again.

Aldon groaned on the ground.

"What money? All I have is what's in my home."

"Don't play with me, old man. I know you hold Rondo's loot for 'em. We been watchin'. He comes out here once a week on the same day, just like clockwork. Where's the fuckin' money?"

Shawn's finger bounced on the trigger; his wrist was feeling tense.

Aldon propped himself up on his elbow and groaned again; shaking his head.

"What? You—"

Aldon's forehead wrinkled, and his eyes danced across the carpet in a daze. He rubbed the back of his neck, then had a realization.

"You talkin' about my grandson, Randall?"

Aldon laughed, "That boy ain't never gave me any money. Hell, he comes here to watch the game and eat up all my food. Only money that I got comes from Social Security, and it isn't much."

Shawn froze, his fingers danced on the handle of his pistol. He licked his lips. His glare maddened and burned.

"You tryin' to tell me all he comes out here for is fuckin' football games?"

Aldon laughed, and nodded, "Yes. You kids are fools these days. Always gotta go at it, and steal from one another; ya ain't got no damn honor. Who's there brother's keeper among ya'll?"

Shawn snapped, "I am."

Then he shot Aldon in the head. Smoke twirled in the air from the barrel. Aldon's brains and blood splattered past the carpet onto the tile of the kitchen floor. A pool of red ran from the back of his head. His eyes grew dull, settled, and lifeless. Shawn stare into them, gazing, then stepped over the old man and grabbed his rifle. Making for certain he didn't leave a shoe print in the blood.

Butter stay leaned up against the wall; clutching his shoulder. His jaw was to the floor, and his eyes looked like a cartoons'.

He gasped, "Yo, I wasn't expectin' you to shoot him! Why you do that for?"

Shawn pointed the rifle at Butter, and muttered, "Because he shot you."

The rifle cracked and split at his eardrums; as he wet Butter up, thundering shots into his chest. Butter went limp and fell to the floor by the door.

Shawn let the rifle hang down, pointing the barrel towards the tile. He snatched for the kitchen towel on the stove and wiped his prints clean from the barrel. Then he knelt down and placed the rifle in Aldon's arms; clutching the dead man's finger across the trigger. He stomped toward the door and stopped to look at Butter. *I love the look of the still void in their eyes after they die;* he thought to himself. He bit the corner of his lip and spoke to Butter as if he could still hear.

"You's a fuck nigga, bro. Always talkin' too much. You too loud, man, too wild—"

I couldn't let you fuck this up for me, Shawn thought to himself as he licked his lips; staring down at Butter's crippled corpse menacingly.

"Bread gonna miss ya, but don't worry about a thang—because I—am—my—brother's— keeper."

Shawn stomped towards the door, and he flung it open with his sleeve. *Best not tamper with the scene; you'll leave more evidence behind if you do—no need for a cover-up. It's a clean calculation.*

Sirens echoed far in the distance. *It's time to go.* Shawn flipped the light off and left the bodies in the dark; the '70 Chevelle revved. Men lie across the floor dead, right where they bled. Shawn had an escape to make.

Moments later, the source of the sirens pulled up, but it wasn't the cops; no they'd be a few hours, maybe even days at least.

Private Investigator Dale Dickson and his partner Donald rolled upon the scene in an all black Chevy Subaru. They caught wind on the police scanner that shots were fired in the region, and figured it sounded like a job for them.

Detective Dale Dickson stepped out of the driver's seat first. His polished shoes crumpled in the gravel, and he lit up an old corn-cob pipe. He wore a black fedora and a long trench coat, like a detective from the 1930s, too. This guy was dressed for the job.

His partner Donald clambered out next with his writing pad. His sole job was to take note of everything his partner said. He had quick hands and could do fast scribbles. His only problem was he stuttered a little, and his stature was short. Donald asked his partner, "A-are you sure t-this is the right place, Detective Dickie?"

Detective Dickson took a puff of his pipe as he studied the scene. He bit the tip as it hung from his mouth.

"Of course it is," he replied, "can't, y'see, there's still smoke in the air, Donald."

"Y-yeah," Donald said as he stumbled over towards his partner's side, "I can still smell it."

"Let's take a look inside," Dale said, as a cloud of smoke crept up from his pipe.

Dale took the first step, and Donald followed; scribbling notes along the way, and painting the environment of the crime scene. When they came upon the victims on the floor inside the home, Donald gasped. It didn't matter how many bodies he'd seen, they always startled him.

"Detective Dickie, are y-you sure w-we shouldn't call the heavies in for this?"

"Absolutely not, Donald. It wouldn't be any use. I know now and you should, too. We've been thoroughly scanning the surrounding area for weeks now, and we have yet to see a patrolling officer."

Dale took another puff from his pipe and heaved, "We are the heavies around here, my dear boy. It seems we've come to a lawless region, a job has been delivered unto our hands, and it's our duty to bring order to it."

Suddenly, Dale's neck snapped towards Donald, and his mouth followed along.

"Are you writing this down, Donald?"

"I sure am, Detective Dickie. I'm w-writing as f-fast as I can."

Dale walked in and studied the scene. He studied the bullet holes by the door frame first, then Butter, and finally the old veteran, Aldon.

He stood up straight and studied the scene between the two. His shadow cast across the floor by the pale moonlight. The detective relit his pipe, and took yet another puff, then said, "What we have here is a cold, calculated serial killer on our hands, Donald. Perhaps he is the devil himself."

"W-what do y-you mean, Detective Dickie? It looks like b-both of these guys shot each other."

Detective Dickson winced and pondered upon the scene more.

"Stop being simple, Donald, you're wrong. That's why I'm the detective, and you're the note keeper, my dear boy, but no."

Dale froze and rested his knuckles on his hips. Then he continued, "I wish it were as cut and dry as you say, but we aren't that fortunate. There are three different types of shell casings lying on the floor in this room, and they're embedded in the wall, as well."

The detective stopped and thought more while he took a thick drag from his pipe.

"Yes," he continued, "what we have here is cold, calculated, and cunning. Genius tactics sewn by a quick mind."

Dale Dickson's voice began to trail off, but he cleared his throat, and made a final assumption.

"What we'll do in this case, Donald, is take a mold of the shell casings in the wall and get a sample of each. Once the coroner identifies the bodies, we can go onward and interview their loved ones and relatives. Did you get all of that down, Donald?"

"Y-yes, Detective Dickie, I sure did."

Donald smiled and glowed with admiration. He counted the detective as his greatest mentor and he was surely his best friend.

"You're the best, Detective Dickie, h-honest."

Dale smiled. He always appreciated compliments from others.

"Well, I've told you it all before, Donald. There must always be a Dale Dickson around to get the job done. That's what my father told me. He was named Dale Dickson as well. Along with his father before him, and his father before him. It is the collective covenant that my blood holds with the universe. There's always been a Dale Dickson around. Even in Ancient Egypt, perhaps even before the great flood might I presume.:

"Wow," Donald said in astonishment, "you're the detective of the ages."

Detective Dale Dickson took another draw from his pipe, and agreed with pride.

"You got that one right, my dear boy."

Eventually, Rondo caught the news, too. His grandfather was dead, and word was the cops were combing the place through and through. They found two bodies, and of course, the poor dog.

Rondo laid back on the couch sobbing to himself; dialing a number. They found the money, too. His girl tried to cozy up to him and kiss his neck, but Rondo jerked away fast, and snapped, "Get off me! I ain't in the mood!"

The phone rang on the other end three times, then the call was picked up.

"What's good?" the voice on the other end answered; it was Rondo's boy, Pats.

All Pats heard was sniffling on the other end.

"Ey, you good, bro," Pats asked, confused. He was chillin' at the bar; kickin' it with his boy, Ronnie.

Rondo's voice shook in the phone, and he moaned, "Man, these fools just won't quit. T-they—t-they—"

Pats barked on the other end, "You talkin' about those fools that came at you at the club? They at it again?"

Rondo's lip quivered by the receiver.

"M-man, they shot Muffie, man; they killed my dog."

Pats flashed Ronnie a menacing glare.

"They at it again," Ronnie muttered. Pats motioned a silent cut against his own throat, flaring his nostrils and nodded. Then he said, "Word? That's fucked up. I know you loved that dog."

Rondo cried; growing more angry with each tear. He clenched his fist, as one fell down his cheek, and screamed, "I'm sick of this shit! These niggas done shot my pawpaw, they killed Muffie, I ain't—"

Pats motioned his hand up to stop Rondo from talking almost as if he were there in person, and interrupted; getting more confused with each second.

"Did you just say pawpaw?" Pats asked quickly smiling, and muffling his mouth, trying not to laugh. Ronnie threw him a "what's goin' on" type of look; and mouthed the words—"pawpaw."

Rondo fixed his shirt, and cried, "Yeah. that's what I said; my pawpaw! They shot my pawpaw! He's dead."

Ronnie heard it that time too because Pat's held the phone between both of their ears. Ronnie threw his head on the bar quickly and lost it. Pats couldn't help himself either; he laughed, too.

"Ey, you can't be sayin' that, man. You—"

"Pawpaw," Rondo snapped on the other end, "I'll say whatever I want to! What you want me to call him? Grandfather all proper and shit or what?"

Ronnie was crying from laughing so hard; he was about to fall off his stool. Pats just shook his head and muffled his laughter in his elbow. Then he collected himself, ushering Ronnie to keep it down a little. He got serious again, too.

"Nah," Pats wrestled to keep it down, and sound sincere, "you good, dog. We finna get at 'em."

Rondo yelled back,"Yeah, we are. I want everybody lookin' for 'em. They gotta pay."

Rondo paused for a minute, then asked, "You saw Breezy, lately? He ain't been pickin' up."

"Nah," Pats replied, "I ain't heard back from him."

"We gotta find 'em then; we gotta get a handle on this shit."

"Word, word," Pats replied, "we about to pull through."

Rondo was cool with that; they ended the call. Pats shot Ronnie a grin, and said, "Pawpaw, for real? This muthafucka really still call his grandpa pawpaw, like a little boy and shit."

They both lost it again.

Through the laughing fit, Pats jingled his keys out of his pocket and cackled, "Man, this fool is slippin', bro."

Ronnie bellowed back hysterically, "He's gonna end up like pawpaw if he don't watch it!"

Laughter cackled towards the entrance; and the door to the U swung open. They were about to make a move.

CHAPTER XXIV:

SLAM

I didn't have the courage to take the cash we'd gotten from the wreck on the road and run. I was racing down the interstate, and ready to go for it, but the thought of the unknown was too crippling, and it was almost as if—I couldn't leave. It's hard to believe; *it's like something has it's grip on me.*

The blackouts have been growing more fierce these past few days, too. The colors of the world seem to flow together, and it's like I'm stuck on replay, restarting every afternoon on the same level, *stuck in the same game; man with no name. I'm failing and falling; there's just no escape.*

I was completely disconnected, unplugged, which was part of the goal, but I didn't like it. *You think of joy; you fake it. You think of love, nobody will take it. It's all empty, and I'm goin' nowhere. I've lost myself.* I gave in to the man in the hat's tempting. My guilt grew ears, and he was the only thing that I could hear.

My fingers stretched in the dark towards the glint of glass that lie beyond; propped up on the edge, leaning against the leg of the coffee table. The crickets hummed outside quietly, and the air danced slow. I unscrewed the cap on the bottle and took a swig. I didn't have a clue where I was or what I was drinking. *Yeagermeister.* It had become a new thing. *That's right,* I thought. It was all coming back.

The cackling drummed away again through the silence. *I made a fool of myself last night, didn't I?*

My thoughts scrambled, and all I had to juggle were the pieces. *Smoke twirling, other kids laughing. Derek got lucky. He made out with her.*

The girl's pretty smile flashed in my mind, but her name—*no, I can't remember her name. I can barely recall myself.*

I took another swig. Sweat grew around my temples and surfaced like a wave across my forehead. The liquor was trying to find a way out, but it couldn't escape. *Nor can I.*

The room spun, and images of my thoughts floated on the edge. Moonlight crept in from the nearby fluttering curtain that hung down across the window. I closed my eyes, and images that I couldn't make sense of appeared. I saw myself back in the old town again; in the place Zanesville used to be.

The downtown district was beautiful and it seemed so alive. People every which way bustled about with shopping bags, kids giggled out of candy stores, and street vendors stood near carts advertising their wares out of barrels. Bulbs flashed around the letters of signs and a simple picture of Main Street could have been mistaken as a classic shot of New York City. Traffic was thick, commerce was the business, and everyone was trying to make their way through a harsh time. The depression left nobody unscathed, but the town still remained bright.

Horse hooves still clattered among buzzing horns, people bustled, and there was chatter. A policeman's whistle blew, and the bell of a door clattered.

I turned my gaze and saw myself facing a red paneled entrance, the knob glinted gold. A record player screeched in my ears, and I could hear Sophie Turner singing, "Some of These Days."

Then came the sign that read, "Knopp's The Hat Man."

Someone nearby yelled, "Come on change up your stride and make your way! Come get yourself a hat and start a new day!"

A boy with dark hair combed back in an undercut was on his knees shining a man's shoes. The boy turned around with a grin. *Classy.*

Next, I saw him standing in front of a large cracked mirror in a shabby room. His face wrinkled and shivered up close. Pools of tears fluttered in his eyes. He trembled as his hand brought up a large purple fedora. The boy placed it on the top of his head. Sophie Turner still crooned, "Some of These Days."

He gasped, and the pools in his eyes exploded. Tears ran slowly down his cheeks to the screeching of the record player. He cried, "Th-that's better," then he pulled the brim of the hat lower.

"Now n-nobody can see m-my eyes; they w-won't know the t-tears that I cry inside."

Raindrops pounded across the concrete; a street lamp burned at the crosswalk, right by a bus stop. The boy was on his knees crying over a bouquet of toppled red roses. The crashing of the fall echoed like dice in the distance.

"P-please."

The boy choked and coughed.

"Into Each Life Some Rain Must Fall," by the Ink Spots echoed through the battling thunder in the clouds; a street lamp blinked nearby.

The boy shuffled on his knees towards a blonde faceless girl's ankles, but she hollered at him, and kicked him away.

"Get off me, Jack! You know, making it to New York City has always been one of my dreams! You're not respecting my boundaries."

The boy heaved, trying to catch his breath. His hand shivered towards one of the roses. He clutched it to his chest, and stuttered, "J g-gave you all t-the best that I h-had. I really did. N-now I'm ruined."

I saw the street sign for Brighton Boulevard, and the vision grew black. Car horns blew and the sound of brakes running across a rail screeched through the air. Then came the high-pitched wrecking of a crash, but I couldn't see a thing; only hear. It was the only thing that would bleed through. The terrible screams tore at my skull and ripped through my brain. They reminded me of the same screams I heard the night my father died. There's something about screaming some people don't know; they've never heard it. It rips at your soul and tears away at your heart. Not even the horror movies can get it right. *A real scream is* something *you can never escape.*

"O-oh! O-oh! No!"

The man wailed like a child.

"No! No! No!"

He groaned and roared; pant legs shuffled towards something. *If I could only see, I'd understand. I'd be able to piece together who he actually is.*

The man gasped, then screamed.

"I can put it back! Oh, god! I can put it back together!"

The man groaned, and the shivering shrills came again. They grew and grew until I fell completely into them. The screaming wouldn't stop. My body shivered, and I rocked with my head lying in the palms of my hands. I was splitting, and I felt my skin burn. My cheeks flared, and my eyes popped open.

He stopped it again.

As his presence grew, so did the bleeding effect of the old ghost's memories. In the visions, I couldn't only see him, but I was him; walking right in his own polished shoes. His heart beat just like my own; as if we were twins. *One being of light, hawk-headed of the sun, the other of the crow; shadow on the run.*

If I could only sink deeper and figure him out more, I might discover a way to beat him, I thought to myself. The barrier of my thoughts may have been weakened, but it still remained.

He can't hear my thoughts when I'm in control, I told myself, *but I have to sink deeper to know him. I have to discover the secret of my shadow.*

I layed back down and sought the gate to the old town again, but I couldn't find it. I saw the golden knob, but I'd drifted off too far. The shadow of sleep had caught me again.

The next day I awoke to Von and Derek bickering back and forth on the game. I got up and went for the bottle again.

There wasn't much to do with the day, besides continue the binge. It had been that way ever since the wreck. Derek and I didn't discuss the incident after it happened. Julian tried to call me up later the next day, but I didn't answer. He texted me and asked if I knew what happened and, of course, I lied. I mean, what was I supposed to do? Tell him the truth? I'm not trying to make myself look that bad. I knew how terrible it was, but I couldn't let myself care. Brian was in a coma, and his girl wouldn't talk, at least to the cops, that is. We left the bag of meth in the car after all, so I guess it was a good thing the guy was takin' a nap because if he weren't, he'd be in jail anyway. It's not justifiable by any means, but I try to find the positive light behind everything. *What else can a fella do?*

We still had cash left to spend, which is another positive point. Money is great too, so it's all good. We've never attempted to rob anyone. We might do bad things, but we're good guys through and through to tell you the truth.

By this time, we'd found a house, too. One of Derek's friends knew somebody, that knew somebody, and maybe they knew somebody, too—I'm not sure, but somebody had a house and we were staying in it; the place was pretty much abandoned. All it had was an much TV, a couch, a chair, and a mattress in the living room. Apparently, they didn't mind us crashing there, or so I was told.

Either way, not all the occupants got the memo because one night some random crazy guy walked in with patches missing out of his hair and gave us all the death stare. Ellie peeped him first, and she gasped. Then we all froze. There was a staring match between us all for about forty-two minutes, or seconds, at the time I couldn't tell which. It was the most random thing ever, and I didn't take a breath the whole time. Eventually, he slowly backed away, in an awkward shuffle, and left, but it didn't help. I can't speak for everyone else, but I was shocked nonetheless and in a bit of a panic.

"Who was that?" I nervously asked.

Derek was the only one laughing, "Oh, shit! I think that was Charlie. Man, he just got out of jail."

"I-is h-he dangerous," I stammered back.

Derek couldn't stop laughing. He nodded, "Yeah, he's crazy. Charlie is gonna kill you."

I shuddered behind a pillow and squealed. My eyes danced above the corners, and I stuttered, "B-but why me?"

Derek threw his head back and nearly fell out of his chair. The room was spinnin, and I was trippin'. The shadows grew in waves, edging closer towards me from the edges of the room. *It's gettin' dark in here, man,* I thought to myself. My ears rung, and I clutched at Ellie's arm for comfort, but she smacked my hand away.

"Stop it! I ain't about to hold ya ass! I tried to tell you not to eat those mushrooms. Now you just gonna have to go through it."

I clutched my face further into the pillow to muffle Derek's laughter as I shook and sobbed all over.

"Oh, no, oh, no, no, no."

"Man, chill."

I'd learned my lesson quick with shrooms; a truly bad business to conduct if you're not safe and in the proper setting. Charlie was a living ghoul, and I've been watching my back ever since.

Thank god, he hasn't come back, I thought with another sip; fluttering back towards the present moment. It was past the middle of the day and Ellie was chillin' on the couch next to Von rollin' a blunt. There were about six other people hanging out, probably just trying to escape mommy and daddy's house to enjoy a little freedom I assume. When people came to hang with us, they knew they could do whatever; we didn't care. Hell, half of the people that showed up we didn't even know, so it was pretty much anything goes.

I lifted two fifths up in the air and squealed in a cartoon voice, "Badadoo! Look what I can do! I got another shot for me and you!"

Some stared, others laughed, and Von was one of them. He cackled, "This muthafucka is crazy. What you got there?"

I lifted up my right hand and replied, "Got some Crown right here," then I raised my left, "And some Peachie Scnapps, my boy, it's the best in town."

Von sucked his teeth, waved his hand, and said, "Peachie Scnapps? Man, you trippin'."

I was weightless and in the hug of a manic, happy wave. *Perhaps I am bipolar,* I thought to myself, but my thoughts couldn't keep up and my voice ran away with me.

I laughed, "I'm just playin' around. No, it's some Evan Williams, man, you get a lot more for a cheaper price, y'know? I'm tryin' to save some money so I can go fly to South America or somethin' and trip my ass off out in the middle of the wilderness with a tribe, man. Y'know? Like just get completely lost in the wind with a bunch of painted faces beating drums around me runnin' around in a circle and all the while I'm just spinnin' off into another dimension, completely and utterly losing grip on the fabric of reality."

A guy leaning against the wall, puffin' on a black, snapped, "Don't say that. That's terrible."

Okay, no need to get all hostile there, I thought to myself. I didn't even respond. Ellie just shook her head and sealed the blunt with her tongue. Von replied, Ok, then. Well, I'll take a shot or two with you if you want."

Shot glasses clicked, lighters flicked, and dollar bills crumpled, then rolled. Before we knew it Tony opened the door. He was already over Kayla, and thankfully for him, the bruises from the beat down healed. He no longer had to lie to people about running into a door. Yeah. A door with a fist at the other end of it.

He said what's up to everybody, and when he got in the living room where we were playing cards he asked where Derek was.

I snapped my neck towards the staircase and replied, "He's upstairs, with some chick or somethin', I guess."

Tony smirked and replied, "Who else up there? Where are Lee and Jay at?"

Lee and Jay were rollin' with us at this point, too. We pretty much had ourselves a trap. Jay had that polished sawed off of his, so y'know, we needed that; to protect ourselves and all. That gun Derek had was his step dad's, and he got his ass beat like Rocky until he gave it back. We were both pretty much kids without homes at this point.

I shrugged my shoulders and started shuffling cards for fun. I wasn't sure what to do with my hands at the moment. As focused as I was I still replied, "Who knows really, man. I guess they'll be back here eventually. It's hard to tell."

Tony nodded his head and said, "Ight, ight, bet. Well, I'm—hold on my phone's ringin'."

He fumbled in his jacket pocket and pulled out his phone. I didn't hear it ring, and it didn't even sound like it was vibrating either. *I would've known.* My senses were on high alert. Tony put the phone up to his ear and said, "Who dis?"

He paused for a moment, nodded his head, then continued, "Ight, shit we been lookin' for you all day. I'll come scoop you up."

He paused again and said, "Ight, peace."

Tony slid the razor down and threw it back into his pocket. He looked at me and said, "Ey, that was my new girl, man. She need a ride to work. I'm finna go, but when you see D, tell 'em I'll be back."

I nodded fast with the jitters.

"Alright, man. Have a wonderful day, Tony."

A few minutes after Tony left, Derek came downstairs and asked where he was.

I replied, "Oh, he just left to go pick up some chick. He said he'll be back in a little bit or somethin' like that, man."

Derek looked towards the back door and replied, "Well, shit, man, he couldn't have left that quick. I just heard his ass."

Derek made his way to the back door, and I stayed loungin' on the couch next to Ellie, twiddling away, getting' ready to hit another bump, but then I heard wood split, like a door frame came off, and someone yell, "Get the fuck out of the way! I ain't playin' with you!"

People screamed and folks started running around everywhere. I was shocked, but it was sort of funny. I mean, everybody was posted up acting tough seconds earlier, but when they heard that sound—the split, all that cool shit went completely out of the window. Corners shook with gasps in them, and carpet shuffled. I turned my head and a voice muffled.

"Where the dope at?"

At first, there was nothing; not a breath. Just two dark holes, staring back at me, each a path to death. *Two tunnels, each in a flash, burn and maim, just to get the cash.* I never thought it could happen. I was staring down the barrel of a sawed-off shotgun.

The stickup kid muffled again, "Where's the money?!"

Everything paused. No sound, no nothing, just a faint tingling in the wind that it was all about to end. Honestly, I didn't even care. I've never been afraid of death—always welcomed it in fact. I was only upset over the loss of power. Someone else had taken control of my own fate. *I can't stand it; I hate it.*

That's the thing about having a gun in your face; in that moment you have a bond—a relationship between each other. *To live or die, I wanna say bye. I'm sick of this game, I just wanna fly.* Stuck in limbo, the clock ticked, and I started to shake.

My face grew hot, and I bite my lip. My ears rang, and I snorted, then tssked. Then came the sniffle and choke.

My cheeks perked up into a grin, and my forehead ran cold. *He's beginning to settle in.*

My shoulders shook, and I shivered. I couldn't help it anymore. I didn't care. I'd lost myself, so it was fair.

My throat squealed and tears ran out of my eyes. I was laughing uncontrollably. *It's so liberating. I'm gonna die right where I lie.*

Finally, I thought to myself, *somebody's gonna kiss me.*

I could almost feel it, the darkness, and floating away. An end to it all; the good and the bad, but at least there'd be no more suffering.

You don't have the bones for this, Jack, the man in the hat said, *I'm all you got in this world now; your on the outside now. Forsaken since the day. There ain't any miracles out here, kid; look where you are. It's just you and me. It's just—*

I couldn't take the reality of it all anymore. I was in the hole and I knew it. *There's no hope of me getting out of it; there's no path to freedom.* There's something to relish in the sense of surrender; you either sacrifice or you take. I did both.

There'd always been the juggle and the struggle. That didn't start before the party phase; he tends to manifest through a blackout. I'd discovered that through the first.

I'll always follow you. I come from within. Never forget that I'm your best friend. That was our pact. We had made an agreement. Jack's motivations were always vague, but I only wanted one thing. I wanted to patch the hole in my soul, only he tricked me. *There's no way to make it undone. I'll always be the lost son.*

Eyes glittered over the red bandanna in confusion. The hand held the gun pointed at me still, but it shook; *just a tittle.*

A glaze of fear washed across the stickup kids' eyes; madness squealed within my laughing tears.

He couldn't take it or understand it. His face tensed up, and guilt turned to fury. For a moment, he wanted to, but he still wouldn't shoot me. He just wanted an advance, a way out of his own. He wasn't trying to kill anybody. There isn't a game to blame. *My, how the truth of the roots can cause so much shame.*

It doesn't matter if you hop in for a swim or simply stick your toes in the water. When you deal in the underworld, the devils will always find you. *Be keen to not become prey, always operate by a code, a special play.*

For some reason, what happened next still doesn't make much sense. I don't know why, but apparently this particular stickup kid couldn't even shoot a dog, too, because, honestly, hand on any kind of good book, that's all it took.

Y'see, we had this guy's dog down in the basement. He pretty much randomly asked us to watch it—as crazy and unbelievable as it sounds. *Doesn't it all though,* but anyways-- me and Derek had basically been stuck with the thing for days. He was a cool guy that liked to get high. *Blow a little smoke into his nose to settle his woes.*

I loved that dog. I'd forgotten about him. Perhaps we all had, but that hound was muscular. It was a meaty pit bull.

The dog ran up the steps barking and growling; then it charged at the stickup kid's heels. He squealed.

His red bandanna flailed around, patting his chin as he swung the shotgun at the hound's face. The dog wouldn't let up. It had sunk its teeth into his leg and jerked away. The boy screamed.

The other stickup kid was out in the dining room the whole time, holding a pistol to Derek's head. He was in all black and wore a ski mask. The dog groaned, a girl whimpered in the corner, and the other guy flailed in fury, then grunted, "Fuck it! Let's go!"

Just like that, he rushed towards the back and was gone. Bloody murder with the red bandanna was screaming from the gnawing of the hound, and he swung the shotgun into the dog's snout a few more good times and eventually knocked his leg loose. He ran, too.

I'll never forget the last glimpse that he gave me. He looked remorseful and sad, almost as if he felt sorry for me. For whatever reason, he didn't kill me. In a way, he will forever be my brother because we had recognized something within each other.

He hadn't fallen; he wanted to be saved. I had surrendered; death is what I craved. *Surrendering and salvation, together, are two great things. A song to a symphony; together they sing.*

After the stickup kids left, everybody started chattering. There were a lot of tears and sniffles; shouts even.

"Damn, bro! What the fuck, man!"

Calm down, flip-flops.

"Cheese and whiskey! Dammit boy, they 'bout shot us all up!"

Who's the shirtless fifty-year-old redneck guy in the corner?

"Oh my gosh, Ashley. We are so getting out of here."

Bye, bye, Barbie.

"We must climb to the shrine upon the heaves of the mountain and call our banners! War is upon us!"

?

"Ey, yo, anybody get a picture of that shit?! If you did and it got me in it, send me that shit! I was doin' deuces in the back the whole time. I ain't scared!"

I love the positivity.

Ellie shook on the couch, completely stricken with fear not saying a word. Von sat in the chair like nothing even happened. *Perhaps this isn't his first rodeo.*

Derek knelt down in the corner with his eyes towards the ground and his hands on the back of his head. For the most part, everything was cool, and the dust was settling.

Suddenly, a chick came running from the dining room and said, "It's ok guys, I just called the cops!"

Somebody yelled, "You did what?!"

Derek scurried up quickly; hell, all of us did. He yelled, "Everybody, get out of here! We gotta go right now!"

Kids rushed out of the doors to their cars. Meanwhile, I ran upstairs to get what was left of the stash in the attic. I assumed Derek would grab the cash. I ran back downstairs and yelled, "What's going to happen when the cops come here and nobody is around? We can't just leave the house open for them to search."

Derek yelled back, "We can't worry about that right now! We just gotta round everything up and get the fuck out of here!"

He looked over at Von and Ellie, then hollered, "What ya'll doin'?! You hearin' me?! We gotta bounce!"

Ellie got up quickly and rushed to the car. It looked like she was crying. Von just got up cool as a cucumber and grabbed a hold of the bottles I'd brought. I, on the other hand , wasn't there. I was but a mere spectator. During the blackouts, he could take over, but once I felt sober, the crack would seal, and he'd have to go back; *locked afar, clicking away, chattering some, then close to none.*

I knew I didn't have what it took to survive within the world I'd put myself in. Jack is the stronger, the more dominant half. He knows how to keep his cool for the most part, and he's a master when it comes to madness. *Consistently systematic.*

I stood up and winked at Lee and Jay they finally made it back; *just at the wrong time.* Jack, the man in the hat, was speaking through me; I'd blacked out. *I've gone away.*

348

"I'd leave, ya know. It wouldn't be a good idea to stick around."

Jay nodded his head and replied, "Damn, right. My gun is as illegal as illegal can be. We'll just go back down the street and hide out. Everything will be cool."

Von walked over to us, panicked all of a sudden over his most recent realization. He yelled, "Any of ya'll know the girl that called the cops? She can't be sayin' I was here. I'm on fuckin' probation, man."

Lee cut in and replied, "Yeah, I know her. I'll tell her what to say. If the cops call her back," he paused and shook his head, "I don't know. They get calls like this all the time. They don't give a shit. Ya'll should get out of here now, though. Don't worry about it, me and Jay got it handled."

Jack jingled the keys, and the rest followed. They all went toward the Altima. Derek rode shotgun, and Ellie, plus Von, rode in the back.

Jack lit a smoke and winced at the menthol flavor as he took a puff and turned the wheel.

"Those guys sure don't how to steal," Jack remarked.

Von replied, "Shit, you thought the shit was funny. I ain't gonna lie though. I'm kind of glad it happened; just another story to tell, really."

Jack laughed at a low rumble, barely audible. He bit his lip and stare at the yellow lines on the road. I could feel his thoughts. He remembered something; I knew it, but he wouldn't let me see. That's unless there's a vision caused by the bleed. *What do you have to hide? Why won't you let me see?*

Jack shook his head, clicked his tongue, and let out a low chuckle.

Nope.

Suddenly, Derek yelled, "This shit ain't no fuckin' joke! I had a fuckin' gun to my head! To my head, man! And ya'll gonna laugh about the shit?! Fuck that!"

Derek punched the dash and kept going off.

"You think everything is a fuckin' joke, man? This shit might be a game to you, but it ain't no game to me. I ain't out here just doin' this shit for fun. You got this shit fucked up! You can go back to mommy's house whenever you want. You got a momma that can buy you a car, nice clothes, and all that. I ain't got that! This is all I got and I'm good at it! It's the only way I'm gonna get out of here. You ain't stuck here like me! You already got everything and look at me, I ain't got nothin'. This is all I got."

Derek paused and then murmured under his breath, "And you just laughed on the floor, when dude had that gun on you, man, you just laughed."

Derek shook his head and threw his empty hands across his face and paused. Then he said, "Who the fuck would do us like this? I mean, we ain't runnin' up on nobody like that; we ain't got no money except for—"

Derek paused, then he gazed at me—at Jack, I mean. He stare, stuck at the wheel driving; listening with one ear and thinking with the other.

"It's gotta be your boy, Julian. Remember? Its gotta be them because we took dude's money, right?"

Jack replied, "A possibility yes, but a probability no. Those guys aren't a threat to anyone. Great thieves, but they're scoundrels, and that's why I like 'em. Trust me. It was definitely someone else."

"Who you think it was, then?" Derek asked.

Jack shrugged his shoulders as he drove onward, glimpsing long and hard at the bell tower of the old Lutheran St. John church.

"I don't know. Ask Tony."

Derek's eyebrows shuffled in thought.

"You ain't tryin' to say it was him, right? Man, Tony wouldn't do no shit like this. That's my boy, nah."

He paused, onward in thought, and continued.

"Nah, but I bet he can help us find out who did it."

His eyes burned, and his jaw tensed, then he said, "I ain't gonna let this shit ride. He knows where to get guns, too."

Jack snorted, and laughed, "Really?!"

Ellie battled so much for reason.

"Don't you think all this has gone far enough?! I mean, Derek, come on! Did you forget that the gun was on me?! It was on me, too! I could've died today, we all—"

Derek snapped back, "I know, I know! That's why I ain't gonna let it ride! They fucked with me—they fucked with my blood, they—"

Ellie yelled; she was pissed.

"Well, you can just drop me off at home! I don't want nothin' to do with any of this!"

Derek snapped. He was furious.

"Okay! We'll take your scary ass home, then!"

Von chimed in next, "Take me home, too, I'm on probation, man, I can't—"

Jack interrupted, "Don't worry about a thing. If you haven't bought the ticket, you don't have to take the ride."

Here. We're all in; down with a spin.

CHAPTER XXV:

HOW TO ROB

It wasn't hard to get ahold of Tony. We didn't even have to call him; he called us.

"Ya'll good? What's with the popo runnin' up in ya'll's crib?"

We were all still in a daze. We dropped off Ellie first, smoked another with Von, then dropped him off, too. It was just me and Derek; we had nowhere to go, and nothing to do.

Derek bounced his knee in the passenger seat and told Tony what happened during the whole charade.

Tony maintained his cool. All he said was, "Word? Ey, I bet I know where these fools stay at. You say one had a red bandana, kinda tall, and the other one in the ski mask was all built and muscular. He look like a titan or somethin', right?"

Derek shook his head in confusion, then looked at me, and slowly mouthed the words, *No, we didn't.*

He kept shaking his head as his eyes narrowed, and his chin fell towards his chest.

"Nah, man, that ain't what we said. One dude had a red bandanna. He was tall, with some long ass alien fingers, and the other guy was short, kind of stocky, but he might've been a little fat, too. I don't know, man. Sound like anybody you know?"

He was on speaker, and Jack heard what was behind his words.

Tony snapped on the other end, "Man, I ain't—"

Then he simmered down.

"Sorry, bro, that was my little sister. She want a ride somewhere or somethin', but uh—yeah, they sound familiar. I know where they stay at. You tryin' to holla at 'em or what?"

Derek nodded.

"Yuh, you know it, bubbies. We gotta make a house call."

Tony laughed excitedly, and said, "That's my boy, right there! Ey, I told you, all you gotta do is hit a lick, and that's it. Fuck all that nickel and dimin' shit."

Derek grinned. You could tell he appreciated the admiration.

"We about to do it, right? We gonna hit these fools tonight. You still know ol' boy with the guns?"

"Yup! I gots it, bubbies. We finna strap up."

Derek laughed on the other end, and barked, "Who done killed my kid bruddha?!"

Tony laughed, too.

"Man, you a trip. Roll up and scoop me up. We finna catch 'em slippin'."

"Ight, we about to come through, then."

"Ight, then."

"Peace."

We set it, just like that.

We met up with Tony, and he was ready. Jack mostly studied and observed, not saying much. He already saw and knew what was to come because he had studied the pathways within the void, the mirror world if you will, but what he was privy to I wasn't. I didn't have a clue what was in store.

All matter of choices lie upon the pitch of three. There's the way you're going, a way that you can turn, and a bridge that you can burn. No matter which way you're going; there's always two ways that you can turn.

Tony stuffed one gun securely in his pants, and Derek picked up the other, smiling.

"Damn, this shit is nice. You ever shoot it off before?"

Tony's eyes flickered, and he shook his head.

"Nah, that shit clean. I just got it and only used it once."

Derek lifted the nine millimeter and stuffed it into his waist, laughing.

"Shit, it ain't clean no more. What about my boy, though, you gotta gun for him?"

Tony narrowed his eyes at Jack, and he grinned back. Tony didn't like the look; it shook him too much. He looked Jack up and down wide eyed and said, "Uh, nah. You okay, bruh? You lookin' off."

Jack shook his head.

"Not at all. I'm absolutely fine. I'm just enjoyin' the ride."

Tony's eyes pierced Jack as he studied him. He was firm, calm, and cool.

"Okay, then," Tony nodded nervously, "well, you can just be the driver, then, and play lookout while we go in."

Jack clapped his hands together and smiled.

"Oh, I hope there's a high-speed chase. I'm so excited!"

Tony scowled and lifted the corner of his lip, then asked, confused, "A high what?"

Then he tssked through his lips and turned back to
Derek.

"We gonna ride or what?"

Derek pulled the hammer back, and it clicked.

"Let's do the damn thing."

Jack and the rest hopped in the ride. He gunned
down on the gas. *Oh the adrenaline, oh the theatrics. You
can't feel like this in the void. It's what pure life is. The risk,
the danger, you just gotta pick your own flavor.*

The trio parked down the block thought that the
house where the stickup kids were holed up seemed like
quite the shithole and it blended in perfectly with the locale.
The neighborhood was quiet nearly all around. *Winter
seems to do that, folks can't stand the chill.*

"Ready or Not" by the Fugees hummed across the
interior of the car as they pulled up.

"Man, I can't stand no more of this fuckin' radio,
bro, your CD player for real broke?" Tony asked from the
back.

Jack peered at him in the rearview mirror and
nodded slowly.

"Uh huh, yeah, it's definitely broken. Why does it
matter? Don't we—or should I say you? Don't you have a
job to do?"

Tony narrowed his eyes back at Jack as he threw his
ski mask on. He spoke to Derek, but kept his eyes peeled
towards Jack.

"Man, your boys trippin'. Why he actin' so funny?"

Derek threw a bright blue bandanna across his face
that he found in the car that was mine, and replied, "I don't
know, you ask him. He be gettin' in those moods
sometimes."

He turned towards Jack and nudged him.

"I told you, you got that bipolar shit goin' on or
somethin'," Derek laughed.

Jack grinned, still staring at Tony in the rearview. He bit the corner of his lip and chuckled softly. Then, he said, "Y'know, Tony, you look very familiar with that mask on. Go trick or treatin' a lot?"

Tony retorted, "Man, you white muthafucka. Of course, you think all black people look alike."

Jack shook his head. *Never steal candy from friends.*

"No, that ain't got nothin' to do with it. Just a little déjà vu, that's all."

Tony stammered, "Man, you trippin'."

Derek didn't say a word. All he did was stare at the gun in his lap. The reality of it all was catching up to him. There was no laughing or running away from it. To him, there was only one thing he could do. He ran his fingers across the barrel slowly towards the grip and tightened his fist around it. Flames lit in his eyes, and he peered back at Tony.

"You ready to do this?"

Tony sneered and nodded.

"Follow me, watch my back, and we got this."

Jack circled around the brick house and dropped them both off in the alley. Derek shivered a little at first, but he shook it off fast and maintained himself. Him and Tony got out and crept in the back. Jack skittered off down the alley to circle his way around and park back down the block. The radio hummed and "Raindrops Keep Fallin' on My Head" kicked off. Jack turned the knob up; feeling the tune.

"Ooooohhh."

Then he rocked his shoulders about and sang along, mimicking and matching each phrase with a goofy symbolic gesture.

Screaming erupted from the home. Jack turned his head towards the sound and gritted his teeth, then he wiggled the bill of his hat furiously, and turned up the knob further. The screaming ceased and Jack continued to sing along. He pulled his hat off and checked his cut in the rearview mirror. He wiggled his eyebrows as he sang along, and ran his fingers through his hair sensually, humming to the tune.

Jack rocked his shoulders up and down and twisted his hat back on. Then, jerked his hand up, bulging his eyes, and studying his nails. Three bright white flashes thundered across the windows of the house. Jack jumped back in his seat, acting startled, and quickly put the car into drive. He turned the wheel out of parallel park, and shimmied slowly down the road, dancing to the tune again. The door swung open and both of the stickup kids ran out.

Jack danced along still.

The doors flung open on the car and shut quickly, and Tony yelled, "Stab off! We gotta get outta here!"

Jack slammed his foot on the pedal and sped away. He turned the radio down to barely an audible hum. Derek heaved heavily in the passenger seat with the money bag.

Jack's lips twisted, and he winced, then spoke. His voice mimicked the sound of a parent asking their child about their day.

"So how'd it go?"

Derek panted, shivered, and let out a faint whine. He wouldn't even answer. He just continued to heave and stare out of the window. It didn't take long making the escape through the downtown area. Jack flipped the blinker towards I-70. They hit the interstate and headed towards Newark. *Best to take a ride out of town,* Jack thought to himself.

Tony barked from the back.

"Man, why you shoot first like that?! We had the money!"

Derek wailed and wiped his eyes dry. He was crying at this point.

"The gun just went off! I-I I didn't mean to! I—"

357

Tony pulled his mask off and snapped from the back.

"You shoot, I shoot! That's the way it goes. Lucky I missed, but you didn't have to shoot the fool!"

Derek shook his head ravishly, and muttered, "That wasn't them, that wasn't them."

"It wasn't them," he wailed.

Tony shuffled around in the back and jerked his neck around. He slapped the back of his hand in his empty palm, and said," Shit, what you mean it wasn't them? Those was the same boys that tried to get at ya'll. I'm tellin' you."

Derek's chin dropped to his chest. His head shook, and he sobbed all over.

"H-he c-came after me first. He—"

Derek burst out bawling uncontrollably, scratching away at his cheek, and muttering to himself. *I didn't mean to; I didn't mean to.*

Jack bit his lip and grinned in the rearview mirror at himself. He pressed further down on the pedal. Derek continued to moan.

"At least we got those grands up, though," Tony continued; smiling to himself.

Derek cried, and muttered hopelessly.

I didn't mean to; I didn't mean to.

CHAPTER XXVI:

BEWARE

Shawn pulled a square from his lips and blew misty smoke through the cold air; it danced towards the still light of the full moon overhead. The tree branches creaked in the wind and etched across the stars. The crows pecked at their eardrums as they cawed across the hallowed woods.

The same man who had lost teeth at the pull of the pliers lie crouched in front of Bread and Shawn; his knees dug in the mud.

Shawn grabbed the corner of the tape and ripped it from his lips. Breezy gasped and panted.

"Ya'll ain't gotta do me like this! I told you everything! It ain't my fault you believed ol dude's lie!"

Shawn stood still, peering down at him, not moving an inch; smoke danced from the ember at his side.

"Nah, you the one that's lyin'. You knew that muthafucka could shoot like Rambo. You sent us in there to get got. Now look what happened. My brotha done got shot."

Bread didn't say a word. His empty eyes glared at Breezy. Shawn tapped his side and continued, "That was his twin, y'know? Look at the tears on his face. You did that!"

Bread choked and sniffled; Shawn continued, "They been holdin' it down since before birth. How you think that make him feel, huh?"

Shawn tapped Bread again.

"How that make you feel Bread?"

Bread stayed still, unmoving, and not answering. Cripple and hollow from the grief. Breezy struggled in the knot tied around his hands behind his back, and wailed, "Rondo kept his loot with the old man. I'm tellin' you! I seen the shit with my own two eyes. I—"

Shawn interrupted, and hollered, "It don't matter now! The place gotta be crawlin' with pigs at this point. If there's any money there—well, shit, they about to line their pockets with that shit on the low, though. Either way, that shit gone to me and Rondo."

Shawn paused and grinned slightly, taking another hit.

"And so are you."

He nodded his head towards the side and kept his glare fixed on Breezy.

"Bread, get the gas."

Breezy jerked around, and hollered, "Gas?! Gas?!"

His shoulders bounced heavily and he panted, "What ya'll need that for?!"

Shawn narrowed his glare and his cheeks twiddled, perking up ever so slightly. The sound of liquid clonked and shuffled in the gas can as Bread stomped towards Breezy. He stopped in front of him and exhaled heavily from his nostrils.

"This for my brother," Bread's throat cracked, "you took away the best friend I ever had."

Shawn's eyes burned into the back of Bread's head, and he wrinkled his face up in a disgusted glare. Gas began to splash across the man. The swish and slosh of the fuel splattered across his face, all over his clothes, and dripped upon the crumpled, dry leaves on the ground. Breezy hollered again.

"Stop, man! Stop, please! Ey, yo, man, I thought we was cool?! We been up talkin' for days! Ya'll ain't gotta do me like this! I'll help ya'll set Rondo up! He trust me! He believes me!"

Shawn whistled a hushing sound through his lips, and muttered, "Yeah, you sure good at settin' folks up. Next time, ya might just plan right and get us killed."

Bread emptied the gas canister clean and backed away as Breezy continued to whine and pant.

"Man, I didn't set ya'll up! I told you the truth. I—"

The man paused; Shawn's glare told it all. Breezy realized all hope was lost. He had to pay the cost. He gnashed his teeth, and wiggled on the ground, spitting hard, then yelled, "Man, fuck ya'll, then! Ya'll can't see me! Who the fuck ya'll, anyway?!"

Breezy laughed madly to himself as he maintained his struggle with the knot.

"Bread and Butta; who the fuck call themselves some shit like that anyway?! Huh?! Man, ya'll fools a joke!"

Shawn lifted his chin up, glaring down at Breezy, and shook his head.

"Nah, Bread and Butta, that's all I've ever needed."

Shawn flicked half of a lit cigarette at Breezy, and whispered, "Toast."

The man went ablaze immediately, and his shrieks howled with the wolves, through the bare, cold branches circling around. A flock of crows went mad, cawing, and flew away. The fire burned hot, and the man's face melted. His skin seared away from his skull upward, almost as if he were making his last grin. His body crumpled to the ground, and the flames grew higher; dancing across both Shawn and Bread's eyes. Shawn inhaled deeply to get a full taste of the burning flesh. He smiled ever so slightly. He had to be discreet about it. *He was grieving, after all, for the dead brother; the traitor.*

Suddenly, Shawn's phone rang, and he turned to answer it, stepping away from the loud crackling flames. Bread didn't move an inch; he held his empty glare fixed upon the burning corpse.

"Yo, what you want, man," Shawn answered.

A voice on the other end snapped, "Ey, bad news, bruh, we just got hit. Two muthafuckas just ran up in the crib and shot Lil Reese; he dead, man. They took off with all the money, too."

Shawn bit his lip, and grinded his teeth.

"What you just say?"

"They got us, man. They caught us on the sneak, sneak, bruh."

Shawn clenched his fingers into a fist at his side, and it shook.

"You got a clue on who it was?"

"Nah," the voice replied, on the other end, "my brotha down the street saw the car they hopped in, though. It looked like somethin' a bitch would drive."

"Ya'll see who was at the wheel," Shawn snapped on the other end.

"Yuh, yuh," the voice replied, "dude was sittin' there a minute; some white kid with a clown on his hat. My mans only noticed him 'cause he was shufflin' around with the radio blarin'. He wasn't even tryin' to hide."

Shawn's eyes burned towards the dark forest ahead. He licked his lips and hissed, "Say that again. He had a clown on his hat? What kind of car was he in?"

"Yuh, he had a clown on his hat, and his car—shit, I ain't good with this type of shit."

The voice paused in thought, then snapped back on the other end, "He was drivin' a Nissan Altima. Yeah. My sister got a car that look just like it."

Shawn cracked his knuckles and grinded his teeth. He didn't even blink.

Shawn nodded his head slowly, then said, "Ok, then. That's all I need to know."

"You know him," the voice replied, but there wasn't an answer. Shawn's phone clicked.

I'm gonna kill that fuckin' kid, Shawn thought, then stormed off.

CHAPTER XXVII:

LOST AT BIRTH

Despite his cut from the job, Derek had been void all day. The light that had once been there seemed to dissipate in his eyes, and all that remained was the dull glint of guilt: a hunger for the things that he couldn't go back and change. It was like a rebirth into a hollow world. *A tender soul that had become unfurled.*

By this time we had been hiding out for a few days. Bouncing around from location to location, couch to couch, until finally we decided to crash at Ellie's. She wasn't home at the time because she worked the night shift somewhere up in Columbus. So it was just us; there all alone. Flipping through channels, searching without finding. It was as if nothing had happened, and the heat had seemed to grow cold.

As for myself, I was there physically, but gone mentally. I had sunken somewhere; into a dark, hellish place where mind was over matter and the chatter had taken over. I was distant, and he was there, Jack, the man in the hat, acting in my place. *The other half, a different man, speaking from a familiar face.*

Jack shifted on the couch and clapped his hands together. *We need more action.*

He jumped up, and said, "What do ya say we get some fresh air and walk to the corner store or somethin'?"

Jack smiled to himself. *Oh yes, I know what comes about by choosing this. I've seen it all play out before—pictures upon the web within the void; what lies hidden beyond this world. Everything that could possibly happen has happened. Every choice has been made, but with each decision the spider deviates at another turn; each web is created through the Y. The story weaves itself into something else. Every strand runs parallel between one another; alternate realities. All is true, and everything is nothing.*

Derek held an empty gaze towards the TV and flipped another channel.

"Nah, I'm good, bro. I'm just tryin' to chill."

Jack spoke with his hands and ushered Derek up. *Come on, this is one of my favorite parts.* Jack chuckled to himself and licked the inside of his lower lip.

"Come on, why the long face? You ain't gotta sit around and be sad."

Derek scowled in disgust, and he lifted his top lip up in confusion.

"Why the long face?"

He jumped up and threw the remote down; boiling with rage.

"Who even says that? Why you soundin' so different when you talk?"

Jack's eyes danced wildly from left to right beneath the brim of his hat, and he let out a soft shudder. *I have to get better at pretending I'm a moron,* Jack thought to himself, then tssked through his lips, and laughed, "Chill out, dude. I'm just tryin' to like lighten the mood up a little or somethin', y'know, man."

Derek snapped, "Man, you play too much. You wanna walk to the store? Fine, let's go then, bro."

Derek snatched up his red coat and threw on his Cincinnati hat, too. It didn't take long, and they were out of the door.

The breeze blew a chill, and it was cold. Jack threw his hood up over his hat to cover up his stinging ears. Derek's legs shuffled beside him, and his breath became a cloud in the still air.

"Damn, it's cold. Why we gotta walk anyway? Why didn't we just take the car?"

Jack grinned to himself, and his eyes flickered around. *Come on, where is he? Very, very soon. Best to wake up in there; it's time for tag.*

Derek shoved Jack's arm, startling him a tad, and snapped, "Ey, man, you gonna answer me or what?"

Jack replied, "Of course, I'm listening; just thinking a little that's all. We'll be okay. It's just a short walk down the road. Nothing bad could possibly happen."

Derek carried on further, and shook his head while he stuffed his hands in the pocket of his hoodie.

"Man, whatever, it's too cold for this shit."

The night was pretty silent. There was a car going down Pine every once in a while, but they were few and far between. A crow cawed upon the steeple of an old house as we shuffled by, and an engine rumbled from behind in the distance. The tires squealed towards us, then it crept up, following us.

Tag, you're it, Jack told me. Then he whisked away; retreating into the depths of myself. *Black in, black out. Back in, back out.* Cold chills ran up my spine, and sweat seared it's way across my forehead. I stumbled and tried to catch myself during the walk. I clutched my chest and gasped for air as I fell to my knees.

"What are you doin', bro? You alright, man? You been drinkin' all day. You sure you can make it?"

I heaved heavily as my consciousness returned.

"W-where? Wh-what? W-what are we doin'?"

"Walkin' to the store," Derek snapped, then he tssked through his lips.

"Man, I get tired of babysittin' your ass. You gotta get up. We're almost there."

He helped me up, gripping my elbow, and returned me to my feet. My hand fell from my chest as I caught my breath. The car still crept up from behind.

"Damn. I feel like I've been gone for days this time," I whispered to myself. My eyes shifted in panic.

"What?" Derek snapped; he was getting irritated.

I shook my head and carried on the stroll.

"Nothing, nothing. It's all good, man. It's all good now."

Suddenly, Derek stopped and peered at the car creeping close to the curb.

"Who is this fool and why does it feel like he's followin' us?" Derek gritted his teeth and sneered.

Still in a daze, I turned around and looked towards the car. It was dark, but the ride was old—*classy, if you will.* It was a bronzed brown 1970 Chevy Chevelle.

I smiled and tapped Derek on the arm, "It's all good. It's just my buddy Shawn messin' with us."

I waved at him, then yelled, "Hey, Shawn! What's up, man?"

I laughed, "Stop playin' around and give us a ride."

The Chevelle pulled to the left and parked on the curb. The lights flickered off at the touch of a knob. Shawn stepped out slowly and slammed his door shut. He stood at the edge of the hood and stare menacingly towards us with his hands shoved in his sweater pocket. He didn't breathe a word.

I laughed, and said, "What's the deal, man? Ain't you gonna say hi?"

Jack's laughter echoed deep within my eardrums, it was rattling madly. *Yeah, stop lolliegaggin' around over there. Get to it.* I hushed the tone and tuned it down, then yelled again, "You good, man?!"

Shawn stood on the edge of the car still, stiff as a nail, juggling a hand around in his sweater pocket. I laughed to myself, and shook my head, then turned to Derek and told him.

"He's just playin' with us, man. He's my buddy, he's cool, I promise."

Derek's jaw dropped, and his eyes popped out of his head; he shook and tapped me on the arm.

"Nah, nah, nah. That ain't your buddy, man. That nigga's pullin' out a gun!"

I shook my head, and laughed, "What?! He ain't—"

Then I flicked my eyes back at Shawn, still smiling, laughter humming in my throat.

"It's all good. It's—"

Then I saw the gun in his hand.

"Hey, man, what's the deal?! Stop fuckin'—"

Remember, you're trying to clean up your act.

I threw my hands up and continued, "Come on, man. Stop fartin' around over there!"

Shawn's fingers tightened on the grip of the pistol, and he edged towards us.

I turned again and looked at Derek, still confused; shaking my head.

"I don't get it. I—"

Derek shook about and yelled, "Yo, yo, yo, we gotta run!"

Shawn charged towards us.

"What, I don't—"

Derek shoved me and took off, then screamed, "Run!"

It all finally clicked. Shawn wanted to stick that gun of his in our mouths and blow our brains out—definitely. I took off and ran after Derek, wailing back at Shawn.

"I don't get it! I thought we were friends!"

Derek squealed back at me, sort of like a little girl to tell you the truth, and said, "He ain't your friend, man! Get that shit outta your head!"

Derek picked up speed and his legs kicked full steam ahead. I definitely wasn't as quick as him. We ran down the sidewalk and cut across Pine Street. A car nearly clipped him. He reacted fast as lightning, jumped up, and slid across the hood. The driver stomped on his brakes, and slammed on the horn, jerked his head around, and yelled, "Myah! I hate kids; ya see! Myah!"

Or something to that accord.

I hopped the curb, passing the street light; Derek was nearly halfway to the next lamp ahead.

We ran past an old man in a red house, and he hollered from his porch across the street. "What in the willy wally are them kids doin' down there?!"

Shawn was gaining on us, *or just yours truly.* Derek was losing us, or just me. I frowned to myself as I tried to catch my breath. *Awww, why don't I have any friends?* I thought to myself.

My arms waved like jack knives as I struggled to pick up speed. Derek cut down an alley, and I picked up the pace, turning too.

Shawn yelled from behind us, "Bang! Bang! Muthafucka! Bang! Bang!"

He was getting closer, gaining on us. My arms and legs flailed around as I struggled, and shuddered, rippling with confusion in the shadows of the dark alley. *Did the gun go bang bang or just his mouth?*

Gravel chattered under our heels, and Derek turned at a shed, then hopped a fence. Barking ensued, and Derek wailed; he was trapped. He reacted the wrong way and moved to fast. My shoes didn't wave to clean across the road, and I slid by the fence; *doin' the splits.*

"Dammit, man," I hollered.

Well, I can't hop no fence, anyway. Wouldn't want to, with the dog and all.

Derek struggled back across the fence with the mutt still nipping at his heels. He got over and fell at the top, and crumpled on the gravel; groaning. He jerked quick and struggled to get up. The hammer on Shawn's gun clicked, and he hummed in a sing songy tune, "Nah, nah, nah, hey, hey, hey, not so fast."

I groaned, "Gee whiz, man! I almost split myself in two! Man, Shawn, what's wrong with you?!"

Derek went still as a dead bird, and didn't say a word. He stood up stiffly with his arms out and stared at Shawn. The dog still barked on the other side of the fence, and the back door to the house flung open. An old lady with curlers in her hair emerged, and she stomped down the steps, tightening her bath robe. She had to be from Wisconsin, or Switzerland maybe. *There's no hope in telling,* but she definitely had an accent.

"Alright! Alright! Shut up, Mike! Before I beat your hide to hound heaven! Okay?!"

The dog settled and whimpered down. The old lady stomped towards the fence, and backhanded the dog on the snout.

"Get in your house and shut your mouth! I've about had it with you, mister!"

The dog cowered down and walked away slowly across the dark green grass. It made me so sad and it bothered me a lot. I shuffled on the ground, and tiny bits of gravel bit into my palms. I squealed, "Hey, that's not nice! You hurt his feelings!"

Shawn jerked at my elbow, pressed the gun against my back, and snatched me up. Then he muffled with clenched teeth, "Shut the fuck up, man. You hear? I ain't playin no more with you."

Okay, okay, I nodded as I thought to myself. *He's pretty mad.*

Shawn brought a finger to his lips, made a shhh motion with them towards Derek, then mouthed the words, "Don't say a word."

He waved the barrel of the gun from my back, pointed it at Derek, then at my head, and mouthed, "Bang, bang."

My knees shivered and buckled towards the ground. I sniveled and whimpered. I was about to piss my pants; I ain't gonna lie. Shawn caught me, and brought me back up as he groaned, growling deep. The old lady's slippers slid across the fresh dew, and she stopped at the fence, put her hand on her hip, and snapped, "Well?! What the fuck is goin' on in my alley?! Huh?!"

Shawn spoke calm and directly.

"Nothin', mam. I was just huntin' down my little brothers for mama to get 'em on home. Suppers ready."

"You're little brothers," the old lady screeched back, confused, then pointed at me.

"That one right there is whiter than a god damn toothpick!"

Shawn snickered and laughed to himself.

"Nah, he adopted, but he's still one of our own."

Derek turned an inch towards the old lady, and Shawn pressed the gun deeper in my back as he arched forward. Derek froze again.

The lady wagged her finger, and the curlers jiggled, dancing around in her hair. She barked back, "Oh yeah?! Well, the three of you better get the fuck out here before I call the law on ya! Okay?!"

Shawn replied cooly, "No need in doin' all that, mam. I'm finna take 'em home."

The old lady snapped back, "Good! Get the fuck out of here! All of ya are ugly!"

She turned her back, and marched for the back porch, past the still whimpering dog.

Tears jiggled in my eyes, my lips shook, and I gasped. *But I'm not ugly. I thought I was one of the beautiful ones.* My mouth quivered still, and I wept into my hands, soaking my fingers wet. Shawn pressed the gun further into my back. I shivered, sobbed, and I cried; groaning in the dark alley. It was all coming to an end.

The lady slammed the back door, and Shawn said, "Ight muthafuckas. We finna take a cruise".

Water dripped from a leaking pipe and pitter pattered against the cracked concrete floor next to a large dark stain on the tile. It looked a faint red, but it was black to the core. I couldn't tell if I stared at the same spot for hours or mere minutes by the door. All I know is my wrists and arms felt strained from being pulled and tied around the pole.

The large column felt cold against my back, and I winced as the crumpled paint dug against me. I slid back towards the floor. Derek sobbed in the rubble ten feet to the right, and didn't speak a word. He just shook his head repeatedly, and muttered, *why, why, why,* to himself. Jack's influence burned under my skin as I sunk into my doom. He remembered something again, and I could feel the conflict within him, inside of me. Shawn's echo barked across the tall, hollow room in the abandoned factory. We were in the old Mosaic Tile Company down Pershing Road past the Fair Grounds.

Another crumbling old red brick building, magnificence lost; the tattered spire reaches for the empty sky, smokeless, and empty. Everything has been cold here in this place for so long. It's the town; it's the curse. Everything just gets worse.

"I'm finna tell ya'll somethin'," Shawn hollered, "This right here, ya'll took this shit for a game, but you done slipped, and we about to square shit up!"

Shawn's arms flailed as he waved the gun around menacingly; his eyes burned towards me.

"And you. You, man. Why?! Why?! I gave you a chance, kid, and you took me for a fool, man. You—you—"

Shawn bit his lip and tilted his head to the side. His gaze grew empty, and his voice rumbled, low and still. It was like he was possessed.

"You," Shawn laughed, "your colder than I thought. I didn't think you had it in you, but you do, man."

Shawn smiled at me as if he were in a state of proud admiration, then he continued, "You do. It's almost like you're my younger self."

I shook in the dark and groaned, not daring to say a word. *But I don't want to be like you anymore.*

Shawn laughed, "All these years, and somehow we stumble into one another again, and there you are. It's almost like starin' into the mirror; a look at myself in the past."

Shawn's laughter echoed across the empty hall.

"Man, man, man, this shit is funny. Y'know, here in the dark, in what's abandoned, it's just us. Me and you. We ain't gotta play characters anymore; it's just us."

Derek sniveled and shook from the side, tied tight to the pole still.

Shawn's eyes darted towards him, and he hissed, "But there's you, too. What's with you, man? Scared to be a killa? You, the one who pulled the trigga on Lil Reese, right? And then there's that other kid that was with ya'll. Who's that?"

Derek sniveled and shook.

"Just let us go, please. We didn't—I didn't want to hurt anybody. I was just—I was just tired of getting' punked, man. They hit us first, and we hit 'em back. That's it. If—if they—"

Derek groaned, and swallowed, then continued, "If they wouldn't have tried to rob us, we would've never done it."

Shawn barked back, "Bullshit! What you mean they hit you first?! How'd ya'll even know it was them?"

Shawn hummed to himself and wagged his head around; *writing in his head.*

"Let me guess. It's a part of my question that you didn't answer. Was it the other kid that was with you?!"

I rambled in a hushed tone to myself as I hung upon the pole, I whispered, "I just wanna get outta here. I wanna go back home."

I can find myself again. I know I can.

"Just find the light," an all too familiar voice spoke, "I will guide you."

The voice of the one, but I forget. A father from within.

Shawn chuckled, "What are you doin' over there? Prayin'?"

He charged towards me and shoved the gun into my cheek, and gritted his teeth.

"Well, pray on this. You tried to run away, but I caught you. I was in the shadows just behind you."

He chuckled low, humming to himself.

"Yeah, you thought you could just take off and get away, but that ain't how it goes. You got shit to answer for. We gotta fix the karma, so it's straight."

Jack, the man in the hat, whispered in my ears, *What's done is done, and what's fair is fair. An eye for an eye, that's what we share.*

You're too late, Jack whispered further, *he's abandoned you. Why don't you think you can hear or find him anymore? You need me. You know you do. Let me slip in—let me—*

Faith was brittle in my heart, and it was hard to withstand the weight. Maybe the all too familiar voice is fake.

The bonds tore at my wrists, and I cried as the man in the hat cackled continuously in a high whine. *I am abandoned.* I believed the lie.

My shoulder's slumped, and I felt the devil swallow my resolve through sharp teeth; a sword without a sheath. *The wolf hath swallowed me.*

The possession was nearly complete; the shadow swam over my skin and began to settle back in.

Shawn still held the gun to my cheek. Jack's eyes grew dark and his flickering gaze pierced into Shawn's mug.

"Settle it so it's straight, eh?"

Derek whimpered upon the pole, "Man, if I ever get out of this I'm never hangin' out with white boys ever again."

Shawn flipped his head around and screamed, "Shut the fuck up! We're talkin' over here!"

Shawn looked back towards Jack and grinned; he recognized the familiarity. *We are Legion, for we are many.* Derek's head fell as he wept to himself.

"There he is. I see it in your eyes; a leader. Yeah, let's make it straight."

Jack twisted his neck and crooned, "Well, I'm not much of a protector. The kid told us those were the guys that hit us, but I suspect—no, now I know—"

I've always known, Jack thought as he paused and cackled low to himself, *it was just more fun to take the long route. You tend to get more of the picture if you do.*

"Know what?" Shawn barked; pulling the gun away.

Jack tssked his tongue behind his teeth.

"Oh, it all started with a kid named Tony. He's the one that pointed us towards the house. He said, blah, blah, blah, it's these guys. Myah, myah, myah, we gotta go get 'em."

Jack shrugged his shoulders, and continued, "So we did, and I'm sorry about your friend but, well,—why look at the situation we've put ourselves in. I propose that my friend—"

Jack grinned and rattled his head around.

"Me and my buddy here! That we kill Tony to make everything square! After all, he tried to rip us off, make a fool out of us, and now everything is so nasty and twisted. The bucko chose to fuck around with us, so he should get what he deserves."

Derek's whimpering halted, and he went still. He lifted his head up and gazed within the hollow shade.

"I hate ever fuckin' with you, man. You're crazy, but—"

He swallowed, nodded, and continued, "That makes sense. Tony was always low key jealous, peepin' at us. It was always there, and I never knew. He fucked this shit up. That shit sounds true."

Jack hissed back, "But it is."

Shawn stood up, and nodded, "Hmmm, ight then. Ya'll my dogs again now. I'mma let ya'll off the chain to bark, but keep in mind I got eyes watchin' ya'll. If you even try to squeal to the pigs; you'll be getting' worse than a bullet. I'm getting' my fuckin' money back, too. I want every fuckin' dollar in the bag. If Tony ain't dead in the next twenty four hours and I don't have my money. Ya'll gonna smell what it's like to burn some kerosene."

Derek winced, and his mug shook.

Jack clenched his teeth and muttered to himself; talking to me.

"My, how rotten it is to be condemned."

I clawed at my heart from the inside. *No, we can't do this, we can't—*

But we can, Jack cut across the thought. *You underestimate yourself so much. Just watch and see.*

The screams within the trapped womb of my soul echoed silently, and I fell away from myself. Jack cackled, *It's time to have some real fun. Time to settle the score.*

CHAPTER XXVIII:

CHILDRENS STORY

Chilling wind bit the cold air, and blew through the trees; teeth gnashed and chattered in the shadows. Three out of the five guy red g man crew were down by the river. It was freezing; *we're finna catch a cold.*

A pair of new Jordan twelves hit the ground, and doors slammed on a red Chevy Malibu; sweatpants jiggled at the heel. Bread stepped towards the front. His eyes were empty and cold. Kane charged ahead of him, and snapped, "Where these fools at?"

Shawn pressed slowly ahead and cooled him down.

"Ey, it's cool; be easy."

Shawn's eyes burned into Kane's; settling him with a command. It was like he put him in a trance.

Kane jerked his head, and barked, "Well, what they know about Lil Reese?! That was my little man, bro. What these muthafuckas got to do with it?"

"At ease, bruh," Shawn shook his head, glaring madly at him still, but this time he laughed a little.

"They on our side. They didn't shoot Lil Reese, but they know who did."

"Tell me who did it then," Kane snapped; heaving hard with his chest.

Shawn shook his head.

"Nah, we gonna outsource this. We got bigger problems at hand. Rondo—"

"Bigger problems at hand," Kane squealed. It was sort of weird; a little too high pitched for a muscly guy.

"Bigger problems at hand?! Lil Reese got shot, man! He's dead!"

Shawn stepped to him; boiling under the skin, feeling tense.

"He is," his teeth clenched, "and it's gonna be handled; just not by you."

Shawn nodded his chin upward towards Bread, and said, "You didn't give him the word? Tell 'em what a fly told you."

Bread was reluctant; he didn't even want to speak. He crossed his arms and glare towards Kane.

"His own crew is sellin' him out. They want 'em gone; they know about us and they want on. So we made a deal."

Shawn cut in, "They bag 'em, and bring 'em to us, and we do that fool just like we did, Breezy. We settin' this straight for Butta and Lil Reese."

Kane snapped, "So we finna work with the same muthafuckas that been gunnin' for us? They shot Lil Reese and you—"

"Them boys in black and blue didn't do that. It was just some random kid that sniffed out a leak. What I tell ya'll? We need to keep shit tight and silent. The—"

"Man, fuck the Vientos! We don't need 'em. We got shit to rock with. Why can't we do it like we always did, huh? Sometimes you gotta make some noise out here; let 'em know there's a problem. You know that, man, come on," Kane huffed.

"It's handled," Shawn assured him, "we got it all planned out smooth. Just keep your cool; you can get first dibs on Rondo."

Kane froze, mashing his glare.

"I can't believe you won't let me handle this. You know how me and Lil Reese was."

"You to important to be put on the line like that; we need you. You're inside, the extra guns are outside."

Shawn placed his hand on Kane's shoulder and assured him, "We need you."

"Okay," Kane jerked at his jacket collar, flicking it.

"Okay. I'll chill and rock with the plan."

He was trying to convince himself. Shawn knew it. *He's a risk.*

"Okay, okay," Kane backed away quickly towards the car; trying to appear cool with a smile. It was too obvious.

"You comin'," Kane hollered. *Too loud.*

Shawn smiled, and shook his head, "Nah, I gotta meeting with the Vientos."

"Catch you on the fly then, bro," Kane turned his back and shuffled towards the passenger door of Bread's red Chevy Malibu.

Shawn burned a glare towards Bread and made a slow cutting motion across his throat, then flicked his eyes back to Kane as he hopped back in the ride mad, and emotional; he just wasn't paying attention. *Insubordination isn't tolerated.*

Bread nodded and headed towards the wheel. Shawn turned towards his Chevelle and gazed out towards the rumbling river. *The bridge wasn't far away.*

Meanwhile, Rondo lay in bed with one of his girls; her name was Katrina. *Damn, Pats got the hook up,* he thought to himself.

Giggling, and rubbing on his chest Katrina, whispering softly, "You like the games I play?"

"You know I do," Rondo groaned as he held her on his shoulder and rubbed her back.

"You want me to tie you up," she giggled, and asked.

Rondo chuckled, "Damn, you a freak, girl. I didn't know you was into that."

Katrina pulled two sets of handcuffs out of her nightstand.

Rondo hummed and sucked on his lower lip; moistening it.

Katrina climbed on top of him and started kissing him on the neck. Rondo fell into her web and groaned with pleasure.

"Oh yeah, do it to me baby," he grumbled, "do it to me."

Click. One hand to the post.

Rondo groaned for more.

Click. Another to the post.

"Oh yeah, baby! You got me!"

"Yeah she do," Pats and Ronnie waltzed right out of Katrina's walk-in closet. They were there the whole time; *easy peasy.*

"What the—"

Rondo snapped and tried to jerk his wrists free.

"What the—hey what ya'll doin' man! This shit ain't funny! Th—"

Pats slammed the barrel of his gun across Rondo's nose; and cracked him open. Rondo wailed. Pats shoved the gun into his cheek; and snapped, spitting into his old friend's face.

"Shut the fuck up and listen. This is how it's gonna go."

Rondo lowered his groaning and listened. Pats leaned against his shoulder and cleared his throat. The gun was still pointed at Rondo's face.

"We gonna get you off these posts, and you gonna put the handcuffs back on. If you don't cooperate—"

Pats waved his gun towards Katrina; she was standing by the vanity with the mirror.

"Katrina here gonna cut your dick off; so you best cooperate."

Rondo wailed, "But why? Why are ya'll doin' me like this?"

Ronnie hit him with his gun next. He just wanted to participate and get a hit in, too.

"Damn! Come on, man," Rondo yelled in agony.

Pats told him to shut up again. They undone one pair of handcuffs and dragged his wrist over to the other. Rondo cried in pain; blood poured from his face onto the white pillows. The cuff snapped, and the other fell to the floor as it came undone. Ronnie pulled Rondo off the bed from under the sheets onto his feet. The poor guy was still naked.

"Ya'll ain't gonna let me put any clothes on?"

"Nah," Pats snapped, "you getting' in the truck naked."

Rondo whined as his wrists shook in the handcuffs.

"Come on, ya'll, why?! Why?!"

Ronnie snapped, "Because you're a fuckin' dirt bag, bro; you ain't got nothin' together."

Rondo pleaded as they led him towards the steps.

"Come on, man, please, man! Please!"

Pats shoved Rondo hard towards the steps, only it was too much of a shove to give, and Rondo went headfirst down the wooden flight. It sounded like a stumbling rhino as he fumbled downward, limbs banging against the walls; his neck cracked at the bottom.

"Shit," Ronnie muttered, "you think he's dead?"

Pats edged his head over the stairwell. Rondo was twisted up like a pretzel.

"Yeah, he dead, bro. Fuck."

Pats shook his head and hollered at Katrina.

"Ey, baby, you gotta move. This fool done died in the hall."

Katrina squealed, "What?!"

"Yeah," Pats assured her, "don't worry about it, though. Me and Ronnie got the body. I'm just saying it might be bad luck to stay here."

"Damn," Pats muttered to himself; disappointed.

"He done fell down the steps. Ain't that a bitch."

Things were brewing elsewhere, however. *On the other edge of town.*

A cock and a click came from the passenger seat of a Nissan Altima; Derek sat there geared up, with that mask laying across his left knee. Jack sat in the passenger seat peepin' a looksee past the streetlight at the corner of the alley towards Tony's new house; *they were waiting in the night.*

Jack's eyes burned towards the back door, and he bit his lip in a grin. *Just a little more, his pain will reach a level of new strength, then the reaping of the harvest shall come. I will collect thy seed, and plant; then I will be free. A new hat man will replace me.*

In the center of the locked prism, I lie, trapped within the cold and the dark inside. We can't do this; we can't. You can't Jack, you—

The cord was cut; and it was being squeezed. Jack replied internally, *But we do. We have to set things right. The universe operates on a code of checks and balances; it's all about energy. An eye for an eye, those of the breed of iniquity, they are the stalks in the field; with the stroking of the scythe, mine they will forever be.*

But why, but why me? I cried.

The picture of the present vanished, and my ego was draining away; I was drunk off the hate. *It was time to meet fate.* Jack took a hit and stare on. Derek breathed deeply and said, "Are we really about to do this?"

Jack's eyes narrowed, and the corner of his mouth shivered up and fell back down. There was a lot of screaming and pounding inside, but still everything was numb; the air floated calm and still.

"We have to," Jack replied, "there's no other option. Didn't ya see that guy? He meant business. If we don't take care of this, it's gonna be us, and our old friend Tony is gonna be done, anyway. See what I mean? Do you want to live or die?"

Derek's eyes glazed a thick burn, and he swallowed.

"I wanna live," he gripped the gun tighter and declared.

"Well, there's only one thing to do then. We're gonna live," Jack threw his mask on. It was blank white; they both were. *Comedy and tragedy fit the scene, each with a frown and a grin; guess which one each were in?*

Jack pulled his revolver from under the seat and grinned at himself. *Boy, I sure do love thieves; like a poor man's market. Put an order in, it'll be delivered right into your pocket.*

They each opened the doors and shut them silently, then crept toward the back. Derek led ahead. He knew Tony better than I did. The back porch light was off, but they were sure he was home. They saw him come. He went in through the back door. A tall pine tree in the backyard shadowed everything and made it the yard dark. It was nearly one to two am, and everyone's home was quiet. Save a few dogs barking in the distance.

They crept in the grass towards the back door and snuck up the steps of the back porch; barely making a noise in the distance. A cat screeched and shook a garbage can. Derek jerked and looked back. Jack caught his gaze and shook his head; biting his lip under the mask. His grip tightened on the revolver. *I sure do hate cats.*

Derek stood closest to the door. He looked at Jack, and gave him a nod, then tried his grip on the knob. Jack stood still, breathing in this town again. Flashes of his life from before began to spin.

A shot—*bang*. Blood poured across the chipped hardwood floor in Packie's gambling den. The dead blonde dame lie on the floor, warm; becoming a part of the cold, dead within the fold. Jack's best friend Bobby wailed in horror; blood was all over him. Richie the Gambler walked forward and took a hit off his cigar. The smoke curled on the edge of his white fedora hat. His crew of goons stood in trench coats behind him.

"What do ya say, boys? How bouts we teach these boys a lesson?"

"Send 'em to Harvey," Edgar hissed behind his shoulder; licking his lips, "he'll fix 'em up right."

Jack's nails drug across the wooden boards, and his fingertips bled.

"I just wanna go back! I wanna go back," he fought, and wailed.

Chains rattled against the cold, wet stone wall. His wrists were cutting against the shackles. They were there together, him and Bobby, down there in the dark room. *The awful place; it was his playroom.*

Bobby moaned and groaned in the pitch black void; he'd given up.

"I-I'm g-gonna get us out of here, Bobby," Jack's voice rattled in the echo as he hung.

"P-promise, I'm gonna get us out of here."

Steady and slow stomps came from down the hallway, and a ring of keys rattled. A man was whistling the tune to Victor Arden's "Dancing the Devil Away."

Bobby screamed and wailed; he never stopped pleading for mercy. The screams rattled and rung in Jack's ears. I began to see the light, but the door shut again.

Derek turned the knob to the back door, and it swung open. *Always keep your back doors locked folks.*

Then I thought further, *If he can see my memories, I can see his.*

The kitchen was dark, but the living room past the dining area glowed; and the TV blared. "The Chappelle Show" was on. Tony laughed. Derek crept ahead, Jack followed from behind.

The floor creaked with the next step. Tony didn't notice the first, but he noted the second. The TV turned down, and a little girl's voice whispered, "What was that?"

Only it was too late, and they were already in the living room. The little girl threw her doll off the couch and screamed. Tony jumped up and backed away towards the stairs. He threw his hands up as Jack and Derek pointed their guns.

"H-hey, man," Tony pleaded, "what's this about? I-I ain't—what the fuck?"

The little girl's scream rung in Jack's ears; and rattled him to his core. *He's beginning to lose grip.*

Derek snapped, "You know what this is about? You did what you did. Ain't no other choice."

The pistol shook in Derek's hand, and he trembled in all black; even under his mask.

"Is that you, D," Tony asked; he continued to plea.

"Ey, man. Ey, man. Come on, don't do me like this. Don't—"

Derek panicked, his grip tightened on the trigger. A whisper rushed, *So I guess it's true, the man in the hat has a soul, too. Even in the darkness, at his core, a faint light shown; mine did, too.*

A voice came and said, *Remember who you are. You're not him and he's not you. Don't believe the lies he's told you.*

Derek pulled the trigger. I threw myself into his shoulder, nearly at the bang, and the bullet went by, shattering the glass that was behind Tony. The little girl still screamed. There was a struggle between the two. The man in the hat faltered, I'd come to.

We began to fight and struggle on the couch. Tony ran away, leaving the little girl behind; screaming still as she huddled on the steps. That's how it goes. That one thing happens to you when you're a kid and you're never right from it ever again; before and after, in this life, or in the past therein. We are the broken; we are the maimed. We are of the fold that need to be saved.

Derek threw a blow across my jaw, and my back fell into the coffee table; shattering the glass underneath. I fumbled around groaning. The screams shook me, and I shivered.

Derek chased Tony out of the back door, and I fumbled across the floor towards the revolver. I snatched the gun up quickly as my eyes began to bleed with tears. I took one last look at the little girl, and my cries roared.

"I'm sorry! I'm so sorry!"

Then I ran for the back door. My feet nearly slipped on the hardwood floor; I tumbled onto the patio. *He can't do it, he can't.*

Shawn sat at the meeting location that his designated La Sombra had given him. Whispers was coming to meet him herself. *Just like that, I'm in with El Jefe's daughter.* Shawn grinned, as he thought to himself. He turned the dial up on the radio and rapped along to Biggie's "Gimme the Loot." The beat boomed; he was up on the rise, there, at Putnam Hill Park.

His hands tapped on the steering wheel and he rocked his head; gazing around, wondering, *Where's she at? Better yet, why ain't I heard from Bread?*

Things weren't going to well with Bread, however. Kane was standing on the top of Bread's red Chevy Malibu. He jumped on the hood of the trunk again. *The damn thing won't shut.* Kane slid off, and his kicks scraped into the dirt.

Another failed attempt. He tried to slam an elbow down to close lid, but that didn't work either. Then he threw a kick.

"You country fried steak eatin', muthafucka! Why you gotta eat so damn much?!"

He slammed an elbow down on the trunk once more, trying to seal Bread's body under the latch, but yet again, it flopped open. Kane balled his fists up and growled, "I'll elastic band this shit closed if I have to. Damn! Ain't no such thing as friends these days!"

Meanwhile, Whispers crept along up the sidewalk. Her eyes were fixed like a scope on the red taillights of Shawn's Chevelle. The car's radio thumped, and her earbuds hummed Mobb Deep's "The Infamous" album consistently.

A headphone cord bounced across her white hoodie, and it hid her dark face under the edge. Her blue eyes glowed in the shadows, and her small frame rocked on the creep. She was only waiting for Shawn to step out. She passed under the light quick, and hid in the trees to the right of the overlook. Eventually, the engine turned off, and Shawn got out of his car; lighting up a smoke, and walking slowly towards the edge, approaching the rails to get a clear view of the Y bridge.

This town is mine. Shawn smiled to himself as he took a puff, and blew out into the wind. He chuckled to himself. *Far from kingpin status, but I'm on my way. This is where it all starts.*

Whispers crept in the shadows slowly towards him. The white of her sweater didn't even stand out; it never did with any of them. Her black Chuck Taylors crunched softly in the pine bristles. *He's off his guard; lost in thought. He could never be one of us,* Whispers thought to herself.

Suddenly, she was on him, rushing right out of the midst of the surrounding darkness; the light upon the lookout had burned out days ago.

Whispers flung the blade at Shawn's stomach, but he jumped back and dodged the blow; struggling quickly for his gun. The knife in her hand whistled another jab fast through the air; only this last thrust had landed right in his gut.

Shawn moaned in agony as he pulled his gun out. He shot his silencer, and the bullet whizzed towards Whispers during her rash flurry. It landed and hit, but only grazed her in the side. *Pa pa taught me better than this,* she thought to herself.

Whispers stumbled, falling towards the ground, and Shawn ran towards his car, struggling to start it as fast as he could. The engine kicked at first. It wouldn't start at first, but then the Chevelle roared to life. The wheels screeched in reverse and sped out of the park. Shawn's hand clasped at his wound. Each breath brought agony, tearing at his lungs.

Whispers stumbled after him, but he was already gone. If she wasn't mad before, she was vicious now. *I'm bleeding too much. I need time to fix the wound.* She stopped at the fence by the basketball hoops and narrowed her eyes viciously at the Chevelle speeding away. She wasn't that concerned about Shawn; only disliked the inconvenience. He wasn't what she was in town for. *I found the old man. I only wished to see his face. Pa pa's eyes; they have the same trace.* The Chevelle's tires screeched in the distance, and Whispers was left in the darkness.

Not so far away, other tensions rose.

Tony screamed for help down the alley as Derek gave chase. He had that happy clown and frown face; mine just hung all over.

Lights began to flick on in homes; people were waking up.

Derek stopped in the alley, by a rusted out car, and gave aim. *Thank god.* It gave me a chance to catch up.

Derek nearly pulled the trigger again, but I tackled him from behind. We wrestled across the tattered bricks in the alley. I could taste the iron from my own blood seeping under the mask. I struggled for the revolver in my hoodie pocket, trying to wrestle Derek off me. He went for his pistol too. We shoved each other off and stood our ground fast. There we were; two brothers, two guns; there it is—*the end of brotherly love.*

Dogs barked, and Tony still screamed in the distance. I shivered.

"What are you gonna do?" I cried; gulping on my words, "shoot me?"

"We don't have to do this, man. We don't have to do this," I pleaded.

Someone hollered from their porch.

"Hey, what in the hell is goin' on out here?! Shut that hollerin' up!"

Tony still screamed away, but nobody was really listening.

The gun shook in Derek's hand, and he muffled under his mask, and sniffled, "You're the one that got me into this, man. You fuckin' ruined my life. I-I—"

The gun shook harder in his hand, and his head rocked back and forth. Then he jerked, and choked, "Stay the fuck away from me. You're the devil."

Sirens blared towards us in the distance; and Derek turned his back on me, rushing off down the alley, running away into the dark; consumed by the shadows. I ran off, too, not by will, but more off instinct still. I sprinted towards my car, jerking the door open, and stomped on the gas; sirens were incoming.

I sped up the gears and cut down another alley; flying past the garbage, and trash littered along the way. I cut down a side street, going a ways, then I hit old Dug Road and gunned it down; throwing my mask off, panting. *There was blood all over me.*

390

The engine rev echoed and hummed across the falling rock wall. There was a flash and a flicker in the distance; something in the shadows, but I blew past it, whatever the figure was.

My wheels spun down West Muskingum, and I slammed a left onto Ridge. *I can make my escape in the woods,* I thought to myself.

I slapped and pounded the steering wheel; heaving, choking, and my eyes were burning hot. I raced beyond the cars parked on the side, and whizzed past a car pulling up to a stop sign. The hill was dark again. I drove onwards, away, for how long, I don't know. I was in a daze from the drama. *I ruined it all; I ruined everything.*

Derek heaved in the cold air as he ran from the sirens. He'd already thrown off his mask. He didn't know where he was going, he simply let his feet carry him. Eventually, the sirens grew distant, and he stopped. He'd ran so far; it seemed like he didn't even pass Putnam Hill Park, but he did, and he was nearly at the Y Bridge.

With his head down, he kept his hands tucked into his hoodie pocket. Derek didn't want to be seen by anybody; he was still paranoid. He made a left turn at the bridge and walked beneath the railroad underpass. The cold wind sent a chill up his spine. Derek shuffled his shoulders and walked onward; turning left on Lee Street, headed for State Street. There were red taillights of an old car lying up the road. The rear end was still twisted in the road. Derek marched further towards it, and the ride began to appear more familiar to him. *Is it him? The guy who wanted us to kill Tony?*

At first he was scared, but he didn't falter. He tightened his grip on the pistol in his hoodie pocket, and stare through the back windshield, waiting for a sign of movement. He crept up towards the side and heard a groan come from the open window, then a cough.

Shawn mumbled to himself, as his head swung across his shoulder.

"Man, I fucked up—"

Another cough.

"If I just would've—"

Suddenly, a click came from the side, and Shawn's head bounced up., his vision was wavy. All he saw was a man with a gun; no, not a man, *a kid*. Shawn knew just who it was. He cackled to himself.

"You little muhfucka," Shawn laughed, and coughed, "so this how it gonna be, huh? You mista big killa man, now, right?"

Derek gritted his teeth; a flame and a crack burst from the gun. The barrel smoked. The inside of the Chevelle was painted red.

"I ain't runnin' from nobody anymore."

He tucked the gun back in his hoodie pocket and took off again towards the new path he had chosen. He could already feel himself breaking inside; *death is at the end of the line.*

As I drove, I cried at the wheel, wishing I'd just die, but then the air suddenly grew still, and a thick presence fell down upon my shoulders. The radio grew staticky, and I pounded my fist viciously against the dash. *I'm sick of it, I'm so sick of it.*

A tune came on and the volume stuck. Patsy Cline's voice hummed in and rattled "I Fall to Pieces" across the speakers. I shuddered, and the road grew darker, but then suddenly just ahead, a strange man in coveralls appeared in the road. He had a torn one eared bunny mask stitched across his face. I screamed in horror, and my eyes darted towards the rearview mirror. The man in the hat was drawing towards my shoulder, and he whispered, "I'm sorry, kid. I'm just tryin' to save ya from the heartbreak."

I jerked the wheel, and the tires squealed. The front end swung around the man in the mask, the one in the road, and I lost control; flinging myself into a ditch. My head slammed and bounced across the wheel. *Lights out for now,* the man in the hat whispered. *It's time that we meet in the Shadowlands.*

CHAPTER XXIX:

THE OMEN

Breath ran shallow through a sore throat, and a rope sawed across, pulling at the neck. Boots hung limply, teetering in the whistling wind upon the hollow, cracking branches of the ancient tree.

There was a gasp for air then a flash; a memory of an ancient deception. A slim man in a tattered dark cloak edged forward out of the wilderness, and spoke.

"There brother, upon the path lies the giant's well, where all matters of diverse images and knowledge lie. Drinketh from the cup, dear brother, as I have. Let us become one and the same through mind, body, and soul."

A hand with long weathered fingers stretched out from the sleeve of the shadowed cloak, and the same man spoke again, "Come with me; I will lead the way. Let us revive the garden of our forefathers and bring about the time before the fall."

The other, a young man with long whitish blonde hair that hung down to his shoulders; stood tall in front of the other. He was shirtless, nearly naked as a babe without blemish, but his back lie scared and torn; weary from battle. He stretched his hand out towards his brother and clasped his arm.

"Lead the way, brother. Let us become one as we once were before."

The other in the dark cloak took his hand and led the way from the edge of the limitless wilderness.

A sacrifice. The shepherd hath been slain by the thief lying within the kin. Blood of my blood, we shareth the same sin.

Thunder cracked in the sky, and the ether was painted black. Gray clouds hung above the horizon, and giant packs of crows cawed everywhere. I awoke under a tree in—some area; *a very strange space.* The grass was wet with a heavy dew, and the chill bit and nibbled at my skin. I shook, and my eyes popped open. Thin, incongruent fingers stretched out in branches that hung overhead; and I began to see the old runes in the twisting sticks above my head.

Carnival music played and whistled sharply into my ears, carried by the howling wind. Hounds barked, and I shuffled my way up from the ground.

Where am I, I thought to myself.

Lightning rumbled through the smoky clouds, and a rattling cackle rippled in the chilling breeze. The sound made my head pound. I gasped and heaved; spinning around. I was ready to panic and scream, but then I saw a tent in the scene. It lie at the center of the fairgrounds in town; *home, but not.* I stood past the gate; *pushing towards the threshold.*

The front corners flapped, and a glowing light appeared within. I didn't walk, my feet carried me. It was as if I were in a dream; stuck upon the rails.

The vision of the long walk was skipped, and I was in the tent. The crowd applauded, only the place was empty; except for Jack, the man in the hat. He was there standing in the middle of a circular stage; only he was wearing a top hat this time. Jack also wielded a cane with a crow's head on the handle. He spread his arms out and a multitude of dark wings flew out from under his open arms.

"Here yeeh, here yeeh," he laughed, and hollered, "thank you all for coming. I hope you've enjoyed the show!"

Antique bulbs lined the creases across what was sewn; the tent began to strobe. Then, suddenly all around me, I saw them, the shadow men, they filled the tiered seats that abound. They all turned their heads towards me simultaneously. I was locked in my seat and couldn't move. I screamed in horror. *The void is poised to capture me.*

The showman in the middle pulled off his top hat and tapped it with his cane; it turned back into his regular wide brimmed purple fedora. Jack flicked his coat like a magician and the very fabric itself turned back into his original dark duster, too.

"Quiet! Quiet now! Don't be rude up there or I'll let the rest of the audience have at you."

Jack grinned and shook his head.

"They aren't a fun bunch; trust me. You should know."

The creeping ones in the mirror. *How could I ever forget?*

I seized and calmed myself the best I could. *Draw on the strength you have,* a whisper came, *believe in yourself; find the light.*

Jack tssked with his tongue, and hollered, "So where do we find ourselves here? What shall we go over?"

Jack paused, then snapped his finger.

"Oh, yes! That's right!"

Then, he brought his fist up to his mouth, playfully clearing his throat, and carrying on, "Meet our benefactor. He is the chosen one, he is the star!"

Jack clenched his fist, snarling, then snapped, "He wishes. If you were a hero boy, you should have stayed in your tower, Quasimodo. You can't make the cut out there in the real world. I mean, just look at what you've done so far; you're a blind and bumbling fool. You can also stick idiot and degenerate in there as well to get a more full and clear view of the whole tragic charade. You're rotten, boy. You're a virus among the living."

My veins pulsed and rose under my skin; sharp pinching sensations rushed like static through my nerves. I groaned in agony; *he's right,* I thought, *I'm worthless to myself and everyone around me. I've hurt my family, and I've ruined the lives of my friends. I am the poison in the story. I feed the sickness, and I pass it.*

"Ahhhh, I can feel it. I'm getting under your skin, aren't I?"

I jerked, still locked in the chair, and felt the crawling leeches feeding under my skin. There prickles burned like fire. I screamed and fought for air in anguish.

"Your blood is cursed, I dearly apologize. It wasn't all you; I had my hand in the orchestration of a lot of what's happened thus far, but no matter. You still loved and admonished it all. I bring all these pretty gifts and lessons to you, but you don't seem to fully appreciate them for what they're worth. But doesn't it taste lovely? Doesn't it taste sweet? Oh, just let go. Just—

I gasped and fought against the drain. *Maybe I should let go. It would be so much easier. I would be blessed through the shadow, and obtain everything I've ever wanted, but who would I become? What would that make me in the end? I can taste it. It's all so—tempting.*

A monster; a villain in your own story, an all too familiar voice whispered.

But where do I go? Where do I turn?

You know where we have always been with you. A voice I couldn't recall came. It wasn't deep or high; it was somewhere inbetween.

I squeezed my fists and gnawed at the torment from the fire raging under my skin. The voice spoke again. *Remember who you are. You are not him, and he is not you.*

Remember, remember, the voice repeated.

I squealed in agony, and the man in the hat cackled. His face shifted under his mask into a more familiar grin. I've seen it before; in the family pictures, that is.

The man tipped his hat, smiling and said, "Just let go; it's inevitable. You can't fight it; none of us could. It's a mark that's been laid upon us, and we have to accept it. Come on, it won't kill you. You'll be one of us, a shifter, a traveler, a free wanderer within the void. There are worlds outside of this one that are beyond imagination, and they are all ripe for the taking. We feed the hive, and the dark matter grows. The souls are swallowed, but they become a part of us. Never alone, eh? Come on, what do ya say?"

The man in the hat cackled, and his face shifted again. It was the same one I've always known. This one was Jack, but the other one; *it's better not to say his name.*

His gaze pierced hard, and he had an emptier look about him. Only in the Shadowlands can the others influence another; it is the home of the hive.

"That boy," Jack shivered, "he was my brother."

The energy of the crowd fell, and the shadow men began to dissipate. Jack's grip on me loosened.

Remember, remember, the voice came again.

Light flashed, and I was out of the tent. I fell with a thud on the blacktop and grunted. The air was misty, and everything was wet. I lifted my head to look around, and I was in downtown Zanesville. Only it was during the days of the old town; everything was in black and white. Old Tudor Saloons, and Ford Model A's, from the 1930s lined the edge of the sidewalk. Lights hung from the poles, hanging limply in rows, and crossing across the road. Suddenly, footsteps began to stomp and echo across the towering brick walls in the faded distance. "Gloomy Sunday" by Billie Holiday screeched from a record player nearby and echoed through the air. A multitude of crows cawed madly from the rooftops.

Suddenly, Jack cackled in a nearby brick alleyway; a street sign shown under the weathered light. We were upon a corner that lie at the cross of 4th Street and Main. A flash, then a memory came. A burly man in a black suit lay there in that same alley, and Jack knelt down over top of him. His eyes burned a yellowish green glare, and he snapped, "Bye, bye, Gregory."

Then he plunged a stiletto knife into his gut, again and again.

Jack pulled the knife away and grabbed his hat back from the dead man. Still looking into Gregory's empty eyes, Jack wiped his knife clean on his duster, grimacing, and declared, "Vengeance will be mine."

"There you are," Jack said in a sing songy tune, "you can't hide from me; not even if you tried."

I stood up and held my ground. It was only because I knew I didn't have a chance at running anymore. We were both there at last—face to face.

"How long are we gonna go about this, huh?" Jack asked, "I'm tired of this ring around the rosy. "

Jack cackled, and sung, "Ashes, ashes, we all fall down."

Then, he continued in his regular tone, holding a thick sneer.

"It's all gotta burn, kid. It's gotta come to an end. You know it, and I do, too."

Suddenly, he stomped his foot; I could see him clearly in the road. He tilted his head towards the moon, grinning, and barked, "It's all gotta come to an end, my boy!"

Thunder cracked across the dark grey clouds, and the lights all around blinked. The cords hanging across the street lamps shook and wavered hard. A cold wind was picking up, and air rushed. I heard a faint sound within it; the whistling of the sparrow—the young boy with the flat cap was near. I could hear it, but he couldn't.

"This world is evil, it's rotten," Jack hollered over the howl.

"You and I, we both know it. Look what it did to us, look what it's doing to you. I can make you strong. I can give you the strength to survive. Just take my hand and walk with me. I can give you it all, everything you've ever dreamed of and then some. I—"

"If it's so great, then why do you want to escape?" I interrupted.

Jack clenched his fists and chewed his lip. Then he gasped.

"Because I'm tired of it, kid, that's why, and I have unfinished business to attend to. What's so great about where you are? Why do you keep hangin' on?"

Why do I, I wondered to myself. *Why do I care so much about being here?*

Remember, remember, the voice came.

A sudden flash, and I was sitting at a table, scribbling on some paper, singing some sort of song to myself. I was a little boy again, around six, to be exact. I got up from the table, ran to my mom, and handed her the picture.

"Look mommy, you like it," I pointed to it and smiled at her.

She held it and smiled back at me. *I love you so much,* I thought to myself. I gave her a hug, and she told me that she loved me. I fell into her lap, and hugged her tightly.

"I love you too, mommy."

Then, I saw my father sitting down with me. Both of us were cross-legged on the floor, and he was talking with his

400

hands. He was a very passionate speaker when it came to his beliefs.

"Always trust in that light, Hawke. The Lord is always with you. If you're ever in a bind, call on him, and he will be there."

"But what about you, daddy," I asked. "will you be there, too?"

He smiled faintly, and said back, "Of course I will. I'll always be there."

But it's hard because the Lord wasn't there for you. You weren't worth saving. I can't believe the same as you.

I gasped and shook; I saw them all, everyone that I loved. Smiles, jokes, laughs, thrills, adventure, and the wandering; the glory of it all.

"Well, what do ya say," Jack implored again, "are you ready to become something more?"

"No," I muttered, shaking my head.

Jack clenched his teeth and gritted them together. "Why not?"

"Because I stay for the sake of love, the pure joy of the experience. That's what a Wanderer is; that's why we keep coming back. We're souls that come again and again into this world. We sacrifice ourselves out of bliss into life all for the sake of adventure. That's how it will always be for us until we've all went through each of our cycles; until the soul family is complete."

I smiled to myself, and thought, *I've found it. I really think I've found it again.*

I felt the warmness in my heart grow, and my tongue flowed.

"The sweetest life experience to me would be a lifelong voyage of discovery, colored and nurtured through the essence of true love. I want to find that. I want to meet the twin to my soul. That's why I stay. I want to feel that. I want to know that story."

Jack clenched his fist and shook, grinding his teeth.

"You will accept my offer. Either willingly or by force. You don't even know a quarter of what you're capable of yet. You can't beat me. Why, you're a fly on the wall. You're a—"

The wind rushed again, a chattering whisper came, and I heard the whistle of the sparrow again. Vehicles shook, and the ground rumbled. Jack gasped and wailed. I turned around to see what the horror was. Giant rushing waves were rumbling towards us down Main Street, tearing away at all the buildings. Screaming, I attempted to run for all I could, but Jack disappeared, and suddenly I did, too.

Rails screeched, and the scratching wind blew rain across my face. I gasped for air. Jack was there, standing above me, right on top of the rushing railcar.

The train raced and blew its horn. Jack stomped, I rolled, and he lunged forward, trying to grab me. I pushed myself up and got ready. Jack ran towards me, and I charged back. We ran into each other, grunting and fumbling. Jack swung a blow into my stomach, and I threw myself forward, tackling him. Both of us crashed hard on the roof of the car.

The train raced full speed ahead across the tracks. The dam was coming up on the left, and the Y Bridge on the right. We fumbled and fought with one another, punching, hitting, kicking, tooth, and nail. There was a break, and both of us stopped.

"You can't beat me," Jack howled. He couldn't stop laughing. He hunched over, losing himself.

"Do you really think you can win?"

I didn't say a word; I charged him again. It knocked him off balance; and Jack stumbled towards the edge, and slid. He almost flew off the car and into the water, but he caught the edge just in time. Jack screamed and wailed. He was terrified of the water. The dam rushed, and the falls fell. The train blew its horn, and the rails screeched. Jack pleaded for help. I slid over to him; the rain pounded in my face, and the wind nearly took my breath. I caught his hand. He gripped my wrist back, and he dangled there hanging on the edge still. Halfway in my grip, halfway not. The river below glowed dark green and smoky skeletal faces appeared below; *some still looked like us.*

Jack's hat blew off and became lost in the waves. I could finally see his real face. We looked a lot alike, but not quite the same. He had darker hair; it was done in a disconnected undercut, and his cheekbones were more pronounced. His face looked soft; unblemished even. I felt sympathy for him, because I recognized pieces of myself in him.

He seemed so innocent now; as if a different part of him emerged; a piece not given over to the shadow. Jack stuttered, "P-p-please don't drop me. D-don't give me to the Valley of Lost Souls. I'll never find her again."

He began to cry and pleaded as he dangled. I was beginning to lose grip.

"P-p-please."

I pulled him up; I kept seeing that boy with the hat in the mirror. Mercy can be found even for the shadows. It's a way to tend to the light in your heart and prepare it for unification. Jack heaved when I brought him back up safely upon his feet. He whimpered for a moment, but then his face changed again. Jack snatched at my neck, suddenly this time bringing me down to the edge. He knelt down to choke me. His hands were drawing my life away; his yellow eyes burned.

"You will accept, you will. I won't see you become a lost soul, but you will replace me. You will wear the hat!"

I grabbed his wrists and tried to fight him off, but I couldn't. I squealed and gasped for air. Jack's eyes burned as he strangled me. I reached my hand out for hope and closed my eyes. Something dormant had lit up within my soul, and a voice spoke through me that hadn't touched the wind in ages. I could feel it, but I still didn't know it.

Father, Lord of Rivers, one of ice, beyond the gate. You are the eye within the sands of Mara. Your gate lies within the oasis. Do not forsake me in this night. Please do not forget your lost son.

Jack choked me still, and I fought and pounded against clenching arms. Everything nearly went black, but then there was a flash. An old man whispered, *Wanderer in the Wilderness; where hath thou been?*

An amulet fell out of the light, and it glimmered down. I caught it in my open hand. An amulet of nine stones, four on the chain, five on the key. The amulet flashed, and Jack gasped; huddling back.

"Get it away from me! Get it away!"

I brought myself up and held the amulet up like a lantern. All the stones burned a color forward, each to their own shade. Jack backed further away. I stepped forward. The voice spoke again. *Speak the words that I give you and bind this soul. The amulet shall be the key to his prison.*

I pressed further forward, and Jack pleaded more. I held the amulet out before me and spoke the words that were whispered to me.

Dark one, vacuum within the shades, walker between worlds. I hereby bind thee by this talisman. Let it be the key to your cell, here, within the void. I bind thee, Jack, the man in the hat, I bind thee to my charge. May you be locked away, imprisoned, and wander no more.

The man in the hat screeched in anguish and torment as he began to tear away. Then I said the final words.

The banishing failed before, but you are now what you were back then. Your nothing but the monster in the closet.

Dark rifts of energy swirled around the straining figure, and a force pulled the shadow towards his prison; the red door with the golden knob. The hinges slammed shut, and within an instance I fell flat and crashed into the ether; floating away back towards somewhere. I couldn't feel myself upon the cloud, all I could do was peer into the dream.

Lightning flashed, and suddenly boots dangled above from a tree in a vision. A young man with long light blonde hair hung from a tree, staring into a well. One pale blue eye burned as bright as a sapphire, the other was missing. Thunder cracked, an image flashed ahead of a cloaked man in a dark wide-brimmed hat wading across the dead of the battlefield claiming those that be called to his hall. The crows cawed and pecked away at the dead flesh that lay across the blood-soaked ground. Two ravens landed on his shoulder.

A flash again. Suddenly, the tree was empty.

You don't know their true origin do you, a voice whispered, *of the hat men? He was the first, thy ancestor Woden, back in times long forgotten. The curse was passed down the line. Your forefathers sold their blood, not just their souls. There is a stamp for all of eternity upon his line. Many are infected, but the one with the true heart of the Wanderer shall prevail, and drink from thy cup; thy innermost grail. Come now. Thy father calls to you; you've always felt him there.*

CHAPTER XXX:

CROSSROADS

I found myself in an unfamiliar place, a land I'd seen before, but had forgotten. There were mighty oaks circling all around, thick, aligned towards a path. Golden, deep red, brown, and orange leaves fell like rain all around. It was beautiful. *There was peace.* Birds chirped through the air and I could hear a woodpecker in the distance. Past that there was an odd stillness to everything, almost as if time itself had stopped.

I spun around in a circle in complete awe of the majestic feeling that blew through the breeze all around. It was like none of it happened at all. That the scars were no more, and I was back to my original self before it all started. Before I first knew pain; *the shame and the cruelty.*

I turned my head towards a path that traversed through the trees. The wind was carrying the multi-colored leaves along with it, *almost as if they were leading me towards something.* It appeared to be a clearing.

I began walking down the path; following the zephyr. Leaves crumpled under my feet and the sun lit up sparkles of golden dust in the air along the pathway. When I reached the end of the threshold, I stopped dead in my tracks.

There was a man sitting cross-legged on the ground with his back against a mighty oak, with leaves drifting down around him. He had a red book in his hands with some sort of old car on it, but I couldn't really tell. He nodded his head, and whispered to himself, "The pleasure of the unknown. I like that, too."

It was my father; we were together again at last. My voice froze in my throat and I couldn't speak a word. My eyes welled up with tears, carrying all the pain along with it. I gasped and heaved deeply over the unbelievable.

My father looked up from his book, smiling, and said, "Well, there you are. It took you long enough. Where've you been?"

I was stuck in shock upon the opening; frozen in disbelief. Hot tears ran down my melting cheeks. My arms dangled, and shook at my sides. I lifted them slowly and rushed into his open arms. He caught me there and my head fell across his shoulder. Gasping, I let myself go in his embrace, and everything came out; the terrible with the tears. The pain flowed from my cheeks and landed on the crisp yellow leaves beneath our feet. My father laughed softly and said, "Well, I'm happy to see you, too. What have you been up to all this time?"

Through the painful groans and shivers, I couldn't say a word. I was just happy to have him back. *It's all over now; it's finally over.*

"Hey, now," he said, "Calm down, it's going to be alright. There's nothing to be sad about."

I pulled my head up from his shoulder and looked into his eyes. I cracked a smile, with the tears welling up still.

"I thought I lost you. I thought you were dead."

My father placed his hands on my shoulders and smiled.

"You never lost me. There isn't a thing such as death, only a parting of ways, more like a 'see ya later on', never a goodbye."

The wind rolled like a wave of passion before me, carrying away the burden of pain I carried with it.

"I didn't think I'd ever see you again. You don't know what it's been like since you left."

My father replied, "I never wanted to leave you. There was just another plan for us in the way of things. It doesn't happen in every reality, but in this one, it did. I'm still here with you, always have been, even if you can't see me."

He smiled, winked, then continued, "A lot nearer than you think, believe it or not."

I asked, wondering over his words.

"What do you mean it doesn't happen in every reality? What does that mean?"

My father took a few steps towards another path, then turned back toward me and spoke, "You'll come to see it later. It doesn't always happen like this. There's many different timelines and events that run simultaneously; parallel along with one another. Everything is now. The past, present, and future are all interlinked; tangled within the web."

I gasped, "But what does that mean? I don't understand."

My father smiled tenderly and replied, "Say you're at a green light. You have the choice to either turn left or right. In all instances, you choose either or. In one reality, you chose to go left, in another you chose to go right, and so it is with every decision you make. Alternate realities are created in this way, where different versions of the self and various iterations of the same story emerge."

I shivered, and sobbed again, "What does that mean?"

I paused; wanting to believe, but not falling to it either.

"S-so you're saying," I continued, "s-somewhere out there, there's still a me and you? And we're happy together?"

My father's smile fell, and he replied, "It doesn't work out the way that you think. Whatever else exists out there, in the alternate states, doesn't matter. Only now, this one, the one we're in right now. You can't change the past, even though I know you will still try. You can only move forward."

I wiped my tears clean, and my voice drug out; filtering it's way through the hurt.

"Y'know, I always imagined us having the type of bond where we'd be father and son, but also best friends, too. I could see myself going to you for advice, teaching me how to tie a tie. Joking with me, growing old together, and then at the end you could laugh and watch my kids play in the yard with me. We'd even get up and play some games with them, too. I wanted you here for all that, but we were cheated. You were stolen away, ripped from us all, and that's what makes me so sick. All these people that claimed to care for you when you were here; they trashed and drug your name through the mud after you were gone, and these are people I still love. It's like it wasn't enough to bury you, but they tried to poison your memory, too. I guess it's easy attacking and placing a stamp on someone that's not here to defend themselves. Whatever's easier than digging through your own closet, I guess."

My dad planted a soft grip on my shoulder, and told me, "Don't be angry with them; forgive. Don't forget the seed that I gave you; never lose sight of where you came from. People aren't perfect. You can't expect them to be, but there is a greater good that serves a higher purpose within us all. You have to believe and nurture that. Not just for yourself, but for all those around you, too. It's the only way to heal the garden."

"But I can't," I screamed. "It makes me so sick! Everyone lied at the hospital. They all said that they would be there for me. They all promised over you that they would, but that couldn't even be honored and respected; I was too much out of there way."

My face twisted, and he watched me with sorrow, but there was compassion from another world behind it. He pressed on my shoulder again. He tried to console me, but I wouldn't listen; I had to let it all out.

"All these people acted like you meant so much to them after you were gone, but they lied. They all treated you like a dog when you were alive, and that's what makes me sick the most. Everyone who was cruel to you and done you wrong, they get to live on. They get to lead nice, happy lives with all of their families; it's easier for them to forget. Some were even jealous of your calling. You shone with something they wanted to possess, but could never hope to have. You were the humblest, that's why the Lord favored you. They said your understanding was lower than theirs, that you couldn't comprehend the scriptures to their level, but it's not about who can quote Bible the best; it's about love, and I'm willing to bet you know more about that than they ever could. You were too good for so many people. I don't feel like any of us deserved you, really. I—"

I paused for a moment, my voice stuck in my throat.

"It tears me up. Because the only reason why I'm acknowledged is because of the guilt. If I wasn't your son, nobody would pay me a thought at all."

My father didn't say a word. He didn't confirm whether I was right or wrong. In a way, I wanted him, too. *Do they really love me for me or just because of who's son I am?*

"Follow me. I want to show you something," he suddenly said.

I followed him down the trail. The wind was blowing gently at our backs and there was a sweet scent of myrrh in the air. At the end of the clearing was a lake, a dark one, and my father stood at the edge of it. He pointed to the waters and said, "Now don't be alarmed by what you are about to see. Don't say a word, don't ask a thing, until the vision is over."

I gazed at my father and approached the edge of the lake. Suddenly, the unmoving waters lit up like a TV screen and a strange scene began playing. It was almost like I could see through this person's eyes and feel everything they felt.

The desert winds blew, and knees dug in the sand. There were two large heaps of rock with a path leading between them; marking the way. *The Place Between the Stones.* A painful groan screeched in the wind.

"Why didn't it make a difference? Will anyone ever recognize the true intentions of my heart?"

The man in the hat placed his hand on the man's shoulder. He was settled in a posture, stuck in the dark night; gazing into the open flames of a fire.

"Why," the man in the hat asked, then chattered, "Because you have the wrong goal. You wanna fix the world, see it renewed, but there ain't no fixing all of this rot. The world is a wasteland filled with thieves and murderers. This isn't La La Land; it's an arena. Ya see, the fair of heart can't thrive in this place. The world is ran by villains; it's their playground here. They are the ones who thrive. A true loving heart doesn't have a hope to survive."

The thorns seep and tear at the helm of the rose; squeezed within the fist, the petals fall straight past the wrist.

In that lake, I saw a story play out; it showed a man getting the fame and acclaim he'd always wanted. Everybody loved him, but others grew jealous, coveting what he had close by. There was a great betrayal down the line, and it shattered him. Day by day, night by night afterward, the sickness grew under his skin, and he felt the torment. The only way to fix it was by seeing the funny side of things. He began to laugh, and to never cry again. He grew egotistical and played people like they were his pawns. Destroying others as they had him, killing his soul more in the process. *I produce vengeance. I am the rectifier.*

The man had lost all matter of love in his life by the end. He was truly alone in the world. The mass reviled him, but the shadows hugged and coaxed him. *Come with us. We shall bring an end to the suffering. We will bring about the final silence together. An end to all cycles. Come, thy blood is the price. Become one of us. Take your place among our fold; a lieutenant of the Hollow King.* A swimming pool with deep red waters waved under the pounding rain. *The lost son has sunk to the bottom.*

The image disappeared, and I stammered by the lake.

"W-w-what was that?"

"That was you," my father replied.

"What?" I gasped, "h-how, but why?"

My dad crossed his arms and stare into the lake, then looked back at me with a sincere stare.

"That was just one possibility of what can await you in the future. In a lifetime, there are many bridges to cross, and many paths to take. There will always be pain, there always will be in this world, but never forget—what you feed is what you get. A perfected flower in the garden shines for all, and its light spreads. It is a remedy and a seed to help heal the world, just like the one I gave to you."

I shook, and rattled; my eyes began to burn again.

"You gave me so much in the little amount of time we had together. I can only imagine what more moments between you and I would've brought. You're the only one I know that could ever truly understand me. I could feel it then; and I still can now."

My father smiled and blushed a little just like I do. His eyes held so much joy.

"That's because I'm always near, as long as you stay open to me. Don't shut me up in your grief; it weighs us both down. You have to learn to let me go so we can both soar again."

"But I can't dad. There's still so much about it all that I don't understand. Why did she do it? Why did she betray us?"

My father stepped forward and placed his hand on my shoulder, and said, "Son, you have to forgive; even the worst out there, we all deserve mercy. Remember. God sent us to heal the garden for the new children to come. The shadow is encroaching and growing darker upon the world every day. The Lord's children have become disconnected from each other. There is no unity and we hold little love for each other out there. What do you think the world needs more of?"

"It needs more faith, more love, more connection, more joy, that's for sure, but that's not a remedy for the darkness; it only suppresses and holds it at bay. The everlasting cycles of pain keep flowing. I think we should dive into the darkness in a safe way, perhaps through art, and understand it. We have to come to terms with what's in our background, with what's in our shadow, each of us, in order to move forward towards rebuilding the garden. Everything is symbolic and holds a message; think about it. A seed must first be plunged into darkness in order to bloom."

From the ashes and dirt, we shall grow.

"Wow," my father laughed, "you've really thought a lot about all of this."

His gaze grew still, and joyful again, then he said, "Some aren't ready to face those types of trials yet, though. There is a preparation that has to unfold in order for an awakening to happen. Leave the keys where you can. The right people will pick them up and understand them for what they are."

"I really wish I could figure out a way to relate to everybody else. The only thing I can find in common with other people is drinking and doing drugs. It's like outside of that I get lost. I just can't let myself go enough."

"It's not that hard. Just shine, Hawke, that's all you gotta do."

I laughed and pulled my hair.

"I guess I just think about it all too much."

I stood there smiling at him, still in disbelief that he was there. I got excited and marveled at the scenery.

"But what about this place, anyway? Did I die or what?"

"No, you didn't die," my father replied, "there's still a lot in your path waiting for you. More than what you could ever imagine."

"Do you think that because of the dream you had with the Indian? The one who told you to give me this name?"

My father smiled and shook his head.

"No, not him. It's because I believe in you. You just have to believe in yourself. Always remember—have faith and trust in what is good, what is loving, always follow with the heart and never be afraid to be vulnerable. Keep the spring holy. Save the best of it for that special someone you'll meet someday."

I smiled with joy. I always wanted to talk to him about girls.

I replied, "Like a true love?"

My father smiled and reiterated, "Like a true love."

He walked over, patted me on the shoulder.

"Just trust the journey, and enjoy the process."

He embraced me in his arms and said, "I love you, son."

I clenched tightly to him. *I never want to let you go.*

"I love you, too, dad."

He patted my back and whispered in my ear, "Always and forever, right?"

"Always and forever. With all of my heart."

A song hummed in the atmosphere above. The words were muffled in the echo. I stepped back, confused, and asked, "What's that, dad?"

His eyes grew sad and weary, but they had a knowing to them. He didn't want me to go. Neither of us did, but our paths went two separate ways.

"It's time for you to go, son. The other world calls to you."

"But I don't wanna go back, dad; it's terrible there. I want to stay here with you. I—"

The grove slowly started to fade away into the mist, and so did my father. I reached my hand out and ran towards him. The pitch from my screams went mute, and the vacuum came.

I just want to go back.

CHAPTER XXXI:

THEY REMINISCE OVER YOU

My body jerked, and my lungs gasped for air. The blinker was clicking, and my ears rung. I lifted my head up and groaned. The radio was still humming. Air Supply's "Making Love Out of Nothing at All," played; it was the same tune I heard in the grove upon the departure.

For me, that song means a lot; it rests in a different context from its author. It's about me, the people, it's about my father. He knew how to make love out of nothing at all.

I cringed, shook, and snorted; swallowing the dryness away, and smacking my hands against my forehead. *There isn't any blood. I might be okay this time.*

I sighed in relief, *How long was I out for? And my— and my dad; did I really see him? Or was it all just a dream? What about the man in the hat? I can't feel him anymore; he's either been hushed or he's powerless. Brooding somewhere still, in the silence, within the shadows. Now I truly feel all alone.*

The chorus to the song kicked off. I gasped again, and choked. *Why am I back here? Why couldn't I have stayed in that grove with him forever? That felt like home.* The song hummed onward, and I cried.

But you do; believe in the message you were given, an all too familiar voice said. *Follow the instincts within your heart. They will carry you towards the stream of your destiny.*

I gotta keep going; the journey has just begun. I wiped the tears away and flipped the gears into reverse; pressing on the pedal. The front tires spun in the mud.

"Come on, come on," I muttered, pressing harder on the gas wiggling the wheel. Suddenly, the back tires caught the asphalt, and I was back on the road.

When I got out to assess the damage, I saw that the front end had only suffered a minor ding in the bumper. I hopped back in the driver's seat and rubbed my hands against the wheel, staring out into the deep night. The sun began to rise. Images of my father flicked like a reel of film in my head, and the unsettled heaviness of my heart began to sink back in. *I need to find answers.*

I pressed the gas and headed forward. *Grandma's house,* I thought to myself, *maybe she'll talk to me today.*

The clouds hung gray above the cove on the hill; and the empty branches whistled in the fast, rumbling wind. Chimes rung, and the window panes rattled.

Grandma walked in, and offered me some coffee by the fireplace, and I took it; nearly burning my tongue gulping it down.

"Is everything going okay, Hawke?" she asked.

I sat the coffee down on the round table and took a deep breath. *I probably look like I crawled out of hell. She knows; she can pick up on just about anything. No sense in lying.*

I hung my head and watched my fingers dig at one another as they hung between my legs above the floor.

"I don't know. I've been thinking about a lot that's all."

"About your dad?" she asked.

"Yeah," I replied, "it's that time of year you know how it goes. I just—I just wanna know why, y'know? Why did she do it? What really happened that night?"

I watched my hands fall limp, and I fell back into my chair; looking at grandma now, no longer at the ground. She sat there studying me for a moment, then replied, "None of us really know why she did what she did, Hawke; only she knows that."

"I know," I replied, "but I don't have a clue where she is now, and if I found her, would she tell the truth?"

Grandma stared at me, then gazed off to the side for a moment.

"I'm not so sure about that," she turned back to me, and said, "you have to be careful with someone like her. She's not like everyone else. She knows how to turn on the tears when she wants to."

I felt the pull when I thought of it; *it's a part of my path I have to settle. There isn't any other choice. Stay here, and wander, or hit the open road.*

"I have to know, though. I'll never be able to get it out of my head if I don't."

"The choice is yours, Hawke," Grandma said, "I'll support you in whatever decision you make, but you need to be careful. She's a very powerful person."

"Do you know where she is? Does Josci live with her now?"

Grandma divulged all the details she knew. I looked her up online and dug up all that I could. An address, a phone number, a Myspace, and a Facebook. *There she is,* I thought to myself. I shivered all over and my eyes stung.

Why did you do it? Why would you betray us? I thought to myself as my eyes laid frozen on her picture.

Josci.

I went towards the posted photos and flipped through. A picture of a little girl in a tree with bright blue eyes and long blonde hair smiled really big back at the camera; her cheeks were flushed red. My eyes grew hot with tears, and I gasped, "Josci."

It had been eight years since I saw my sister. *I've missed you so much,* I thought, as I studied her picture, trying to find features in her that matched mine; something that we both had that would link us towards our dad. *Does she even remember me?*

I didn't have an answer for any of it. *I have to know. It will never stop eating away at me until I do. I made my mind up;* I'd found a direction. *Time to hit the road.*

I stayed out at Grandma's for more than a few days, and it really helped me out because it felt more like home to me than any other place I could find. My dad lived in that house too, when he was a teenager. Even though all the walls had changed, and the rooms were different, I could still feel his presence there, especially in the basement. They used to have Christmas down there by the fireplace.

Grandma pulled some black and white pictures out down there one day. They came out of this old steamer trunk. We flipped through them, because I was interested, too. There were so many faces that didn't have a name, but after a while I began to notice something. *There's something peculiar about these pictures. It feels like there's something in them.*

I shuffled another photo from the front to the back of the stack and shivered at the next one. I didn't see past the little baby girl in the christening dress yet, but when I did, I gasped and shook.

"What?"

In the corner, above her right shoulder, was a man, a happy one. His eyes were shadowed under the brim of his hat; but his grin was clear and deep, etching its way upward towards his ears.

"G-grandma, l-look, look," I tossed the picture to her hands quickly, eager to be rid of it.

"What is it?"

"T-the man."

I pointed him out.

"Don't you see him? The man in the hat?"

Grandma leaned backward in her chair, studying it.

"Hmmm, that is strange."

"Who is that? When was that picture taken?" I asked her; eager and desperate to know. Perhaps it's a clue.

She flipped the picture over, and nodded, "Oh, that's my grandma. She was my dad's mom. Yeah—"

She paused and turned the picture back over, studying the man in the picture again.

"That is strange."

I couldn't help it. I had to ask.

"Do you think there's like some kind of curse on us or something? I mean, do you ever get the sense that there's something in our family history that we don't know about?"

Grandma replied, "Well, there is a lot we don't know about. That picture was taken in 1903, and her father disappeared when she was just a baby. Nobody knows what happened to him."

Grandma paused, then laughed, "I shouldn't laugh, but they used to tease us when we were kids and tell us he was in the walls of the house somewhere, hidden away, and watching us."

I jumped back, "That's really creepy. Was that the house in Somerset?"

"Yeah, that was the family home for over a hundred years."

"No wonder why I was scared to go upstairs then," I replied, "that attic door always gave me the creeps."

"They used to say you could hear whispers coming from it," Grandma replied.

My hand plopped against my knee, and I stammered, "Come on, really? Are you trying to scare me or what?"

Grandma laughed, "No, that's really what they used to say."

We'd laugh about crazy stuff like that all the time. I didn't know if she was messing with me or not, but she's always fun to talk with. We never ran out of topics.

January was coming to an end, and I was finally clean. I could think so much clearly, and connect things on such a higher level. I was more fluid, and synchronized with myself. I was finally focused on a change. *It all starts with finding my answers.* I couldn't fight the push any longer. It was like the gravity towards it all wasn't just on the inside, but the outside, too. I knew I had to leave even if it was hard to hit the road and leave everything behind. *I just hope everyone doesn't end up hating me.*

A couple of days before I planned to depart. I made sure I said bye to everybody.

I went to Uncle Stallone's first. The house was loud, and there were little kids running around. Aunt Louise did day care. I walked right in. With them, you don't even gotta knock.

"Hey, Hawke how you been? You talked to your mom," Aunt Louise asked from the kitchen table. She had her laptop open and was on Facebook. Tommy's wife Nicole was there, too. She was doing the same thing.

"No, I haven't. Is everything goin' alright?"

"Yeah," Aunt Louise replied, "everybody's just worried about ya that's all."

"I know." I looked to the ground in shame, breathing deeply.

"I'll talk to her sometime."

"Well, you better," Aunt Louise replied, "because you only got one mother, and she loves you. You need to talk to her. You need—

Suddenly, the back door flung open, and Uncle Stallone charged up the steps.

"There's some old guy in a wheelchair out there that just tried to pull his thing out in front of all the kids back there in the yard!"

"What?!"

We all jumped back in shock.

"Yeah," Uncle Stallone nodded, "I just chased him down the alley, and Carl's still after 'em back there."

Aunt Louise gasped, "I can't believe that."

"Yeah," Uncle Stallone shook his head, and continued, "He tried to pull it right out. Hell, he had a whole bottle of whiskey with 'em, and half of it was gone."

I headed for the back, grinning.

Carl was still chasin him down the alley. He looked like Lucky from King of the Hill.

The poor guy was wheeling away, and Carl was over the top of him, barking. His chair was electronic, and it didn't go too fast honestly. Suddenly, Carl stopped and the weirdo in the wheelchair slowly shifted, and rolled away; slurring, and hollering, "I was itching my leg! I was itching my leg!"

"No, you weren't, you sick bastard," Carl barked.

The chair hit a bump in the alley and slowly crept ahead. He was around twenty feet away from Carl now; he stood still in the middle of the alley, flexing up.

"Yeah! That's right, you better get out of here! And don't come back!"

The drunk flasher in the electric wheelchair continued to groan and turtle away.

Carl turned around and shook his head, walking back over towards me and Uncle Stallone.

"Geez, man," he said, "people these days are fuckin' whacko around here."

Yes, they are.

We went back inside, and of course, Uncle Stallone continued the talk. Aunt Louise started on how I needed to speak to my mom, and we need to make up; y'know all of that. I just nodded in understanding, and knew it was true, but they wanted to talk and I listened. We always have good talks when we sit down with each other. I love listening to their stories and a lot of things that they say really make me think. They've always been teachers to me.

Tommy stopped by, too, while I was there. Of course, every time he arrives, he has to make his presence known.

"Okay! I'm gonna need everybody to put their cigarettes out and get off Facebook. It's time to rise and shine and get happy to be alive!"

Tommy danced past the staircase and into the dining room. He paused, frozen solid in the entry, and stare at Nicole. Then he pointed, throwing her the keys to the Jeep.

"You! Store—now," he barked; jokingly.

She tried to react fast and make the catch, but the keys jingled out of her hands; dropping beneath her stool.

"Come on, Tommy," she wailed, "stop actin' stupid."

Tommy pressed her.

"Well, how bout you drop down and give me ten. Then, I'll give you a pass."

Nicole turned her head from the laptop screen, rolling her eyes, and said, "Whatever, Tommy. I'm not goin' to the store right now. I don't want to."

They went on ranting with each other, Uncle Stallone, and Aunt Louise got in it, too. It wasn't an argument; it was a fun bubble. A way to challenge each other in a light way just by joking around. A lot of people can't do that these days; they're just too sensitive about facing any type of criticism about themselves. They wouldn't survive with wolves like us.

I made my exit smooth after a while. It was in the late afternoon. I told everybody bye in a casual way, knowing that it would be a while before I'd see them again. I didn't know what would come after I found my answers. I figured I'd just keep rolling along as a drifter; y'know, a road warrior type of guy. *Yeah that would be fun. Travel the whole country and end it all in 29 Palms. Now that would be an adventure. That would be a story that could turn into a good book.*

I hopped back in my ride and hit the blinker at the stop sign. I pulled a right off Echo Avenue and headed up Pine Street towards Luck. I wanted to see grandpa and grandma, but I figured I'd stop at the gas station first. To my surprise, Uncle Shua was in there standing taller than everybody; he's a giant. You can't miss the guy. He appeared to be arguing a little with the cashier, who was speaking Spanish.

"Español? Español?"

The cashier kept asking.

Uncle Shua shook his head in frustration.

"No, I already told you I don't speak Spanish."

The cashier spoke in a thick accent that sort of sounded like Tony Montana.

"You mean you're Mexican and don't speak Spanish, mayne?"

Uncle Shua shook his head again.

"I already told you I'm not Mexican, man."

The cashier pressed further; and measured with his fingers.

"Not just a little bit?"

I cut in out of nowhere basically, surprising Uncle Shua, and told the cashier, "He's not a Mexican guy, he's a black guy, man."

The cashier nodded. "Oh, okay, okay. Sorry about that, mayne. Jew, just look Spanish, that's all."

Uncle Shua snatched his drink off the counter and told the cashier, "Look at me, man. I'd be the tallest Mexican on planet Earth if that was true."

I busted out laughing, and we walked outside towards the pumps; I forgot what I even stopped for.

Uncle Shua asked me, "So what you been up to, man? I haven't seen you in a while."

"Nothing much, really," I replied. "I've just been runnin' around town, that's all."

"What you getting' into today?" Uncle Shua asked.

I shrugged my shoulders and replied, "I don't know. I was about to ride over to grandma's to see her and grandpa."

Uncle Shua nodded, "Yeah, I'm probably gonna stop over there, too."

Then he paused in thought for a moment, looking past the road, then continued, "But, shit, I'm about to meet up at the gym with Zeus if you wanna come, man."

I figured I would because I wanted to see him, too. It was a blast at the gym because Zeus was about half nuts. When I'd try to push the weight up, my arms jiggled, and wavered.

Zeus was spotting me on the bench, and screaming over me, "Come on! Come on! Get it up! Get it up!"

I couldn't do it; he had to save me.

"Geez, man, what are you trying to do? Kill me?"

All he said was, "You gotta know how to flex with your chest and push. A lot of it's in your head."

He tapped me on the shoulder, and said, "If this is something you wanna do, and it's somethin' you gotta do, then you do it. Fighters fight, bro."

"Did you just quote Rocky, man?" I asked Zeus.

Uncle Shua busted out laughing, "Yeah, he did!"

Zeus tried to defend himself. "No I didn't."

Yeah, you did.

Not soon after, I headed to grandma and grandpa's down on Luck Avenue.

I parked out front and got out quick because the cold was starting to nip. It was February 2nd, so everything around was still brittle from the chill. I pulled the screen door open and turned the knob on the inside, swinging the door open. Shivering, I walked in.

"Hey, Hawke, how you doin'," Grandpa asked.

Grandma said, "Oh, I didn't know you were stopping by. Are you doing okay? It's nice to see you; we ain't heard from you in a while."

I hadn't talked to anybody much, except Paul through text half lit, that is.

We sat and talked in the living room for a little bit, and I pretty much lied about everything I'd been up to the last few weeks. I had to. I couldn't tell them the truth. They'd be to disappointed in me.

Suddenly, grandma broke up whatever we were talking about and shifted the subject. She said, "Oh yeah, I almost forgot to tell you."

She pointed at me from her recliner, and continued, "You left a coat here, I think. It's hanging up there in the hallway closet."

"Really?" I asked, confused.

"Yeah, go get it out of there, and take it with you. You're not wearing enough to stay warm," Grandma declared.

I agreed to look for it, and at first I couldn't find it.

"No to the left," grandma directed me until my hands fell on a hanger. A long, dark pea coat hung from it. I pulled it out of the closet and held it up in the living room.

"This one," I asked. My eyebrows fluttered; confused.

"Yeah, that coat. Is that yours?"

I shook my head, "No, I don't think it is."

A flash, in a second, a laugh came, then a flicker; *a shadow in a hat. The red door with the golden knob.* Everything went silent behind it.

"Well, I don't know who's it is then," Grandma replied.

Grandpa studied the coat on the hanger, almost as if he saw something in it, too. Then, his eyes fell on me. He had that deep glare of his going on. The kind you can tell means something, and he's thinking, but you don't have a clue what it could be at all. Suddenly, he said, "If it's mine, you can have it. Take it with you."

"It looks like it would fit ya," Grandma chimed in,"that's why I thought it was yours. Go ahead and try it on."

I threw off my jacket and pulled the coat from the hanger. My arms slid perfectly into the sleeves, and the tail hung above my knees. I flipped the collar up, pulled it tighter, and smiled. *Classy.*

I laughed, and said, "Hey, grandpa, now all I need is one of those old type of fedora hats to go along with it."

Grandma sat back cool and relaxed on the couch; staring away in a daze at the TV.

"Yeah, I used to have a hat like that," Grandpa replied, still staring away. He was there, but it seemed like he was drifting away in thought somewhere else.

"Back in the olden days," he muttered.

"Well, I like it," I said, "Thanks, grandpa. I'll take good care of it, I promise."

Grandpa nodded his head, and grandma said, "You're welcome, honey."

The shoulders of the coat hung heavy at first, but then the fabric began to settle, and it moved fluidly. I didn't stay too long after, only because I promised Paul I'd take him to the movies. I couldn't wait to see him again. It had been too long.

"What are you, a businessman now?" Paul asked when he jumped in the ride.

I flicked the collar up and laughed.

"Guess so; it's good to see ya, man."

We went to see the new Seth Rogan movie, "The Green Hornet," and we laughed our asses off. It was so nice to have some one on one time with him. Afterwards, we went to Buffalo Wild Wings and got down on some food. We talked about girls most of the time, and how mean they can be. We both pretty much cried about it, honestly. We might look different, but we have a lot in common.

The whole time I was sitting across the table from him joking around, the same thought pervaded in my head that had been there all day. Only it burned more with him.

They're going to be devastated when you disappear.

Paul's lips moved, but I didn't have a clue what he was talking about. I was lost in my own thoughts. *But I have to,* I thought to myself. *I'll just keep bleeding from it if I don't. I have to know why.*

When I pulled up to the driveway of the house, Paul's head jerked over at me, and he stammered, "You mean you're not gonna pull in?"

"No," I shook my head slowly, and muttered.

"But why?" Paul asked, his face was growing sad.

"Because I can't," I told him.

She'll take one look at me and know something is up. Plus, I really can't. My thoughts ran on. *If I see mom I might not be able to go through with it.*

"J-just tell mom I — tell her I love her, a-alright?"

Paul nodded silently; he looked like he was going to cry.

"Okay, bub. I'll see ya in a couple of days, okay?"

Silence fell, and I held my face tight. *Don't cry, don't cry.*

"Give me a hug, man," I told him. We hugged, and I held him tight.

"I love you, man. Okay?"

"I love you, too," Paul replied.

I patted his back and let go.

"I'll see ya soon," I told him. He opened the door and went to get out.

"Talk to mom sometime, please," Paul said.

"I will, I promise," I told him.

We said our final goodbyes, and I glanced into the rearview mirror, rushing off. Paul had his head hung as he walked through the bitter cold down the driveway. *I know they'll miss me;* I thought to myself, *but this isn't about them, it's about me. Everybody will be okay, but this way of life, this town, I can't do it. I want something more. I need a new place. After I get my answers, I can go anywhere. I have enough money to last. It's time to see the world.*

Derek's cut from the lick was still in the trunk after all, and I wanted to give it back to him, but he told me to stay away so--I was just trying to respect his wishes. I figured Shawn was probably hunting me down somewhere, too, but I had been out of the loop so I didn't have a clue. *Just another reason to leave.*

The next day, I bought a Garmin GPS and a burner flip phone.

"Hey, nice coat," a passerby in the store said.

"Ey, yeah, thanks," I waved; the leather finger gloves I found in the coat pocket; they felt pretty snug, too. 1 gotta admit. *Now all I need is a hat to go along with it.*

429

I parked at the landing by the railroad crossing just by the vicious gap at the end of the Y-Bridge. I walked up towards the middle column, and a crow cawed, squealing upon the light. My peacoat blew in the wind, and the rumbling waters upon the dam crashed ahead; the falls. My phone rang suddenly and it was an unknown number. I stare off for a moment towards the raging river and chose to answer the call.

"Hello?"

The voice on the other end hissed, "We know what you did to Brian and when we find you you're fuckin' dead! Dead! Understand you mother—"

I hung up abruptly. I couldn't feel fear or anything really, only the words in my head. *Catch me if you can.*

The bird croaked above my head on the light pole once again. I stare at the barking crow, and my gaze grew. Losing itself into the midst of the long night. Suddenly, I jerked and scared the old crow off.

"Those things are the devil," I muttered, then I cracked my phone in half and threw it into the river. *Good riddance, old life,* I thought to myself.

Suddenly, footsteps loomed closer; quietly towards my right side. I was on edge enough over the call, plus there was still Shawn, or even Derek, but when I allowed my gaze to creep over towards the clicking of the steps growing ever near, I saw him, he was there, the Grey Man; waltzing closer with an all too familiar smile.

"Hello there," he waved casually as he stopped by my side. His eyes glimmered with compassion into mine, and his fine polished shoes rotated with a slide towards the sight of the falls. He took a deep breath and exhaled upon the vision.

"Beautiful, isn't it?" The Grey Man asked casually. "This place and the bridge is the only thing that seems to endear here."

430

I was dumbfounded, but I wasn't afraid by his presence. I felt like I needed to talk to him, and honestly, I kind of wanted to.

"Yeah, it is pretty, I guess. I mean, this town is kind of shitty and there's nothin' to do most of the time, but it's home, y'know?"

"That it is," the Gray Man affirmed with a smile.

"It's a place you will always hold dear in your heart, but there will come a day when it will hold nothing for you. Those that you love, your family, one day none of them will be here anymore. That's how it is with life, though. Things change, people get older, and then of course fate does it's duty. The wheel has revolved without mercy already. You can see that can't you?"

My eyes grew heavy, and I gulped. I hung my head and muttered, "Yeah, I know. That's always been my biggest fear—when that day comes, I mean. When I'm an old man and all the people I love are gone. I don't know what I'm going to do then. That's why what I'm about to do is so hard. I don't want to leave them behind."

The Gray Man rubbed his manicured beard gently, and pursed his lips a tad, then swallowed. For a moment it appeared as if he were going to cry, but the heaviness in his eyes drowned itself out of sight quickly.

"Everyone has their path. They have given you so many tools throughout your life that you're going to grow to be so thankful for. You couldn't possibly know the gravity of it all in this moment."

The Grey Man edged his chin downward at my wandering gaze, and he smiled faintly.

"I know, trust me," he continued, "you have some of the best people anyone could ever ask for."

I chuckled under my breath.

"Even, though, we're kind of goofy and crazy?"

The Grey Man nodded quickly, his hands were locked together behind his back, and his shoulders rocked a little. His voice rose, and he laughed, "That is definitely so, but very right!"

He laughed to himself, and I wanted to say more, but I could tell I needed to wait. The Gray Man settled back down and his gaze stretched onward into the horizon.

"Always cherish them, Hawke. There is still time before you part ways beyond the next, but still, love them now. What you are setting out to do, getting your answers, it is a crucial part of your destiny. It can not be avoided, and things will not go as you expect. Be vigilant, and always trust in your instincts. Thy breath hails from Zi, the all keeper."

There were so many questions that I wanted to ask him, but I didn't know how. It was like I couldn't find my voice to speak. The Grey Man turned from the river and looked me in the eyes. There was so much compassion there. I could have mistaken him for my father, but I knew he wasn't.

"You should be easier on your mother, too, y'know," the Grey Man continued. He was hiding something in his eyes and holding it back. I could tell, but I couldn't place it. His gaze softened more, and he muttered, "She's the biggest and best supporter you'll ever have."

My eyes fell towards the pavement, and I nodded slowly. *I should've said goodbye, but now it's to late.*

"I know she is, but I still have to do what I have to. I never wanted to hurt her, but I—"

I looked up and the Grey Man was gone. It was as if he vanished with the wind. I shook the cold breeze from my shoulders and stood there no more. I couldn't get lost in wandering about the strange man. It was as if he still spoke within my mind. *All questions will be answered in due time.*

I began walking back down towards my car. I was at the landing still, getting ready to cross the bridge, and then the thought came again. *Do I really want to do this?*

Then the assurance, *I have to.*

I turned the radio up and over to 107.3, and the host was chattering. Then came some strange sound effects, and Rod Stewart's "Young Turks" kicked off.

I turned the knob on the radio, lifting the volume, and smiled to myself. *This music will forever remind me of you, dad.*

The song whistled across the speakers, and I pulled out. Crossing the same bridge yet again, the Y; where it doesn't matter which way you're going, there is always two ways that you can turn.

EPILOGUE:

PENNIES FROM HEAVEN

A wrist relaxed in a lap, the other hand steered. A solid gloss wooden wheel edged slowly towards the right, bending around the corner. The front end of the car bounced softly at the turn, and street lights flashed through the window across a shadowed face. A dark blue '69 Chevy Caprice cruised down Main Street, past the old, archaic brick buildings. *That's all that's left. Downtown used to be the heart of this place, but now nearly nothing from the old days remains. Cold, empty, desolation, the Y-Bridge city has lost its soul.* The six story Masonic temple gleamed in the night to the left on North Fourth Street. The glass in its windows reflected the moon.

Speakers in leather hummed softly inside the ride, and a voice rhymed. Eminem's "Infinite" played; *reminds me of back in the day.* Thoughts conjured in the mind of the driver, and his dreams replayed.

Rushing forward, upon the mountain high, towards the tip that reaches the sky, he whispered to himself.

I was there; the Wanderer thought to himself; *I saw it, it's still in sight, but my shoulders grow weary, and sometimes I run out of breath. There's always a struggle, and yet that one. The cloaked one broods, and still, there's him. He's near, always in the shadows; tapping on my shoulders with a grin. There's still the man in the hat I have to contend.*

Did I make the right choice by coming back? It's been ten years, I thought to myself as I drove through the town, feeling the same weight resting upon my shoulders. *I want people to get*

434

something out of my writing. Someday, maybe. I just want to be somebody.

At the end of every journey, there appears to be only one certainty. A new beginning rises upon that timeless horizon.

The uncertainty of the following steps grows ever unsure across the teetering beam of existence. Sometimes it may take forever to find one's balance in their chosen path, and it could take a lifetime to find the way, but through this story unfolds many. *Mine and others, all fitting together, forming the grand scheme of a message; a guide to the mazes of many worlds. The message lies in the keys to the word. Paths to study in a song unheard.*

The same seeds are at the heart of all my quests. To find myself, and to discover true love. At the time of my return, I wasn't sure what led me back to the town of my birth, but it was something, some sort of reason. The steps lie unsteady and I was as blind as an old hermit, but still I trusted that feeling; the all too familiar voice. Through my stumbling, I found it. Through the unknowing, I found her. After the return, everything came together, and it only took a mere month.

It all started with a new job. I didn't notice her at first, but during one of the first pre-shift meetings I attended, I saw—*her, that is.*

A blonde girl with pigtails came waltzing through with her hands tucked in her front hoodie pocket and she was chewing some gum. She was only about 5'2, and she was beautiful, too. The glint in her eyes burned different from the rest. She had this knowing to her, I could tell it. An edge of certainty that cloaked itself casually behind her soft lips. I could feel the magic hidden within her. *Untapped and untamed; I can feel the wild energy of nature within her. That girl is a flame.*

She stoked the dead fire inside of me. From the start, I felt close to her even if I didn't actually know her—*but I do. It's sort of like Déjà vu.*

People surrounded us, but there was some strange magnetic draw that kept pulling me towards her. I continued looking from the side and wondering about this familiar feeling I was having. *Did we know each other as kids?*

I couldn't pinpoint this one of a kind pull, but the intensity of her flare, her energy, it stuck to me like glue. I was enveloped by it, especially when I saw her smile. It looked like she had apples in her cheeks, and her eyes glittered. I wanted to approach her, but I couldn't bring myself to do it. I watched her still, though.

The first time I actually heard her laugh and speak, my heart fluttered. *She has such a lovely sounding voice;* I thought to myself, *and that laugh.* It made me feel like a little kid again, but I was still scared to approach her. *She'd never go for you, boy. Pipe down your horses,* the man in the hat said; and of course I listened, but still, I couldn't help myself. *I want that girl.*

"Better Days" by the band, Citizen King, whistled through my eardrums as I spun around a corner on my electronic pallet jack. Then I heard a crash. One of my carts had spilled.

I was flustered, and hopped off the jack to pick up my boxes to re-stack it all again, but suddenly a helping hand rushed towards me. *It's that girl again.*

I stopped stacking, frozen in my tracks, and I blushed. She was smiling from ear to ear. Her cheeks burned red, and I thought to myself, *There are those sweet apples again.* My stomach churned, and the butterflies fluttered.

"It looks like you need some help," she laughed, and went on to stacking the boxes back up with me.

"I need a lot more help than you think," I replied, laughing, too. *She smells so sweet. I wish I could get closer. Next to her would be best,* I thought to myself as we both put it all back together.

"Take it easy," the girl said with a grin. Then she ran back to her jack. Her petiteness made her come off as a tad ornery. I smiled to myself, and my cheeks burned. *I think her and I might have a lot in common.*

My heart burned for her from that very moment. I spun around another corner, and the beat kicked off through my earbuds to "Here Comes the Rain Again" by the Eurhythmics.

From night to night I danced around corners to show off for her, and she was peeking through the stacks at me, too; smiling with those big cheeks of hers. *I think she loves me already, and to be honest with myself, I think I love her too.* It was love at first sight for the both of us, but, still; I was terrified of getting burned again. *Should I really let myself go?*

That's how it all started. Of course I was approached first. She asked me what my name was because she couldn't find me on Facebook. I told her my name was Hawke, and she told me hers was Auburn. *I feel like I've always burned for you.*

After she got my info, I blurted out, "Do you read?"

Auburn looked confused and a tad irritated. *Do I read? Of course I read. What kind of question is that?*

"Yes, I can read," she replied with narrow studying eyes.

"No, no, no, that's not what I meant," I replied, laughing. "I meant do you like to read? I've got a book out, and it's called "29 Palms: An American Odyssey for True Love". It's about the journey I took across the country."

She smiled again under those wandering embers of hers. *I love the way you look at me.*

Auburn replied, "Sure, I'll check it out. Where can I find it?"

I told her it was on Amazon, and she ordered it, but didn't read it right away. From then on, we spent every moment we could with one another. When she began reading the book, she asked me, "So what am I dealing with here? Do you check everybody out everywhere you go or what?"

"No," I shook my head quickly in defense, then shrugged my shoulders, "I just--I don't know I was a single guy, and I was trying to make the book funny, I guess."

I took a deep breath, and thought to myself, *Yeah, there are a few cringy things in there, but at least I'm honest about my thoughts.*

Auburn sat in the passenger seat of my beat up blue truck and took a draw off her smoke.

"Well, it doesn't really make any sense that you would travel across the country to get someone to fall in love with you, but you're flirting with other girls the whole time."

"Yeah, but I," then I paused, in thought, *She's right, but I didn't intend for it to seem that way. I just wanted to show that I had plenty of options.*

"So you don't like it?" I asked sadly and disappointed.

Auburn replied, "I mean, yeah, I like it, but all that has me kind of worried."

"Well, you don't have anything to worry about. My heart belongs to you. I don't care about anybody else."

She smiled, and done a goofy voice as she fluttered her eyebrows.

"Awww, does that mean you love me?"

I laughed and brought her in for a kiss at the red light.

"Of course I do; with all of my heart."

We got lost in each other's lips until horns honked behind us, bringing us back to the world. I screamed out of the window in my New York accent, "Quiet back there! We're talkin' business up here!"

I mashed on the petal and gunned it through the light. Auburn laughed, "You're somethin' else, man."

I blushed. It would be a lie to dispute.

"I guess I am."

Eventually, Auburn moved into an apartment with me, and our kids play great together—*sometimes, that is.*

She has three, two boys, and a girl, plus there's my two. Five kids, and they're all running around. It gets crazy, but wherever we are together is home to me. In my head I like to think of them as the Sparrows, but I never say it outwardly. They might not like it or think I'm weird so I just keep it to myself.

I've found it; home and true love. I did all that traveling for nothing. All I had to do was come back here.

We were, and still are, perfect for each other as a family, and I hope we always will be.

Auburn makes me feel alive, and the core of my soul shines outward and bursts every moment our lips meet. *With every touch, I tingle, and I will give myself to you forever.*

Time passed from the beginning; a year full of growth. *Seeds were planted with the pen, with a tap, then a stroke. I am the Wanderer you have read the second part of my tale. Now follow me into the void and watch me sail.*

Another night fell, cold wind whistled past the window. Chimes clattered and blew from the force. The Wanderer sunk back into the sand with his true love's cheek resting upon his chest as she slept. *The love I have for you forges the barrier between him and I, but still there is much to be settled in the vast deep within due time.*

He dove into the star, dropping towards the dark water. There was a crash, then a splash. Fog crept across the thin pool, and an antique lightbulb flickered at the end of a gloomy tunnel. Black vines grew across the red panels, and the golden knob shone. The Wanderer fixed his dark pea coat, flicking it dry. The tail near the bottom bounced over his knees. He patted the top of his head, running his fingers through his slicked back undercut; the hair was shaved down on the sides. This time he'd left his hat behind.

The Wanderer's footsteps echoed and the buckles on the side of his black leather boots jangled as he gradually edged down the shaft towards the dreaded encounter.

Above, in the empty, cavernous, void scenes played from the beyond. The Wanderer stopped, watched, and heard. They had been there in his head since he asked. *It all came to me when I touched grandpa Gene's old shoe shine kit.*

1952. A battle of the Korean War.

Bullets thundered in the vision above. Men in camouflage rushed together through the jungle. A grenade exploded, blowing dirt and shrapnel everywhere. A young man's voice screamed again.

"I got ya, Eddie! I got ya!"

Bullets riddled fast, and another explosion rocked the landscape. Boots dug in the mud, and another voice pleaded in horror.

"I'm in the hole, Gene! I'm in the hole!"

The Wanderer couldn't see the man's face because he was running too fast, but he knew who it was. *It's grandpa. They used to call him Geno when he was younger.*

The scene faded to black, and the last scream from the battle became an echo.

"Help me cover him, Anthony! Help me cover him!"

Another image flashed, and an original vision came; the year was 1972. An engine rumbled in the desert, and a dark blue

1969 Chevy Caprice was gunning it down a desert road. A boy with long blonde hair was at the helm of the wheel, and a girl on the passenger side of the bench seat screamed, "Step on it, Danny! Step on it!"

A dark Lincoln was chasing them, and two mobster looking guys were in the car.

"The sons of bitches can't run forever! I'm gonna scalp that blonde when I get ahold of her."

A thundering motorcycle sound came from behind them. It was coming upon them quickly. The desert sand blew behind the wheels of the steel horse, and the rider's long dark coat flailed in the wind. Tina Turner's "River Deep, Mountain High" screeched in the breeze, and the man's dark face shone with a freeze. Vengeance burned in his eyes. Men were about to meet their demise.

The mobsters in the dark Lincoln heard the motorcycle in the distance, and one said, "Oh, hell."

Then the driver mashed down on the pedal further, and barked, "It can't be him! The son of a bitch should've been dead by now!"

Geno Anderson pulled a sawed-off shotgun out of his saddlebag as his right arm held the bike steady. I heard the sound of the blast, and the shattering of the glass. Wheels screeched with a crash, then the vision disappeared, and the darkness of the vast void returned.

The red door with the golden knob lie ahead, and an old record player came on. Tommy Dorsey's "I'll Never Smile Again" twinkled along with each slow step.

The Wanderer reached for the knob and threw the door open. The man in the hat cackled as he leaned forward in his chair, pressing his elbow into the labyrinth upon the square. Flames danced in the fireplace behind him, and he took a puff of his cigar.

"Oh, how nice of you to join us," he teased from his seat.

"I was startin' to think you forgot about me."

The buckles on the Wanderers' black leather boots bounced and clattered as he made his way down the red, golden rug. The checkered floor was busted across several places, and

440

vines nearly took over the whole room. They snapped and slithered towards the vibration of the steps. The Wanderer sat down at the table, calm, bolstered with assurance. He rested his elbows on the edge of the etched maze.

"Your jokes really aren't that funny, y'know," The Wanderer spoke, "and you're not that dumb. You don't shut up long enough for me to forget."

The man in the hat cackled, "Come on! You aren't gettin' tired of me now, are ya? You know you love this game of ours. You'd be destitute without it."

"I don't need you anymore," the Wanderer replied, "I'm tired of your infection. Our time together is coming to an end."

"Is it now," the man in the hat sneered, "you can't get rid of me; there ain't a chance in you figuring out how. Face it, boy, your stuck with the curse."

The Wanderer's chin fell, and his eyes studied the swimming vines on the floor.

"Y'know, it never occurred to me," the Wanderer lifted his head, holding a firm glare on the hat man's grin.

"What's that," Jack snapped.

"I've tried to shut you out for all of these years; I tried to forget about you, but that's never going to work."

"You got that right," the man in the hat replied.

"So I'm here to make a deal," the Wanderer continued, "just tell me what you want. You can't have my body, you can't overtake my soul. You know that's off the table. All I seek is a parley. A path for you to walk your way, and for me to walk mine. So tell me, Jack, what's it gonna take?"

The man in the hat leaned back in his chair, and his grin turned to shadow as he brooded. Dark ether swirled off his shoulders and around the tail of his coat.

"Why don't you just set free me then," the man in the hat growled.

The Wanderer grinned and shook his head.

"You know as well as I do it doesn't work like that. There has to be an exchange for things to be concrete. It can't just be given; it's a part of the law."

The Wanderer leaned back in his chair slowly, throwing a leg over his knee. His hands rested in his lap.

"So what is it gonna take, Jack? What will it be? We can't do this dance forever."

"Don't call me that," the man in the hat snapped, jumping forward, and slamming his fist into the table. His voice grew shrill.

"You don't know the story behind that name."

"But I do," the Wanderer replied, "I've seen flashes and memories of who you once were. In my dreams, and in the waking hours. What happened to you, Jack? How did you become this?"

Jack's grin grew into a frown, and he bit his lip.

"W-why do you w-want to know?" he stuttered.

"Because I want us both to walk away free."

Dark lines swam up Jack's neck, highlighting his veins, and pressing around the corners of his mouth.

"There's no hope," Jack groaned. "I'm already lost."

"But there is. There's always hope; as long as you don't lose your faith."

The man in the hat burst out suddenly, cackling.

"Wow! Could you get anymore corny?"

He stood up and clapped his hands.

"I almost had you, too!"

He lost himself in a maniacal wave, dancing around the table, and slammed his fist down upon the wood in front of me.

"There won't be a parley," the man in the hat growled, "your stuck with me."

The Wanderer didn't shiver a bit. He kept his calm, hands still folded in his lap. He had grown a lot in patience.

"Don't you want to find her? Don't you want to find"—the Wanderer paused, then resumed, "Layla?"

The man in the hat edged back, and despair fell across his shoulders.

"Don't speak that name," he growled, "I don't want to hear it anymore."

"You were in love once too, Jack, just like I am. You have it. It's all not completely gone; I've seen you, and her, but there's still something I don't get. How did you know my grandpa?"

"Shut up, about him," Jack growled. "I hate him for what he did to me!"

"Well, what did he do? What did—"

Jack threw his chair into the fire and groaned as the flames overtook it, then he snapped, "If he were as weak as you are; I would've had him back then. I was at the height of my power in this realm, but he stripped me clean."

He clicked his tongue against his cheek, and turned back towards me, grinning again.

"We played the same game, him and I, y'know? The same one I do with you; only I didn't have him in my grip like I thought I did. We knew each other in life, too. He—"

Jack paused, remembering the little boy with the flat cap at the Avondale Orphanage. He used to visit the children there, and shine their shoes. He shook and gagged from the memory. *I was so weak back then.*

"Jack," I asked, "what did he do?"

He stretched his hand out, and another chair snapped to him. He dragged it across the floor as he clicked his tongue behind his teeth.

Jack sat calmly in the chair, and folded his hands in his lap as he sat back, grinning still.

"So you really want to hear the tale? You wanna know my story?" he asked.

"Yes, I do," I nodded my head eagerly.

"Are you gonna turn it into another pretty little book of yours?"

"I just want to know," I replied, "you deserve justice. I've seen who you were before. Perhaps, by telling your story; you'll rediscover your own light again."

"Ahhhh," Jack tsssked, "a little sympathy for the devil. I like that. Are you sure you're ready to walk in my shoes, boy? You might just lose yourself along the way if you do."

"I feel like I have to. You are a part of whatever all of this is. I can't get to the others if I don't pass through this gate."

Jack crossed his leg over his knee, lit up a cigar, then took a draw.

"Well, then, get your typing fingers ready, boy. This one's gonna be a doozy."

As I wrote the first words to his book, a news alert popped up on my phone. A fire erupted on North Fourth Street. The masonic temple caught ablaze. I tasted iron in my throat, and my mouth began to bleed.